SHRIKE

BOOK ONE OF THE DICHOTOMY DUOLOGY

CHARLA AYERS

Book Cover by Decky Yuriadi

Illustrations by Decky Yuriadi and Charla Ayers

First Edition: October 2025
Second Edition: January 2026

For every soul who feared the dark, only to find themselves amongst the shadows.

And for Caleb because you have always been my home.

Time & Distance

T-earrach: spring
Samhradh: summer
Fómhar: autumn
Luan: Monday
Chéadaoin: Wednesday
Aoine: Friday
Nollaig: December

Aecers: acres
Míle: mile
Hawr: hour
Wyth: week
Wythnos: weekend
Menoth(s): month(s)
Yehr(s): year(s)

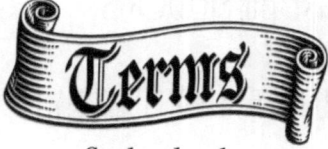

Terms

Scol: school
Scoler(s): student(s)
Scolemaster/Master: professor
Scyrte: shirt
Léine: ankle-length tunic
Raiments: clothing
Baíníns: woven wool sweater
Notorum: known/familiar
Buinín: cattle/cow
Tá sé in am: It is time
Mhargadh: bargain
Tairseach: portal
Roghnaigh: chosen
Mo céasadh: my agony
Brandálaim: brand
Soitheach: vessel
Mo céasadh: my agony

Spells

Briseadh: break
Éadaí: clothed
Nocht: naked
Sedes: seat
Ceilt: veil
Oscailte: open
Ampligh: amplify
Bloc: block
Solas: illuminate
Dorchacht: cover in darkness
Rois: blast
Spreagadh: move
Tine: fire

Pronunciation Guide

Eregahl: air-eh-gaul
Danumhar: dan-oo-mar
Skean: sk-een
Draíocht: dree-oct
T-earrach: ter-ahk
Samhradh: sow-rah
Fómhar: for
Mo céasadh: mo case-uh
Míle: m-ee-luh
Mhargadh: mar-guh
Notorum: no-tore-um
Tairseach: tar-sha
Sídhe: Shee
Failinis: fall-in-ish
Caolán: keel-an

Briseadh: bre-shu
Éadaí: ae-dee
Ceilt: kelt
Rois: rosh
Tine: ten-eh
Oscailte: os-cult-tah
Dorchacht: dar-hact
Spreagadh: spreh-guh
Roghnaigh: roh-nuh
Scyrte: sheer-tuh
Luan: loo-in
Chéadaoin: kay-deen
Aoine: hee-on-a
Nollaig: null-ug
Ogham: ow-uhm

Tá sé in am: Toh shay in ahm
Oidhre an Domhain: Eye-duh an du-in
Oidhre an Cinniúint: Eye-duh an kin-oo-it
Oidhre an Cnámh: Eye-duh an cnawv
Oidhre an Spiorad: Eye-duh an spee-ruhd

Playlist

Music was my first love and remains a large part of my life and creativity. This story was born from music—born from the feelings that certain songs and musicians have made me feel.

At its core, Shrike is a culmination of art that I have consumed for years. It began with a feeling, an inkling, and grew. Here is a hand-selected discography for your reading pleasure. I hope it aids in your journey through the halls of Adonien.
Enjoy.

Content Warnings

This book contains mature themes and content that may not be suitable for all readers. Reader discretion is strongly advised. If any of these content elements may be triggering or uncomfortable for you, please consider whether this book is appropriate for your reading preferences.

Please be aware that the following elements are present throughout the story:

Strong Language:
Explicit profanity and coarse language.
Sexual Content:
Sexually explicit scenes and mature romantic content.
Violence and Death:
Scenes involving death and violence.
Blood Consumption:
Scenes depicting the consumption of blood.

PART ONE

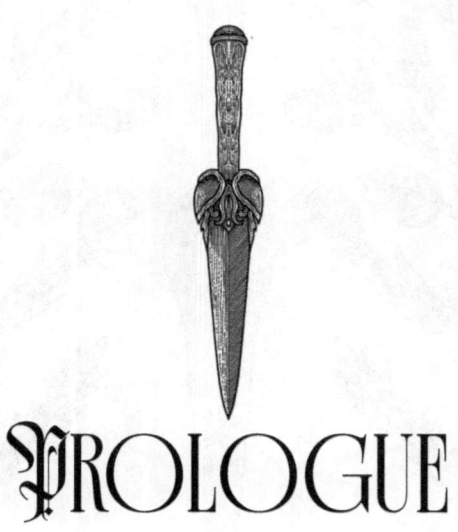

PROLOGUE

I am dying. Except I know I am not. The rational, intelligent part of my mind reminds me that this has happened many times, and I will survive. But the physical part of me, my body lying in a sweating, convulsing mess on the floor, my chest cleaving in two, my salt-burned face, my nails digging into the stone floor; those parts never remember. Every yehr, the eternal cycle repeats itself. Days of dread and grief and emptiness followed by a night of my body feeling like it is trying to shed its skin—like it yearns to turn itself inside out. Every single yehr since sixteen.

My parents relentlessly searched for answers. Acolytes blessed me, alchemists concocted tinctures and teas, physickers would leech me, and once, when I was eighteen, my mother even brought in a witch healer under the cover of darkness to assess me. I remember her rubbing my forehead and wrists with a thick oil that smelled warm with spices unknown to me and placing a round stone with holes in it atop my navel.

It was when she threw bones at my feet that something in the room changed. Wind wound around us in the enclosed space of my childhood bedroom. The air bulged with suffocating energy that hummed so loudly I had to cover my ears. It rattled my teeth and curdled my blood. The threads of my pale lavender quilt pulled from each other, threatening to burst. The fire in the hearth burned ravenously as blazing flames licked the wood of the mantle, leaving scarring burns.

I will never lose the image of the whites of her old eyes turning cloudy when she looked at me, or how she seemed not to look at me at all but through me. Into my past. Into my future. Seconds later, the fear evaporated, the humming dissipated, and her eyes were clear again. Then she laughed. Laughed in my face and packed her stones and bones and anointments back into her worn leather bag.

I could have let it go. I could have trusted my mother when she told me that the healer had a rare gift from the goddess. I could have lived my life ignorant, never knowing more. But then the healer paused in the door frame to say in her unusual lilting accent, "There's nothin' I can do for you, dear wain. Nothin' anyone can do. You are bound by the gnarled hands of fate, and there you shall stay. May the Seren bless your soul and guide your footsteps."

Then she was gone, leaving us more confused than before. Who were the Seren, and what did they have to do with my fate? My mother said nothing as she shooed me back into bed, kissed my cheeks, and left my room. Hyacinth wordlessly snuck in moments later, climbed into my bed, and wrapped me in her arms. She hummed as she brushed long strokes up and down my back—how she had gotten me to sleep since I entered this world.

Mother died a yehr later. The day before an episode. The way they all did. It took me far too long to realise they were connected. That I, that whatever this is, had caused their deaths. Parts of me, most of me, died with each of them. Mother took my love of the earth, Hyacinth took my laughter and carefree spirit, and Father took my light. My warmth.

Since then, I have been cold. On the outside, I have been nothing but words in books, dealing in facts and knowledge and priding myself on being the smartest person in the room. Internally, I have spent every moment since searching for the connection between my episodes and their deaths. I caused them, I am sure of it. Mother was unaware of what she was doing by bringing in the healer. She had no idea of the chain of events that would follow or my insatiable hunger to find the answers. I cannot stop now. I must live through this. I am too close this time.

The ringing tolls of my thirteenth episode clang through me now, violent and hungry as ever. I had two of them the yehr I was twenty-two, and this singular moment trumps them both, mocking me for finding the others debilitating. Hyacinth, cold in her grave, offers no warm fingers to soothe me now. No one does. The episodes are advancing in their affliction. Like parts of me really are dying. It's drowning on land. Burning underwater. Like my soul is trying to leave my body. A summoning I cannot answer. I do the only thing I can and surrender to the ceaseless storm quaking in my bones. A desperate sob thunders through

4

me, and I press my forehead harder into the grout between the rough stones, clutching myself around the middle. Their cool, hard surface usually anchors me. Tonight, they are the bars of a cage.

The experience of the episodes remains largely unchanged. It is the most desperate form of grief and need and rage and desire roiling together in my blood, dancing to its own melody.

Squeeze, swell, squeeze, swell.

I am empty; I am flooded.

I am nothing; I am infinite.

No one should ever have access to the severity of so many emotions at once. And now, visions have begun to accompany the horror of the enthrallments. At least, I assume the hallucinations are a way for my body, my mind, to process the episode.

I have lost sense of how long I've been here on the floor. Minutes, hawrs, days. I slip in and out of consciousness sometimes. I remember finishing my packing, bathing, and lying down to read a book. I confirmed the departure time appointed by the sea master for the morning, scribbled in the tattered, leather-bound journal on my desk. Then I blacked out.

No, no. There was something else. A smell. A thought. Maybe a dream. Maybe a hallucination. The smell of earth, of samhradh rain, an odd frequency—some strange melodical sonation. Then a blade between my ribs and a sudden, delicious finality. A dream, maybe. A nightmare, surely. Then I was in the middle of the fit, lost to the nausea and vibration of my skin.

I force my swollen, tear-stained eyes open at the memory. The room is spinning, or I am falling, or maybe I *am* dead. I crawl my way through the quicksand of my mind on shaking limbs to the basin and vomit my dinner, an undeniable relief of pressure releasing with it. Maybe I will survive this one. Taking long moments to breathe, I try to bring my seizing body back to this realm, but time evades me, slipping in and out of my hands like vapour as my bones rattle in my skin.

At some point, I realise I am on my feet. The scent of petrichor wraps around my body again, carrying me to bed. As I turn to lie back down, I swear there are moss-covered footprints behind me. This is a new development. I try with my entire body to turn back, to trace my fingers along the moss to confirm I have not yet gone mad. I cling to my consciousness as if it were smoke on the wind, and when my body collapses on the bed, I am already gone.

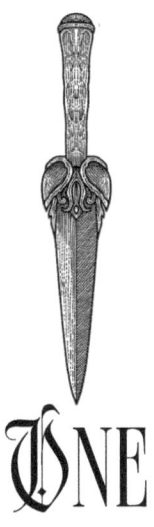

ONE

Miss Alder,

I pen this missive to convey our most profound gratitude and unequivocal approbation regarding your proposal to the Adonien Academy of History and Art. It is with the utmost rarity that we encounter such spirited and distinguished enthusiasm for our ongoing intellectual endeavours.

Your academic and professional credentials have been scrutinised with the greatest care and have proven most remarkable. Following extensive deliberation with our esteemed sector heads, we are pleased to communicate our wholehearted approval of your project for next term. Adonien Academy shall undoubtedly reap immeasurable benefits from your proposed journal on The Origins of Eregahl's Myths, and we take great pride in welcoming a distinguished expert from Albion to our hallowed halls of intellectual discourse.

As Chief Editor, your pursuit shall be guided by the venerable Master Dominus Shrike. Upon your anticipated arrival, a carefully selected coterie of research assistants shall be assembled to support your work. Herewith, I have enclosed the formal contractual documentation, and I eagerly await our future correspondence.

We await your presence with the most profound anticipation.

Yours most sincerely,

Headmaster Connally

I have read the letter until I have committed it to memory, tracing the flicks and swishes of the ink and wearing the parchment thin. All preparations are complete. I have packed up my little cottage and dismantled my sad life here. I have readied to say goodbye.

Yehrs, decades. I have worked so diligently for so long to get here that it is nearly inconceivable. Endless obstacles previously preventing me from leaving flood my mind. The deaths, the horrors, the grief. Ceaseless, maddening loneliness, so unaware of how close I was to losing my battle for survival, for my life.

The memories are all distorted now, a little blurry, perhaps hazed over with the passing of time or simply by my ageing. I wish I could share the news with my family. I imagine standing hand in hand with Hyacinth, jumping up and down on these very floors, squealing with excitement. I can see how Father's warm eyes would brighten, shining all glossy with pride as he squeezes my shoulder, looking for words that portray how he would feel, which would, no doubt, be a carefully crafted conglomeration of eloquence and humour. Mother's touch would be gentle and warm. Her whispers of, "I knew you could do it. I never doubted," would linger with me long after my feet abandon these shores.

"Are you ready, my dear?" Vivian's voice is quiet, exploratory. Like someone looking in on the scene of a crime, not knowing what to say, and I suppose that, really, she is.

I allow myself a final moment on the doorstep of my childhood home. A finite amount of time and space to compress an entire life into a box of memories to bury deep beneath the ground of my mind. The reality of it strikes me violently, but not in the way I had expected. I can see it now, from the threshold of goodbye, how desperate I have been. Their clothes still hang in the wardrobes, thick with dust now. Rolls of leather age in the corners of the rooms. Skeletons of herbs and flowers long past their rot still litter the pots out front. I never erased them; I could not bear it. It is as if one of them could walk into the room at any moment, pick up their favourite book, or resume their most recent pursuit, and exist outside of my imagination.

Nights with wits abandoned and delusion flooding my aching heart float through the room like living memories. How many times have I rocked in that ancient chair, talking aloud to a room of dead people long since buried? Keeping them alive in this way likely only made it worse for me, but what else could I do? Who else have I had to walk through grief with me? Grief, alone, is perhaps the only thing that remains. My perpetual, unwanted lover.

Vivian quietly clears her throat behind me, and for the first time since they left me, I allow myself to release them. To let them remain here, in our home, while I finally begin my search for what took them from me.

"Yes," I whisper, turning toward her. Her hair has greyed over the yehrs, and the skin around her eyes and mouth hangs gently now, but she is still my light, my saving grace, and all I have left.

"Thank you for seeing me out and for keeping an eye on the place. I am not ready to be rid of it just yet."

"You have nothing to worry about, dear. Nothing at all. It is your time." She pats my hand, and the heaviness of goodbye coils between us, tense like an asp ready to strike. She continues, "Your time to get away from here, to find what you have always been looking for, or what has always been looking for you."

It is not lost on me that it's a miracle she stands here at all. I have diligently kept her at arm's length for yehrs, but her role in my life is paramount. And now, following my yehrly episode, I am all the more grateful that she remains—that this episode did not take her, too.

My obsession with folklore and tales of magic began at sixteen when my tutor had me complete a history essay about a lost people. I can still remember standing in our town's antiquated library yehrs later when I first smelled that now too-familiar smell of after-rain that haunts me. On the very bottom shelf, wedged between *The History of Kells* and *The Lost Apollons,* I found a small, leather-bound book, torn and layered in arid dust. The writing looked like it was once gilded. It hummed in my hands, calling to me without words that it somehow belonged to me, and I was instantly lost to it. I remember peeling its cracked spine open, revealing a word that shook me to my core: Seren. The healer's thick accent resounded in my mind like the swinging of an executioner's axe.

"Miss Vivian, do you know what this is?" I asked the archivist, who would soon become the closest thing to a friend I have ever had, shelving ancient tomes a row over from me. Vivian was in her early thirties at the time. She quickly became my research conspirator once my compulsion ensued. She was kindness, warmth personified, and the reason for my herbal tea obsession.

Vivian took the book from my hands, gently dusting off the mounds of cobwebs. "Hm. I don't recognise this one. Let me see if we have any record of it. If I can get it cleaned up enough to decipher it, that is."

Vivian spent half the day showing me the basic steps of properly cleaning a book. She walked me through brushes, solutions, and how to store them so that the moisture in the air would not cause them to mould and rot. She had no catalogue or history of the tome in the library, but after many wyths of research, we were able to make out the title: *Oidhre an Domhain.* No colleague or resource of hers knew what it was or where it came from. It took us three fortnights and many awful translations to figure out that the title loosely translates from the language of Eregahl to "Heir of Earth." I confirmed it later at university. Even further, I was able to decode its secrets of magic, creatures, gods, and power, unlike anything I had ever learned of in Albion. Things far from the gentle goddess, Cyfrif, who crafted our island.

The book even told how the Seren would imbue their favourite humans with small amounts of power, allowing them to do simple magics, minuscule versions of their great creations: seers, healers, menders, shapeshifters, warriors with uncanny abilities to wield a weapon, and even those able to cast curses. It has been my anchor. Fruit to my unbridled hunger. Water to my unquenched thirst. My own map of self-discovery.

And now, I am finally here with nothing and no one to stop me as I voyage to the island of Ereghal, searching for answers.

For magic—the secret I hope to find.

Real magic. The thing that twisted through the wooden floorboards of my room and pressed itself into every pore of my skin when the witch healer cast those bones at my feet. Someone who might help me figure out why everyone around me dies. It must be a curse. A hex. Some remnant of a crooked finger pointed at an ancestor of mine. Luck, gods, fate—surely none of them have such a bloody, twisted sense of humour. I have searched for yehrs and found no other reason. No rumours or research of magic exist in Albion, and I have found no woman like the healer in my homeland. But Eregahl is teaming with lore and a rich history of once-practised incantations and mystical creatures that roamed amongst the people. I can only hope my studies might provide some answers. That maybe, that island holds untold truths that might set me free.

Vivian's gentle voice pulls me from my internal inspection. "Promise me that you will write. Promise that you will share with me the answers to the questions we discovered all those yehrs ago."

I am not sure how to say it—how to swear to someone about anything in a future that I am not sure I exist in. But Vivian is somehow still here, and this, this, I owe her. I would not be this far without her.

"I promise." My voice is hoarse and coated in longing that I cannot allow myself to feel. Instead, I let the bargain clang through me, and I swear to Vivian and myself that I will find something—anything—that offers us both solace.

My singular hope is that it does not kill me first.

TWO

Eregahl is a country with a rich history steeped in folklore, mystery, and blood. Which is precisely why I am here. More specifically, why I am in Danumhar, its northernmost region. Living a sea away, I have spent the last ten yehrs studying the people and history of this place. The magic, the creatures, the lost ways of life so unknown to its current inhabitants.

I have scoured countless catalogues of mythical beasts and the precise locations where they lived, memorising Eregahl's varying origin stories and forgotten magical histories. The understanding I have gained is that the people of Eregahl are proud of this history. They believe all these things to have once been true and lean into the reality that they once *were* real. But not anymore. What has always puzzled me, though, is that there are no accounts of what happened to them all. No text, book, or piece of fiction addresses where the magic all went. If it *did* exist, where did it all go? Where is the line between reality and fantastical storytelling?

Instinctively, my mind snaps back to *Oidhre an Domhain.* I carry that ancient book I found with me everywhere. I carry it with me now, tucked along the inside of my overcoat. The rough tweed snags on the dry skin of my fingers as I reach to graze the cover, my own object of comfort that I cling to like a babe in a crib.

Even with the t-earrach giving birth to samhradh, the weather is still rather insufferable on the seas. The last few days of travel have not been easy on my body. Though I do not particularly think it is the sea to blame. I seem to be taking much longer to recover from my latest episode, the worst I have ever felt, and the closer I inch to the shores of Danumhar, the more wretched I feel. The only relief I find is in the fact that I have a full yehr stands between me and another episode. If my episodes were to ever consort with luck, I would say it was rather fortunate that this one came before my journey. I hope that allows me a modicum of safety.

Physical discomfort aside, I have never seen a more beautiful view than the one the vastness and loneliness of the open sea offer. The joy of nothingness has wrapped me in its embrace every night, lulling me into the most serene sleep. Now, the morning yawns and stretches its way across the sky, casting the foggy sea in hazy golds and blues. If the mist were any thicker, it might feel as if we were sailing on the clouds above.

I am eager to begin my work for the journal. My goal is to research and record a comprehensive history of the lore here, specifically for the scolers at the academy. Creating a record of who discovered or developed what and when allows researchers to receive recognition for their contributions. Journals maintain a permanent record of alchemical and academic work, preserving knowledge for future generations. Specialised journals like this one help define and advance particular disciplines or subdisciplines by concentrating relevant work in one place. Though there are endless history books on the lore of Eregahl, there currently is no fully encompassing system for the many complex parts of the research. My goal is to begin that process for Adonien and allow the scolers and scolemasters to continue to hone and craft the recording of history as it continues to unfold.

Aside from this being the pinnacle of my career, I am even more keen to discover if anyone else surmises truths about the lore here. My work will be headed by the infamous Master Dominus Shrike, and I cannot help but wonder what he will be like in person. He is an expert in all things Eregahl. He has published a manuscript and several essays about the history of this island, and I have read every word of his I could find, as well as the critiques he has written of other historians.

Rumours of scrutiny and stubbornness shroud his reputation. He is brutal in his examinations, offering no pleasantries in his absolutes. Other authors often retort about his sharp tongue and lack of respect amongst his peers, but he is the expert on these lands and people and one of the reasons why I am here. I have crafted him many thorough letters, attempting to build a rapport that will aid in communication upon my arrival. However, I have yet to receive any word from him. Being the renowned elitist that he is, he likely finds me so far below his station that he need not attempt to interact with me at all. Though I am curious how he might manage that as my point of contact. I truly hope he is more willing to work alongside me than against me.

"You might consider cutting your hair off for the journey back. I am not sure that you will ever get those knots out."

I quickly twist about to find Orvander, the kind and knowledgeable captain of this fair ship, staring at me. I have rather enjoyed the many hawrs of conversation we've exchanged over the past few days. It has helped keep my mind distracted. And yet, having small, simple talks with a man the same age as my father would have been only adds to the concoction of emotions twisting my middle.

I thoroughly enjoy Orvander's thick, black moustache that curls gently toward his nose. When he smiles, his whole face alights, and he turns a very delicate shade of pink when he laughs. His age is not the only thing that reminds me of my father, who never took anything with too much seriousness either, perhaps to a fault. His blasé often irritated my mother to anger, and she would bat him about the kitchen with a thick hand towel. It would leave me and my sister in prickling laughter with tears welling in our eyes. Giggles that Hyacinth and I both knew fueled his flame. Then he would wrap Mother in his arms and whisper things into her ear that sent redness to her full cheeks. She would swat him about some more before he would pinch her behind and wink at me with his warm eyes, the colour of buffed leather, as he left to tackle another task that needed tending.

Orvander's eyes, bright and blue as the sea, peer over my

nest of thick, wind-whipped hair. The chaotic mass of mushroom brown sweeps him from my vision, and I pull my long, wavy tresses back and stuff them into the nape of my jacket.

"You might be right," I say, tucking the shorter fringe pieces behind my ears. "Perhaps I will use the cuttings to make myself a moustache like yours."

Orvander bursts into that rosy laughter. "G'wan. I'd love to see that. We're near shore yet, lass. Keep your eyes on the bow there, through the fog. Not on my glorious facial hair."

I beam right back at him and turn my eyes toward the sea again. Not even half an hawr passes before tiny balls of light begin to appear in the thick, hazy landscape like little glowing orbs forming from thin air. Moments pass in silence with only the lapping of the water and the whooshing of the wind around us as more and more of them begin to shine brighter. As the steep shores creep nearer, the fog begins to recede, and I begin to make out the silhouette of the academy. It sits high on the cliff, overlooking the waters. Achingly beautiful and old, she perches stoically like a woman waiting for her lover to return.

Adonien Academy of History and Art was built nearly two hundred yehrs ago, and its construction remains shrouded in mystery. Legends claim its architect believed there to be wild monsters on the island—deamhans—so, he secretly built precautionary survival details into the scol. Hidden hallways, secret dungeons, weapons hidden within the stones. It is unknown to me if any of the scolers or scolemasters have found any over the yehrs, or how many of the local people believe it to be true, but I, for one, *will* be keeping my eye out for the hidden treasures.

I was not prepared for how beautiful the island, or the academy, would be. It looks as if it has been plucked from a dream—an ethereal painting created by an ancient Danumhar artist. A beautiful castle full of knowledge and wonder and, perhaps, even magic, right in front of me.

A gentle thud pulls me from the inner corners of my mind, and I realise we have docked.

"Ya know, not many people get to see this view the way I often do on the seas, and one thing I can tell you, lass, is the feeling you get when gazing upon that castle is truly immortal. It hasn't lost a single ounce of wonder since the first time I laid eyes on it. If you find nothing here other than this, I think the travel would be well worth it." His eyes devour the scene before us as the sun finally crests over the mountain range, casting its spotlight directly on the academy. The fog dispels rather quickly in the light of day, and an enormous flock of birds swarm up from behind the scol, flowing and swaying, waltzing around the dawn.

"Beautiful," I breathe.

"Butcher birds," Orvander informs. "They are native to this island. Showed up around—"

"Three hundred yehrs ago. Shrikes. They are shrikes, Lanius meridionalis."

"Right. Historian. I forgot," he chuckles.

I watch the shrikes dip and dive, their song loud enough to reach us at the shore, mystifying and beautiful. Their appearance is striking. Though their heads are a pale grey, a black mask extends from their beak through the eye to behind the ear coverts. A slightly hooked black beak reveals its carnivorous nature, perfectly designed for dispatching small prey. Their wings have prominent white patches that flash conspicuously during flight, and the long, graduated tail is black with white outer feathers that create a beautiful pattern when spread.

"Eamon is a caregiver here, and he will take you up the cliffside. He's coming down now," Orvander says, motioning me to gather myself.

I abandon my study of the shrikes to turn my gaze toward the cliffside. An older gentleman with a single horse and a small, open carriage with two small lamps hanging from either side of the dash slowly moves down the carved path in the stone's face, leading to the castle. "Ready to be rid of me that quickly, are you, Orvander? And here I thought we'd bonded."

"Aye, we have, Miss Alder. It's only that I have a special engagement this evening that I need to prepare for. If you need my assistance at all, just inform Eamon, and he will see to it that word reaches me. I will be here at the dock, ready and willing to adventure with you again." He offers me that rosy grin, and I find that mountain of grief beginning to shift in the back of my throat. I clear it immediately.

"Thank you, Orvander. You have been the most gracious host and formidable captain." I salute him then, earning that booming laughter I have come to love in the days we have spent together. No, not love. I cannot *love* anything.

Orvander masterfully angles the boat gently to the dock's edge. "I have a sneaking suspicion you might cause a bit of a ruckus here, Miss Alder. One I look forward to witnessing." He moves to anchor us.

"'No fun worth having can be anything but chaos,' Captain.

Words I shall leave you with from a man wilder and smarter than me." I wink at him then, and he stretches out his hand to help me step onto the dock.

"I think I might adopt that one," he says, placing my luggage on the dock behind me. He effortlessly hops up, taking my bags to the carriage now waiting at the edge of the quay with Eamon at the reins.

Once Orvander loads me and my luggage into the carriage, we say our parting goodbyes, and he sails off again as Eamon and I make our trek back up the long and winding cliff.

"There's a wool blanket under the bench for you, wain. Some tea as well."

I reach below the wooden seat to pull out a dark brown wicker basket, indeed packed with a blanket, a glass jar full of a hot, golden liquid, two cups, and a gingham tea towel full of still-warm scones resting atop heated stones.

"Well, sir, you certainly know how to treat a lady." I see his broad shoulders shaking on the bench in front of me. His thick, wool coat trails down behind him, a match to the scally cap atop his hairless head.

Like Orvander, he has facial hair, but where Orvander has only a large moustache, Eamon has an impressive, white beard that nearly touches his chest. It is well groomed, and when he turns, the sun makes the oil in it glisten. I take the basket in my hands and throw a leg over the bench, making sure my pants and overcoat do not catch on the rough wood, to sit alongside Eamon at the front of the carriage.

He smiles at me. "Not one for tradition then, are you, love?" I shake my head at him. "Glorious. We need some entertainment around here. These authors and masters are not without wit nor intelligence; however, they do suffer greatly from prudency and tameness that is rather dull and disinteresting. Perhaps you can stir some earth, Miss Alder."

"It would indeed be my honour, sir."

"Call me Eamon, please. Did I not just explain my distaste for formality, Miss Alder?"

"Alright, Eamon. Thorne, then. My name is Thorne." I pour him a cup of tea before my own and hand it to him.

"'Tis nice to meet you," he says, and I cannot stop the smile from stretching across my face. He looks me over cautiously. "You remind me of my wife," he says, rolling his eyes and taking the tea. "Thank you," he adds.

"Then that is a woman I am eager to meet."

"I have no doubt you two will acquaint yourselves soon enough, Seren bless the island," he says, murmuring the last part into his cup. I only grin at him. "So, from what I have gathered from my debriefing of your arrival, you are here to help create a new journal for the academy?"

"Why was there a full debriefing of my arrival?" I ask, handing him over a scone as well.

"From my understanding, it is rare that the academy retains any overseas researchers. Especially one of such esteem and fame," he says, wiggling his thick, white brows up and down at me.

"Ah, not at all. A woman simply graduates from university in a male-driven field of study with distinctions, a published collection of essays, and a rather dense brain, and she becomes such an anomaly in her village that she generates enough talk across seas. Rather impressive yet wholly uninteresting, in my opinion." I pop a scone into my mouth, immediately overtaken by its deliciousness. "I would rather think the person who concocted such perfection that is this divine pastry deserves far more decoration and notoriety than me," I say, taking another bite.

"Elowyn will be delighted to hear that. A woman with a sharp tongue and a sense of taste, she'll adore you immediately."

Realising Elowyn is his wife, that monster roils in me again. I remind myself to keep distant. I cannot create meaningful relationships. Instead, I only smile at Eamon and continue to eat.

"How long have you worked here?" I ask as we wind the mountain at a meagre pace. My greedy gaze takes in all the sights of the island and the cliffs beginning to come into view as we rise in elevation. The breeze becomes stronger, and the salt-drenched, musky scent of the air wraps around us.

"I have lived in Eregahl my entire life. Elowyn and I are originally from Eden, but as you can deduce as to why, Elowyn was hired on as a cook for the academy. It has always been her dream, and I can bladesmith anywhere, so we came. A few yehrs here, and the headmaster at the time became aware of my many talents," he says very smugly, mocking himself in a way I find endearing. He takes a sip of his steaming tea before continuing. "So, he asked if I would become a caretaker of sorts. I maintain the castle itself and have hired dozens of staff to manage the entire eighty aecers it sits on. Elowyn oversees many cooks, gardeners, and service staff as well. We've lived here for over three decades now. This is our home."

"That is wonderful, Eamon. But, if you so unofficially run the academy, then why are you chauffeuring around the likes of me?"

He smiles and says, "When they told me a famous lore researcher was coming to study for a while, well, I wanted to see you for myself. Call it vain curiosity." He gently bumps his shoulder against mine. "Thankfully, you showed up instead." I bump him back a bit harder, and our laughter shakes the carriage.

We arrive at the academy gates half an hawr later with empty cups and not a crumb of Elowyn's blueberry scones in sight. Even though I slowly watched the academy come into view for the entire journey, it still did not prepare me for the full experience of it up close. Huge, magnificent, and expertly maintained, it physically embodies the atmosphere of prestige. Endless rows of stone and brick climb high to the numerous spires. Balconies, archways, and ancient stone footpaths all fight for my attention. Regardless of my humility with Eamon earlier, the reality that I am truly standing on these grounds overcomes me.

I made it. I fell in love with this island in a book nearly ten yehrs ago. I have dedicated my life to studying the history, lore, and literature of this land. I have spent endless nights by candlelight, uncovering secrets in forgotten texts. I have taken on the life of a people and of a land I have never actually witnessed. I played pretend for a long time. Now, I get to immerse myself. I will witness firsthand the culture, the history, and the magic of Eregahl. The yehrs of failure, of death, of obstacles in my way remain a distant thought now that my boots are on

Danumhar soil—on the grounds of the academy that harbours all the answers to my questions. That might offer something to help break my curse.

"Well, you won't accomplish much by simply staring at it, Miss Thorne. This way, lass," Eamon remarks. Servicemen begin to appear, taking my bags, the blanket from my shoulder, the teacup from my hand, and disappear into the towering, arched doors.

As I take my first step through the gate, a shrike swoops in front of me, flapping its wings violently. I halt, nearly toppling over at the abruptness of my feet. The shrike eyes me curiously before whistling an eerie coo and taking off into the mist.

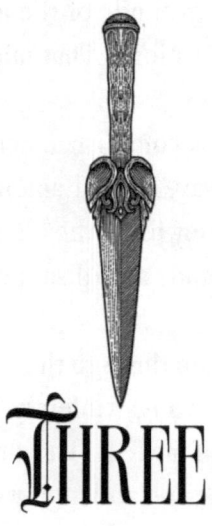

THREE

Moss and ivy cling to the rough-hewn stone on the exterior of the archaic doors. Steep black turrets reach toward the sky like the fingers of some long-forgotten giant. Stepping through the towering doors of the academy, I am immediately enveloped in a timeless aura. Sunlight filters through enormous stained-glass windows, casting kaleidoscopic patterns onto the polished marble floors below. The scent of aged parchment mingles with the faint aroma of ink and beeswax candles, and the entry hall is overwhelmingly opulent, with two monstrous staircases flanking either side of the grand entrance that wind up and up to unknown levels. Large sitting rooms adorned with rich, dark wooden hearths and reading tables can be seen through giant sliding doors on opposing sides of the stairs. The stone walls drip with tapestries and paintings depicting scenes of battles and triumphs from ages past, the history of Eregahl littering the halls.

Towering stone pillars line the passageways, their surfaces intricately carved with the likenesses of fearsome beasts. I want to spend the rest of the day running my fingers and eyes over the carvings, learning what the creatures are. Some of them I recognise, some I have never seen before, and I immediately wonder if any of them depict the deamhans said to run these lands. Each carving tells a story, a testament to the craftsmanship of the building.

"You did arrive early in the day, even for these uptight hoots. So, I will show you to your chambers where you can settle and rest for a while. Then you are to meet with Headmaster Connally at ten. Aileen, Connally's assistant, will fetch you then and bring you to the hall."

Attempting to digest the wonderment, it takes me a breath to remember who Eamon is and that he is speaking to me. "Lead the way, sir."

One of his eyebrows shoots up at me as he takes the lead to the staircase to the left. "Now, you will be getting your exercise up and down these monstrosities, so I hope you brought comfortable footwear. I tried to tell Connally not to put you on the top floor, but he insisted. Something about offering you privacy along with all the grandeur of the view. I will inform you that there are few scolemasters in the west wing. Most of them stay in the east wing, closer to the grounds and borough. However, you are not fully alone up here."

"There are masters who reside on the grounds?" I ask.

"Absolutely. Most of them do. Through the wyth anyway.

Those without families. We have everything we need on the grounds, but it is twelve miles to the nearest borough of Kilmainnun. Some masters have homes closer to the borough but will stay here through the wyth."

We are three flights in, endlessly going up, and I struggle to keep pace with Eamon, trying to fill my lungs to their maximum with each inhale so he might not hear the exasperated extent of my windedness.

"Gracious, Eamon. How are you this fit?"

Eamon booms with laughter six steps ahead of me. "I damn well better be for having to climb these bloody stairs for the past thirty yehrs. You'll find it easier each day. After a fortnight of your arse being on fire." We both laugh at that.

Eamon spends the remaining trek showing me portraits, tapestries, and architecture that adorn the halls. He points out the shared lavatories, classrooms, studies, and more. My legs are gelatin in my boots when we finally arrive at my quarters.

"Here you go. Top floor, west wing, back corner. Hopefully, you will not get too lonely here."

"Oh, thanks," I say sarcastically, dropping my leather bags and heaving for air.

Eamon procures a brass skeleton key from one of his many pockets and places it in the corresponding brass lock. The door, giant and ancient-looking, is crafted with dark oak and carved with more stories, like the towering pillars in the entryway. My brief inspection discerns what looks to be flitting birds and ornate floral filigree. Eamon pushes the door with both hands, and it offers a resounding yawn of a creak. I would have guessed that it had not been opened in decades, but the inside of the room is stunningly clean.

My hands wander their way to cover my mouth as I take it all in. This room is nearly as large as my entire cottage back home. Giant stone floors run into wooden slat walls. The back two are lined with enormous windows. Straight ahead, I can see the ocean, and the right view offers me the courtyard behind the academy. The windows are slightly cranked open, offering a cool morning breeze that dances with the endless floating alabaster drapery hanging from them.

My bed sits in the corner of the room, directly between the views, and is the most remarkable work of art I have ever seen. Made of solid wood, the headboard is crafted in the shape of a giant half-moon. The wood sideboards run down to the matching footboard, and I ache to run my fingers along the worn grain. Plush, deep green down linens cover it, reminiscent of a bed of moss. With this thought, I notice the smell. Rain, salt from the sea, and something else mingle in the air. Something faint. I inhale deeply, closing my eyes, trying to place it.

"That smell..."

"Ah, you catch that, do you? It's vetiver. Grows loads around the island. Many of our residents make oils from it, from many of the plants here."

I know of vetiver from my studies. I could smell its warmth on the wind during the small voyage with Eamon. This smell is something else. This is lighter, almost citrusy. "It's incredible."

"On the morrow, I will have a footman bring you up some oils made from the local plants and herbs. They may be different from those you grew up with. Might be nice to have or study even, in your case."

"You are too generous, Eamon."

"Och," he waves me off. "Your bathing chambers are through the door to your left. That bookshelf to the right of it, there, is actually a door. It opens to your study."

I was hoping for a broom closet out of the way, and this is what I am provided with. I decide this is all my dreams made tangible.

"Alas, I will let you get settled, and I will see you on the morrow."

I turn to Eamon, my heart doing flips inside my chest. Placing my hand on his arm, I say, "Thank you loads, Eamon. I thoroughly enjoyed our ride, but more importantly, you come and bring me to Elowyn the moment she is free. We must discuss those scones—amongst other things," I say, offering him a strong wink.

He only grumbles and hands me the brass key. "'Tis at the top of my list," he says, turning to make his trek back down the stairs.

My pocket chronometer reads a quarter past nine. I have explored every inch of my rooms; looked through all the books in my study, which houses an enormous desk and large, arched windows overlooking the sea; unpacked all my items once they were brought up; bathed; put on fresh raiments; and made notes in my journal of how I got to my rooms—just in case.

Although the wear of my travels and the lingering bite of

exhaustion from my episode are beginning to blur the edges of my mind, I am far too excited to sit still. I stifle the pinching between my eyes and the shaking of my hands and decide to wander the upper floor for a bit before finding myself some tea. I pop my timepiece back into the pocket of my jacket and check myself over once more in the gilded floor-to-ceiling looking glass on the wall between the windows that overlook the sea. I take pride in my appearance. As a leading woman in my field, the painstaking attention to my wardrobe is worth it every time I see a man sweat.

Since I started university, I took it upon myself to retire my favourite gowns and loose trousers for the harsher lines of fitted coats and tailored pants. My seamstress and I have spent many nights sketching, sewing, and inventing all sorts of wicked things. It took us two full moons alone to prepare for this trip, and I spent a small fortune on fabrics, knowing good and well I would encounter egotistical, insecure men who would be infuriated by what I have between my legs as well as between my ears. My wardrobe is full of suede, tweed, linen, silk, and wool, all expertly crafted to tell a story. My story. And though I do not find myself able to love many things, I certainly relish that.

I finger and tousle my hair once more, adding a bit more volume to my long, loose waves. My reflection stares back at me, appearing far more confident than I feel. My pale brown hair falls below the curves of my full chest, heaving nervously. My wide hips are hidden beneath the shin-length overcoat. Beneath it, a black fitted, velvet dress meets the edge of the coat below my knees, and toned legs run into black leather boots. My own golden eyes shimmer with the light of the morning sun reflecting on the glass. I add a bit more tint to my pouty lips, a special blend made of beeswax, sweet mint, and pigment from dried flowers that my mother always made growing up. The thought reminds me of her. Of Hyacinth. I abandon the looking glass, bounding out the door before I have another moment to sink.

Sunlight streams in ribbons through the corridor. I walk slowly, taking in the view of the sea. I make my way down the six flights of stairs, finding my way back to the main entrance on unstable limbs. Scolers are now bustling around. Chatter, laughter, and footsteps fill the space the more I venture in. I stop to study the carvings on the pillars again when I am immediately interrupted by a small hand on my shoulder.

"Miss Alder?" I turn to see a middle-aged woman with dark brown hair, flawlessly secured in a thick plait wrapped in a low crown, smiling at me.

"Yes. I'm Thorne. Nice to meet you," I offer, extending my hand. She takes it eagerly, placing her other hand atop mine.

"Welcome! I deeply apologise for not coming to you sooner. I'm Aileen. I was just on my way to your rooms to bring you down."

"Ah, well, in that case, I am elated that I saved you the trip."

"No, no. 'Tis no problem at all. I rather enjoy the walks. It is nearly time for your welcome meeting. Allow me to show you the way? We have refreshments waiting."

"I would be delighted." I ignore the throbbing in my eyes and the twisting of my heart and allow Aileen to set the pace.

She leads me through the staircases and down a passage that opens into a giant arched room. "This is the Grand Hall where scolers and masters take their meals. The kitchens are in the back. This is where we host scol balls and an end-of-yehr feast each Nollaig."

Littered with scolers eating and chatting, the Grand Hall is lined with long, wooden tables and benches, and brass candelabras hang from the ceiling and cling to the stone walls. The scolers all don matching garb of some sort. Dark pinafore style dresses, long skirts, ruffled shirts, tailored pants and jackets, and all of them wear some sort of deep green, plaid raiment. The colours and pattern of Adonien.

"We will be right through here." Aileen leads me through a corridor off the Grand Hall that opens into another room. Though significantly smaller than the Grand Hall, the chamber is equally impressive. The far side of the room is made of solid windows that overlook the grounds. Large, leather reading chairs sit in front of the windows, and a buffet table loaded with delicious-smelling food rests in the centre. A man with peppered grey hair and a herringbone jacket sits in one of the seats, and a cup of tea rests on the thick arm.

"Headmaster Connally," Aileen lilts. The man turns, and a manicured moustache, straight teeth, and styled, waxed hair greet me. He stands immediately, securing the top button of his jacket. When thinking of what the headmaster of Adonien would look like, I did not picture someone so dapper and suave.

"Miss Alder," he reaches out for my hand, placing a kiss on my knuckles. The act makes me grind my teeth. He would not lick the palm of a man when meeting. I struggle not to swat at the headmaster.

"Headmaster Connally. It is truly my honour to not only meet you but to be here. I am beyond thrilled to have such an opportunity. I cannot express my gratitude."

"Och, you have no one to thank but yourself, Miss Alder, for it is your work alone that brought you to these shores. Your proposal for this project truly inspired and impressed many here. We are delighted to bring you on to complete it."

"Perhaps, but I know this is a rare occurrence, and I am deeply elated to be the one to help create this study for Adonien. It is quite literally my life's work."

"Exactly. You were the only choice for this. We are honoured to have you, Miss Alder."

"Please, call me Thorne."

"As you wish, Thorne. Master Shrike should be here at any moment. Help yourself to some refreshments, and I will be back with you shortly." He turns to pour me a cup of tea and places it in my hand with an unnerving amount of grace before striding off through the corridor.

I immediately begin gorging myself with the architecture and artwork on the walls, ignoring the small feast on the table. I sip my tea, turning to view a quite exquisite Danumhar landscape. Delicious, warm spices coat my tongue, and I unintentionally release a moan.

As I do, a man walks into the room. I do not see him enter, but I feel him. The air leaves upon his arrival, the walls seemingly aware of his presence. The frequency of the room alters, and that barely noticeable sonation hums somewhere in the distance. I hesitate for the briefest of moments, breathing through the remnants of the episode before turning my gaze fully to see Master Dominus Shrike.

He is nothing of what I expected—much younger than I

thought. How old is he? He looks to be maybe in his thirtieth yehr or so. None of the abstracts or even his widely disseminated works mention his age. I assumed, by the number of his publications and notoriety, that he would be much older. His dark, wavy hair lies at the nape of his neck. He looks as if he has gone a wyth or so without a fresh shave, and the dusting of dark hair defines his sharp, strong jaw. My fingers twitch, rattling my cup, as my gaze dissects his sparkling leather boots, tailored trousers, and crisp linen scyrte. I inhale deeply, breathing through the shaking, begging for the ceaseless tormenting dregs of this episode to free me.

Unbuttoned at the top, his black overcoat fits tightly to his sculpted arms. I study him hungrily, all the way to his eyes. Eyes of the palest green I have ever seen, bright and shocking.

He is the epitome of tall, dark, and handsome—if his tallness is the way he towers over me, if the darkness is the shadows that lean closer to him, and if handsome is the way he looks every inch primal, near animalistic, with his sharp features and wild appearance. He is a walking contradiction; somehow equal parts soigné and rawness. My eyes beg me to take in every inch of him while my blood urges me to lower my gaze.

Dangerous, very dangerous.

Seconds pass before I am aware that I have yet to inhale. When I do, I find my mouth dry, and suddenly, I am quite without the ability to swallow.

"Miss Alder, I presume," he says, his voice like audible night, pulverant and alluring, and so wholly disinterested. I attempt to clear my throat, to tame the insolent and immature beating of my childish heart, to offer a coherent, professional response.

"Yes, Master. It is quite the honour to meet you."

Thump, thump, thump, thump.

"Yes, I am sure it is quite the momentous event for such a menial researcher as yourself," he quips, plucking a plump, violet grape between his fingers, and though I am deeply offended at his comment, my eyes do not deter from watching as he slowly brings it past his full lips to his sharp, white teeth and bites. A throat clears from my left, presumably from Headmaster Connally. I refuse to tear my attention from Shrike to confirm.

Never take your eyes off your opponent. My father's words echo in my mind.

"Ah, your reputation precedes you indeed, Master, though I was truly hoping the gossip had you wrong. Unfortunately, it seems your mind is far more beneficial to society than your mouth. Such a shame," I offer nonchalantly with a shrug of my shoulders and an insincere smile.

Another choke from the headmaster sounds beside me, though I dare not look away from Shrike as he stops his languid chewing to sharpen his gaze on me. I see the tiny remnants of what may be a smile, so quickly I doubt I saw it at all, before he plucks another grape from the bowl, rolling it around his fingers. A small smile does begin to bloom this time when he responds, "Miss Alder, I assure you those who have the delight of benefiting from my mouth find it no such shame."

Heat rises from my neck to my face.

"Master Shrike, regardless of your station, you will refrain from speaking to our guest in such a manner for the remainder of her time. I will accept nothing less than your utmost professional and accommodating demeanour towards Miss Alder. Am I understood?" Headmaster Connally's tone is demanding, though his delivery is velvety smooth.

Shrike's eyes never leave mine as he raises his hands as if accepting defeat, a show I am certain is only for Connally. "You have my word, sir. Miss Alder, please forgive my insult. And please, call me Dominus," he says, reaching those long fingers down in an offering. I hesitate before placing my hand in his. We shake once with equal grip, causing the skin of our hands to whiten. His fingers, coarse and unnaturally warm, wrap around my hand as if it were a child's.

Connally huffs and walks away, but Shrike promptly drops my hand. His eyes darken, and his brows quirk together, forming a stony look of frustration. I dismiss the expression, realising we have been abandoned. I assume my tour has been rescheduled, and that does not fit into my carefully crafted planning. I smile as an idea comes to mind.

"Well, I assume, since you have so wonderfully riled the kind and generous Headmaster Connally, it is now your responsibility to finish my tour," I say, plucking the very grape from between his fingers and popping it into my mouth. His eyes narrow as he watches me, and I can see in my periphery that his fists are clenching at his sides.

Abrasive, rude men are not surprising to me. However, I do find it far more difficult for one to avidly try to conjure such hatred in others when I think it is far more natural for humans to want to work together. There is a balance and harmony to life that Master Shrike appears uninterested in taking part in. That comes from a woman who has witnessed more death, grief, and sorrow than most. Yet one who has also witnessed beautiful, selfless love. I do not seek pain, however intent it is on finding me, yet it is not easy to disentangle from its addictive thralls once we dance with it. I know that insidious tête-à-tête with grief well.

I am reminded that he never returned my correspondence, though meeting him now, I am not surprised, nor do I remain disappointed. Avoiding such behaviour is my preference; although, it might have been amusing to pen my responses, flaunting my capabilities to such a fragile ego. I sense pain in Shrike, and he is eager to dance. I cannot wait to reveal to him that he has met his match. I turn on my heel, placing my cup of tea on the table. I easily glide my hands into the pockets of my overcoat. Propping against the door frame, I glare back at Shrike, waiting for him to make his move, taking the lead in our first pirouette.

Shrike only huffs a breath as he steps around me, staring daggers as he passes. As he breezes by, I am covered with the smell of him. Rain, earth, and...

"Bergamot." Wholly unaware that I spoke the word, it causes Shrike to freeze in his tracks directly in front of me, wedging us both in the doorway.

"Excuse me?"

It resonates then. This was the smell I noticed in my room, only it was so faint I could not place it. Now, this close, his scent climbs its way into my nose and slithers in the pulsing air around us. I force a swallow.

"You...you smell like bergamot. A citrus fr–"

"I am aware of what bergamot is, Miss Alder," he says

smoothly, looking down his nose at me. Tilting my head to meet his gaze, his warm breath caresses my face. I hope my hair is hiding the way it has caused the skin of my neck to prickle. "Perhaps you can control your nasal cavity and the impertinent hole beneath it for the remainder of this torturous tour?"

I swallow the smile and respond, "Only if you stop thinking about my impertinent holes, Shrike." I step in front of him again, not allowing him to see the grin on my face. He thinks a few sharp comments might bruise me. I thought he had a brain to be envied. "I would like to see the grounds, the library, and wherever you will be having us meet, oh, gracious leader."

"Oh, I am beginning to see you could not be led if you were bound and gagged, Miss Alder."

"You would still like to give it a try, though, wouldn't you?" I spin to look at him with crossed arms and a single brow raised in question.

"I assure you, Miss Alder, that would be your fantasy, not mine."

Giving him an exaggerated sigh, I say, "It may be," before offering a hand in front of me, suggesting he leads the way.

"Impossible," he mutters, walking by.

I tell my blood to stop pumping so violently. He is only a bloody man.

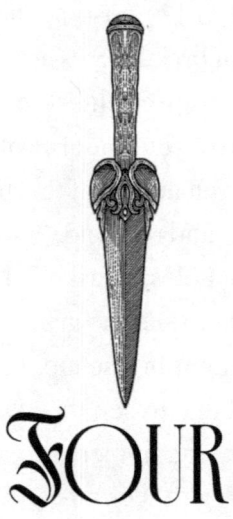

FOUR

Shrike begrudgingly gives me the tour. We have spent over two hawrs alone walking through the castle. He shows me classrooms, the library, and the infirmary, and now we walk to where we will hold the group meetings.

"Though I am overseeing this journal, you will lead the group. My goal here is to offer my guidance and support, not do the work for you," Shrike quips at me.

"I have a feeling I am only here because of the work you refuse to do," I volley.

"Excuse me, Miss Alder, what are you implying with that statement?" he demands, whipping around to me, hands in his pockets.

I straighten my spine, standing tall. "Your aptitude and knowledge are obvious, Shrike. As someone who has spent an incredible amount of time studying your work, I am very aware that you could complete this project in no time. Could have already done it yehrs ago. Maybe that is why you refused to deign a response to my letters. Do not get me wrong, I stand here with nothing but gratitude for your unwillingness. With that understanding, please know that I will only work twice as hard to prove that I can do it just as well as you. You may have a lot of people fooled here, but I know you more than you think. I do look forward to your guidance—believe it or not."

"I can assure you, Miss Alder, neither you nor the rest of the blubbering fools around here know me. I intend to keep it that way. And your incessant letters were burdensome and unnecessary. There is no need for us to develop a relationship for you to complete your work. But, perhaps, the desire to become aware of everyone's privacies is a product of your sex." He turns around, dismissing me. "As I was saying, since you will be heading this project, you have been provided with three others to help you develop the academic journal. Orla Rafferty, Norine Quinn, and Thair Torin. Rafferty has been attempting to climb the ranks here for some time now. She is on track to become tenured in history. She has a sharp brain yet often forgets how to use it. Torin joined us about six menoths ago and has been an utter rawgabbit since. He is an anthropologist who spends an incredible amount of time trying to convince everyone who will listen that he is smarter than I am. He does a poor job.

"Quinn will be most valuable. She has been a scolemaster here for ten yehrs. You have a very similar background; her concentration is ethnology. She released a riveting essay last fómhar which analyses the characteristics of the Eregahl peoples and the differences and relationships between them. She even breaks down the intricacies between the territories here. I am sure you have already read it." I have. Many times. "I will warn that you might have to keep a tight rein on the other two imbeciles, but they can, at the very least, find your books and make you tea."

"What do you teach here?" I ask.

A sly grin. "I thought you knew everything about me, Miss Alder."

I cross my arms. "I asked for a record of courses taught here. I was told an updated list for this term would be provided upon my arrival. I have yet to see it, though. Perhaps a product of my sex."

A slight smile. "I teach an Eregahl History Seminar, Ancient Literature of Danumhar, and Mythology."

"Will you be working with us often, or will I have to find you if I need assistance?"

Another grin, exposing those sharp, lupine teeth. "I am always around. Never too hard to find." A non-answer. "Come. I will show you the meeting hall and introduce you to your faction."

We round the corner to a set of wooden double doors. Shrike effortlessly pushes them open. Inside is what looks to be a large study—or a small library. The walls are lined with bookshelves; two of them have rolling ladders that go far higher than I would want to climb. The back wall is a row of giant windows overlooking the east side of the scol. I make a note to figure out how to get from my room in the west wing to here. In the centre of the room are four large worktables littered with books, parchments, and some of the most exquisite fountain pens I have ever seen. I wrote with reeds until university and only now own one of my own. A gift from my father.

At one of the tables closest to the windows, three people sit, now staring at us.

"Thair, Norine, Orla, this is Thorne Alder," Shrike says, striding over to the group. I follow him, eager to meet them all.

"Hello, everyone. I am delighted to meet you." Each one of them shakes my hand and introduces themselves. There is a warmth that radiates from Norine, Orla looks me up and down with cold eyes, and Thair nearly purrs his hello. Maybe Shrike wasn't wrong.

"Thank you all for your contribution and assistance to this project. I look forward to learning from you and creating a lasting journal that distributes knowledge on the latest studies, research, and breakthroughs of Eregahl."

"We are equally excited for this project, Thorne. And we are very happy to have you," Norine responds.

Shrike breaks his stare from the window. "Right, while we are here, you all must take a moment to decide on your meeting times and days. Be sure they fit well with your teaching schedules; your duty is foremost to your scolers. I will return momentarily."

Shrike turns to leave, but I stop him. "Master, do we not need to work around your schedule as well? It might help to know what that is."

"Do not bother," he says, striding out, loosening his tie. Strange.

"Is he always like this?" I ask.

"Indeed," Thair responds. "However, he is correct. Do not waste your time trying to communicate with the prick. 'Tis a moot venture." His russet skin, high cheekbones, and dark chestnut hair mark him as someone from Caledon, where it stays significantly sunnier and warmer than Danumhar. Most residents here are pale from the constant fog and rain that the northern tip of the island possesses almost constantly. The other territories house endless variations in skin, hair, dialect, and culture.

"Thair," Norine sternly chastises, "Could you at least pose as the professional and intelligent scolemaster you are supposed to be for a single moment? Thorne just arrived."

"Tell me I am wrong. 'Tis best to warn her now so she doesn't take it personally. He is an insufferable man. Nothing more to it."

"Oh, I believe I have already deduced as much," I add.

"See, Thorne has already discerned as much, Nori."

"Refrain from calling me that, and figure out a way to cease your gabbing. We have actual work to do."

I notice Orla eying me, suspicion lurking between her scrunched blonde eyebrows. She's a petite woman with long golden hair that frames her sharp face. Her hazel eyes study me, unimpressed. I try to dissuade her. "And what about you, Orla? What are your thoughts on the impossible Master Dominus Shrike?"

Her eyes soften a bit. "I think his talent and knowledge far outweigh his lack of social niceties."

Ah, a devotee. "Good to know. Alright, if you all wouldn't

mind going over your teaching schedules with me, we can meet when you all are free. I can move my work around meeting times."

It takes us half an hawr to work out a good time between us all, but we settle on meeting three days a wyth at five o'clock, making them supper meetings. Thair agrees to see to the kitchens about providing our meals here. The next hawr is spent getting to know our backgrounds a bit, discussing what works we've read of each other's, and the plan for the journal.

"So, Thorne, tell me how a woman from Albion finds her way to study Eregahl history and folklore. I mean, we are all from here, have a background in it, and went to this bloody scol, but what possesses a girl to want to learn about the mythical creatures and stories of magic an ocean away?" Thair asks.

"I think a part of the answer lies in your question. What little girl doesn't dream of magic and faerie tales?"

"I do not think monsters from the pit, evil witches, and generational curses are the things anyone dreams of."

"Maybe not, but it is exactly what I have been looking for either way. There is something about this place that has always called to me. I hope to find many hidden truths while I am here. Speaking of that. Thair, would you be interested in doing a few archaeological unearthings while I am here? I was hoping to search some specific locations along the coasts. I have read many reports that there have been remains found, and since that is your expertise, I thought it would be beneficial to take advantage of your qualifications."

It is an odd sensation having menoths of preparation coming to fruition. A tiny shimmer of pride flickers in my chest.

"You can take advantage of me all you want, Thorne." Thair grins naughtily at me.

Orla is quick to step in. "How does that contribute to the work of the journal exactly? We are here to write, research, record, and compile."

"I suppose it contributes as much as Thair does being here at all. His knowledge of the day-to-day lives and tools of ancient civilisations is paramount to this journal. I was hoping that if we find any artefacts, we can write an entry about them, and present what we find and the writing somewhere in the academy. Our own contribution to the journal, perhaps. The work we are doing here is very important to this scol and all of Eregahl. Together, we can compile and provide a rich source of history, lore, and resources for scolers and future generations. That is something that has never been done before. Any way we can deepen our well in what we provide can only help. If any of you have any other ideas on how to do that, I would love to hear them. Maybe, together, we can even unveil some secrets of this land."

Orla half rolls her eyes at me, but Norine begins to beam, "Indeed, I do have a few ideas."   Her warm brown hair lies in heaping curls around her head, landing gently just below her chin. Her round face and soft amber eyes make me feel like I've known her for yehrs.

"Wonderful, let us hear them."

"Since we are going to ask each scolemaster in the history sector to write an essay for the journal, I was thinking perhaps we could allow scolers to submit a piece as well. We can create specific themes or topics for them to write on, but I thought it would be progressive and motivating for scolers to potentially have the opportunity to contribute to the project."

"I think that is a wonderful idea, Norine. Perhaps that is something that can continue as well once I am gone. We shall explore that more at the next meeting."

"Speaking of exploring," Thair begins, "has Shrike given you a decent tour of the place yet?"

"I have indeed, Mister Torin," Shrike says, gliding back into the room, smoothing his hands through his loose hair. Waves of midnight tumble around his ears and neck, messy and wild. He attempts to nonchalantly dust himself off, but I do not miss the now dirty stains of his hands before he slips them into his pockets. "As I have told you countless times, there is no need for you to worry about my responsibilities."

"Nice of you to join us. Now that we have completed the meeting," I say, taking in his shaken appearance. Where had he gone?

"Good, you can catch me up as I escort you back to our hall."

Our hall?

"If you are busy, Shrike, I can take Miss Alder myself. It would be indulgent to study her mind a bit more."

"There will be plenty of time for that in the meetings on Luan, Chéadaoin, and Aoine, Mister Torin. Miss Alder needs to eat and rest."

I cannot help my pinched brow and the sour set to my mouth. How did he know about the meeting times? Has he just been standing outside listening? And what's it to him that I eat and rest? And *our* hall?

"It was great talking with you all. I look forward to seeing you on Luan evening. Please let me know if you need me before then."

"Indeed, we will, Miss Alder. Have a wonderful rest of your day." Thair grins at me before we turn to leave.

In the hallway, I begin my barrage of questions. "How did you know about the meeting times? Where did you go? What do you mean by *our* hall? Why are your hands covered in filth? Did you slip away to the gardens? Does the infamous Master Shrike dally with dahlias?"

Shrike looks sideways at me, his pale green eyes peering out from behind his dark curls. "Because I am a rather brilliant individual. That would not be considered any of your business. And yes, *our* hall. Our lodgings are unfortunately next to each other. Yes, I already tried to remedy that to no avail. I have no idea why Connally would put you up there in the middle of nowhere, next to nothing. And, again, that would not be any of your concern, but since you asked, no. I much prefer bramble and briars to fleeting, flourishing beauty."

He would adore the violent things. Although I have more questions, I choose to play the mugwump to attain answers. "Why are you in the west wing, then?"

"I like my privacy, Miss Alder, and my space. So, do make yourself as unnoticeable as possible."

"You and I both know that is not something I can do."

"Cannot or will not?"

"Take your pick, Shrike."

He releases a deep sigh, and I think we have both had enough chatting. We walk in prickly silence for a bit. It is a decent trek, nearly from one side of the castle to the other.

Between these walks and the stairs, I might need some more comfortable footwear. I will query Eamon as to where I might acquire some leather to make some slippers with. Thinking of Eamon reminds me of something else I have noticed upon my arrival.

"I have a peculiar question," I start as a thought from earlier revisits me.

"No doubt."

He's insufferable. "Are none of them wed? I have found it very odd that Eamon and Orvander are the only wedded people I have met here."

"I think that you will find, Miss Alder, that Eragahl differs from Albion in many ways. A few of which include progression and advancements. Where your tiny island has nothing to focus on other than breeding and sustaining life, we in Eragahl, Danumhar, especially, prioritise our studies and societal contributions. You will find many individuals here dedicated to their work. Like-minded individuals who think and speak and live more freely than what is allowed in your ramshackle village."

Ouch. "Perhaps you might find you are not quite the unique specimen you might be in your homeland. Perhaps you might find yourself feeling quite ordinary—maybe even lacking."

A buttery laugh rumbles through me. "No, I do not think I will ever consider myself lacking, Master Shrike. However, it is rather refreshing that no one here is concerned with the status of my coupling. I suppose I am considered a spinster at home, already surpassing my twenty-eighth yehr without a husband."

"Do not consider it too much, Miss Alder. I am sure those who have associated with you are very known as to why you remain unwed." My eyes widen at his response, but before I can respond to him, we arrive at my rooms. "Here you are. Your midmeal is waiting inside for you. Eat and rest. Enjoy your wythnos. Work will begin first thing Luan morning."

Endless possibilities swirl in my mind. I have two days of free time before meetings start, and I cannot decide if I will spend them roaming the castle and the grounds, visiting the borough of Kilmainnun, or reading as much as I can of the books in my study. Maybe I will try them all.

Shrike turns to leave, but not before adding, "Oh, and Miss Alder, under no circumstances are you to be outside the walls of the academy past nightfall."

I laugh. I laugh because he thinks he can tell me what to do and because this is a bloody boarding scol. What does he think the people who live here do at night? "Why is that, Master? Will the deamhans eat me alive?" I ask, raising my brows in sarcasm.

"Yes." He spins on his heel, taking ten long strides before opening his door and slamming it behind him.

"Impossible," I murmur before doing the same.

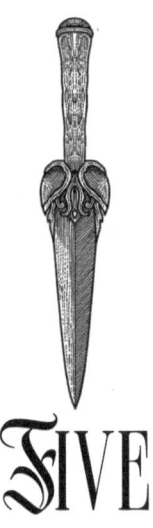

FIVE

The bed is, indeed, delectable, but sleep still evades me. I spent the evening reading until my eyes were finally exhausted enough to be able to close. I toss and turn now, not used to the stillness of the room. In my cottage at home, I could always hear the sounds of nature outside, the calls and croaks of small animals lulling me to sleep. Here, in this stone fortress, the quiet is too loud.

I huff a breath and toss the covers back, moving to crank the levers on the giant windows, letting in the sounds and smells of the night air. The beautiful song of the sea and the cooing of the breeze immediately calm me. Danumhar is painfully beautiful, even at night. The large moon, seemingly much closer on this island, shines brightly with the twinkling stars, illuminating the cliffside. My room rests high above the new bloom of the trees below, and I can see parts of the carved path from the gates to the cliffside. I glide across the room, dancing with the breeze now winding through it to open the windows that overlook the grounds. Warm, glowing torches line the top of the stone walls that surround the walkways and large quadrangle, casting a haunting radiance on the barren grounds. The yard is tremendous. Its walkways end in lofty archways that lead to other parts of the castle and the path to the forest beyond the grounds.

I am at home here in ways I did not expect. Academia has always been my haven, my safety, my passion. It is where I have found hope and security when the world around me has been anything but that. Being able to stay and study in the most renowned and architecturally resplendent institution is beyond a dream.

As Orvander said, if I find nothing else here but the opportunity to witness the history and art, the wonder of the academic life, then maybe I could find some sense of contentedness that I previously had not allowed myself to consider. I could live this life, alone and happy with my books and my research and perhaps even alongside the company of like-minded people, sharing in rich, profound discourse.

I should be happy at the realisation. Most people would be. But like any other instance in which I recognise the space that could harbour a small amount of happiness in my life, fear rushes in to pry it from my shaking hands. A terrible, horrible fear of seeing what I could have here and knowing I likely never will. I am not allowed happiness.

As if in response to my thought, lightning scatters across

the sky, bathing the yard in quick flashes of light. Something catches my crying eyes, drawing my attention from the sky to the fountain in the centre of the quadrangle. Thunder booms in the wake of the lightning, echoing in my chest. Rain begins to fall in viscous, heaving drops. Even from this height, I can hear it splatter on the stones below. I squint my eyes to focus through the darkness, waiting and listening. The smell of the rain wraps around me like an old friend, but it carries a different tone here, made warmer by the flora of the island.

Another streak of lightning barrels through the sky, bigger and brighter, causing me to startle, causing me to almost miss it. But there! Something is there. Along the back wall, nearly too far from view, darkness, a moving shadow, blurs through the yard. Is it coming onto the grounds or going into the forest? I cannot tell. It stills in the threshold of the yard. I wait with bated breath, forcing my eyes to focus in the dimness. Another crack of light, another fraction of time to see it, but it's gone. I scan the entirety of the grounds, looking for it. Nothing. My mind flashes back to the pillars in the entryway—to the unknown beasts carved in there. Surely, if they were indeed on this island, they certainly would not make their way this close, would they?

I search the darkness for a moment longer, and when I find nothing else, I allow myself to resume my breaking, letting preemptive grief prepare me for inevitable heartbreak, dressing in self-crafted armour. I let it sound through me, crying along with the rain, as I lace it up to my neck.

An earth-shattering roar sounds from the forest beyond, hauling me away from my spiral. I squint, focusing my stare into trees of darkness coating the ascending mountainside. Nothing moves, nothing sounds. Nothing remains but the seething of the rain screaming against the earth. I move swiftly to my bed, diving in and bringing the covers to my chin. I listen and listen until the wind and rain harmonise into a mystical crescendo that finally lulls me into sleep.

I dream of that shadow and that harrowing bellow. It replays in haunting repetition, each time getting closer and closer to my window, unspooling more dread from my gut. I dream as it loosens again, this time shattering the glass windows on my feet.

I bolt from sleep. My breaths saw raggedly in and out of me. I am drenched from sweat and the sodden air of my room, wet from the downpour that still has yet to cease outside. I vault from my bed, searching the windows again. The sun is moments from cresting the sea to the left, but night still clings to the courtyard—still has its claws embedded, leeching every moment it can.

Muddled footsteps pound against stones in the hallway. I scurry to the door, keeping the sound of my own feet as quiet as possible. Squeezing the lock, and with a forceful turn, I beg it not to make a sound. The weight of the door is nearly immovable with the slow pull I give it, cracking it barely open. I angle my head just enough to get a single eye out. Just enough to see a dark, towering figure move toward me in the corridor. The candles dripping from the wall go out with every stride it takes past them. I watch them all die out as my heartbeat pounds in my ears. All but one. The one that hangs beside Shrike's door.

I want to scream, to warn him, to scare the thing away, but my voice refuses to bend to my command. The shadow stops in front of his door. Its laboured breaths echo to me, the shaking, ragged gait of it sending my hair on edge. As it turns and places its hand on the door, the light from the single, flickering flame reflects a shimmering, red wetness across its arm.

No, *his* arm.

The shadow *is* Shrike, and he is covered in blood. What is he doing? Before I have a moment to study him further, he whips his head toward me. I dart back into my room, using my full strength to quickly but quietly close the door. I lean my back against it, intent on not moving until I am certain he is gone. Nothing happens for a moment, then his steps sound again, getting closer and louder. All the way to my door. I close my eyes, hoping he doesn't begin to pound it, demanding to know what I was doing, why I was spying on him.

Just barely, I hear him place his hand against my door. I hear him as he slides it down the wooden carvings of the flying birds. Then he takes off back to his room. The slamming of his door rattles my bones, and I hurry to jump back into bed, my heartbeat running with me. Was Shrike the shadow in the forest? That is impossible. That shape, that shriek, belongs to something unholy.

Deamhan, my mind whispers. I wrap myself up and wait for the sun to rise, running over the possibilities. Then I remember who I am. I am not a woman easily frightened. I am not a woman who shrinks in fear of men or monsters. So, I rise and prepare myself for the day ahead.

SIX

My hands ache with soreness. It has been yehrs since I have worked with leather. My heart bleeds alongside my pricked fingers as I finish the final work on my new slippers. I can still hear my father's smooth baritone in my ears now, "Tighter stitches, my love, or your toes will burst right through the top."

The borough of Kilmainnun was beautiful, and the people there were very kind and helpful. Cobblestone streets echoed with the clip-clop of horses' hooves and the rattle of carriage wheels. Ladies wrapped in shawls and gentlemen donning baíníns promenaded past elegant shop fronts and manicured gardens. The tang of salt air from the bay wafted through the streets, mixing with the earthy scent of peat smoke from countless hearths. In the marketplace, the vibrant colours of fresh produce and the glint of fish scales sparkled in the sun. I was able to purchase a full hide, securing excess in case I need to craft anything else while I am here. Memories of my family followed behind me like ghosts as I wandered the streets, running my hands along materials, smelling the fresh herbs and spices, and tasting freshly baked bread.

Something about Eregahl is opening me up. I have been able to think about my family more than I have in recent yehrs. The pain is still fresh, still marring me with each moment. But being here, I can nearly see it from the outside, as if I am finally beginning to distance myself from it. Being an ocean away has allowed me to look at the memories with more introspection and less dismay.

I finish my slippers, leaving them to soak in warm water in the copper tub so I can fit them properly to my feet. Staring out the room of my window, I wrap my aching fingers in small strips of bandages I found in the cabinet of my bathing room. The moon is full and bright tonight, casting my room aglow. I fill my lungs with the night air, breathing in the delicious scents of rain and that warm, woodsy musk of Danumhar. The citrus still lingers in this room.

For a moment, I consider taking a walk, but then I remember the shadow and the howl. I cast that fear aside quickly because looking for monsters and magic is what I came here for. Shrike's warning of being out past dark rings in my head, causing sheer defiance to rise in my blood with it.

Do it. Go. He can't tell you what to do.

I run my wrapped, bloody fingers along the stone wall beside the window, digging my nails in contemplation. As I increase my grip, a stone moves beneath my aching extremities.

Excitement washes away my petty desires, flooding me with suspicion and curiosity. I try wiggling the long stone free. It moves but does not release. I scour the room for something to help remove it. It could simply be a loose stone, but it could be more. It could be one of the hidden designs of the academy.

My heart gallops in my chest. Frantically, I run to the study and palm the sharp letter opener on the desk. Running back to the window, I begin to dig out the dry mortar from around the stone. I pause every so often to wiggle and pull on it. My hands become more battered, but my curiosity pushes me on. Finally, the stone clamours to the floor, only just missing my bare feet. I take the candle from my bedside, holding it up to the opening, my heartbeat coming to a pinnacle in my ears. The glow of the candlelight presents a neatly wrapped piece of cloth bound with a decaying leather strap.

My hands shake as I reach inside, and my breath heaves in and out of me louder than the waves slapping the shore outside. I bring the mystery object and the candle to the windowsill for more light. Slowly, gently, I unwrap the cloth. A gasp leaves my mouth as I fully uncover a dagger. My mind begins hurling questions before I can comprehend them. How old is this? Who made it? What was it used for? Who knows about this? Are there more hidden objects in my room, in the scol, on the grounds?

Working to calm the frenzy, I grip the handle, bringing it to the light. Its weight is a sturdy comfort in my hand as I close my eyes and let it all rush in. Yehrs of swordplay with Father beneath the giant cedar trees. The way he would pretend to attack Hyacinth and me, only to be beaten black and blue with our wooden weapons. The yehrs after when he gifted me a dagger of my own. How he crafted a sheath for me to wear around my neck, the embossed hyacinth and irises along the edges of it.

This dagger, however, is not the sleek and agile weapon my father had made for me. The handle is wider, fitting my now adult hand comfortably. Where mine was a poker, a glorified butter knife, this was crafted for a warrior. My mind, rattling around in my skull, considers the history, lore, and traditions of the land, and spits out a word: skean.

This is a skean. The wooden grip is aged and worn with natural finger grooves worked into it. The handle blooms into the quillon, opening as if birthing the blade. The ricasso is expertly carved with an intricate knot pattern that looks vaguely familiar to me, but I cannot place it.

The dagger gleams in the candlelight, its double-edged blade singing a promise of both protection and peril. I run my thumb along its razor-sharp edge, relishing the whisper of steel against my skin. A thrill races through me, awakening something primal and ancient in my bones. Without command, my body begins to move. Scraps of supple leather left over from crafting my shoes find their way into my grasp.

Time passes without my recognition, and I now stand facing the looking glass with the sheathed dagger around my neck suspended by a thick chain from a pendant brought with me—a poor substitute for proper weaponry, but it will suffice until I can venture back into the borough. I unsheathe it, cutting through the air behind me, spinning on my heel, and leaning into a fighting stance as Father taught me. I flip the blade in my hand before sheathing it again. With wicked fire burning in my chest, I tuck the skean beneath my gown and don my overcoat and boots. Armed and alert, I take to the stairs and out to the woods. The forest beckons, dark and wild, and I must answer.

I need space. I need the night air filling my lungs and tangling my hair. I need to feel small. I need to feel nothing, lest the memories begin to eat me whole. I need to see what's out there. I take the path through the trees that leads straight to the cliff overlooking the Draíocht Sea.

The nights have usually begun to warm by now in Albion, but here, high up in the sky, they still possess that small bite of coolness. I let it pebble my skin, soak through to my bones. The sea calls to me, closer and closer now. I can feel the water in the air and the salt on my skin. I am acclimating to how different this place smells. I notice more now the warmth of the vetiver and the citrus in the air. Citrus...

There is a blur of darkness up ahead. I barely see it as it runs across the path and disappears off the cliff. Suddenly, I am on the ground, and pain renders me frozen. Pain all over my body, but mostly from the side of my head. There is a heavy weight on me, unmovable and paralysing. I wince, scared to open my eyes.

"Gods, Thorne! What are you doing out here?" I peel my eyes open to find Dominus Shrike on top of me. His bare chest presses against mine, pushing the sheathed dagger into my skin beneath. His arms frame my face, and one of his hands reaches back to cradle my neck. "Are you alright? Thorne, speak to me."

"Get. Off," I wheeze out. The man is huge. I have no air left in my lungs. On my command, he jumps up in an instant and is on his feet before I even blink. I am beginning to think I am concussed. Shrike leans down to pick me up. He gently places his arm under my neck and at the bend of my legs and lifts me as if I weigh nothing at all. He moves to sit me on a large stone beside us, one we barely missed in our collision. I wince, thinking of how much worse this could have been had we not.

He leans over to me, placing both hands on either side of my face, inspecting me with more concern and intent than I can stomach to see reflected in his eyes. "Thorne, I need you to speak. Tell me that you are alright, or if I need to get you to the infirmary. Your head is bleeding." There is a strange humming coming from somewhere that I cannot make sense of. Like the aftershock of an ancient gong being hit.

His eyes are glowing. Glowing with pale green light. "I hit my head, and your eyes are glowing. So, you tell me."

"Shite," he murmurs, closing his eyes and taking a deep breath. When he looks at me again, they aren't glowing anymore—just that bright, pale stare blazing into me.

"Whoops, never mind," I chuckle.

"Can you take a deep breath for me? And let me look at your head?" I do what he says, breathing deeply, filling my lungs with his earthy citrus scent. "Does anything else hurt?"

I take inventory, thinking about all the places we made contact when we hit. This leads me to think about all the places where we are currently making contact, and his skin is hot as he touches me, roving my body, looking for any injuries. "No," I say breathlessly but unsure. Everything is a bit hazy. "Just my head, here." I turn to show him my temple and the blood running down to my chin. It's a slow drip, and I hope it is not too deep.

He grunts. "What were you doing out here? I explicitly

told you not to be out past nightfall, Thorne."

My insides begin to war. My gut reacts, telling him what he can do with such commands, "Listen here, Shrike—"

"Dominus. You will call me Dominus."

I expect his demand to only further my rage, but this time, the defiance shrivels to ashes before it fully catches fire. What is wrong with me?

"Listen here, *Dominus*," I bite out with as much spite as I can muster, "You do not get to tell me what to do. I was out here because I wanted to be. There are no scol rules against it, and do you wander around berating everyone else for being out here? Wait, why are you out here? And where is your scyrte?"

He licks his thumb before wiping away the blood from my head, causing me to whimper. "Be still. I need to see how deep this is. And it is none of your business what I am doing out here. Nor is the whereabouts of my raiments. Can you stand?"

"Then my location and lack of raiments are not your concern, either," I respond and immediately regret it.

"Not your best retort, I am afraid. Might have done some damage here." I jab him in the ribs. He refuses to acknowledge my act of violence. "I am going to pick you up and place you on your feet now."

"No, you are not. I can stand." I move to stand on my feet, only to stumble back a bit.

"You are not walking anywhere." Shrike dips me back in his arms again and begins to walk back to the academy.

"Put me down, you insufferable heathen," I demand.

"Not a chance. You nearly fell over back there. I am taking you to your room."

"Shr—Dominus, what if someone sees this? I do not need the talk this will cause. I am a professional, and this is obscene."

"No one will see," he assures.

"How do you know?"

"Because no one else is foolish enough to come out here at night except you. Notice how you did not see another soul on your little walk?"

Thinking about it, I had not. But why is that so? What are they afraid of? What was he doing out here? "Why are you so unafraid then?"

"Because I have the means to protect myself."

"With these big, dumb muscles?" I say, poking at his shoulder beneath me. I close my eyes, wishing I could summon the words back in my mouth. I sound like an absolute imbecile, and my head is pounding, and his skin is so warm, and I want to lay my cheek to it.

"Precisely why," he replies without a hint of sarcasm in his voice.

"Oh," is all I offer.

Dominus carries me into the castle and all the way to my room without us seeing anyone else. Something is strange about it. There should be scolers bustling about looking for late-night food or studying or embracing in the corridors. It should not be abandoned. As we ascend the final flight of stairs, I find myself staring at the side of his face. His breath is even, unchanged, and unbothered by carrying me up an endless number of stairs. My head still spins a bit as we arrive.

"I am going to sit you down so you can unlock your door. I will be right behind you to keep you stable," he says with that unnerving calm he has.

"It is unlocked, but you can still put me down."

I feel his teeth grinding beneath my fingers that hold onto his neck. Without putting me down, he reaches to swing the heavy door open. He closes and locks it before slowly walking me to my bed and sitting me down with painful softness.

"Do not move," he growls before stomping off. I hear him step into my bathing chamber, and I take a moment to gather myself. My coat is covered in dirt, twigs, and leaves. I gently peel myself out of it, becoming more aware of the stiffness setting into my limbs. My fingers are nearly immovable at this point. I should have paced myself after so much time out of practice.

I hear a crashing sound and look to find Dominus before me, an empty bowl spinning on the wet floor. He holds a dry cloth in his hands. His eyes roam over my body, and I remember that I am now down to my silk gown and muddy boots. He clears his throat before kneeling to retrieve the bowl and leans to wipe the water from the floor. Once clean, he looks up at me from his knees, those green eyes a beacon in the dark. "Apologies. I will hastily return."

Thankful that I am not standing, I wrap my arms around myself and offer him a nod. A rush of wind floods through the open windows, fluttering the drapery and wrapping my long hair around my face. I brush it out of my eyes and away from my blood-soaked skin. Finding a discarded scrap of leather on my bed, I tie my hair into a mass on my head, welcoming the breeze on the back of my neck.

Dominus rounds the corner again, white-knuckling the clay pot in his hand. A fresh cloth dons his right shoulder. He kneels before me, and sitting on the bed, we are at equal eyesight.

"I am going to get this cleaned up. If I find it does not need stitching, I will leave. If not, back down to the infirmary we go. Do you understand?"

I only roll my eyes at him—the only answer he needs since he dips the cloth into the bowl, squeezes it out, and gently grabs my chin to turn my face to the side. With great carefulness, he begins to wipe the blood away from the wound. The cloth is warm and soft on my skin but still stings, and I wince, pulling away from him.

"You must be still, Thorne. I need to assess this." He grabs my face again, holding me in place as he returns to his maintenance. I look around the room, concentrating on everything I see: the books on the floor, the leather scraps everywhere, my dark raiments hanging in the open wardrobe, and the way the moon casts blue light that dances on the walls. The flickering of endless candle flames. I think of everything else happening other than his hands on me. "This looks fine. It has already clotted. I am going to get the rest of this blood off you, alright." Not a question.

Unable to meet his eyes, I nod my head slightly forward anyway. Dominus rinses the cloth again, bringing it to my cheek. He makes soft, slow strokes. Wipe, rinse, repeat. He works his way down my chin, across my throat, to my neck. Before I realise what I am doing, I begin to lean into the touch, the warmth, the care of another. Feeling someone else's hands on me is—

"What is this?" He pulls the chain from the inside of my gown, revealing the skean. I watch as he takes it in. As his brows furrow together. As he pulls it from the sheath. "Where did you find this?" There is anger in his voice, but it is laced with curiosity. Perhaps even disbelief. I study every twitch, every move he makes. I examine him like an insect in a glass, dying to know what he will do next. I briefly consider lying to him—telling him I brought it with me, that it was the dagger from my childhood. But my traitorous heart flips in my chest, and I suspect he would know if I were being truthful or not.

"I found it. Over there," I nod toward the hole in the wall, the loose stone still lying on the floor. He moves to inspect it, still holding the skean in his strong grip. Still assessing him, I realise how effortlessly he carries it and how *right* he looks with it in his hand. Rage suddenly begins to fill me as I realise I do not want him to keep it. *I* want it. "I made a sheath for it. I had spare materials from making some slippers. I was not unarmed in the woods." I don't know why I need to justify myself to him. It is none of his bloody business either way.

"With or without a weapon, you are unarmed unless you know how to wield it."

"I know how to wield a blade. You assume, because I am a woman, that I could not cut your tongue from your mouth where you stand? Why don't you hand that back and let us see?"

Warm, velvet laughter escapes him, cresting the ebb of a genuine smile and revealing a small dimple on his right cheek that I had not noticed before. I swallow before standing and turning my hand out for the blade. He considers it, flipping it end-over-end. He pauses, bringing those haunting eyes to meet mine. Then he sends it. The skean flies past my head, and its tip thuds as it sinks into the wood of the headboard behind me.

"Keep it, Thorne. You will need it."

Shrike

I stand unmoving, absolutely baffled with my mouth gaping open and my hands to my bare chest as Dominus Shrike storms out of my room. He stops only to turn, staring me down, pure hatred turning his eyes to the deepest green of the forest floor before saying, "And stay out of the fucking woods."

He slams the door behind him, sending a shock through my bones.

Your move, his footsteps echo down the hall.

SEVEN

If I slept at all the night before, I cannot tell as I open my eyes to the growing light of the sun casting its golden rays into my room. I stretch, taking inventory of how I feel. My hands are sore and stiff. The ache in my head has subsided, but my back and side remain sore from where we landed. Thoughts of Dominus Shrike fill my head, setting my anger to a raging flame. He threw a bloody dagger at me. I understand the competitiveness and even his downright disdain for me, but attempted murder is rather excessive.

I decide to wash my mind of Shrike and take advantage of my last free day before my work begins. Since the sun is just rising, it will be hawrs before I can send for bricfeasta. Instead, I bathe, scrub my teeth, get dressed, and boil some tea over the hearth. Taking my tea into the study, I begin to work through the books. Most of them are on Eregahl's history. There are books in languages I do not know, and some are in languages I suspect are ancient and forgotten. Many I recognise as the modern Danumhar dialect; others are old versions of it. I turn over all I have learned of Eregahl in my head.

There is no known date of when people first settled on the island. The lore states the island was created by four gods known as the Seren when they first inhabited this realm. There are a few unregulated texts that speculate that arrival was around two thousand yehrs ago. The widespread, factual history only speaks to human existence for the last few hundred yehrs.

What we do know is that the island has always been prosperous, flooded with vegetation and wildlife, and home to many plants and animals found nowhere else, like the vetiver and the shrikes that flutter in droves outside my window now, singing their morning song to the sun. I have always been amazed by the shrikes. Unlike other birds, they do not swoop to attack their food. Instead, they impale their prey on thorn bushes or sharp trees. They kill more than they immediately need, storing the food for later. They skulk through dense bush, stalking their prey, waiting for the best time to attack. As Orvander stated, many texts refer to them as butcher birds.

But they are also songbirds. Their particular melody is soft—a long, complex, thrasher-like series of haunting coos. It is an interesting dichotomy being able to produce lilting, ghostly lullabies while also possessing such violence. I wonder if Shrike's family was part of the first group of people to settle here. Were they named after them, or is it a mere coincidence that he shares the moniker with the butcher bird? After last night's display, I find the name fits perfectly.

My mind shifts back to the lore of Eregahl. The general history states that these four created Eregahl in their own vision, making art and light of it. It tells that they came here from a distant place, wanting to create a new world. Eden, Noreg, Caledon, and Hellas are siblings, and the territories of this island are named after them. I found that small fact to be a bit boring and egotistical, but then I questioned what I would name territories if I were a god, and well, I suppose it could be worse.

Together, the siblings indeed created many beautiful and wonderful things. From their own blood and bone, they crafted powerful beings to look after the land. Texts mark them as "Mistéir" or Mystics. They were their first and favourite creations. Beautifully crafted with incredible strength, healing, and many other supernatural abilities, the Mystics were a powerful cadre of lethal and dangerous beings that did the bidding of the Seren. The Seren created many other beings, too: faeries, kelpies, selkies, merrows, keeners, all the way down to humans. It was even said they created bunúsachs, which were spirit-like beings crafted from tiny slivers of their essence and used to see all parts of their lands. Some stories say they used them to spy on their creations and even each other.

I run my fingers along the pages of my book, a needed weight against my chest, *Oidhre an Domhain.* The lore varies in the distinctions; however, these tattered pages hold a story unlike anything else I have ever read about the origin story of the Seren: a prophecy that one of their creations will rise against them one day, take their throne, and reign over the earth. I have never been able to discern if that was a positive thing or not. The prophecy is seared into my consciousness, its words etched deep onto my bones. Through countless recitations over the yehrs, it has transformed into my sacred invocation, my prayer. I sip my still-steaming tea and recite it to myself.

"In the crucible of sorrow, forged by blood and bone,
one shall rise, by anguish known.
Against the shadows, they'll wage their war,
to claim a birthright long before.
Through valleys deep and mountains high,
this Heir of Earth will rule the sky.
But heed, for power comes at a price:
A heart surrendered shall suffice.
Vicious eyes that pierce the night,
aglow with ancient, eldritch might.
In sacrifice, true strength resides,
as destiny's thread swiftly glides.
Only when the self is shed,
and on the altar, tribute bled,
shall the Seren's heart be won,
and darkness' reign be undone."

I have found no other instance of it in all the books I have scoured, nor do I have any idea what it means, but it twists something dark and unknown within me.

This is just one of the very answers I aim to find here. Maybe I can find another being, maybe a seer? Can I find someone like the woman who cast magic upon me nine yehrs ago? Can I find answers here about my curse? Can I break it? Will I ever be able to love another and have another love me, or am I destined to live my life alone?

I shuffle stacks of books around, noting the titles I want to come back to. Breaking to finish my tea, I move to the window, hungrily taking in the view. Unlike many people here, I know magic is still real. It has to be. There is no other explanation for what that woman did that night. If I can find someone, deep within the mountains or sea of Eregahl, who does practice, who does believe, then maybe I can solve this. Maybe I can someday know the peace of a full home, of full arms, of a full heart.

A knock sounds at my door, pulling me from the books. I tap the top of the stack I separated to investigate when I get back. They are ancient-looking tomes and dusty parchments. They look older than this world. Maybe they hold some secrets.

I wrench the heavy door open to find Eamon standing on the other side. "Oh, Eamon. Good morning!"

"Good morning, yourself, Miss Thorne."

"What brings you all the way to my wing?"

"Elowyn is dying to meet ya. You wouldn't mind joining us for a bit o' bricfeasta, would ya? I figured, being the wythnos, you might have some free time before your busy sets in."

My gut sinks, but I plaster on the biggest smile I can. "If Elowyn is cooking, there is nowhere else I would rather be."

"That's just grand. Come on then."

Eamon takes me in the horse-drawn carriage to his cottage on what feels like the other side of the eighty aecers.

"If you two work in the scol every day, why live out here?"

"Like most at the academy, we will stay there during the wyth. On the wythnos, we like to take a step away. "'Tis a difficult thing to live where you work and work where you live.

You need the separation. It can be hard on the mind if not."

"That makes sense, I suppose. Does that mean if the next few menoths begin to weigh on me, I can come hide away with you and Elowyn?"

"Don't you dare mention that to her. She will love it too much, and I share her enough with you lot at that scol as it is. For two glorious days, she is mine."

"Oi, Eamon, a bit ruffled this morning, are we?"

"Oh, not at all, my dear. Just a man determined to spend every moment he can with the woman he loves."

A knot begins to form in my chest, seeping with envy, but I only reply, "Very admirable, Eamon. Very admirable."

The endless ride is, realistically, just short of a half hawr. Eamon and I talk so much about Elowyn during that time that I feel I already know her. We arrive at their beautiful stone cottage nestled atop a sloping hill. The morning sun shines brightly on it, but warmth radiates from within before we step inside.

A lovely woman steps out. Her dark hair is grey at the roots, and she wears a baby blue cotton dress with a linen apron that she's rubbing her hands on. Her blue eyes sparkle at me. An uncomfortable knot starts to form in my chest. She resembles what my mother's sister might look like. Or what Hyacinth might appear at her age if she had ever lived to see it. They radiate that same warmth, that same kindness, that same kind of unconditional love.

"Well, you must be Thorne." As I step down from the carriage, she walks to greet me. Surprisingly, she wraps me in her arms, and for a single breath, all I want is to stay here forever, to lean into her and give way to all the emotions that have risen within me since yesterday. Instead, I squeeze her gently with my gnarled hands and pull away.

"Elowyn," I greet her, offering her my most genuine smile. "It is truly an honour to meet you. This one has spoken of nothing else, and I feel like I know you already. Also, I must thank you for your tea and scones. I would never want to be welcomed to an island in the middle of nowhere any other way." Elowyn offers a buttery laugh, squeezing my hands in hers. I unintentionally wince, causing her to look down.

"Och, lass, what happened here?"

"Oh, I made myself some slippers. It has been some yehrs since I have sewn. Right humbled myself, I did." I try removing my hands from hers, but she only investigates further.

"Eamon, put the horse up and join us. I am going to fetch some salve for Thorne, and then we will eat." Eamon rolls his eyes as if he already knows he has taken to the background for today.

I want to poke my tongue out at him, but instead offer him a warm, "Thank you, Eamon," and smile. Elowyn pulls me inside and sits me down at the kitchen table, which is brimming with food, and my mouth begins to water instantly.

"Please tell me you did not do all of this for me, Elowyn. I would be truly upset." She rifles through an old, wooden cabinet in the corner of the room. Above it, echinacea, lavender, arnica, and chamomile hang to dry. I close my eyes, not wanting to take in any more. Not wanting to realise how familiar this is.

"You worry about nothing besides filling your belly, dear wain."

I swallow again, searching for something humorous to say.

Something to keep the mood light. Something to make her like me. Something that does not reveal the broken woman I am.

"I can do that." It comes out flat.

"Ah! 'Tis just the thing. Massage this into your hands twice a day. It will help heal the cuts and the soreness." She saunters the round, palm-sized, silver vessel over to me. I open the tin, inhaling the balm.

"It has—"

"Calendula. For the wounds." I breathe again. "And lavender and rosemary for the soreness." I meet her eyes then as she smiles at me with pride.

"Good girl. Where'd ya get a nose like that?"

I clear my throat and begin to remove the bandages so I can apply the salve. "Uh, my mother. She...made these kinds of things constantly for me and my sister." I cannot meet her eyes as I rub the soothing, cool balm into my aching hands.

"I see," she says, slowly sitting down in the chair beside me. "And how long has it been...since your mother made a salve for you?"

I meet her gaze, wholly unable to blink back the tears as I answer quietly, "Nine yehrs."

"My deepest apologies, dear." She gathers my still-bandaged hand, gently unravelling the soiled cloths. She takes a spread of the salve from the tin and massages it in. I have not been soothed like this since Hyacinth died. I have not been healed with personalised balms since Mother died. I've not been touched tenderly with care and love since Father joined them both.

As if she heard my very thoughts, she asks, "What about the

rest of your family?" Her voice is concerned but not pressing.

"All dead, I'm afraid." A single tear rolls down my face. Elowyn reaches to wipe it away, taking my face in her soft, warm hands.

"You poor thing. I cannot imagine. I know there is nothing I nor anyone can say to lighten your grief. But do know that time, well, it doesn't heal anything, but it softens it. Slightly. One day, you shall find yourself able to take a deep breath again. You will be able to walk around, carrying all the pain, and it will not be quite as heavy. I promise." She grins at me.

I wish she were right. I wish I were any other person who has lost loved ones. But I am still waiting for that day. Still aching to take a deep breath. Still waiting for the guilt to release my throat.

I hear Eamon approaching the open door, and I can only imagine what this looks like. Pulling myself together, I turn to Eamon before he has a chance to speak and say, "Eamon, you did not tell me that your wife is a goddess."

He offers me a small smile, and I think he knows. I think he knows her well enough to know how she moves. How she loves and cares for others. He takes his cap off and asks, "Didn't I, though?" as he flops down beside us. We all grin and begin to eat.

Elowyn is without a doubt the best cook on this and every other island. I find it horrific having lived twenty-eight whole yehrs without tasting her food. Bangers, hash, eggs, toast, even apple cake, tea, coffee, and freshly squeezed orange juice were prepared. It is the bricfeasta of my dreams.

"Eamon, I mean this in the kindest way possible, but what

did you do to deserve such a woman?" They both giggle at that, and I relax, being back in control. Being able to turn everything into a jest and a deflection away from me.

"Och, gods, something right, I suppose. I know I couldn't live without her. Wouldn't want to."

"Well, I certainly now understand why you try to hide her away here on the wythnos all to yourself." Elowyn and Eamon beam at each other, and it makes me wish my body would slip away to nothing and disappear through the floor.

"You are welcome anytime you want, Thorne. Here or at the academy."

"Och, let us not go too far, Wyn, love. We've only just met the girl. She might not be all sorted out and whatnot."

Elowyn and I both gape at him. "Eamon," we huff together. He offers us a sly grin.

"You'd better get yourself together. Besides," she says, leaning across the table to grab my hands—my hands that I realise do not hurt at all anymore, "I like her. 'Tis something special about this one, Eamon." We grin at each other.

"The feeling is mutual. Though the jury is still out on Eamon," I add, sending us all into laughter.

I stay most of the day. I help Eamon with the horses and help Elowyn prepare the midmeal. We eat in the garden, watching the shrikes fly overhead. They tell me stories of their lives. We laugh and talk and eat, enjoying the presence of one another. It is a perfect day.

Eamon rides with me back to the scol where I spend hawrs crying into my pillow, knowing that everything I want exists on these grounds, and I cannot have it.

I realise, with a banging on my door, that I must have fallen asleep. I jolt awake, finding my room dark and stuffy. I wipe crust from my swollen eyes as I run to the door that is *still* being pounded upon. Half asleep, I pry it open, shielding my eyes from a candelabra burning brightly in my eyes.

"Where have you been, Miss Alder?" Dominus Shrike stands before me, dressed—finally—in what looks to be riding raiments.

"Frankly, I do not see how that is any of your concern. Now, if you would so kindly remove yourself from my doorway, I would like to go back to sleep." I attempt to shut the door, but he stuffs his large boot in the way. "After throwing a dagger at my head, you will not be surprised to know that if you do not move your foot, I will break it with this door."

"You certainly may try."

I try to slam the door, but he catches it effortlessly with his free hand.

"Please, just bloody relent, would you?" I turn on my heel, not concerned at all with what he's doing. I fling my windows open, looking for the cool night air. I hear him step into the room, and the door shuts behind him. His audacity should not be as surprising at this point. "One would think a man as smart as you could discern when he is imposing on others. I am tired, and I wish to sleep. If you must stay, you can watch."

"Where have you been?"

Opening the last window, I take a deep breath of sea air. The coolness of the breeze washes over me, sending chills along my skin. I spin on my heel to Shrike. "Are you dense? I specifically said it is of no concern to you. I may be your subordinate, but you are not my caretaker. You do not need to concern yourself with my schedule."

His eyes roam up and down my body, and I can see the disgust turning his mouth down. Glad to know I cause such vitriol in him as well. "It is my concern since you have a death wish, and your death is the absolute last thing I need on my hands, so if you continue to traipse around these grounds as if they were your private residence, then I do, indeed, need to keep up with you. You are not the only one with something to lose here, Miss Alder."

Unfathomable. The absolute gall of him. Not deigning to offer him a proper response, I only do what I know will make him leave. I slowly shake my head back and forth in disbelief. "That is precisely where you are wrong, Shrike," I say, pulling my gown over my face, exposing my bare body fully to him, knowing it will send him running. "I have absolutely nothing left to lose."

He spins immediately toward the door. I toss myself onto my bed, already drifting back to sleep, my mind beginning that strange hum. I crack a single eye to see his large frame standing in the light of my open door. His entire body is tense, and his free hand is clenched at his side. The other white-knuckles the stem of the candelabra. He growls, actually growls, before stomping out, slamming my door.

I realise every encounter between us since my arrival has

ended in the slamming of a door. And then I smile because he has been the one to slam them all.

Your bloody move, Shrike.

I barely have time to drift off to the humming in the back of my mind when the door sounds again. Thinking he could not be foolish enough to return, I drape myself in a robe before answering. No one is there. I look down to find a silver tray full of food. I pick it up and bring it inside, shutting the door with my foot. A folded piece of parchment rests on the tray. I lift it to the candlelight, finding the word, "Eat," written in expertly formed handwriting. I instantly know who it belongs to. What is his obsession with my appetite? Perhaps like the shrikes outside my window, he is only feeding his prey, waiting for the precious moment to attack.

Oh, dear Shrike. Don't you know I am not the sufferer? I am the thorns on which you will fall. I smile, knowing this game is far from over. I eat roasted chicken and smashed potatoes under the light of the moon until I am full and quickly drift back to sleep.

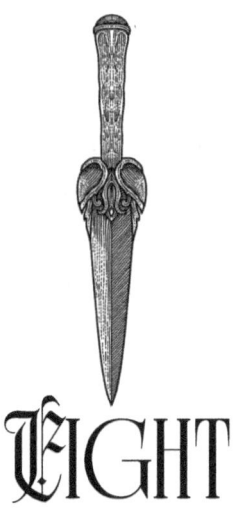

EIGHT

The next few wyths pass quickly, and I find myself sinking into a joyful routine. I spend my days engulfed in books in my study, the evenings meeting with Norine, Orla, and Thair, and the wythnos with Eamon and Elowyn. We have discovered we rather enjoy each other's company, each of us as passionate about rhetoric, etymology, history, mythology, and ethnology. We spend the evenings talking or in heated debates about our favourite books, theories, and findings. Shrike has yet to join a meeting, and I have seen very little of him since my display.

A display I am still reeling from. I am usually not so abrasive. Finding empathy and understanding for others is important to me, but Shrike has done nothing to earn my respect, and honestly, I do not think he can be dealt with any other way. Shock for shock, another stylistic aspect of this dance we do.

That was nearly two fortnights ago. I occasionally see him walking to and from class, and each time, I ignore him. I could have sworn he tried to stop to speak to me yesterday as I walked past his open classroom, but I breezed on by, not giving him the chance. I can hear him go in and out of his room. All hawrs of the night, his door opens and closes, and his boots slap up and down the stone floors. I do not dare look outside the door again, though I do stay up watching out my windows, looking for signs of him, signs of monsters, too. I have not heard that cry or another since the night I arrived.

"Right, but hear me out here. If that were the case, if what you say about magic being a living thing is real, Thair, then how would one access it? And what qualifications must one possess to be able to wield it? Are they born with it? Is it a genetic trait?" Norine asks Thair as she pops a small tomato into her mouth. I love watching their battle of wits. I am but a spectator enjoying the throes.

"Not exactly. See, from my findings, I have the instinct that magic has no rules. No bounds. I think people can be born with it. I also think that it can be gifted. However, I suspect that it exists in ways our human brains cannot understand."

It is an interesting thought. I have been gulping down their theories like a parched woman, becoming a sponge, soaking up everything I can and comparing it to what I know and the comforting weight sitting in my chest pocket.

"What do you mean, our *human* brains? What other kind of brains might there be?" she volleys.

"Well, if we continue with the theory that magic is real and exists in Eregahl, would we not be incredibly naive to assume that we are the only beings still here that the Seren created? If the magic comes from them and is still here, would all their other creations not be as well?"

It is something I have considered myself. But where is the proof? What are we missing? "One would think so. But would you not also assume there would be a record of it? That is what has always been missing from the equation. There is no proof of these things existing among us. Not in centuries. No explanation of where they have gone. Where are they?" I offer, throwing myself into the fray.

"Ah! But that is only if we conceive them to be creatures as the lore describes them. But what if they exist all around us? What if they look just like we do, hiding in plain sight?" The tension in the rooms rises as the child-like versions inside us all beg for this to be true, wanting the magic to come alive before us.

"Do they have a secret society? Because wouldn't you think someone would know? Or one of them would get close enough to a human to spill their secret?" Norine asks.

"Maybe they are sworn," Orla finally offers. She spends most evenings judging us while offering menial commentary. Sometimes she has great points, but mostly she's just ornery. When she gets into the theory, like she is now, her facade of boredom and disgust fades a bit. "Maybe they are all cursed from being able to tell a human the truth."

Thair only shrugs at her, shooting his eyebrows up as if saying, "Maybe."

I pull my pocket chronometer out to check the time. It is half past ten, and though that is early for me, I am itching to get back to my room to finish a particularly thrilling piece on the early civilisations here.

"Though this is truly riveting discourse, I am afraid I need to retire for the night," I say, popping my timepiece back into my pocket. "But before I do, I want to run something by you all. I want to travel to the four other territories while I am here to speak with the locals and the other academics to see what information they have. I want to know how it correlates to what we have. Would any of you be interested in going with me?"

Thair eagerly volunteers himself to be my private tour guide, and the others agree as long as it fits into their schedules. We decide to talk about it at the next official meeting.

"Why don't we all go out for a drink this wythnos? We can show Thorne around the borough more and talk about something other than monsters and magic. What do you say?" Thair asks.

Orla quickly offers her stern, "No."

Norine looks at me wearily. "Alright. I suppose we all deserve a bit of a break after wyths of work. It would be nice to get away for a bit, anyway. And Thorne here deserves to see what you turn into after too many spirits."

"If you mean a devilishly good time, then you would be correct, Norine," Thair says through a smile.

"I mean the type of arse that becomes obnoxiously loud and terrible at jests," she retorts. I struggle to maintain the laugh rising in my throat, a rare emotion that I acknowledge.

"Was it not you spewing ale from your nose the last time, or did I hallucinate that?" Thair asks, tonguing his cheek.

"Aye, it was. But I was laughing at the embarrassment you

were making of yourself, not your extensive wit."

"Well, I am a right good laugh either way, am I not?"

She laughs, "I suppose you are, Torin."

"Count me in. That is a version of you I want to see," I say. And though I mean it, my chest aches at the thought.

"But not the only version, I am sure," he winks at me. I roll my eyes and offer my goodbyes to the group and head out for the trek to my rooms.

The walks are no longer daunting, and I thoroughly enjoy wandering the castle, especially at night. I take my time, meandering down hallways I have never been before. I stand, spending long moments taking in the tapestries and sculptures that line the path in the eerie quiet of the halls. This one in particular has caught my eye each night that I have walked by it, but I have yet to let myself pause to take it in. Until tonight. I stand as slow, warm tears begin to run down my face.

It's simple, really, though entirely complex. It is an oil of Adonien, resting high on her throne with violent waves smacking the cliffs beneath. The academy itself looks as if it has just been built. It lacks the salt stains and the heaps of climbing ivy that I love. A dark storm brews in the clouds above. The colours are all dark and sharp. The contrast of the shadows and highlights makes my gut sink. There's a wrongness in it. It is just a painting, a landscape of the very castle whose halls I now roam, but something about the small creature distantly falling from the sky, far above the highest spire, with its hand stretching, reaching toward the clouds as dark wings hide its face, breaks me.

The longing.

The fall.

The aching.

The loneliness of it calls to the very solitude in my soul.

Footsteps pull me from my moment, and I turn to see Shrike pacing down the hall towards me with powerful, long legs. He carries a stack of books in his arms and is dressed impeccably in dark raiments per usual. He squints his pale green eyes when he sees me. I grunt and turn back toward the artwork. He has ruined the moment I have waited wyths for. A private moment to absorb invisible emotions crafted with paint and lines and shadows. He doesn't make an effort to stop. He breezes on by, and I think I am safe...until he speaks.

"Best get back to your rooms." His voice is low and stern.

"Excuse me?" I whip around to him, anger surging through my blood.

He stops then, inhaling and broadening his shoulders before turning slowly to look at me with the eyes of a wolf, with eyes of a predator gazing upon his next meal.

"I said," he growls, "you had better get back to your rooms."

"Or what?" I question, stepping up to him.

He smiles a wicked smile at me. "I know you think your defiance is power, little one, but in fact, it is ignorance. Listen to me, and get back to your rooms. Now."

Red. I only see red as my arm raises to smack Dominus Shrike right in his insufferable mouth. He catches my arm, pulling me into him. Our faces are close, too close, as our rapid breaths mingle with each other, and my heart begins to pound.

"If you ever try that again, you had better land it. Because I do not miss, Thorne, and I will gladly reciprocate what you give. It seems you need to be taught a few lessons."

A wild, deep laughter slithers from my throat, surprising me with its unheard tone. "I know you think you have me all summed up, but I promise whatever narrative you have crafted of me is wrong. I never relent. I never submit or stand down—especially to the likes of you. You think your contention and aggression will frighten me or force me into submission." I huff an honest laugh then. "You know nothing of me. That only stokes my ire." I bring my other hand to his chest to push away from him and out of his grip. "And I will do what I bloody well please. If that means spending my nights in these halls or beyond them, that is my choice. I suggest you stop assuming that I am yours to worry about."

I turn, taking off down the long hall before he has a chance to respond. I have never met a man, or anyone for that matter, so infuriating. So full of disdain. Such an...equal adversary. He angers me, pushes my limits, and causes me to act in such inappropriate ways. I must keep my distance from him.

I do not allow myself to look back, though my mind claws at me to. I do allow myself a small smile. It is a minuscule victory, but it did not end with a blade spinning toward my face or a slammed door—and the last word was mine.

NINE

Thoughts of Shrike stab incessantly into my mind as I dress for the day. I wonder what sort of life he has lived—one of luxury, I am sure—to make him think he can treat people the way he does. It must be lonely being so miserable.

I would know.

I settle for plaid, high-waisted trousers. I tuck a sleeveless, linen scyrte into them and secure them with a leather belt. I don a chunky, heeled boot, and exchange my overcoat for a light cardigan. I tousle and oil my hair, letting it flow freely nearly to my waist. The comfort of routine has made me complacent. I need to get back into the search, to venture onto the grounds at night again to see what I can find.

A knock sounds at my door, and I pray that it isn't Shrike. I open it to find Norine waiting for me. Her beautiful curls are especially bouncy today. Her bright eyes and round, defined cheeks rise as she smiles at me.

"Oh, thank the gods," I say, pulling her in.

"For what?"

"That you are not my cantankerous neighbour."

"Ah, that's fair. Gods, Thorne. This room is amazing." She walks around inspecting every inch of it, the way I did on my arrival.

"Have you never been in here?"

"I have never been to the west wing. No one really does. Shrike is—was—the only one over here. I stayed clear of it, as does everyone else." She thumbs through a stack of books on my bedside table as she speaks.

"I see."

"Alas," she says, finally making eye contact, "I came to retrieve you."

"For what?"

"Shrike is giving a lecture today. Connally has asked you to sit in on it. He thinks it could be beneficial and a 'real treat.'"

"Has he met the man? The very last thing I want to do is listen to him literally lecture me for an hawr."

She huffs a laugh. "He is a master for a reason. I promise it will not be terrible. I will take you there."

"You aren't even going to suffer with me?"

"I am afraid I must send you into battle alone. I have my own lecture to give."

"Why can I not attend yours? I would much rather listen to you ooze wisdom and passion for a session."

She smiles at the compliment. "Because he is the all-powerful and wise sector master, not me. Come now, put your war face on." I smile wickedly at her. "There she is." She loops her arm between mine and leads us down the hall.

She deposits me at the threshold of a large classroom moments later and leans in to whisper, "Do not kill him, and all will be well." Then she pecks me on the cheek and pads down the hall away from me. I take a deep breath and turn to enter the room. Only a few scolers have arrived. They sit in rows of sturdy wooden desks and benches arranged in regimental formation, each adorned with tattered tomes and magnifying glasses of varying sizes. My eyes are immediately drawn to the arched ceiling soaring overhead, its weathered beams crisscrossing like the ribs of a great beast. At the front of the room, an imposing lectern awaits its master, while behind it, shelves groan under the weight of ancient volumes and peculiar artefacts, including bare skulls and worn vertebrae of animals—or beasts.

Windows of leaded glass allow thin streams of daylight to penetrate the chamber, their diamond-shaped panes creating a patchwork of light on the worn floorboards. Dust motes dance in its ethereal beams, sparkling like miniature stars. Scattered about the room are bizarre contraptions: a towering perspective glass pointed out one of the windows, a massive pendulum swinging in hypnotic arcs, and tattered maps and scrolls. Aged wood permeates the air—the rich, deep smell of centuries-old oak from the desks and beams. This is underscored by an earthy scent and bergamot.

I am honestly in awe of it all. This classroom is not merely a place of learning, but a portal to another time and realm, where the boundaries between lore and truth blur, and every lesson holds the promise of unlocking the extraordinary. Parts of me ache to have been a student here.

More scolers begin to shuffle in, and I take an empty seat in the very back, close to the windows. I watch nearly forty scolers settle, waiting for their master. A large chalkboard stands to the left of the lectern. "Mythology" is written on the board in perfect, familiar script.

The hum enters the room before he does, and I force myself to stare at the plaid green banner of Adonien hanging from the left wall. I watch him in my periphery take his place in the front of the class, resting his leather bag on the small table beside it. His gaze is on me, searing my skin. I try, but I cannot force my eyes away any longer. Instead, I slip on a mask of disinterest and sit back in my chair. He indeed stares at me through squinted eyes as he rolls the sleeves of his scyrte up.

"Welcome, class," he booms, still looking at me. My neck becomes warm, and I toss my thick, long hair behind my back and remove my cardigan. Look at us, preparing for battle. I want to laugh at it, but I refuse to quirk my lips up at him. It might send the wrong impression, and I do not want him to think he has taken the lead. If I am forced to be in this presence, then the least I can do is make it miserable.

He finally peels his eyes from my face, assessing the rest of his pupils. "In the past few wyths, we have discussed the physical locations of the territories in Eregahl and how the mythology from each territory might be different. Today, we will pull the scope back and look at what we know of Eregahl as a whole. Then we will take that and apply it to some new theories."

He walks to the board, picks up a half-worn piece of chalk,

and jots down some points. "Eregahl mythology is a rich tapestry of ancient tales, legendary heroes, and supernatural beings that form the foundation of its cultural heritage. This body of lore is typically divided into four main cycles. First, the Mythological Cycle: This cycle deals with the earliest mythical inhabitants of Eregahl, including the Mystics, a supernatural race with godlike powers. Key stories include the creation of these beings, along with those that follow."

Having studied these very points in my own education, this experience is somehow infinitely more authentic, and I cannot help but lean in on my elbows, fixated on his every word.

"The Seren Cycle: Set around one thousand yehrs ago, this cycle focuses on the life of the Seren while they were here. This era explains how they lived amongst their creations and how they led their courts. The Hellas Cycle: These stories revolve around the god Hellas and his band of deamhans that waged war against his siblings, causing chaos and betrayal that upended all ways of life before. Finally, the Historical Cycle: Also known as the Cycle of the Kings, these narratives blur the line between myth and history, explaining how the territories of Eregahl abandoned their gods and took on their own leadership, selecting leaders for each province as we know them to be today."

The Cycle of the Kings is the only connection between myth and history, showing how Eregahl obtained its now human rulers.

Shrike makes eye contact with me briefly, and I force myself to lean back into my seat; the vision of indifference.

He continues, "Key themes in Eregahl mythology include magic and the way the Seren crafted their creations to use it, mythological creatures, the importance of poetry and prophecy, and the interplay between the mortal world and supernatural forces."

I watch him speak with such power and sureness. Surprisingly, he treats his pupils with respect and oofers encouragement as they ask questions and converse their way through theories. A creeping, slimy reverence slithers its way through me while I watch in wonder as he lectures his way through the hawr. It is not at all surprising why he is here or why he holds the place that he does. He is enigmatic, brilliant, and truly inspiring. I am lost in thought, gazing at the way he fills out that buttoned vest when he speaks...to me.

"I am sure many of you know, but Miss Alder, there in the back, is here to aid the academy in creating a journal that focuses on the lore and mythology alone. She works alongside myself and a team to research and preserve written stories. Miss Alder, why don't you share with the class your favourite story of myth?" He leans against the lectern and crosses his arms.

Interesting.

I initially want to comment that he works alongside no one, having completely abandoned all connections with my project, but I digress. I am curious to see what his angle is here. I take a deep breath, knowing my answer immediately, allowing the fond memories to flood me.

"Well, thank you for the unnecessary introduction, Master. I will share with you all a story you might not have heard. One of my own scolemasters shared this with me once, and I have rarely seen it in many texts. Long ago, in the misty realms of ancient Eregahl, there lived a creature of many talents named Lugh. He was known as Samildánach, meaning 'skilled in many arts,' for there was no skill or craft he had not mastered. Lugh was born of unusual parentage—his mother was a shapeshifter, one of Caledon's children, but his father was one of Hellas' deamhans. It is uncertain how the coupling happened, but it was Lugh's existence that caused much discourse on what Hellas' creatures truly are. Legends claim that Lugh had a very interesting life. Though incredibly talented, he constantly warred between the good and evil inside himself. Hellas worked to get him to join his war, but he would not turn on his mother's people. Lugh was a great warrior in the battle between Hellas and his siblings. They still lost, but his sacrifice and glory are why we know him today."

For some reason, I pull my attention from the many faces pointed at me and set my eyes on Shrike before finishing, "His story is my favourite because it is a reminder that no matter what we deal with, no matter the darkness inside us, we always have a choice of who we want to be."

Shrike stares at me with clinched eyebrows, examining me to the very bone. The room becomes deadly quiet, and he does not move his eyes from me as he says, "Class is dismissed." Scolers immediately rise and scramble from the room. I allow them all to exit as I am in the back before I follow suit. Nearly to the door, Shrike stops me. "Miss Alder. A word."

I grind my teeth in defeat. I was nearly free. I walk my way to where he stands, still leaning against the table, and mimic his form on a desk in the front row, crossing my arms, too. He uncoils his own, moving to grip the edge of the table. We stare without speaking, both of us waiting for the remaining stragglers to clear the battlefield.

"Did you find your observation satisfactory?" he bites.

"It was not my idea to be here if that is your assumption. Connally sent me. Thought it would be a good idea. I will admit, I was...surprised."

"By what?" His gaze sharpens a bit.

I breathe deeply and slowly let it out, trying to form the compliment in my mouth. It tastes like coal. "At your...ability to teach. I found it baffling that you are capable of self-expression and conversation that possesses kindness and respect. Lucky them."

He smiles at me then, showing off that bloody dimple, and runs a hand through his hair. I look away at anything else. "I am very capable of that, and much more, for those who earn it. For those I find worthy."

"Worthy?" I snap at him. "How have you found me unworthy of your kindness?"

He leans slightly toward me. "Maybe because the only thing that comes from that vexing mouth of yours is foul and incorrigible."

I open my arms, mirroring his lean. "Oh, please, Shrike. It's beyond you to insult me now, is it not? Especially without true effort. If I am too great an adversary, you can accept your defeat. I do have a knack for being more than most can handle."

He steps close to me, placing his hands beside me on the wooden desk. It groans as he leans onto it. His scent envelops me, causing my head to swim. "Yes, Thorne, you are too much. Too defiant, too mouthy, too persistent, and far too intelligent. You command everyone in your presence to rise to meet you, and that—" He pauses, leaving me on the very edge of his words, sharp as the blade I carry. His eyes devour me, searching for something I know he will not find. Truth. "I have not witnessed before," he finishes, and I free-fall from the edge, spiralling toward my demise. "You make me feel such violent, curious things." His voice is low and coarse, and I cannot tell if he wants to kill me or kiss me. The thought sends my heart pounding in my chest and makes my mouth dry. Just when I think I have secured the victory, he spins me into unknown movements, causing me, again, to doubt my abilities...or to improve them.

"Show me," I dare, my voice sounding far bolder than I feel. His eyes begin to shine as they stare at me, as they trail a path from my eyes down to my lips, to my neck. I hold my breath as he leans in and runs his nose along the side of my throat. He inhales deeply, releasing a low growl that crawls along every part of my skin. All thoughts dissipate, all guards drop, and I become defenceless. A blubbering fool. Just as I begin to lean into it, a knock sounds at the door. We remove ourselves quickly, and he immediately walks to open the door. Norine pops in, and I am beyond thankful for her.

"You survived!" She holds her hands in the air in congratulatory excitement. I clear my throat and tighten the grip on my cardigan in my hands.

"Indeed," I say, and I grab her arm and lead her out the door, not daring to glance back.

"Are you alright? You seem...startled."

"Yes. It wasn't terrible. You were right. He is a miserable prick but a fine scolemaster. It was nice to witness."

She only offers me a knowing glance and a smile as we take

off to the Grand Hall to eat. The heat of the encounter fades with each step I take away from him. I remind myself once again that he is only a man playing a game.

A game I intend to win.

TEN

The rain batters the top of the carriage so violently, I can barely hear Thair speak over the sound of it. "It's just up here," he nearly yells to Norine and me.

I look forward to seeing Kilmainnun at night. I even look forward to letting loose a bit. These wyths of work and research, diligently remaining perfect and brilliant and making all the right choices, well, I am ready to take my mask off for just a moment. To settle more into myself, or what remains of me, anyway.

I have not gotten to explore as much as I would like. No new information has been uncovered from the books in my room. The only mysterious things I have witnessed yet are the howling shadow in the forest and Shrike himself. Darkness shrouds him. Besides his uncanny ability to be a renowned arse, something else hovers at his edges. Something I cannot place. I would need to get closer, speak to him without burning fury roiling in my veins, to study him further. That is an unlikely option.

The carriage thuds to a bumpy stop. Thair exits first, holding his long coat over his head for Norine and me. We quickly follow, trying to avoid the torrential downpour by hiding under his thick arms. It only fractionally works, but we are inside the tavern before the rain soaks through our raiments.

We push open the heavy oak door, and the tavern's warmth and raucous ambience wash over us. Flickering torchlight dances across rough-hewn beams overhead, casting long shadows that twist and writhe with each gust of wind from the hearth. The air is thick with the mingling scents of ale, roasted meat, and pipe smoke. To our right, a group of men hunch over a table, their beards tangling with foam as they drain massive tankards. Their rich laughter punctuates the low hum of conversation. Across the room, a hooded figure sits alone in a darkened corner, fingers tapping rhythmically on a worn table. The bar stretches along the far wall, its polished surface gleaming dully in the firelight. Behind it, rows of bottles catch and refract the amber light, their contents shimmering like liquid gems. The barkeep, a burly man with arms like tree trunks, wipes down mugs with a cloth that has undoubtedly seen better days.

We step in, shaking off the rain. A whimsical sound wraps around me, and I notice a minstrel plucking at a lute near the hearth, her melody nearly lost beneath the clinking of coins and the scraping of chair legs against the uneven floor. The scent of tonight's stew wafts from the kitchen, rich and inviting, making my stomach growl in anticipation. As I move further into the belly of the tavern, my boots stick slightly to the ale-soaked floorboards.

I can tell this is a place for the locals. This is somewhere people go to enjoy the company of one another. To drink and eat and laugh. Where everyone knows each other and can exist in a common place with ease and enjoyment. That is something I have never done. I swallow at the thought of it, suddenly regretting my decision to come. Thair pulls us along, ruining my exit plan, and quickly secures a table not too far from the hearth. We are close enough to enjoy the flames and the music while still being able to hear one another.

The barmaid makes note of us. She is slightly younger than me, and her tight, dark curls bounce as she walks her way over to us.

"What poor victim did you bring with you tonight, Torin?" she asks, and her large, round eyes sparkle at us beneath long, dark lashes.

"This is Thorne Alder. She's a researcher from Albion here to develop a journal for the academy. It just so happens that she was gifted a disgustingly handsome and equally genius anthropologist to aid her."

"Ah, where is he, then?" I ask, looking around the room. The barmaid and Norine both roll with laughter.

"I retract my statement calling you a victim, lass. That might be Thair in this instance. Good for you."

"I will gladly be her victim, Aoife." Thair winks at me. I roll my eyes at him. Aoife does the same.

"What can I get for you this eve?" Aoife asks. I stare blankly at Norine for help.

"Stew and a loaf for us all," she answers, and I am grateful for the rescue.

"And ale," Thair adds. "Lots of ale."

What have I gotten myself into?

We eat the delicious stew and drink frothy, thick ale long into the night. Norine offers me her history of how she came to Adonien. Her family are hedenks, those who still believe heavily in the Seren and hope for their return. They pray and worship and take part in offerings and rituals that many gave up long ago.

"It wasn't that I ever questioned their existence. I just watched as so much of my family blindly believed and partook in things without question. I always questioned. I wanted proof of them. I need to see the things I believe in. That wonder took me down the path of history and lore and to study the relationships between the people of Eregahl and our cultural and religious beliefs," she says very matter-of-factly.

A thread of understanding tightens between us. "And have you found what you were looking for? Are your questions answered?" I ask.

She laughs breathlessly at me, her amber eyes turning glassy from the ale. "I fear I only find more of them."

"I understand what you mean," I offer, and she looks at me as if she believes I do.

"And what of you?" I ask, looking at Thair, though I am beginning to see two of him. I smile at the sight.

"Me? Well, I do not think there is enough ale in this tavern to work through my family affairs. Besides, that would thoroughly ruin the lushy look in your eye, and that would break my heart." He takes my hands and pulls me from my seat.

The wood of the walls swirls and blends as he spins me around. Laughter, unadulterated and uncensored, sounds from my throat—a sound I have not heard in a long, long time. The ale washes away the panging in my chest to stop, to refrain from it all. I allow Thair to spin me around and sing a lilting bar song loudly in my ear. I wrap my hands around his strong shoulders, tipping my head back to smile. I smile like the drunk I am, and for once, my inhibitions are missing. I finally know the feeling of a night in the borough with friends. I know how it feels to laugh and talk with fear abandoned. Maybe it's the ale, maybe it's the magic of Eregahl, but I feel free. I feel like I am coming alive.

ELEVEN

We spend the ride home in such laughter that my stomach hurts with it. I begin to come down from the high of it as we pull through the giant iron gates. Guilt begins to twist through my sore abdomen; that thing that never lets me be happy is back with a vengeance. I part ways with Norine and Thair on the first set of stairs, echoing empty promises of doing it again soon.

"Thorne," Thair calls, jogging to catch up with me. I notice how the full muscles of his chest rise and fall with each thud of his feet. If I am being honest, Thair Torin is a beautiful man. He is nearly as large as Dominus, but his strikingly handsome features are more natural, more human, and less carved from stone. He beams at me with that sideways smile he has, coming to a stop in front of me. He runs both hands through his thick, wavy hair, which is much shorter than Shrike's. And suddenly,

I find myself completely irritated for comparing him to that chiselled arse.

"Yes," I finally answer him, a bit breathier than I would have liked. Thair is an unapologetic flirt. I have discerned enough in the time I have known him to understand it is less about his intent and more about his self-confidence. Sure, it borders on egotistical, but most of the time, he is genuinely being himself. And if I am honest, there is little I love more than someone who can jest about and make others laugh or blush with embarrassment—especially if it's inappropriate. We share a twisted pleasure in making people squirm with the abrasive things that come out of our mouths. I think, since I am one of the few people who encourage his foul behaviour, he has inherently gravitated toward me. And that is acceptable. I can handle the banter. I can wade in the shallow friendship. Thair is the perfect person for that. Plus, he is nice to look at.

"It is late, and I know you know your way and that you are beyond capable, but would you please allow me to escort you back to your rooms?" he offers with more sincerity than I have seen of him these wyths.

I sigh deeply at him, making him squirm a bit. "Fine," I finally say, shoving my hands into my pockets. "But no funny business or your future privileges will be revoked."

"How can you say such things to me? No funny business? While you just made me aware that you are already thinking of the next time. You wound me. I would not have thought you to be so keen." He offers me a crooked smile and loops his arm through mine in my pocket. I allow it to remain.

"I think we both know which one of us is *keen*, Torin, and

it is not me."

"Are you so certain of that, Thorne? Not even for the famed Dominus Shrike? I see the way you look at him, the way you search for him in the halls."

"You are absolutely correct. Except you mistake lust for disgust and my searching for avoidance. He has been a right pain in my side since my arrival."

"Ah, don't take it personally. That is just who he is."

"So you have mentioned. How do you know him so well?" I am suddenly grateful Thair is leading me because I pay no attention to the turns and stairs we take for thinking of what he's saying.

"I don't actually. I assessed his type quickly upon my arrival. I decided it would be quite fun pressing his buttons. Turns out, he doesn't have any buttons to press. He remains incessantly miserable. Perpetually stoic."

"He certainly is."

"Besides, I do think I am ripe competition for him, and since I plan on staying here for a long while, I thought it would reveal more about him to shake his tree a bit. He is painfully unprovokable. I do not think I have seen the man smile once."

"You do not want to. It's terrifying." We both giggle and sway our steps. "Where are your rooms?" I ask.

"I reside in the east wing. As far away from Shrike—and you, unfortunately—as the castle allows."

"Why *unfortunately?*" I push my eyebrows together as I peer over to him.

He stops walking then, and I realise we have turned the corner to my corridor. Or *our* corridor, I suppose. Thair slowly and gently backs me against the cool stone wall. I allow him, curious about how far he will take his play. He tenderly takes my face in his hands, curling his fingers through my hair. "Regardless of our shameless entertainment, you must know that you are the most beautiful woman in Danumhar—on this entire island. Your brain is equally as stunning, and I would be tremendously delighted to get to know more of you. The true parts of you. As I would like for you to get to know me truly. Not the versions we save for the world, but the broken bits beneath." My heart begins to race at his words, at his surprising and beautiful declaration.

"I do not think that would be most appropriate, Thair. Though not wholly unwanted."

He offers me that delicious, crooked smile again and gently runs his thumb across my cheek. "I hold you to no expectations, Thorne. I want nothing from you that you are unwilling to give. I simply want to enjoy a few honest moments with you. And please know that you can have whatever you want from me."

Oh, the want. I want. I want things I have not wanted in a long time. Heat blooms beneath my raiments, making the weight of them become unbearable. I never seek love from a partner. Only brief joinings of bodies, teeth, and tongues. I learned early on that physical connection is the only kind I can have with another, and a quick goodbye must follow. Never stay long enough to develop feelings. Never give them enough truths to hold onto.

But standing here, beneath the blazing stare of his warm brown eyes with remnants of ale swimming in my bloodstream, I realise it has been far too long since I have touched and been touched. Since I have ravished another. Since I have found sweet release coated in sweat and the night air. Since I felt someone else's hands on my skin.

The quandary is, however, that I still have menoths here yet. And Thair is indeed keen. We would have to keep this discreet, occasional, and without wanting anything else from each other. A battle brews within me. Part of me screams to refrain, to stay professional, and not to do this. The other part aches for physical interaction. It has been so long, and I fear I am beginning to lose that part of myself, something dancing with Shrike does not aid in.

"I have a counteroffer," I say, bringing my hand up to his chest.

"I'm listening." He leans closer.

"No feelings. No honest moments outside of tangled sheets. You cannot know me, and I cannot know you. It's better this way. And we must be discreet. No one can know. This is what I can offer, Thair. This is the only part of me I can give. Is that enough for you?"

I see the thoughts tumbling in his mind for a moment. It feels like forever before he finally answers, "I will eagerly take what I can have of you."

"Deal," I say. Then boldly, daringly, and terrified, I lean in and press my lips to his. Thair meets me with equal want, and before long, we are a knot of limbs and tongues. A whine escapes my mouth as I become less patient with the amount of raiments we have on. Thair's large hands begin their exploration of my body, working their way from my hips to my backside.

"Gods, you are delicious," he purrs.

Before I can respond, I register a familiar sound of boots, slapping against the stone floor. I push Thair away from me, landing him against the wall on the other side of the hall. Dominus Shrike steps out from the shadows, the lit candelabras lining the halls illuminating his stone-cold face. His hands are in the pockets of his black trousers. His white linen scyrte is half undone, exposing his chest. His hair is in hand-torn waves around his face, and he looks exhausted. With deadly calm, he looks us over. Those pale green eyes inspect every inch of me before moving to throw proverbial daggers into Thair, and I hope he hosts no real ones.

The tension rests at a dangerous pinnacle. Shrike takes a slow breath, then pierces through the anticipation. "I have one question," he says through gritted teeth. "Was this consensual?"

Thair immediately responds, "For fuck's sake, Shrike, of course it was consensual. What kind of monster do you take me for?"

"The kind that would make a move against a colleague, knowing full well the repercussions this could have." Shrike and I lock eyes, and I cannot seem to move.

Thair speaks again. "We are both consenting adults, Shrike, and there is no policy against it."

"Something I will rectify with the sunrise, I assure you, Torin."

Thair runs his hands over his face. "Honestly, this has nothing to do with you."

Shrike finally breaks eye contact with me, and I allow myself a breath. Games aside, Shrike is still my superior, and this is embarrassing. He slowly walks to stand in front of Thair.

Not quite eye-to-eye, Shrike makes a point to look down at him. "Everything that happens within these walls is of my concern. I suggest you swiftly find yourself in the east wing of this fucking castle before you become the very centre of that concern."

Thair laughs in a deep tone I have not heard before. "I wish I could say that your actions surprise me, but you have this unyielding delusion in your mind that everything belongs to you. But maybe you are simply teeming with fear, Dominus. Maybe you stand there, shaking in your boots, knowing full well Thorne has a mind of her own and that she chose this. She chose *me*."

Shadows quake in the corner of my eyes as Dominus stalks closer to Thair. Not wanting to see these two puffed-up eejits shed blood tonight, I step in. "Go ahead, Thair. It's not worth it. We will talk on the morrow. Thank you for tonight. It was truly lovely." He meets my gaze, looking back and forth between us for a moment, considering whether it is worth what will undeniably transpire if he stays. "Please," I add.

He nods his head and offers Shrike a crooked smile before turning around and walking away from the corridor. Shrike stays facing away from me, staring at the stone for a long moment. So long that I do not know what to do.

"Goodnight," I bark before turning and walking to my door. I open it, and before I can turn to close it, Shrike steps in behind me, walking his way to my open windows.

I close the door and follow him. "You cannot be serious."

He turns on me then, pure fury blazing in his glowing eyes. His glowing eyes. So, it was not my injury that night. Why are his eyes *glowing?*

"I knew you were selfish and inconsiderate of the lives that go on inside this academy, but I did not expect you to be *this* incomprehensibly stupid."

Per usual, his words ignite me. I point my finger at him, nearly touching his nose, and unleash all that has been building inside me with every encounter we share. "You know absolutely nothing about me, you arrogant miscreant. I do not know why you seem to equate your existence to that of the very gods that constructed this land, but you do not have the right to demand anything from me outside the bounds of my role here. The fact that you continually put yourself in my way—to insult, belittle, and shame me—is disgusting behaviour. I have lived a far more difficult life than you can imagine, Shrike. So, your immature, petulant involvement in my business is more like the existence of a persistent gnat flying about my face than whatever delusional influence you think you have. If you continue to make yourself my problem, I will go to Connally and see to it that changes. My whereabouts, my diet, and where I find release are *none* of your concern. Have I yet made my feelings for you completely obvious? Or do you need me to continue?"

I swear I see shadows roll off him as he bites his bottom lip. His large chest rises and falls in quick, shallow heaves. "What is clear here, Miss Alder, is that you are bound and determined to cause such detrimental problems for m—this academy. Forgive me if I will not stand by and allow hundreds of yehrs of work to go to waste for some woman with a smart mouth and shapely body that she intends to offer up to every man in this castle."

I slap Dominus Shrike across his stone-carved face with every ounce of my strength, and this time, I do not miss. His head whips with the contact. I move my hand back to my side, my heaving breath the only sound in the room. Dominus slowly turns his head back toward me. As he pushes his hair out of his face, I see that his lip is bleeding, and I wish I could harbour any sort of remorse for it.

"If you intend to draw blood, Miss Alder, then—" I do not let him finish his sentence before unsheathing my blade. I press it to his neck, pushing him back against the open window. I realise that, regardless of my position, I am at a disadvantage here, lifting myself to the tips of my toes to hold the blade against him.

"Don't you ever speak to me that way again, Shrike, or I swear on your gods I will shove this blade into your throat." For emphasis, I push it harder, causing a small bead of crimson to slowly roll down his neck.

I am fully out of control, but I do not care. I have never done anything like this, but this man evokes more anger in me than I have ever felt, and I truly want to shove this skean deep into his skin to see if he really is made of stone.

He holds his hands up toward me, a sign of surrender. Murderous tears silently stream down my face. I am a storm of anger, madness, and...shame. I have never felt such shame as he has made me feel tonight, and I hate him for it. I bloody *hate* Dominus Shrike.

His eyes begin to soften, which only makes me more enraged. The very last thing I want now is his pity. I push myself away from him.

"Leave," I demand, pointing the dagger toward the door. "Never step foot in this room again. The interactions we must have from now on will be fully professional and in the presence of someone else. Get the fuck out of my sight, Dominus."

"Thorne, I—"

"Get out!" I scream, losing control, spiralling under the weight of my emotions. Shrike moves to the door, pausing on the outside with his hand on the doorknob.

"Forgive me," he whispers.

"Never," I say, and to truly prove to him my rage, my sudden frenzy, I lick his blood from the knife before walking to shut the door in his face.

Game over.

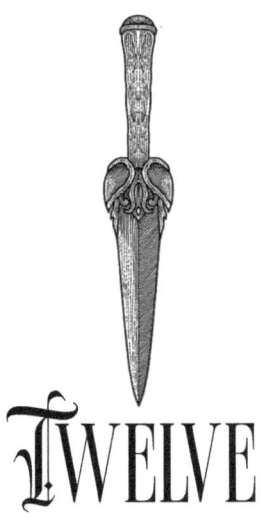

TWELVE

It takes hawrs before I finally calm the war within me. I pride myself on control. On presenting myself exactly the way I want. I always have the upper hand, building walls of safety with nonchalance. Shrike does something to me. He unravels me, sets me alight, and fills me with fury. I have never felt such rage. I need to change tactics. This dance does not work if I cannot keep a level head around him.

I pace the floors of my room until I finally release the rage and spend the rest of the night staring out the window, watching the midnight blue waves ebb and flow, bathed in moonlight, over and over until they evolve into a shimmering aquamarine, considering what comes next. I stare so long that the bloody sun rises. The sun always rises, though, does it not? The promise of a new day that never falters. Proof that whatever happens in the darkness, the light will always come around again.

I bathe in cool water and dress, not knowing what I will do with the day. The group does not meet again until morrow evening, and I am thankful for the time and space after last night.

I rerun all our interactions through my mind. I suppose I have never had anyone treat me with severity the way he has, and regardless of whether my actions were justifiable, I still regret them. I wish I had stayed in control. I wish I had not allowed a man to unravel me. I wish I could take back last night with Thair.

Because Shrike was right.

It is completely unprofessional. I was being selfish, wanting what I cannot have, especially here. I have been naive, and, yes, he was right, idiotic. I have spent most of my bloody life working to be where I am. I will be dammed if I let a man—or two—ruin that for me.

I decide to put a stop to the pity and self-destruction. I will keep my distance from them both. I will offer them my apologies, and that will be the end of it. I will keep my head down, focus on my work, and figure out the mysteries this cursed island hides.

Feeling marginally myself again, I take a moment to secure my thick, unruly hair into a long plait. I select a comfortable pair of dark trousers, a light linen scyrte, and a leather harness that my seamstress and I crafted together.

My fingers hover over the sheathed dagger for a moment before I place it over my head and tuck it beneath my scyrte. I pack a book, my journal, and a fountain pen in my satchel and strap up my sturdier boots made for longer walks. I have no idea where I will go today. I simply know I am going. A troubled mind is a sign that I need to work my body. I need to sweat and breathe and exhaust myself. Then the answers might reveal themselves amongst the silence.

I take the water skin that Eamon let me borrow and strap it across my shoulder as well. There is a fresh spring a few miles away. I remove the map of Danumhar from the wall, roll it up, and place it into my bag. I swing my large door open to find Thair standing in the doorway, knuckles raised as if he were about to knock.

"Hello," he says, running his outstretched hand over the back of his neck.

"Good morning."

"I—I wanted to come check on you after last night. That was bloody insane. I have no idea what Shrike was doing, but—"

"But he was right, Thair. Oh, do not look at me like that. I do not agree with his actions either, but I spent the entire night thinking about it. What we did was a mistake. It is not for lack of wanting, but I do need to consider my role and my place at Adonien. I have spent so long working to be here, and I do not want to jeopardise that. If it comes down to ruining my career or rutting with you, well, no offence, but I choose my work." Thair's eyes shift from sadness back to their normal, deviant posture as I speak. I recognise he is allowing me out, choosing not to pressure me, and I respect that.

"Ah, you can only say that because you, unfortunately, did not get the experience of *rutting* with me, Alder," he offers with a wink. I let a small smile shine through then, thankful for his good reaction.

"And maybe I will never experience the grandeur of it, but I would still appreciate your friendship, Thair. I do enjoy spending time with you."

"As do I, Thorne. My offer does not change. You can have whatever you want from me."

"Well, I still need you—platonically. So, if you are willing to be my friend, I would like to resume our antics."

Thair shines that beautiful, crooked grin at me and brings me in for a hug. He pats me on the back, effortlessly and unwanting, and I appreciate the gesture. "There is no other soul in the castle whom I would rather haunt with."

"Then it is a deal." Removing myself from his grip, I reach my hand out for him to shake it. He does so very dramatically, making us both laugh again.

"Where are you headed, anyway?"

"Out. Not sure where. I need some space and not to be within the confines of these walls. I have not had much time to wander the island yet, and today is the perfect opportunity."

"Ah, I see. Well, I want you to enjoy that space, so I am not going to ask to join you, but please be safe. And be back before nightfall. Don't get lost on me, Alder."

"I'm no anthropologist, but I do know how to read a map, Torin."

"I do not doubt you for a minute, but I cannot have my new *friend* dying because she got lost in the middle of the woods and starved. Or worse."

My stomach flips at his words. "What is worse?"

Thair bunches his eyebrows together before stepping closer to me. "Just be back before dark, alright? I shall come check on you after supper. Just for my own sense of peace— don't flatter yourself."

"Alright then," I offer, wondering if Thair knows more than he lets on. That makes two people who have told me not to be out past nightfall, while no one else has mentioned anything about it here. I intend to question him further, but right now, I do need that space.

By the second mile, my thoughts become slower, clearer. Rolling green hills dotted with grazing sheep sweep down to meet cascading cliffs that rise majestically from the churning sea. Their sheer faces are weathered by centuries of wind and waves. Vibrant patches of purple heather and yellow gorse add splashes of colour to the verdant landscape. In the distance, I can make out the ruins of an ancient stone castle perched atop a craggy outcropping. The sky above is a dynamic canvas of blue and gold, littering sporadic sunbeams through the white, puffy clouds, making the sea sparkle like diamonds. Shrikes wheel and cry overhead, riding the strong ocean breezes. This scene spectacularly inhabits the raw beauty, rich history, and untamed spirit of Danumhar, and I wish I had the artistic ability to paint it, to capture its likeness forever.

I stop atop the knoll to sit for a while, taking out the food pack that Elowyn prepared herself. I visited the kitchens for some morning tea and scones, and she asked me where I was going. She would not let me leave without provisions.

I soothe my growling belly with a large apple, some cheese, and freshly baked bread. I leave the cured meat for later, only eating a small amount to not make myself nauseous. Samhradh is in full heat now, leaving me dripping in perspiration. I gulp greedily from the waterskin full of cool, fresh water from the spring I acquired on my way.

I can still see the academy from here. It casts a stark silhouette against the colour-drenched, radiant landscape on which it lives. Its weathered grey stones, creeping ivy, and giant arched windows peek through the constant mist that shrouds it.

Away from it, I grow empty. Or maybe just wholly alone. I cannot determine at this moment if that thought comforts or terrifies me. I am used to being alone, but I have quite enjoyed the bustle of the academy. Living with people whom I do not need to know, whose safety I do not have to worry about because I will be gone before I ever affect them enough to put them in harm's way, has been a welcome experience I never thought I would have. I do not think I can say the same for Eamon and Elowyn, though, and a deep, dark part of my mind whispers that I need to distance myself from them.

Finishing my meagre midmeal, I check my pocket chronometer before setting off again. It's only half past noon. I have many hawrs left before sunset. The samhradh sun has yet to fully reach its peak, and I made great time getting here. I decide to venture further, keeping to the coastline with the academy in view to avoid getting lost. According to my map, there should be ancient stone ruins about three more miles north. I want to try to reach it before I turn back.

I spend the trek to the stones picking flowers and plants I have never seen before, pressing them into the pages of my journal with notes scribbled beside them, studying unknown shimmering pale rocks, and letting my chest unwind itself. Another two miles in and I feel better, restored, and my legs begin to shake with exhaustion. I know the journey back will fully do the job, and I look forward to a hot bath and a good night's rest. Maybe I will begin to dig into the journal writings that the scolers and masters are already submitting.

The trail from the cliffs veered gently right toward the centre of the island and into a thick forest a bit back. I can no longer see the cliffs, but I can faintly hear the sea. The forest is vivid and lush. Blooming flora sprout everywhere. Shades of blue, yellow, and pink I have never seen before freckle the soft, rich grasses. The dirt path turns back to the left before revealing the most enchanting sight I have ever seen.

In the distance, two monstrous ash trees stand as silent sentinels on either side of the path. Their weathered trunks, large enough that a small gaggle of grown men could easily fit inside, are covered in thick, winding strips of moss-covered bark. The branches between them have grown and twisted together in an intricate pattern, forming a perfect circular opening framed by their gnarled limbs. The natural archway, measuring half a metre above my head, appears almost deliberate in its symmetry.

Glancing down at my map, I see no indication or note of anything in this area, and the stones should be much further up ahead. I pen a circle quickly on the parchment before stuffing the map into my pack. I slowly move closer to the opening, coming to an abrupt stop after only three paces.

Lights. Tiny, glowing balls of light begin to shine beneath the shaded cover of the wooded mammoths above. My breath hitches in my chest, and I slowly reach my hand to my sternum to the safety of the sheathed skean beneath.

The wind suddenly whips through the trees, moving like an arrow down the path of the forest. It dances around and in front of me. *Go,* it seems to say. I walk slowly, roving my eyes back and forth from the trees and the opening to the glowing lights. As I pace further, the wind increases its encouragement, rushing past me fast enough to loosen hair from my plait and whipping it about my face. As I tuck the loosened strands, cupping my ear, I notice a very faint noise. I move both hands behind my ears, increasing the sound. A long, slow, gentle moan comes from the direction of the trees on the path I came down. The wind must be causing the long limbs to rub against each other. The large pines of my hamlet would sound like desperate sobs in violent winds.

Daring a few more steps toward the opening, I can finally make out that the glowing lights are mushrooms, casting an ethereal glow in the gathering darkness. My mind begins to churn. I have not read anywhere that Danumhar has bioluminescent fungi. If so, I would think they would be closer to the sea, not high up on the cliffs. I will have to introduce myself to Cathal, the botanist, when I return.

The mushrooms vary in size and shape. Some are small and delicate, no larger than my fingertip, their caps emitting a soft, pearl-like radiance. Others grow in shelf-like tiers up the trunks of the ash trees, their edges trimmed with a brighter amber light that pulses softly with an inner life. Larger specimens dot the ground. Their broad caps glow with a mesmerising shade of pistachio and copper. The light they emit is strong enough to illuminate the intricate patterns of moss and lichen on the nearby stones and tree bark. As the strong breeze rustles through the forest floor, the mushrooms flicker and dance, their collective glow ebbing and flowing like bioluminescent waves. The living light show reflects off the still dew-laden grass and leaves, creating shimmering sparkles that complement the fungal display.

The lights cast a kaleidoscope of colours into the darkness of the opening. I move closer, staring into the void. Where the path should continue, only darkness exists. Confused, I walk around one of the ash trees. Behind it, the path continues. I go back around, daring to place the tip of my boots on the threshold of the opening. Darkness again. A great absence. The pit of nothing.

What is this? What have I discovered? Is it a cave of some sort? A magical portal? A den of deamhans?

The wind begins pushing violently around me, almost urging me into the opening, but fear turns my body in the opposite direction. As I begin to take a step away from the trees, a deafening scream pierces my ears, dropping me to my knees. My hands push hard against my ears, trying to muffle the shriek. The smell of rotten flesh stuffs itself up my nose. The frequency of the air changes, and I suddenly feel like hunted prey.

The screech stops, and I heave over, my hands landing on the grass-covered floor, eviscerating mushrooms and splattering the luminescent mucus onto my palms. I quickly wipe them down my pants and unsheathe my skean as I rise on shaking legs. The wind slows to a barely noticeable breeze, and the forest hushes to a deadly quiet. The only sounds now are my jagged breathing and blood rushing in my ears.

Thump. Thump. Thump. Thump.

Clouds cover the sun, darkening the forest even more. I squint my eyes, forcing them to focus. A flowy figure steps out onto the path a short distance from me. My grip of the wooden handle tightens so hard I fear splinters, and I anchor my weight into both feet, taking a fighting stance. My blood pumps unbelievably harder, and that distant hum begins to echo somewhere. The shadowed figure steps closer. Long fingers dipped in inky black spiderwebs pull back the hood of their floating cloak, revealing a woman as pale as the moon with jet-black hair and solid obsidian eyes. Her full mouth is blood red, and she smiles a serrated smile at me. She is painfully beautiful. I have never seen anyone like her. *Anything,* my mind whispers. I start thumbing through the catalogue of mythical creatures in my mind, studying her carefully.

She opens her mouth, and I think she will speak to me, but that same bloody screech comes from her instead. Before I have time to raise my free hand to my ear, she charges and is upon me instantly. I try to strike, but she catches my arm, looking at me with her cold, dead eyes. Her stunning lips twist into a terrifying smile before she snatches my arm to her mouth and bites.

I scream and thrash against her to no avail. Her sharp teeth dig deep into my flesh, and now it burns. It burns, it burns, it burns. I strike her jaw with my free hand, but she remains unaffected. My body begins to weaken, caught in sinking sand. I can no longer feel my feet, my legs, my hands. We slide to the ground together, and the woman hovers over me, forcing her teeth even deeper. My vision begins to blur as she makes strange gulping sounds. Gods, she is drinking my blood. The numbness moves further up, and I open my mouth, but no words come out.

Dearg due, I hear the whisper somewhere in my mind. And if the myths offer any truth, she is currently pumping venom straight into my body that will kill me in minutes. I am losing consciousness, on the brink of blacking out. This beautiful monster is going to drain me dry, and I will be here, dead in the middle of the woods, where no one will find me. Maybe she will take me with her and eat me whole. Maybe nothing will remain of me but a trail of my licked-clean bones.

I try to tell myself that at least I found her. Or she found me. At least this is proof that there are monsters on this island—that magic must be real. This is proof that there could have been a way out for me. I barely feel the tears slide down my numbing face. I look over to her once more, watching her sharp cheeks concave to her face as she sucks the life from me.

I found you, I think, and I hope she sees the smile I try to form.

A loud boom sounds behind her, causing her to release my arm from her latch. Tossing me away, she stands with her arms wide and prepared to fight. She opens her mouth to scream, but I hear no sound. I close my eyes. They are so heavy now, and the blood in my ears pumps so slowly. I force my eyes open once more, giving way to my end. When I do, her detached head stares back at me. Her black eyes now have iridescent shimmers and whirls of red in them. Her open mouth is a gore of blood and sharp bones.

I close my eyes for the final time, allowing the growing hum and citrus smell to take me under.

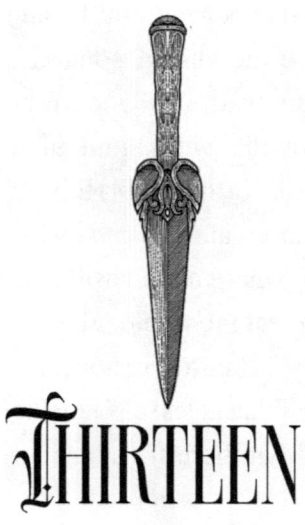

THIRTEEN

Everything is muffled. I feel inside myself, lost somewhere below the surface. A voice sounds distantly behind a thick door, but I cannot make it out. I wonder if it is the goddess of Albion, Cyfrif, calling me through the veil of death.

That voice grows louder, clearer now. A deep and pleading song. The thrum of it coursing through me, down to my very bones. I become more aware, and shining lights flicker across my closed lids. Feeling slowly returns to me, though with it comes the agonising burn of the venom, searing me from the inside.

Then my hearing sharply returns to me as if someone opened the door. I must not have been breathing before because air violently rushes into my lungs, causing me to gasp and wretch. That familiar sonation vibrates through every inch of me as more and more of my awareness crawls back to me. I painfully force my eyes to open. Dominus Shrike hovers over me, his eyes glowing brighter than I have ever seen. A melodical incantation sounds from his full mouth. Words and sounds I have never heard before flood through me, and something deep within responds to the song. Something takes hold of my ravaged arm, and I use every bit of strength to turn my head. Vines, lichen, the earth itself is *moving*, covering my arm.

I feel it as it crawls inside me. The gritting of the dirt against my open wound. The scratch of the moss as it winds its way through my veins. The grip of the vines as they squeeze tighter and tighter. Dominus holds my arms down as the earth consumes me from wrist to shoulder. I have no voice. I have no thoughts. Utter shock has numbed my mind, and I hope that I wake from his horrid dream. Blood spurts from my mouth with an uncontrollable cough, causing Dominus to break his trance. His eyes are full of fear and pity, and I want to laugh in his face because I know the tongue-lashing he wishes to give me.

"Hold on, Thorne," he begs me. His voice is deep and rough and laced with desperation. "Everything will be alright. Just breathe. Don't give up. Fight." He leans over me, running his large, hot palm across my face. Something inside me twists at his plea. It breaks loose in my chest, and I am sinking again. Darker, darker, total darkness as Shrike resumes his haunting chant.

"Dominus." His name slithers from my mouth like a prayer before I am wholly consumed again.

I am sheathed in darkness. There is no time, no space, no one.

Only my mind, suspended and lost. I have no sense of how long I have been here or how long I will remain. I have no wants, no desires, no intent to move. I am weightless and infinite and everything.

At some point, moments, centuries, aeons, warmth surrounds me, pours into me, and I become aware of who I am outside of this plane. I still see and feel nothing other than the warmth and light that cling to me as if I were its very child. It is unlike anything I have ever felt before. Such comfort and security have been lost to me. I never want to leave here. This light can consume me and hold me forever.

Not yet, a voice, my own voice, speaks into my mind. I push back, questioning it.

I *am your past, your future, your legacy, and your destiny. You have much left to do. Much to suffer. Much to gain.*

I do not know what that means, and I honestly cannot find the desire to care. I just want the light to stop talking and hold me until I fall into oblivion.

No, my voice demands. *You will claim him. You will claim them all. It is your duty, cursed one.*

This piques my interest, forcing me to slightly pull myself from its blissful caress.

Yes, you are cursed, and you are blessed. You have the right to decide your fate, though the path has already been carved. All you must do is pick up your weapon.

A thud begins to distantly sound.

Thump. Thump. Thump. Thump.

That is the beating of your heart. Listen to it. Let it guide you. And live, child. Live.

ℱOURTEEN

Infinite sadness fills my waking body. I want to return. I want the comfort and love of the light. A sob breaks through me, forcing me to realise how raw my throat is and how my body aches.

I peel my eyes open only to find darkness. No, not total darkness. There is light, and it dances. Fire. I begrudgingly roll my head to the left, making eye contact with Shrike. He stokes the flames, dropping logs onto the fire, sending tiny embers floating through the air. I blink, and he is in front of me. "You must teach me how to do that," I whisper with a shattered throat.

Shrike drops to his knees before me, running his hand over my forehead, no doubt checking for fever. "You mean to tell me that you wake half dead and the first thing you do is jest?"

"If you think death will stop me from my attempt to disarm you, then you have learned nothing about me, Shrike."

Laughter, deep and warm, rumbles in his chest, and I want to drink it. "Oh, I have learned enough about you. Enough to know you have earned your namesake. Since your arrival, you have done nothing but bleed and torture me. Thorne does not do you justice. Perhaps Shillelagh would have been more accurate, for you are a multi-functional pain." I wonder if he knows how right he is about my namesake.

"Your bedside manners are unmatched, good sir. Truly, you must go on."

"A chonách san ort."

"Serves me right? I nearly died. Wait, am I dead? This is not what I expected."

"No, you are not dead, you imbecile. Thanks to me." Silence folds around us like a warm tartan.

"Help me sit up," I whisper.

Dominus wraps his large hands behind my neck and knees and does all the lifting as he sets me up. He gently releases me, letting me lean against a cool stone. Stone. I force my eyes to focus harder in the darkness. We look to be inside a cave. The stone walls are carved in a dome shape, large and spacious. The fire flickers in the centre of the room. There is a makeshift bed on my left, stacked with battered, frayed blankets that look worse than I feel.

I look down then. The glow of the fire reveals a stained, torn, and matted version of myself. My harness has been removed, and my raiments are mangled remnants that cling to me with dried blood and mushroom goo. The full cloth of my right sleeve is nonexistent. Fear pangs through me as I remember my arm. I bring it close to my eyes in the darkness. My heart begins to rap against my rib cage. Nothing. Nothing but two faint half-moon scars. Bite marks. I run my fingers along the scars, along my healed skin. I whip my head to Shrike in disbelief. "How?" I demand.

He rocks back from his knees to stand on his feet. He paces for a moment, pokes the fire with a large stick, and lets out a deep breath. "I–healed you."

"How?" I echo. He must think I am completely incompetent. Of course he does.

He throws the stick into the fire, causing it to blaze brighter. "It's complicated. And not entirely information meant for you."

Knowing Shrike offers nothing freely, I comb my mind for what I do know. I replay the events. I was bitten by what *had* to have been a dearg due, red blood sucker. Descriptions from lore fit it perfectly: hauntingly beautiful, lifeless skin, bloodthirsty, and ruthless in their kills. It attacked me, and Shrike somehow killed it right before it finished me. He *beheaded* it. Which means he is more powerful than a dearg due.

Then he healed me, using what? *Magic.* An incantation, a spell, a ritual of some sort. The earth listened to him, crawled towards and into me as if it had consciousness. And those damn glowing eyes. That thing begins to move inside me again, speaking to me. I realise that something within is now different. I am no longer wholly alone in my mind.

"What are you, Shrike?"

His head whips up to me, his eyes intent and beginning to gleam. We stare at each other for long seconds. The rise and fall of his chest mirror my own. I study him again. He wears a black leather jerkin, battered and worn, over a simple linen scyrte. His broad shoulders taper to a lean waist. A dagger, not too unlike my own, rests on his right hip. Dark trousers disappear into high boots caked with mud. Across his back, two swords are sheathed in a double scabbard—one steel, one silver—their hilts protruding over his shoulders. The muscles of his arms bulge, hinting at the immense strength I now know he possesses.

His fists clench at his sides, covered in what I assume to be my blood. The strain causes the muscles of his forearms to ripple beneath his skin, cords of sinew shifting like taut ropes. Scars crisscross his exposed skin, pale lines etched into the brawny landscape of his arms that I have not yet noticed. Dozens, countless, pale scars shimmer in the glow of the fire. He does not look like a scolemaster. He looks like a warrior. Like the gods crafted him themselves. Maybe they did.

His hair is loose. Tendrils of midnight frame that carved, stoic face. His strong jaw is pebbled with dark hair, and those green eyes study me as well. We're taking score of each other, playing the mental game we are so good at. Only, I am sure that what he deduces of me is weak, half-dead, and the gallows around his very neck.

His eyes darken, and I am uncertain if he is becoming angry. I need to keep him focused long enough to supply me with answers. Changing the subject, I say, "That was a dearg due, wasn't it? The thing that attacked me. You can hold your secrets for now, Shrike, but no other explanation exists for what happened to me. If you have answers, give them to me, please. I need to know. I need to understand how that thing exists and how you brought me back from death." He turns his head from me, biting his bottom lip. Oh, to be in that mind of his. I want to crawl inside, turn over, and inspect every thought he has ever had. I want to know what he knows. I want his truths—need them. "Please, offer me something."

Shrike moves, and I think he will leave, but he leans down to retrieve my pack and brings it over to me, placing it with the skin of water at my feet. "Eat."

"And we resume this. Gods, I thought I told you—"

"You nearly died," he booms at me, his breath quickening. "You nearly fucking died. For once in your bloody life, stop being so insolent and do what you are told." I open my mouth to tell him 'fine', but he stops me before I begin to speak, holding his callused, bloody palm up to me. The man is covered in my blood from saving my life. A life he attempted to take himself not long ago.

My head begins to swim.

"I need you to get your strength up. You lost a lot of blood. Indulge me." The muscles in his jaw clench and release a few times before he sighs and adds, "Please."

"Alright." I open the pack, somehow still in one piece, and take out the meat, the other half of the bread, another apple, and a small satchel of nuts.

"Would you like some?" I offer him.

"No, please eat every bite that you can."

Another strange moment of silence passes as he watches me consume my food and drink deeply from my skin. He relaxes a bit in what I assume to be satisfaction and finally begins to speak. "Yes. It was a dearg due that attacked you. One I had thought was...gone. There are many creatures on this island. Many things from lore that you would be delusionally delighted to know exist.

They—this is rare. They do not attack humans, especially in broad daylight." A mixture of surprise, satisfaction, and fear barrels through me simultaneously.

"That night, the night we collided, I saw something. A shadow, diving off the cliff. What was that?"

Shrike exhaustively runs his hands over his face, seemingly annoyed to learn that I had seen the thing. "Something far darker, and had I not been so close, you would be much worse off than you are right now."

"Do not speak in riddles. I am not a child, Shrike. I have spent my life studying, searching for these truths."

"Searching for something and finding it are very different things, Thorne. And you nearly just died. Can you not take this a bit at a time?"

I snort, causing him to cut me with his eyes. "You mean to tell me my nemesis holds all the answers to the questions I have asked for decades. Fate really is a bitch."

He kneels beside me, plucking a sliver of salted meat from my hand, and pops it into his mouth. Watching me, he places his thumb onto his tongue and sucks it clean. His bloody thumb. He closes his eyes, taking a deep breath. "Delicious," he whispers. Leaning back to a full seat, he asks, "Do you truly believe in fate, Thorne?"

I turn away from him to gaze into the entrancing flickering embers. "There is no other answer."

"For what?"

It is my turn to recede, and I realise we stand at a stalemate, refusing to reveal ourselves to one another. I gaze over to my right to see a sea of stars and the light of the moon casting a faint light over the gory scene of my attack. There was no cave near the path. This view should be impossible.

"Where are we?" I try to stand but tumble back into Shrike's waiting arms.

"Somewhere safe, I promise. Nothing can reach us here."

I piece it together quickly. The archway, the darkness. I went around it. The path continued—no sign of a giant, bloody cave. "Is this a portal of some kind? We are in the opening, are we not? The twisted branches that form a circle? That is what I was inspecting when she found me. What is this?"

Shrike releases a breath of what I hope is surrender. Still in his arms, he walks us closer to the opening, revealing more of the forest. "I won't—I cannot offer you everything tonight, Thorne. What I will say is this is a haven. A veiled place safe from the things that wander the woods at night. He leans closer, his mouth touching my ear, and my skin prickles like gooseflesh. "If you had stepped in, it would not have been able to hurt you." His voice is laced with a curious kind of sadness. Daringly, I turn my head to meet his gaze. Standing an entire head taller than me, he lowers his own to fully look at me.

"The wind. It—this sounds absurd."

"Tried to protect you. The wind tried to save you. But of course, you are too bloody defiant."

My body warms at every place we touch: his chest against my back, his hands wrapped around my wrists, and his body encasing mine. His heart begins a steady rhythm that echoes my own. That not-quite-my-own voice whispers to me to lean into him, gently push myself back into his embrace. "You may release me now."

"Right." Shrike gently releases me before moving to stoke

the fire again. I glance beyond that invisible barrier, forcing my heart to quiet its insistent beating.

Magic. Magic. Magic. Magic.

"Are we trapped here?"

"No, but we do need to wait until sunrise. If that thing attacked you under the sun, I do not want to tempt the trek back under the moon." Fair point. So, we are spending the night together. Wonderful. I stretch, trying to relieve some stiffness in my body. "You need to sleep. We have a long walk back in the morning, which will be infinitely more difficult in your condition."

"How early can we leave? I don't want anyone to see me like this."

"Do not worry about that," he says, leaning back against the wall opposite me. It feels like there are miles between us, and perhaps there are. Miles, secrets, entire worlds. My traitorous mind brings me back to our last encounter, and I am reminded that I currently owe him an apology *and* my gratitude for saving my life.

"Shrike—"

"I thought I told you to call me Dominus."

I am taken aback by his interruption. "You did, but Dominus is too familiar, too friendly for whatever we have going on."

"Too familiar?"

"We have tried to kill each other, and you saved my life, which I suppose I should thank you for, by the way. We are intimate strangers, intently aware of the deep disdain we hold for each other. Calling you by your first name feels...wrong somehow."

He tries to hide the smile blooming on his full lips. "If we can get through all of that, then surely it is no such awkwardness to say my name. Try it. Say my name."

The air in the room seems to change, to charge. I clear my throat, fully unable to deny a challenge. "Dominus," I say breathier than I mean to. "Dom," I follow for reasons unknown to me. Our eyes both widen at each other. My quick mind swoops in to save me. "Perhaps that is more suitable. Since you work so hard to dominate everyone around you." I bite the apple, hoping the deliciousness of it will help me forget the moment.

"Touché," he offers, playing into my game.

"As I was saying, about last night. I–"

"Have absolutely nothing to be sorry for. I was an insufferable, foolish, emotional bastard who should not have treated you or Torin that way." I raise my hand to my chest, bewildered by his admission. "Oh, contain yourself. Even an immature, petulant gnat such as myself can possess enough morality to admit his faults. Though I will admit, it is quite rare, so indulge in this while you can."

Immature. Petulant. Gnat. My own words from the previous night clang through me with shame. "Dominus, I did not mean that. Well, I meant it. I only wish I had not said it. If given another chance, I would not have acted that way. I would have restrained myself and retained control. My actions are inexcusable. I held a bloody knife to your throat. For that, I apologise."

He offers a small grin, and the light of the fire pools in that single dimple. "Do not be sorry for that, Thorne. That was glorious, and I savoured it. Had it not been for the grief reflected in your eyes, well..." He stops himself, seeming to realise he said that aloud. "What is more," he adds, clearing his throat, "it was owed. For the one I threw. Strike for strike is fair enough."

"That does seem to be our way," I say, pouring water from the skin over my face and hands, trying to clean the dried blood from me.

"What do you mean?" he inquires.

"I call it a dance, actually. But perhaps it would more appropriately be considered a duel. We strike and parry, disarm and deflect, only to offer a hand up to start again."

"Hm."

"What do you call it?" I ask, meeting his gaze again.

He pauses, something raw flickering across his face before he says, "Surviving. I am doing my best to survive you."

Thump. Thump. Thump. Thump.

I clear my throat. "Well, then, I should warn you, good sir. I have only gotten started."

He loosens a small laugh. "That is what I fear most."

"Do I sense hesitation, Dominus?"

"You sense fear, mo céasadh, doubt certainly, but no, not hesitation."

"Good. That would be rather boring."

Dominus offers me a grin as some sort of understanding passes through us. Battle mates? Yes. Enemies? Not quite certain anymore. Maybe this was laying the ground rules. Yes, please still challenge me, but maybe we can be less murderous about it. And yet, there is still so much I need to learn from him. So many answers I must coerce from his devious mouth.

"You know that I will not stop. I will not let you live a single moment of peace until I know the truth. All of it."

He releases a deep sigh. "I am fully aware. But that is not going to happen tonight. So, sleep." As he says the words, a wave of exhaustion sweeps into me as if my mind were only holding out long enough to find an explanation of what happened. Satisfied— for now—I slowly lay myself down toward the warmth of the fire, using my pack for a pillow.

"Absolutely not. Move to the bed. I will help you."

"I am not sleeping on that. It must be infested with a myriad of questionable things."

A deep chuckle sounds from him. "I can assure you it is not." Dominus helps me stand and settle into the cot. It's surprisingly comfortable and smells strongly of citrus. Of him.

"Will you sleep?" I ask.

"No. Tonight, I stand guard. Tonight, I lay my sword down at your feet for a moment of reprieve. Of safety."

"Only if you promise to pick it up again with the sun."

"You have my word."

I cannot help myself. I stare into those pale green eyes, my mind cycling an endless list of questions. One of them sleepily tumbles from my mouth—one I would not have chosen had my eyes been open and my body not already half asleep. "Will this glowing goo come off my skin?"

I hear stillness before Dominus quietly asks, "You can see that?"

"Of course I can."

I do not hear a response because I am already gone.

FIFTEEN

I wake to the sound of birdsong whistling outside the cave. Sunlight shines through the invisible barrier, causing a honey haze to wind through the domed room. As my sore body becomes more aware, I find I am in the same position as I went to sleep: on my left side, facing the now-dead fire. Except, unlike last night, Shrike sits with his back against the tiny wooden frame of the cot. The deep pattern of his breathing reveals to me that he is asleep.

His head rests against my chest, and my right arm lies over his right shoulder, gripping him to me. His jerkin and swords lie beside him, and only a slip of linen rests between our skin. I rack my mind, considering the events of the night as to how we might have ended up in this position. I remember nothing after I fell asleep. I fear movement, fear waking him. I fear what the day might bring, what I will learn, and what might transpire between us. I still, deciding to remain longer in the parlay that we have created. To soak in the warmth and feel of another. To let his heat sink into my battered body. If he isn't good for anything else, at least he makes a great warm compress.

I cannot even say that about the man who saved my life, the only reason I still breathe. As I replay yesterday's horror, I unconsciously begin to trace small, smooth circles against his broad chest. He moans in response, nuzzling his head deeper into my body. Our heads are now only inches apart. His reaction makes me startle, causing him to awaken.

"Oh, hello," I start. Shrike stares at me for a moment. His eyes search mine as if he is looking for something. My traitorous fingers itch to brush his dark hair from his forehead. Before I become bold enough to dare, he jumps up quickly to redress in his jerkin and scabbard.

"You, uh, had a rough night. You kept sobbing and thrashing in your sleep. You calmed to my touch."

"Touching me in my sleep, are you, Shrike? And here I thought you were supposed to be my great protector."

"Needy for the touch of a man, are you?" he parries. we are back to our game, and he does not intend to play nicely. Good. I let the pain shine through for a moment, offering no response to him. He runs his fingers through his hair and down his face. "I apologise. That was harsh."

"Maybe I would not be so hungry for touch had you not ruined my night with Torin," I retort, standing to stretch my aching legs. He grits his teeth, looking out into the growing daylight.

"Seek him out upon our return, then. If you must. But do know that the moment it becomes a problem is the moment I shut it down."

Something whines inside me. It thrashes with anger and betrayal that I do not understand. "Now you offer your permission after you so royally mucked it up the other night? Typical. Unfortunately for me, I already expressed to Thair that it was a mistake and that I would like to remain friends. My position here means too much to me."

His gaze searches my face for deceit or something else. I am not sure. "Good. Smart."

"Good." We stare at each other blankly for a moment.

Shrike swallows. "How do you feel? Are you able to walk?"

I move about, taking inventory and assessing my pain levels. "I am sore. Stiff, like I slept on a haggard cot last night. Otherwise, completely normal." I bring my arm up again to examine the wound in the light of day. Unbelievable. Still healed. Still two small half-moon scars. Dominus moves over to me, taking my arm in his large hands. He grazes his thumb over the puckered flesh, sending a full-body shiver reverberating through me.

"Sorry for the scar. Nothing to be done about it, I'm afraid."

"A scar is a minute trade to still be alive. Plus, my father always said that scars offer stories, histories, a map of one's life." I pull my arm free from his grip, reaching to bring his own up to my hands. I flip it over, examining the scars that litter him. "I cannot imagine the stories these hold," I say, running my fingers across the whirls and slashes.

"No, you cannot," he says through gritted teeth.

"Though I would like to," I say, pretending to be intently studying his arm to avoid meeting his eyes, "hear what you have done to gain these."

Shrike pulls free of my grip without a word and walks to the opening of the concealment. "If you are well enough, we should go. We are already behind." I gather my pack and water skin. I use my skean to cut my remaining sleeve off as Dominus kicks dirt over the already dead fire. We move to stand at the edge of the opening. "'Tis a long walk back. We are going to move as quickly as we can. Follow my lead, stay quiet, and keep your eyes open." His eyes move from my own down to the blade hanging from my neck. He gently thumps it. "And that close."

As we pass through the safety of the veil, my body quakes with a strange vibration. The moment we step out, it's gone. "What was that?"

Shrike looks at me curiously. "What?" he whispers, scanning his eyes for a suspected threat.

"That...feeling. When we passed through. It felt like an earthquake in my body."

"You felt that?" Confusion wrinkles his eyes.

"Did you not?"

"Of course *I* did. But you shouldn't."

"Why not?"

He releases a deep breath, running a hand through his hair. "Honestly, I haven't a bloody idea. Let us move."

As we begin to walk, I notice my torn harness in a bloody heap of ravaged earth. I pick it up, dust it off, and place it into my bag.

"I believe that has seen its final day."

"I can mend it."

"You can?"

"Yes, I can. I can do immeasurably more than you know."

He offers a soft smile. "I am beginning to see that."

I return the gesture.

We walk in silence for a long while. Dominus constantly scans the woods. Every so often, he reaches his arm in front of me to stop us. He listens for a moment, and then we move on again. We do this for miles, reaching the spring before we take a break, my thirst an aching scratch in my raw throat.

"Sit for a moment, drink plenty of water, and fill the skin up. The rushing of the water will cover our voices. We can speak while we are here."

The myriad of questions I thought of as we walked disappear from my mind as Dominus kneels to place his head directly into the small waterfall. He lets the water wash over him, down his body, before using his hands to drink from it. He rises, running his hands through his inky wet hair. Sunlight reflects on the rivulets that drip from him like crystal-coated midnight, and suddenly, I am parched.

I peel my gaze from him, heat flooding my cheeks to do the same. The water bites with cold, but I welcome it. I let it run down my head, face, and body, letting it seep into my bones. I wipe water from my eyes, finding Dominus glaring at me. I look around, wondering what he sees. Then I follow his eyes as they trail from my face to my neck and down to my chest. I follow his gaze to find my peaked breast nearly completely revealed through the soaked remnants of my white, linen scyrte.

My mind whirls with possibilities. Do I embarrass him, encourage him, ignore him? I make no move to do anything because my body is frozen in his gaze. Dominus quickly turns around and stalks off into the woods. I continue drinking and fill my skin to the brim before resting on a large rock beside the water, taking in the view. My feet ache in my boots. I cannot imagine what I will find left of them once removed. I roll my neck around and stretch my arms and legs.

Dominus is beside me instantly. "If you need to relieve yourself, now is the time." I realise I had not done so since the walk to the stones yesterday. The glorious stones I never got to see.

"Right." Afterwards, I dip my hands into the water once more and hobble on aching feet to sit back on the boulder with Dominus.

"Ready?"

"Just another moment. My feet are barely keeping me up."

"I can carry you the rest of the way."

I look at him, unconvinced. "No, you cannot."

"I can. Whether or not you would like me to is your choice."

I consider it, wiggling my toes, feeling torn bits of skin come free. "Just give me a moment," I say. We sit in silence, watching the shrikes fly overhead, diving and swooping. "Are you named after them?" I ask, nodding my head toward the bright, blue sky. Dominus follows my direction.

"Yes."

"Your lineage must be impressive to retain your surname for so many centuries."

"I have no family here."

"Ever?"

"No." We sit silently for a moment as I consider his answer. Surprisingly, he offers more. "These birds were my only friends when—for a long time. They became as familiar to me as myself. It felt fitting."

I notice that the lack of my prodding incited more from him, and I decide not to push further. Instead, I offer him something in return.

"I have this book. It is a work of fiction I have carried with me since childhood. I have never found another like it, but it's about the Seren. It tells stories about them that I have never seen elsewhere. It talks about the shrikes. It mentions they followed them here from their homeland."

Dominus snaps his head towards me. "What book do you speak of?"

I wish I could pull the words back from the ether, shove them back into my stupid mouth, and keep them there. That book is *mine*. My haven, my secret. Something not to be studied by anyone else.

"Nothing. It's just a silly book of faerie tales."

"Can I see it?"

"No," I bite out.

"Why not?"

"Because it is mine. It is the only thing that has ever been mine. It is inconsequential to you but everything to me." Again, I regret my words as soon as they are spoken. I just revealed my weakness to Dominus Shrike. Gods, help me.

"Alright," he concedes.

"Let us go." I stand to move.

"Are you sure you can walk the rest?"

"Yes," I bite. Dominus says nothing else before turning back onto the path toward Adonien.

I nearly make it all the way back. I push and push. I work through breaths and gulps of water, but I cannot take another step. I collapse atop a grassy knoll, the academy resting on the hillside ahead.

"Come here," Dominus says, reaching for me.

"No, I am fine."

"No, you are not. I have listened to you grind your teeth since the spring. Stop being so stubborn and let me help you."

"I can do it."

"Trust me when I tell you, as someone who loves seeing how far you will go, this will cause more harm to your body than to your pride. Concede to this one thing, Thorne." I roll my eyes, knowing he is right and terrified my boots are now melded to my feet with my blood and torn skin. "Either way, we have to go now."

"Fine. Fine. Just get this over with."

Dominus lifts me easily and cradles me in his arms like he did that night by the cliff. My feet, thankful for the reprieve, still throb incessantly. He wordlessly and effortlessly carries me to the bottom of the hill before moving right, toward the sea.

"Do not tell me, now that you have me secured, you are going to steal me away to your murder dungeon beneath the scol?"

His laugh rumbles through my body. "Honestly, you are not far off."

"What!"

He laughs again. "I need you to trust me. I am not going to murder you. Why would I go through so much trouble to save you only to kill you?"

"Maybe you wanted to do it yourself. Maybe you would rather cut my insolent tongue from my mouth rather than let the dearg due drain me dry. Maybe *you* want to drain me dry."

"Your mind is very troubled."

"Well, it isn't a far-fetched idea from my perspective, is it? I don't even know what you are. Do you drink blood, too?"

"Are you offering?"

My eyes bulge at him, and I begin to squirm in his grip as his laughter reverberates through me again. "You are demented."

"And you are far too naive to be so damn brilliant."

"Dominus Shrike. Did you just call me brilliant? I thought I was nothing special, *perhaps even lacking.*"

"You showed more gall yesterday than I would have assumed. Though that could be brilliance or exceptional foolishness. I have yet to decide."

"Touché."

"But my aim is not to harm you. I am taking us through the tunnels to avoid detection."

"The tunnels?" I nearly shout. "What bloody tunnels?"

"The secret ones built into the scol. The ones that lead into the armoury."

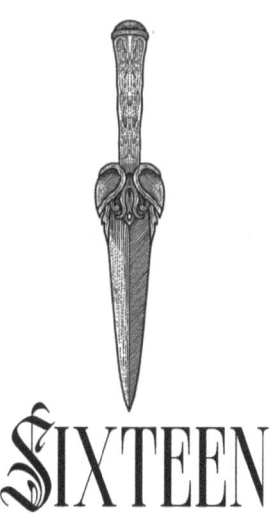

SIXTEEN

A bloody armoury! I am as giddy as a little girl as Dominus carries me down and around to the northwest corner of the academy. He gently sits me down on a pile of stacked sea rock.

"Don't be too excited." He squints at me.

"You mustn't be serious. I am belligerently thrilled at this moment." He offers a half smile and a roll of his eyes. Then he turns to the wall of the castle. This side is fully covered in ivy and moss. So much so that no one would have been able to see the hidden door revealed as Dominus cuts away the green covering with his dagger. I cannot help but slacken my jaw at the revelation. Behind the moss curtain is an ancient wooden door. The strips of metal reinforcements running horizontally across it are covered in rust and sea salt. Dominus heaves a weighty board up that secures the door.

"Step in," he says. I stand on shaking legs to enter. Dominus steps behind me, taking what looks to be a large iron fire poker, and places it in the crack of the door before closing it. He then slowly lowers the iron bar until a thud sounds, sliding the board back into place with it, locking us in. As he closes the door, all the light in the room goes out. He takes my hand, leading me through the dark to another door. Beyond it lies an expansive stone hallway fully lit by torches that line the entire length of the walls.

"Why are those burning?" I ask.

"Because they always are." Of course they are. Dominus takes my legs out from under me to carry me again. He carries me the length of the hallway before taking a right. Without releasing me this time, he throws me over his shoulder, narrowly missing the hard impact of my chin with his silver sword, before heaving open two hulking iron doors.

"Brute."

He puts me down on the inside of the doors. Amazement floods my body, spiking my heart rate. The stone room is vast. Burning torches line the walls all the way around, illuminating rows and rows of glistening weaponry. I take a few slow steps forward to see wooden tables lining the middle of the room, brimming with smaller knives, daggers, and many other ghastly things. Mauls, axes, longbows, war hammers, bludgeons, maces, spears, javelins, and even devices I have never seen before litter the room.

"Where...who...what?" I cannot form words.

"The person who constructed the place. He—"

"Believed in the deamhans. So, he constructed secret

rooms and weapons hidden within the walls."

"You have found that particular piece of lore, have you?"

"I have found them all," I say, dragging my eyes from the pointy things to grin at him.

"I will give you the full tour later. For now, you need to bathe and get back to your rooms for a proper meal and some rest." Dominus leads me to the back of the armoury through another door. This one opens to a small room with a bathing tub, a matching cast iron basin, and a small wooden wardrobe. "Take a quick bath to remove the blood and...everything else you're covered in. There are raiments in the wardrobe. I will warn you, they are mine, so do not expect them to fit, but they will get you to your room."

"And you?" I ask.

"What of me?"

"Do you not need to bathe as well?"

A strange emotion flashes across his eyes, and his brows narrowly draw together. "Do not worry about me. Let us get you cleaned up and back to your rooms." He closes the door and leaves me to it.

I bathe quickly, not even letting the tub fill, but wash under the hot water, thoroughly scrubbing my scalp and skin twice with the delicious soap that smells of palo santo and rosemary. My poor feet are indeed torn and bloody. Wincing, I pull off loose bits of skin, leaving open wounds on my heels and toes. I dry myself with an oversized bath sheet that is deliciously plush. I leave my hair down to dry and peruse the wardrobe, running my fingers through the dark raiments. I lean in, smelling a thick, black wool pullover. It smells of him. Rain and citrus and earth.

First, I put on a black sleeveless tunic, likely something he would use for sword fighting. It hits just below my knees. I layer the pullover atop it and pull on a pair of knee-high stockings over my bruised feet. I neatly pile my soiled raiments into my pack and carry my boots out with me. There is no way my feet are going back in them for a few days—or wyths.

I walk out to a freshly cleaned Dominus dressed impeccably in a dark wool suit. "So, you get to look like that while I get to walk the halls looking like I rummaged through the wardrobe of a giant?"

He does a poor job of hiding his smile. "You look fine. Come with me."

Dominus takes my stuffed pack, waterskin, and boots to carry for me. He leads us back out of the armoury and across the other end of the second hall. He opens a door to an endless spiral staircase. I silently curse him. Silently, because I know that if I complain, he will offer to carry me, and I have had enough of that. Step after step after step, we go. We pass two landings with doors before finally stopping at the third.

"This will take us to the very end of our hall. This is the only door besides ours in our corridor. No one should be there, so go out of this door and straight to your room. Understood?"

"Got it."

Shrike takes a skeleton key from the front pocket of his coat and unlocks the door, only opening it fractionally. "The door is behind the tapestry, so slide out, staying close to the wall."

I let Dominus take the lead, and I follow behind him, pushing myself as flat as I can against the stones. He peeks around the side and waves me on. The only candelabras burning in the corridor are right beside our doors. The rest of the hall is darkened. We move silently. Ten steps. Fifteen steps. Twenty steps. We are nearly there when a shadow jumps up from the floor near my door. No, not a shadow. Thair bloody Torin.

"Thair! Goodness, you frightened me," I say with my hands to my chest.

"Bloody spirits, Thorne, where have you been? I was so worried about you. I came to check on you last night, and you weren't here. I was terrified something happened to you out there."

Steps sound from the darkness behind me. "And yet, you are here. Considerably not worried enough to search for her."

"Shrike."

"Torin."

"What's going on here, Thorne?" Thair asks, hurt brimming in his eyes. May Cyfrif harvest my soul this very moment. I let Thair down to show up with Dominus, in his raiments, only a day later.

"I swear to you, Thair, this is not at all what it looks like."

"Really? Because it looks like Shrike doesn't know how to take his own advice. Rich, is it not, that you can berate me for something that you now do? But perhaps that was the reason. Perhaps it was out of jealousy and not at all from your morality."

"Thair, please listen to me. Shrike—"

"Dominus," he corrects.

I whip my head to him. Now is *not* the time. "*Dominus* just happened to find me and—" He cuts me off again.

"It was indeed from jealousy, Torin." He steps up to my side. "I could not stand to see your foul mouth on what is mine."

"Excuse me—"

Dominus takes me by the back of my neck and turns me into him. Then his mouth is on mine, hot and wanting. It's needy and punishing. Claiming. My traitorous body responds, though my mind screams to stop. And I bloody well find myself kissing him back.

It only lasts for seconds, but those seconds last a lifetime. My mind whirls. It twists and warps, and behind my closed lids, I see something. I see the same vision I had the night of my last episode. A blade—my skean I now recognise—slides through my ribs, scraping gently against my heart. Only now, the vision progresses. My point of view pulls back to see that the skean is in someone's hand. Someone's large, callused hand that leads into a scarred arm. The vision warps again to show me Shrike's face as he holds my body in his arms, as he kisses my neck, and pulls out the blade.

Instantly, I am back in my body. Our lips separate, and Dominus and I pull apart to stare into each other with pure astonishment.

"Right. Consider me unsurprised," Thair deadpans.

I slowly turn my head back to Thair, still reeling. "No, truly, Thair I—"

"I understand. I do. I simply hope you made the right choice." With that, he turns on his heels and walks away. I promptly turn and barge into my rooms.

Of course, he follows. I turn on him once the door closes behind him. "How could you? How *could* you? You belittled me not days ago for kissing a colleague, and now, you do this? In front of him? What do you think will happen now? Do you honestly expect him to keep our secret?"

"No, I certainly do not." His response is nonchalant, and it boils my blood.

"Then why would you do it?" I plead with outstretched hands.

Dominus places my things on my bed and slides his hands into his pockets. "To save him, Thorne. Because you were considerably close to telling him what happened. Or at least that I found you in the woods, and I cannot have that. I cannot have another person knowing anything about what is going on. It has already nearly cost your life. It could cost me everything. Do you want to risk Torin as well?" My breath settles a bit then. I bloody hate it, but again, he is correct. I was going to tell Thair the truth, and I honestly don't know if I could have stopped myself from telling him about the dearg due.

He steps closer. "Whatever we are doing, whatever I divulge to you, it cannot leave us. You can tell no one. To get the truth, you must abandon everything you have ever known—everything you have ever worked for. Because this world is not ready for this truth, Thorne. Can you commit to that? Can you leave it all behind to have every question you have ever had answered?"

I consider it, but not for long. Because I never did this, worked so hard, carved a name for myself, and became who I am for recognition. I never did it for praise or for anyone else. I did it to find the truth. My truth. And he might have information that can help me. He might know someone who can break my curse. "Yes, of course I can. Do you find me so vain?"

"I do not. But this must be your decision."

"I have made it. I choose this. I choose the truth."

"Good. Then we keep the ruse with Thair going. Let him believe that whatever sneaking we do in the night is because I cannot stop myself from devouring you."

My heart skips a bit. *Devour.* That word reminds me of the vision, and maybe that's what he wants to do. "Fine, but offer me a truth. What are you?"

"Not that. Not now."

I try another angle. "Did you see that? When we...when we kissed?"

"Yes." His eyes darken.

"What does it mean?"

"I don't know. I—"

"What do you mean you do not know? Don't you know anything? Can you not offer me something?"

Dominus closes the space between us, placing his hands on either side of my face. "I can tell you that I thought I knew it all, that I had it all figured out until you showed up. Now I have more questions than I have answers. And I am working hard to figure them out, but I need time. I promise I am not withholding." His stunning green eyes plead for me to believe him. I become transfixed, wholly enamoured.

"Do you want to eat me? Is that something your kind does? Because I honestly cannot determine if I am misreading things."

A rich laugh sounds from him, sending warmth to my blood. "I would be lying if I said I did not have thoughts of consuming you. But not the way you are thinking." Too much. Too serious. Too...raw to come from his mouth.

I step from his embrace. "The vision. Can you tell me why

you would want to kill me? Other than the obvious reasons?"

"Is that truly what you believe?"

"The attempted murder and constant attacks on my person have crafted a reliable narrative to make me believe so." I shrug.

"Is that not part of our dance, our duel, this addictive game we play?" He leans close to whisper into my ear, "Is that not the very part that you revel in? What makes your blood pump and your knees weak?" Yes, but I am not telling him that. Because I cannot decide if he is playing now or not—if this is a feint or an offer of honesty—and I would rather have the higher ground if we are again at war.

"Yes, it does," I whisper seductively back to him as I slowly run my hand up his arm to his thick hair. "With rage," I add, and pull his hair roughly, dragging him away from me. He laughs again as I release him. "I have had two visions of you killing me now. Regardless of how beautiful you are, Dominus, I think I will keep my distance until I figure out why."

"Two? When did you have another?" His eyes turn from playful to concerned instantly.

I hesitate to reveal too much, but then I realise there is a connection of events here that I cannot believe to be a coincidence, and the quicker I figure out why, the better. "The night before I left to come here." I leave out that it came after an episode.

"Are you certain?" He runs his hands through his hair.

"Yes. Well, that night I did not see you. Just the skean in my rib cage. This very one, actually," I say, tapping the blade under my—his—raiments.

His brows quirk together as he studies my face. "I do not

believe I was killing you in the vision. It felt like—" A breath. A pause. "Like something else." I know what he means. It was something else. Something I have never felt before. Something like...surrender, which does not grow my confidence. "I need to go. Your bricfeasta will be here soon. Eat and rest. We meet with the team tonight."

"We?"

"If you think I am letting you out of my sight now, you are mistaken. I do not know what you are or what any of this means, and if there is one thing I absolutely loathe, it is not knowing something."

I understand what he means, except I have always lived in the unknown, searching for answers. So perhaps, there is a soft familiarity I have in that space that he does not. "I am but a woman, Dominus. Just a *woman with a smart mouth and shapely body*. What is there to fear?"

The dimple makes an appearance before his smile fades. "Everything." And with that, he spins on his fine leather boots and closes my door behind him.

Gently.

SEVENTEEN

A soft knock brings me from a deep sleep. I roll myself over to find the sun beginning to set. I have slept all day.

Tap, tap, tap.

I drag myself from the bed, wincing at my sore feet. My energy was nonexistent after eating to apply the salve before immediately falling asleep.

I open the door to find a not-so-rested Dominus. "Did you not sleep?" I ask.

"No, too much to do. I am a very busy man," he replies smugly. I roll my eyes and walk back to throw myself atop my bed. "We do not have to attend tonight if you are too tired. I can only imagine how the last few days have been for you—"

"As a human, you mean?" I mumble into my sheets.

"As someone who was violently attacked by a bloodthirsty

monster, nearly died, perhaps actually died, then came back to life to trek endlessly across unforgiving terrain. The physical and emotional consequences of that should not be taken lightly."

Well, when he puts it that way. I roll over and sit up, pulling the thick down cover nearly to my chin. "The strange thing about it is, I do not feel like it happened to me. What I mean is, I do not harbour those repercussions. I wait for the shock of it to arrive, yet it has not, and I believe it won't. I am not numb to it, but I do have peace about it." I chew on my lip in contemplation. Dominus remains quiet, letting me find my thoughts. "I had a thought when I was dying that at least this was the way I was going to go. That, at least in my death, I found truth. I found a monster. Irrefutable proof of all I have searched for. Perhaps that makes me a delusional sycophant, but it remains the truth. It is difficult to fear the things you have searched so long for. Even when they are pumping you with venom while gorging on your blood."

"That is exceptionally dark," he says.

"I know." I smile at him.

He rolls his eyes. "I suppose I do understand, though. But I shall keep a watch on you still, lest those deep, dark emotions decide to boil to the surface and cause you to run loose, screaming of dearg dues through these halls."

"Fair enough, and honestly respected. I assume you will be escorting me to the meeting. Ever the doting lover?"

"Indeed. So, get ready or go back to sleep. Choice is yours," he offers.

"We will go. I have something important to ask the team," I say, tossing the covers that had just begun to warm away.

"Care to enlighten me?" His eyes squint suspiciously.

"Yes. At the meeting, oh gracious overlord," I say, offering an exaggerated bow.

"You're wretched."

"I know." I cannot help the smile stretching across my face.

Dominus keeps to my room while I wash and dress in the bathing chamber. I never changed out of his raiments. Honestly, I could bathe in his scent. It is calming, soothing, and somehow also powerful. It makes me feel safe. I shove that thought away as I run a bit of lemon and cedarwood oil through my hair and lather my dry lips with the sweet mint and lavender balm. My feet, thoroughly coated with Elowyn's salve and thick stockings, feel better already. As always now, my skean rests against my sternum, the chain living between my breasts.

I emerge shortly, wearing a high-collared scyrte with light, billowing sleeves that taper at my wrists under a fitted vest and a pleated skirt, the hem of which rests a daring amount above my knees, paired with dark, heeled boots that come nearly to my thigh. When I open the door, Dominus is standing at one of the giant windows, staring out at the sea. He turns to me as I enter, my boots sounding with soft thuds against the stone floor.

"Tell me, do all women of your hamlet dress like this?"

I smile internally. "Like what?" I ask, looking down at myself as if I don no more than a potato sack.

"With such awareness of themselves," he says, walking slowly toward me. "With intent. Like an artist with a blank canvas creating masterpiece after masterpiece."

His words nearly make me stumble, but I straighten my spine and toss my hair over my shoulder. "No. Most women in my home have rarely even had the sun on their ankles."

"Well, I thank the Seren you are not one of them."

I roll my eyes at him. "You are taking your subterfuge a bit too seriously, don't you think?"

"Oh, I am merely practising. For the witnesses. It is unusual to pay you compliments rather than insults."

"It certainly is."

We arrive at the meeting before anyone else. Some kitchen staff bring beef stew, cabbage, and fresh rosemary bread for supper. Dominus requests that they bring a few bottles of wine up as well.

"Here's to skullduggery," I say, holding my goblet up. He grins, nods in agreement, and raises his as well.

I drink deeply, needing the liquid courage. The wine is a light and sweet aromatic, a complement to the warming season. Orla and Norine enter together. Thair follows behind them.

"Well, well," Norine beams. "Look who decided to grace us with his presence. Let me guess, you let us do all the hard work these many wyths only to come in and take the glory?"

"Not at all, Miss Quinn. I only came to observe and thoroughly judge, maybe offer some much-needed guidance, and to make sure the academy's coin is being well spent."

I do not hide my disdain when I glare at him. "Detestable," I murmur into my wine. Dominus winks at me.

"Sounds about right," Thair murmurs, louder than me.

"That would be your cue to catch me up, Miss Alder."

I do exactly that. We spend over an hawr explaining to Dominus what we have already accomplished, like working to edit and review the submissions from the scolemasters, and Norine offers up her implementation of the student submissions. Thair and I work through the plan for the unearthing and so on until he is fully aware of every move I have made since I have been here.

"Well?" I ask, watching Dominus bring a bite of stew to his mouth. He swallows and looks at me as he turns over his spoon and licks.

"Well, what?"

"You're here. You have heard all we have done. Offer up your unaltered wisdom. Pass your unyielding judgment upon us, your eminence."

He covers the quirking of his lip quickly. "You will be surprised, very surprised, even I am surprised, to hear me say that I have no criticism." Dramatically, I bring the back of my hand to my forehead and fall back into my chair.

"Someone mark the day, the time, the very hawr," Norine says just as dramatically as I act.

"I can only say that because this is the team that I assembled. So, I suppose if you were not doing well, it would be my reflection."

"There he is," I say. "He finds a way to take the credit for all our hard work."

He does grin then. "I only jest, Miss Alder. Honestly, you all have done a wonderful job, and I look forward to seeing the final project and witnessing how this legacy lives through

Adonien."

My heart jumps in my chest. If what he offers is honesty, then regardless of all the other things going on, that means I am doing my job and doing it well. And maybe I have even impressed Dominus Shrike.

"Here, here!" Thair offers, raising his goblets to mine, and we all clink them in unison. I am thankful he does not appear angry with me. Or at least that's the part he is playing with the others around. I must talk to him—alone. Not to change my story, but to try to make peace with him.

"So, Thorne. What did you want to talk about tonight?" Dominus asks.

I clear my throat. "As we have discussed in the past, I would like to visit the four other territories of Eregahl while I am here. I want to record, share, and cross-examine lore and history with the other territories to see how certain myths and legends might change across the lands. I would love to extend the offer to any or all of you to join me. Master Shrike, I understand that would require you to release your well-managed masters from their duties—only briefly, I assure you. If it is not feasible to reach them all, I still think it would be beneficial to visit Eden and Caledon since they border Danumhar."

"I think that is a very clever idea," he offers. The compliments are beginning to chafe, I think.

"I was thinking we could start with Eden next wyth, if everyone is available, and we could plan the following territories based on everyone's schedules."

"It works for me, as long as my overseer approves," Norine says, looking to Dominus.

"Same for me," Thair offers.

Orla, who has been awfully cheerful tonight, walks over to sit on the arm of Dom's chair. "I look forward to spending more quality time with you all," she says, but she is only looking at him.

I clear my throat, unreasonable anger boiling my blood. "Well, what do you say, Shrike?" I use his last name purposefully, knowing it will anger him. It will anger him as it angers me to see Orla brushing her bony backside against his arm.

Dominus rises, pours himself another glass of wine, and walks over to look out into the dark sky. "As long as none of you neglect your priorities, I can make it happen." We all whoop and cheer, and we spend the night sipping wine and planning the jaunt.

We talk for hawrs, thoroughly enjoying ourselves. Even Dominus lets his guard down a bit, joining in on our conspiracy theories and wild ideas. Of course, this conversation is different now that I know more about what really exists. At least now that I know what it means to be one of their meals. Orla has made it a point to stick close to Dominus tonight, and by the end of it, I find myself wishing I had teeth like the dearg due to rip her throat out. I am not sure why.

A yawn escapes me as I stare out the open window to the forest beyond. The nights are getting warmer, and I look forward to samhradh nights and bonfires. Or maybe not, as I remember the nightmares brought to life that roam these woods at night. I scan the trees, the grounds, and the mountains beyond, searching for things I likely do not want to find.

"Thorne, I will escort you back to your room now. It is

late." I find it odd that his presumptuous and assuming demands do not incite immediate rage in me. Indeed, I am exhausted, and my head swims from the wine. I want to fall into my bed and slip into nothing.

"Goodnight, everyone. I will see you after the wythnos."

We all offer our farewells, and Dominus leads me out. I consider staying to speak to Thair, but I am not confident I could form a coherent sentence, and I need to be especially mindful of what I say to him.

Dominus walks me back to our corridor. At some point, his arms are wrapped around me, and I am certain it is because I keep stumbling. "We're nearly there," he whispers into my ear, and an ache builds between my legs.

Moments later, we are in my room, and Dominus leads me to my bed. He helps me sit, and I immediately relax in the comfort of my room with his scent wrapped around me. My head becomes clearer and my breaths easier.

I kneel, attempting to undo the buckle of my boot and fail. Maybe I am not as sober as I thought.

"Here," he says, helping me to the bed. His voice is like wine, and I want to continue to drink. Dominus kneels and begins to unlace my boots. I do not stop him, infinitely curious about his move. He removes them swiftly with inhuman grace and places them next to the bed. Then he looks at me with those painfully beautiful pale eyes. I play my move in my mind, trying not to smile.

I slowly bring a leg up to place my toes on his shoulder, encouraging him to remove my stocking as well. His eyes begin a gentle, low glint, and I struggle to contain my smile. He brings his hand to the top of my stocking at the middle of my thigh. He loops his warm fingers inside the hem and slowly, painfully so, begins to pull it down. We cease to break eye contact as he brings it down to my ankle, taking my foot from his shoulder to remove the stocking before gently placing my foot on the floor.

Dominus gives me nothing. No indication if he likes this, if he hates it, if he's playing along. I cannot read him. Nothing other than that barely noticeable glow. He remains still but kneeling. I place my other foot on his other shoulder, and as I do, I let my knee fall away from me slightly, offering him a view of the lacy underthings beneath my skirt. He stills—not moving, not breathing.

I begin to feel embarrassed and ashamed. Perhaps he is not playing tonight, and perhaps I have taken it too far. Then, as if he lost a war with himself, his gaze slides languidly from my eyes to my mouth and trails down to beneath my skirt. He sucks in a sharp breath and closes his eyes. Liquid pools in my core at the sounds of it. I want to press my legs together, but I dare not move or breathe.

When he opens his eyes, they are blazing, casting a bright, pale light upon my exposed body. He bites his lip so hard I am certain he will draw blood as he grips the hem of my other stocking and pulls it down achingly slow, drawing it out. His warm fingers glide down my smooth skin, sending lightning to skitter across my body. "Thorne." His voice is raw and deep as he says my name like a plea.

"Dominus." I do not recognise my own voice when I respond. It is breathy and powerful in a way I have never heard.

"I need you to move. I need you to remove your leg from

me and move onto the bed." My heart sinks in my chest. Perhaps his repulsion looks akin to desire. Maybe he was playing too, and I fell for it. "I need you to do it because I cannot. I do not have the willpower to move away from you, and you have had too much wine tonight to be making any decisions."

My breath hitches in my chest. I no longer feel as if I have had too much. Maybe before we got here, but now I am clear-headed. I feel like I want his hands over every inch of my body, but maybe he's right. Maybe this would not be a good idea, for a multitude of reasons, like the fact that I still have no idea what he is. That thought brings me closer to my senses. I hesitate, though, tempted to drag him closer to me, tempted to see what would happen if we kissed again. Then I am reminded of the bloody vision and become completely frustrated by it all.

"Thorne," he begs. I slowly remove my leg from his grasp, though he does not move his hands, letting his fingers graze over my skin as I pull from his grip. Only when my leg is free and I move to the top of the bed does he stand, running his hands through his hair, something I enjoy watching him do. "My apologies," he says.

I am suddenly irritated. Or maybe the right word is frustrated. This is the second time I have nearly been able to give in to my desires, only to have the opportunity seized. "You have nothing to apologise for, Shrike," I bite.

He is over me in an instant, one knee on the bed, one arm squeezing the headboard behind me, and the other grips my chin firmly but not painfully. "What did you call me?" he growls.

Fire blooms inside of me, ravaging my veins. Defiance dancing with it. I smile between his fingers, "Shrike."

"I will give you one more opportunity to correct your error. Then I will be forced to teach you what happens when you defy me. Do not think this very same misstep with the others tonight went unnoticed, mo céasadh."

Temptation overtakes me, urging me to make the worst kind of decision. My heart begins to pound against my rib cage as I consider what to do. I know I should call his name, satisfy him, and let him leave. But when have I ever been one to do as I was told? And I am just as interested to see how far he would go because I sense he is playing now. This is not how it would be between us if we ever put our weapons down, but it remains a thrilling dance. And he is letting me decide. He is asking for permission to keep our performance going. So, I oblige.

I slowly run my tongue across my teeth, considering, before answering, "Shrike."

Before his name fully leaves my mouth, I am on my front, lying face down across the end of the bed. Dominus has both of his hands on the backs of my thighs, and he is slowly moving them up and up and up until he pushes my skirt to my waist, exposing me fully to him. He loosens a low growl at what he sees, and I smile into the bedding. His hands move further, kneading my endowed bottom. Then, the spanks it, once, twice, three times. The strikes are not painful but deliciously sharp in their delivery. He kneads where he struck, soothing me, but I want more. I arch into him, a silent offering.

"Gods, Thorne," he says hoarsely, before giving me another three strikes on the other side.

I become clay in his hands. His to mould, to knead, to form into whatever he wants. A low moan escapes me, a desperate desire for more. He leans his body down, pressing himself into me, and I become intently aware of everywhere we touch and how exactly into this he is, too.

His weight on me is exquisite, and I want to turn, yearning for the full brunt of him against me, between my legs, pushing against my ribs. He pulls my long, thick waves to the side, exposing my neck. He kisses and licks and sucks, sending me spiralling before he bites my shoulder. He slowly drags his teeth across my skin, releasing an audible gasp from me. One not of pain but pure pleasure.

In an instant, his comforting weight is gone, leaving me cold and wanting. I quickly reach for him, but he's already across the room to the door.

"Wait, please," I beg.

"My deepest apologies, Thorne. I should not have done that. I—"

"That was not a cry of pain, Dominus." His eyes glow brighter as he clenches his jaw. "Trust me, you would know if I did not like something. I'm not afraid to tell you what I want."

"What do you want, Thorne?" His tone is desperate, frustrated.

It all becomes too real, too revealing. I cannot speak the words. I cannot tell him that I want him to throw me back on the bed and show me more things I do not know. I cannot tell him that I might break if he leaves. I cannot show my hand. I cannot give him my throat. Because what if, instead of kissing it, he cuts it open? What if he strips me of my vulnerability only to laugh in my face? The lines have become too blurred. I cannot determine if we are dancing anymore. I refuse to drop my guard, not now, not knowing what he would do.

I take a deep breath as tears fall down my face. "Go," I whisper. "Just go."

He nods his head, the flame going out in his eyes. "Goodnight, Thorne."

He slowly shuts the door behind him.

EIGHTEEN

"It will either make our next night there horribly uncomfortable or exceptionally delicious," Thair says, grinning at me behind his wooden cup as he sits with Norine and me in the Great Hall for supper. I try not to envy his escapades with Aoife as I press my thighs together, thinking of last wyth when Dominus pushed me against the bed and spanked me.

"I cannot wait to witness it either way. Are we going this wythnos?" Norine asks.

"Let me check with Elowyn what day she plans for me to come, and I will let you know."

She turns to me, placing her fist beneath her chin. "I find it extremely adorable how you have bonded with them. Of all the relationships I would have expected you to make during your study, theirs was not one of them." Norine smiles as she says it.

"My thoughts exactly, but there's something warm about them. An ease that I have not felt in a long time."

"You must take me one day."

"I would love that, and I am sure they would, too. Well, Elowyn would. Eamon might skin me alive for it." Our chuckles mingle together.

Someone clears their throat behind me, and I do not have to look to know with the drop of Thair's face and the humming in my ears that Dominus stands behind me. I am not sure how to face him after what we have done. After what we didn't do. Heat blooms in my core.

I slide my mask on and turn to smile at him. "What can I do for you, Master?" I ask sweetly, looking up at him through my lashes, suddenly aware of where my eyeline would fall if I look straight. I smile internally and let my gaze do just that, lazily running down to his waist and back up.

"Miss Alder, I need to see you for a moment. In private." Gods, the heat takes me over, but I try my best not to let it show.

"Alright." I rise to follow him. The way he moves is art—a dance within itself. I choose my words carefully, edging the pinnacle we stand on. "Where are you taking me?"

He glances back over his shoulder, those green eyes looking me up and down. "I have something to show you." My mind wanders, thinking of all the things he could show me. We do not speak any further as I follow him out of the entrance and through the giant front doors of Adonien. I stay a few steps behind him, watching and studying every move he makes. I still have no idea what he is or is capable of. The thought shakes me with fear and...exhilaration. He leads me out of the entrance gates, still silent as ever. I refuse to speak first. He brought me out here. He can be the one to make the first move. My stubbornness is wasted because he refuses to even act like I am here as he leads me down the path winding through the craggy cliffside.

The sea thrashes against the rocks, and the sky slowly begins to fade from the bright blue of a sunny day to the deep indigo of a day-old bruise, threatening to fall at any moment. Still, we do not speak. Thunder begins to boom far out at sea as we reach the waterfront. We walk along the sandy shore for a while as darker skies roll closer. Tiny pebbles of cool rain just begin to fall when Dominus takes a sharp left into the mountainside. I slow my pace, wondering if he brought me out here to silence me. I figured something out about him. Maybe he wants to keep his secret. I round the edge of the stone wall to find him standing under the cover of a cavern carved into the cliffside with his hands in his pockets, staring at me with those eyes.

"Bring me all the way out here to kill me, Dominus? At least you chose somewhere with a view." I stop in front of him, crossing my arms.

He smiles. "If I wanted you dead, Thorne, I would have done it the night you arrived. I would have snuck into your room after I found you spying on me." Embarrassment envelops me, but I refuse to let it take over.

"I heard howls in the woods that night. I saw—I saw a shadow. I fell asleep, and then I woke to your footsteps. Imagine what I thought when I saw you stomping down the halls covered in blood. Who—what did the blood belong to, Dominus?"

"Do you ever tire of inserting yourself in affairs that do not involve you?"

"No. It's my favourite pastime."

He huffs a laugh, removing his hands to turn them up and spin around slowly. "It was an afanc, and this was its home."

A bloody afanc, living at the bottom of the cliff on which the academy sits. Gods. The afanc are terrifying water beasts. Their descriptions vary, but they are often portrayed as a crocodile-like creature, sometimes with elements of a beaver or a dwarf. In some tales, it is simply described as a giant beast, but they are always depicted as dangerous and destructive, causing floods or attacking those who come near its waters.

"It found itself on the grounds. I chased it away from the water and into the mountains. Where I killed it."

"Dearg due, afanc, are all the creatures of mythology real?" I ask, the possibility of it nearly sending me to my knees.

He nods. "Most of them. There are, of course, the occasional ones that have been made up by humans over the last few centuries. Some of the others have gone extinct."

"Which ones roam this island?" The question stirs an equal concoction of fear and thrill within me.

He runs his hand through his hair, looking out into the storm that has now fully let loose. "Are you never satisfied with what I give you?"

I snort at his words, considering how he left me wanting the last time with were together. "I will let you know when you have satisfied me, Shrike. You cannot just keep offering me crumbs when I am starving."

His eyes alight at my words, and I don't know if we remain

talking about the creatures. "What do you want from me?" he asks through clenched teeth.

I want the truth. I want him to cease withholding from me. I want to twist my blade in his gut. I want to watch him writhe. I want...his hands to sear my skin. My chest heaves at the thought.

"Nothing. I want nothing from you," I say and abandon him in the cavern to stomp off into the pouring rain and the cracking of thunder that echoes the booming inside of me. Dominus grips my wrist and spins me around roughly. I collide with his soaked chest. The heat of his body bleeds through our wet raiments. His chest rises and falls as mine does. I look at him through the thick wall of rain, daring him. He loosens a growl as if in defeat and kisses me. He kisses me with anger and frustration, and I meet him with the same fervour, never one to back down.

He pushes me back suddenly, and I stumble but stay on my feet. "Say it. Tell me what you want."

I refuse. I refuse to say it, to give him the victory. We stare at each other through falling rain and heaving breaths. I move to push him back, placing both hands on his chest and pushing with my full might. He takes one small step back, and I know he gave it to me. I grunt at him, full of anger and hate and want. "What you will not give me!"

He grabs my throat and pulls me in, resuming our battering kisses. Then, he reaches for my hips and hauls me up. I wrap my legs around him instinctively. He tastes of rain and citrus—a salty, sweet concoction of the best and worst desire. A delicious dichotomy. Emotions wage a violent war inside of me. The hate I have for him is nearly levelled with the desire hollowly aching inside of me. I bring my hands into his dark, wet curls and pull roughly, causing us to break our kiss. His wide eyes glow as he assesses me. He drops to his knees and lays me against the wet sand. Raindrops pelt every inch of me like kisses from the sky. The coolness of it is a blissful harmony with the warmth of him on top of me, between my legs.

Dominus looks at me as he reaches his hands to the top of my scyrte and rips it down the centre in one powerful pull. A moan escapes me at the sight of it, encouraging him, I realise. He's on me again, moving his cruel mouth to my neck and chest. He runs his sharp teeth across my collarbone, and I think I might combust with need. I wrap my arms around his shoulders, but he grabs my wrists and pulls them to my sides, where he holds them. I want to touch him. I want to run my hands through his hair and across the hardness of his muscles. I want to dig my nails into him. I want to taste him.

"Let me touch you," I beg. He looks up at me from my navel, pausing his exploration.

"No," he commands.

I grunt in frustration, trying to remove myself from his grip. He does not budge. I hate myself for it, but I add, "Please."

I watch as he runs his tongue along my rib cage. "If you touch me, I will not be able to control myself. And I have needs to satisfy." He moves to take both of my wrists in one of his hands, holding them above my head. With his now free hand, he reaches beneath my skirt to rip away my underthings. He drops the black pile of lace beside my face. Setting his gaze on me again, he reaches back and runs a finger down the centre of me. I arch into it, contorting beneath his frame in pleasure. He purs in response before plunging that finger into me, and I cry out, the sound muffled by the rain pounding down on us. He works in and out of me as he rests above me, watching me with intent. I try to squirm out of his grip to touch him, but he holds me tighter.

Then he moves to his knees. "Hands to your side, Thorne. Now." I want to retort, but more than I want to conquer him, I do not want him to stop. If he stops now, I might die. So, finally, I do what he asks. "Do not move them. If you touch me, I stop."

I nod at him, waiting for his resume. Slowly, eyes still on me, he leans down and wraps his hands around my thighs, digging his fingers into the bare, wet skin at my hips. Before I have a chance to prepare myself, he replaces his fingers with his tongue, and I think I might die at the pleasure of it. Dominus feasts on me desperately and fiercely as if he were a starving man and I his only meal. I writhe beneath him, and without thinking, I reach to run my hands through his hair. He stops, and I whine at the absence of him.

"Thorne," he warns. I slap my hands down to the sand in a rage and clench my fingers in the earth, needing something to anchor me. "Good girl," he croons, resuming his pursuit. He works me from top to bottom in long, hard licks and adds his fingers, sending me into a fit. My gut clenches, my body begins to shake, and that humming wraps around me, flowing into me, resonating the climb.

"Dominus," I beg, needing the release, needing him to consume me whole. He growls at my plea, and the vibration of it against me sends me falling. I squeeze my legs around him and quake around his fingers. I fall and fall and fall, harder and longer than I ever have. I cannot breathe. I cannot think. I let the pleasure thunder through me as lightning scatters across the sky and watch as he takes his time, committed to the delivery, down to the final second.

When I finally float back down, Dominus rises to me. He rests some of his weight on me, but not nearly enough. Leaning close to my face, his hair dripping on me, he whispers, "Satisfied?" His hardness presses against me, all of him, and I wrap my legs around his waist, pulling him closer

"Not even a little," I whisper back. It's a half-truth. It was exactly what I wanted. It stopped the throbbing need, but it also worsened it. It made me hungrier. It only grew my craving for him, and I bloody hate it. And now he has had me. He made me come undone beneath him, and I could not even touch him—could not even give it back and drive him to the brink of insanity. I lie beneath him, a storm of hate and desire, planning my next move. He has the upper hand now.

I cannot have that.

I pull him into me and kiss him deeply. I kiss him in a way that we both know is bloody dangerous. In a way that somehow goes further than what he just did to me. He pulls back, running his eyes over my face. I can no longer tell if I am even playing the game anymore.

"Let me touch you," I beg. Something happens then. It is a modicum of time, but so much transpires. I watch his pale green eyes as they nearly give in, as he nearly surrenders to me. I watch as he begins to kneel, to drop his sword, remove his walls.

Then they suddenly haze over, becoming colder. He smiles a wicked smile, looking at me as he says, "Never," and plunges his sword through my core. He is on his feet the next time I blink, leaving me a broken mess on the sand, and walks toward the rising cliff of Adonien.

I cleave at my chest, forcing it not to break. I stifle the pain and let the warming comfort of anger flood my blood instead. I rise quickly, snatching the remains of lace, and stalk off after him. I follow him, raging, all the way to the top. He pauses, turning toward me. "We need to go through the tunnels," he says with a stone face as if everything that has just transpired never happened. I will not allow it.

"No, I am going through the front door."

He gapes at me. "You cannot be serious. Look at you."

I look down at my torn scyrte, soaked to the bone. Sand grits in my hair and beneath my nails. "What, Dominus? Are you ashamed of what you've done? Don't want everyone to see what you are capable of? No. You do not get to kneel before me out of sight and look down your nose at me in front of others. Believe it or not, I have more respect for myself than that."

"That has nothing to do with it."

"Then this should not be a problem for you." I toss my underthings at his feet and wrap the two halves of my scyrte around myself. "A trophy for your victory," I spit and stomp off through the iron gates.

ℭINETEEN

I have no time to think about days ago with Shrike as I sit at the table with Eamon and Elowyn, devouring yet another divine bricfeasta. This is the warmest day yet, and I stretch back against my chair, a satisfied glutton, thankful I wore a simple léine. However, I find myself consumed by the fact that it happens to be the same pale green as some monster's eyes.

"How are the studies going then?" Elowyn asks as she sips from her rose hip tea.

"Really grand, actually. We leave in two days for Eden. We shall attempt to make it to the other territories for a closer look at their resources as well."

"Oh, that is wonderful. Eamon and I are from Eden. We try to travel back every full moon if we can. You must visit my dear friend Oona while you are there. She's a Spicer. She specialises in the spices and salts of Eregahl. You would love her flavours. I cook with many of them. She is also a very interesting woman. You would enjoy conversing with her. She keeps a stall at the town market. I will send word to her tonight to look out for you."

"That is incredibly kind, Elowyn. Thank you. I look forward to meeting her."

Eamon leans to peck Elowyn on the cheek before rising. "'Tis time for me to get to my chores. Will you be joining me today, wain?"

"Absolutely. Give me a bit to help clean up in here, and I will be right out." Eamon leaves us alone, and Elowyn begins to clean the table.

"Elowyn," I say, nervous for what I am about to ask. "Since you are from Eden, I was hoping you would not mind answering a few questions I have." She settles back into her seat and refills both our cups.

"Of course, dear; ask away."

"I know this might sound strange, but part of my work lies heavily in folklore, myths, and legends. I know it is well-known that Eregahl might have had, or might still, possess some type of...magic." Her eyes begin to shimmer a bit, and I take it as an invitation to continue. "I was hoping you might tell me what you know of it or if you have experienced anything in Eden. I read—somewhere—that the goddess Eden is known for imbuing her favourite humans with soft magic. Eden specifically offers powers of divination, gifts of foresight." I pause there, unable to ask what I need to, but it is unnecessary because Elowyn takes over for me.

"Oidhre na Cinniúint. Heir of Fate, she is called."

All air leaves my lungs as my mind immediately jumps to my book. *Oidhre an Domhain.* Heir of Earth. I bring my hand to my chest, looking for its comfort, but I remember that the warmth of the day caused me to leave my jacket behind. In all my desperate attempts, I have never encountered any other information relating to my book or any others like it. How does Elowyn know of this?

As if reading my mind, she answers, "The Seren are very unknown entities. Everything we know about them is based on what they want us to know. When I was a wee lass, my father would whisper stories to me, long since forgotten. There is a particular story he told me once and never repeated. It was said that when the Seren came to this realm, they left behind a sibling, a sister. She was the collateral damage it took to get them here. Her sacrifice in the great war of their world gave them enough time to slip away undetected."

Inaudible music fills my ears from inside of me. A savage beating of war drums. Screaming, the clanking of metal, and noises unlike anything I have ever heard. Something tells me it is the sounds of magic, the sounds of fatal attacks by powers I cannot understand.

"What was her name?"

Elowyn smiles at me like I asked the right question. "Her name was Danu." As she says it, my vision blurs, burning my eyes. "The story depicts her as an ethereal beauty, but she was also a warrior far stronger than her siblings. She was the goddess of nature and wisdom. The other Seren loved her very much. So much so that they used her namesake for one of the territories in Eregahl. Danumhar."

My head swims with the realisation. "How is this not known?" I question.

"Like I said, I only ever heard it once. And it died with my father—well, I suppose it dies with you, now. "Tis the thing about myths and legends, though. Without proof, they remain just that. No one I have encountered has ever heard the story either. So, who knows if there is truth to it, or if it was the work of a mad, old man." She takes a sip of tea, and I follow suit, considering her words.

"But there has never been any record of how Danumhar got its name. And that one certainly sounds convincing."

She shrugs at me, taking another sip. "Perhaps. Keep your eyes open. Now that you have something to search for, perhaps more will turn up in those books of yours."

"What you said earlier about the Heir of Fate, what does that mean?"

"Ah, each Seren is said to be a royal heir in their home realm. Each royal child would possess a certain power. The power is not born, though. It is gifted. However, the Seren can live for, well, maybe forever; who knows? So, the exchange of power is rare but is still very much kept in the family. The exchange was known to be very ritualistic in nature."

"How will being here alter that exchange? Will it be through offspring they make with their own creations? Will they make it at all?"

"Possibly. Though the exchange itself only needed to be between blood, and since we are all creations of the Seren, I suppose they could choose to gift their reign to any one of their chosen. Though I doubt they ever will. I assume they will let the power of their homeland die with them."

My mind races, starving for the new information to consider. "And I am assuming their titles correlate with their specific powers?"

"Precisely. Eden, the Heir of Fate, possesses the ability to look into the future and the past. She converses with the cosmos and is gifted to see signs that others do not. She imbues others with that same power of sight as well as other mental abilities. Noreg, Oidhre an Spiorad, Heir of Spirit, has the power to manipulate the spirits of others through her tongue. Thus, her chosen ones have the ability to curse or bless others."

"Curses?" I cut her off. This. This might finally be a crumb, a trail, something to pursue about my episodes.

"Oh, yes. Though they are very specific to the individual and often pass when the inflictor dies."

If this is the case, it might be unlikely that I bear a curse. Unless the person to cast it is still alive. Before I have a chance to ask, she continues. "Caledon, Oidhre an Cnámh, Heir of Bone, can heal and destroy anything made of bone. He can also animate wicked things with them. His chosen are healers and menders. And then there is Hellas."

She takes a deep breath before continuing, but I already know this part. After their arrival, the Seren began to build and create a world, something very different from their home. They worked alongside each other for a long time in harmony, creating many new beings. But while the others remained happy with their new families, Hellas remained perpetually unsatisfied. He pushed the others to go further, to expand, to experiment. They were not interested. They had their beautiful creations and their many other things to play with.

So, Hellas began to secretly build an army of monsters. The band of deamhans. No text explicitly names them, but careful consideration through study, and my recent, very personal accounts, have given an idea of which ones are most likely his: dearg due, failinis, afanc, and sea raiders at least. He filled his entire territory with the things and took off to wage war against his own blood. Rumour claims that he killed Noreg and Caledon in the process and sent Eden running forever. I do not think that to be true. I think that might be the version he wants to be heard, but if he did kill his siblings, then he could have easily taken over and be reigning all territories—and show himself.

The Seren used to intimately rule their territories. They held court, threw parties, and committed all sorts of magic and miracles. Since the war between them, things have gone quiet. Or as quiet as I would assume. I have never met anyone who has spoken directly to them, thus giving more credence to the theory that they never existed.

"Hellas was always the troubled child and one that Danu protected the most. She understood him more than the others and was able to keep him leashed. In another world, though, without her there to keep him in line, well, he went back to his hunger for power. And with Danu dead, he was next in line for the throne."

"Do you think he killed Noreg and Caledon?" I stiffen on the edge of my seat, desperate for her answers. The lump in my throat softens a bit as I can now justify my closeness with her and Eamon. Answers, research, and nothing more.

"I have no idea. And there is no way of knowing that he

could offer them a true death."

I spin her words in my mind, chewing on my cheek. So many of these were things I have spent yehrs studying. Only, coming from her mouth, they sound significantly more like truths than myths, and I wonder what more she knows and how she knows it. Perhaps she converses with the gods.

"Elowyn, pardon me if this is inappropriate to ask, but are you imbued? Are you one of the gods' chosen?"

She stares blankly at the table for a moment. I fear falling off my seat as I lean closer, anticipating her response. She looks up to me then. "Of course not. Though I thought there was a time when I did receive messages. But it has been yehrs. So long that I even doubt if they were real or not."

"Maybe not. You seem to know a significant amount about them."

"Maybe." Her stare becomes distant, and I wonder what memories she is recalling.

I realise that now is the time. This is what this entire journey has led to. I place my hand atop hers and allow the sincerity, the desperation to shine through. "I need to be honest with you. I am searching for a seer. I know that it is rare and that it sounds mad, but, well, I might just be incredibly mad. I do believe in all of this, Elowyn. I believe magic is real. I have witnessed it for myself, and I have something I need help with. Is there any way you can help me?"

She smiles at me then, resting her hand atop mine. "I knew there was something special about you."

I spend the rest of the day like I do every other wythnos: with Eamon and Elowyn in effortless harmony. Today, they tell me more about their children. They live in different territories now, scattered all around.

We pick vegetables from the garden, and she promises to use them to make me something hearty for next time. I spend some time with Eamon in the stables brushing and feeding horses. I even climb atop the roof to help him mend a worn spot in the thatch.

"I had better get you back before sunset, wain. Say your goodbyes, and meet me up front," Eamon says, taking a blunt hammer from me. I walk inside to find that Elowyn has a basket full of food packed for me to take.

"You know, you are the very reason why my backside has doubled in size since I arrived. Well, you and those bloody stairs."

"Thank you for letting me cater to you, love. It can be hard with the wains, well, the wains not being wains, and them being spread across the lands. It makes a mother's heart happy to feed bellies."

I want to say that I love her for it. I want to tell her that I will be her pseudo-daughter during my stay. I nearly forget that doing so would most likely secure her death, and that is something I cannot bear. So, I do the only thing I can, which is wrap my arms around her and breathe in her warm, maternal scent. "I am very grateful to you both."

"As are we, dear."

Not able to stand in this house that feels like home, not being able to allow myself to love and be loved, I turn to go. I stop at the threshold, something tugging at my mind.

"Elowyn, you didn't mention earlier, but what was Danu's title?"

She stares at me, her eyes slightly glazed, before nearly whispering, "Oidhre an Domhain. Heir of Earth."

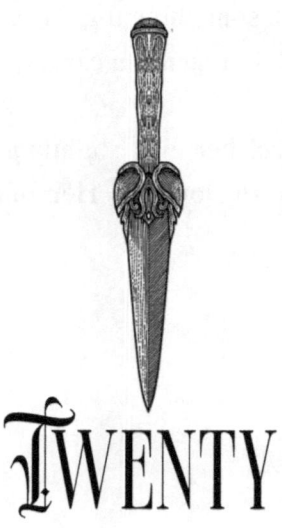

TWENTY

I spend the ride back with Eamon in near silence, my mind reeling over the new information, turning it over and speculating how this compares to what I know. I plan to question Shrike as soon as I return to see what he knows about this. The disseminated information is chaotic and contradictory, and I wonder if we will learn more unheard-of tales in Eden. All my hard-earned knowledge is now a bit unsteady. And what does my book mean? Is it a story of Danu? Could it be true? Are there more books out there?

I feel like a child playing a game of gods, and I will never understand the truth. And maybe I don't need to anymore. Maybe I just need to understand enough to break this curse so that I can spend the day with Eamon and Elowyn without constantly silencing my beating heart. Maybe I can be bold enough to figure out what is going on between Dominus and me in those rare moments of truth.

"Are you sure you're alright, lass?" Eamon asks as the silhouette of Adonien comes into view.

"Yes, just very tired. I'm sorry I have been lacklustre this ride. I promise to be back to myself next time." He only smiles and pats my leg, but I know. I know this is the last time in a while. I know I need to distance myself from them. I must.

Eamon safely gets me inside the grand entrance, and I leave him to take off up the endless stairs. I am surprisingly more agile and stronger, finding the stairs not so difficult, but I am still winded at the top, and I take deep breaths as I head down our corridor.

I knock on Shrike's door, waiting a few moments for an answer I do not get. I give up and move on down the hall. I reach for the handle, but the door is already open. Dominus sits on the floor with his back against my footboard. Parchments, books, and my raiments are scattered around my room.

"What happened here?" I ask, running to him, dropping my basket of food on the floor. I stop before I make it because in his hands is my book. He rifled through my room and is reading my book. I move, snatching it from his hands. He looks at me with anger-filled, shadowed eyes. His hair is a mess as if he's been running his hands through it.

"What did you do?" My voice is only a whisper, but it is laced with betrayal.

"I did what I had to. I have been racking my mind, trying to figure out what is going on, and when you mentioned this, I needed to see. I wish you had given it to me when I asked, but I needed to see this, Thorne. You have no idea what this means."

"I have a theory, which I was on my way to talk to you about before you betrayed my privacy and my wishes. How could you do this?"

He stands too fast, his tall frame towering over me. "Because that is who I am, Thorne. I do what is necessary. I hunt and kill to survive. Because I have a family to get back to. Because I have a job to do."

I am shocked and confused at his revelation, but it cannot make its way past the anger. The anger that is really a mask for the pain because he broke my trust. "And isn't that so typical of you? Looking out for yourself. Surviving at the expense of everyone else. I am not a stepping stone for you, Shrike. I will not be walked on!"

"It's just a fucking book, Thorne."

"No, it's not!" The words leave my mouth before I choose to say them. "This is my entire life. This is the only bloody thread that held me together through the deaths of everyone I have ever loved. This is the only reason I am alive, and it is up to me who I get to share it with." I suck in a sharp breath, reining in the loosening threads of my composure.

A crack in his anger. Concern bleeds through. "What do you mean?"

"That is none of your bloody business. You lost the privilege of learning anything else about me the minute you entered this room."

"Thorne, forgive me. Not knowing this drove me mad, and there are things in here we need to discuss. Answers we have both been looking for."

"I do not care anymore."

"You do not mean that."

"I do for now. I need some time."

"You need me."

"Ha! I need no one," I bite.

I don't give either of us time to slam another bloody door. Instead, I take my book and leave. I run the halls, through corridors, down stairs, and across balconies. I let my pain rip through my body as I go faster and faster, not caring who witnesses me.

My feet take me to the library, my place of refuge, and I plop myself down in an oversized leather chair. A snap and a cloud of dust release upon my landing. Before I can break, the chair beside me is taken by someone. I breathe deeply with frustration.

"Miss Alder! Nice to see you," Headmaster Connally croons at me. I slip my mask back on, ever the calm and collected lady.

"Headmaster, is the library one of your common haunts?" I am disgusted with how smooth I sound.

"Well, I did not become headmaster because of my good looks. Though it did help," he grins beautifully.

"I am sure it did."

"I will not bother you, but while I have you, I would love to hear how your work is going." He could not have picked a worse time for this conversation.

"Honestly, it could not be better. I have had the most incredible time here working with the team. The journal is—"

"Something special to hear Shrike speak of it. Our briefings have been wonderful. He speaks very highly of you. I am not sure how you manage to impress him, but that is a talent in and of itself."

I shove down the maniacal laughter bubbling in my throat. "I find Shrike to be like a stubborn ram. He wants to bleat and attack, but if you refuse to back down, if you do not run, then his horns become less scary."

A singular laugh. "Fine way of putting it, I suppose. How are you enjoying the scol? I do apologise for putting you on the third floor. Master Shrike insisted. He said he wanted to make himself available to you and be able to have someone close if you needed anything. I hope he has not been much of a bother."

Fucking prick.

He said it was Headmaster Connally's doing to keep me locked away up there. It was him all along. I wish I had stabbed him after all. "Ah, it's not so bad. I enjoy the long walks, and no, he has kept to himself with no surprise." I shouldn't be covering for the bastard.

"Look, I understand that he is, well, difficult to say the least. But there is another side to him that few know. Trust me when I tell you it makes putting up with his prickly side all the easier."

That should have made me feel better. Yet I find myself envious of Connally's knowledge of Shrike. The side I have yet to see. "It's not my place to ask to see it. He is allowed to portray whatever version of himself that he pleases."

"Oh, I understand. It is simply— Well, I think he is so accustomed to playing the villain that he does not know how to be the hero."

Because that is who I am, Thorne. I do what is necessary. I hunt and kill to survive. Because I have a family to get back to. Because I have a job to do.

That's a fair assessment. One that cools my anger marginally. "That may be so, but it's up to him to decide who he wants to be."

"And maybe it is our duty, as humans, to reach out a hand—to be the example. A testimony of change through our own acts."

My heart sinks at that. I have never given Dominus a chance to be anything but cruel. That is the game we play. Maybe it is time for a change in refrain. "Perhaps, you're right."

He smiles at me, "I should be off. I have a meeting to get to. I hope you enjoy your reading," he says, nodding to my book. I bring it to my chest, wrapping my arms around it.

"I always do."

Connally leaves me in the library. I look around to see I am nearly alone, other than a few scolers at the writing desks. I find it odd there are not more until I remember it's the wythnos. I open my book to the page Dominus left off. I know because he bent the bloody corner, an absolute vexation for me. I read the passage again, as I have hundreds of times.

"Vicious eyes that pierce the night,
aglow with ancient, eldritch might.
In sacrifice, true strength resides,
as destiny's thread swiftly glides."
Eyes that pierce the night.
The prophecy.
Realisation barrels through me. I know who the Heir of

Earth is. I slam the book. As I rise, something slaps against the floor beneath the chair. I lean on my hands and knees, pressing my face nearly to the wood to find a book there. I pull it and a cloud of dust into the light and bring it to an empty study desk, dusting it off. It's a deep ochre leather journal, dried and old. I pry the brittle pages apart, recognising the flawless handwriting immediately.

"I have lost hope that they may return. I have spent yehrs in the darkness. I will wait no longer. I will live whatever life I have here."

I slam the journal closed, refusing to betray his privacy the way he has mine. Instead, I take off, armed with new information. Up and around, twisting and turning through candlelit halls, my heartbeat synchronises with the slapping of my feet. I make it to our corridor, pushing even faster, and slide to a halt at the front of his door. I bang and bang and bang.

"Dominus, open up. I've found something. Please."

No answer.

Bang, bang, bang.

"Dominus." No answer.

I test the door, certain it will be locked, but to my surprise, the knob turns freely. I hesitate for a moment, not wanting to invade his privacy, but then the image of him and my tossed-about possessions fills my mind, and I push the door open.

The size and layout of this room are similar to mine. We both have those large, arching windows that overlook the sea, but his lacks the wall of windows that overlook the scol, allowing for less moonlight and more darkness and shadows.

Those strange, ever-glowing torches stand watch against

the walls. Impressive candlesticks, tall as me, drip with pale wax in the corners, illuminating his bed. Where mine is made from a gentle wood with a soft, pale stain, his is solid and dark as the night outside the windows. Four thick, spindly posts climb high above me from each corner of the bed. The solid white bedclothes sharply contrast against them. A vision of thick, red blood staining the ethereal cleanliness of them flitters across my lids.

Books and weaponry litter the space. My eyes scan the room, committing it to memory, feasting on it as if it were some forbidden, dark secret. A thick, woven rug of the same deep green of the forest floor covers most of the area. I am surprised to find that beautiful paintings litter the walls and stand stacked against each other in the corner. I slowly walk towards them and run my fingers gently across the canvases.

They are eerie pieces. A single eye in great detail. A darker one with black scales, twisted horns, and dripping blood. Another that looks to be the night sky from this room, or perhaps from mine. I flip through them all, spending long moments staring into them, searching for meaning, searching for pieces of a man I cannot understand.

I inhale sharply as I make my way to the final painting. It's a portrait of a woman. The view is half of her naked body. A sharp chin, a swollen, peaked breast, the curve of a stomach, a full hip and thigh. Her arm is extended above her head as if she is stretching or reaching for something. I search for confirmation in her face, but the top of the canvas stops right at her plump bottom lip.

My bottom lip. This cannot be. The painting looks like

me. My mind tries to find differences, tries to justify the eerie resemblance, but my blood pumps with the truth: he painted me.

I run my fingertips over the curves of my body, coating my fingers in thick dust. How long has this been here to acquire this amount of grime? I run my hand across more of it, brushing away yehrs of cobwebs, revealing the vibrant colours beneath. The few menoths I have been here would not be enough time to develop this much build-up, especially if it has sat behind all these others.

Emotions swim through me. What does this mean? Has Dominus had visions of me, too? I abandon the achingly beautiful artwork to rummage through his wardrobe. Endless amounts of dark raiments fill it. Linen, wool, pristine suits, neckties and cravats, sweaters, cardigans, and tunics in varying shades of black, grey, deep green, and brown. I pull the drawers open, revealing mounds of black fighting leathers, sheaths, and holsters for unknown weapons.

These were expertly crafted with fine leather. I have never seen anything like them. My heart does a flip in my chest as I wonder what these might look like on him. How they might mould to the dips and ridges of his carved muscles. I slide the drawer shut with a thud, ending my wrongful intrusion.

I sit on the upholstered settee at the foot of his bed, its enormity a creeping creature behind me. I sit for a while, wrapped in warmth, in citrus, in serenity. Before I know it, sunlight blooms to life through my eyelids, casting splotches of bright light in the darkness. I awake with a shock, remembering where I had fallen asleep. I stand, twisting around and looking for signs of Dominus, but he's not here. A bitter ache grows behind my ribs. The sun illuminates the room in a way that is wrong, like it shouldn't be here. As if it should only be witnessed in the light of the moon.

I hesitate at the door frame, my body pulling me back in. I turn to the wardrobe, snagging an exceptionally made moss-colored cravat, before exiting and making my way to my own rooms.

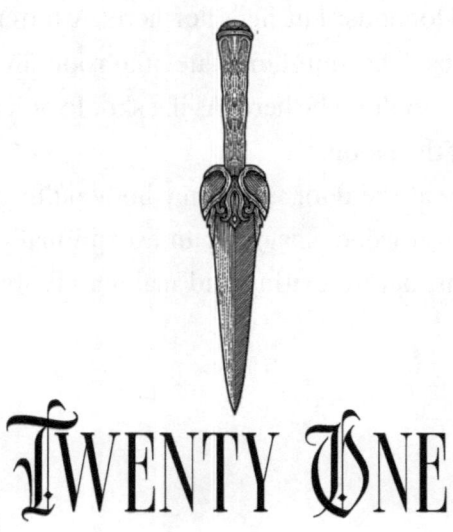

TWENTY ONE

I do not see Dominus for a wyth. I spend days looking for him, waiting to hear his footsteps in the corridor, but they never sound. He seems to have dismissed his classes as well. My heart aches to speak with him, to resolve our...misstep and to share with him what I found.

I stand in the meeting room bathed, fed, and with an overnight bag packed, ready to set off for Eden. I have a plan. One that involves a seer. My hands shake at the thought of it.

Thair enters first, his luggage in tow as well. "Good morning, Miss Alder." I'm glad Thair was the first to arrive. I need a moment alone with him.

"How are you?" I ask

"Well enough. And you?"

Looking down at my wringing hands, I reply, "I could be

better."

"Trouble in paradise?" He quirks his eyebrows at me in a way that shows he is not in the least bit surprised.

"Thair, I need you to know that..." That what? That I am not rutting with Shrike either. That we do, in fact, loathe each other. I think. And actual monsters are running loose in the woods. My heart flutters in my chest with the truth I cannot give him. Instead, I offer all that I can, "I'm sorry. Truly sorry. I never meant for any of this to happen, and I never wanted to lose your friendship. Please forgive me."

I watch his guard drop as those warm brown eyes soften towards me, a look I had not realised I missed seeing. "I understand. I do. And, frankly, it is none of my bloody business. The choices you make are your own. I must deal with how they affect me, but that is not your problem, Thorne. There is nothing to forgive."

I reach across to place my hand on his. "When did you get so emotionally intelligent?"

He winks at me as familiar boot steps thud behind us to the cadence of that humming. Though I don't need to hear those to know when he is nearby. The air tells me with its vibration. He clears his throat, no doubt seeing the intimate moment we are sharing.

"Master," I say, making delayed eye contact with him as I take my time to peel my gaze from Thair. It's childish of me, but that is what Dominus does. He brings out the ugly, petty, monstrous parts of me that no one else has ever seen. That I, myself, have never seen.

"Am I interrupting?" he bites. Those powerful hands are

fisted in the pockets of his dark pants. His raiments are more casual today, and I recognise the cotton scyrte as one from the armoury, and I cannot believe I did not think to look for him here.

"Would it matter if you were?" Thair bites back.

"I suppose not. I am secure enough to know Thorne would never betray me. Would you, mo céasadh?"

He makes four long strides across the expanse of the room to where we sit near the windows. I want to scream at him. I want to bring up which one of us he thinks would betray the other first, since he already holds that honour. But I refrain. Because I recognise that this is his version of a public apology. This is his way of extending his hand. Thoughts of the conversation with Connally fill my mind, and I decide to extend mine back. Though I do regret that Thair must witness such behaviour from us both.

I stand then, letting him see the full view of me in his tunic that I cut on the side up to my thigh. The cravat I liberated this morning tied around my throat. The knee-high boots I know he likes. The newly crafted black leather harness strapped around my chest and ribs, with an addition: a new sheath for my skean. I let him see me, dripping in solid midnight, covered in his scent, and reflect my eyes with as much certainty as I can and say, "Never."

I relish the way his breath leaves him as if he were physically struck. The way those pale eyes threaten to praise me. I offer him an innocent smile as I strut toward him and place my hand against his chest. His heart races against my heated palm. "Where are the others?" I ask, allowing treasonous lust to coat my words.

He clears his throat. "About that." He takes my hand from his chest and leads me to sit back down. He takes a seat across from me next to Thair. "Norine has taken ill, and Orla has been assigned an urgent, unforeseen task she must prioritise." I roll my eyes, knowing that the "unforeseen" task was likely assigned by him to keep her from coming along, a circumstance I cannot truly be bothered by.

"So, just Thair and I will be going to Eden then?" I ask.

"You will not postpone?" he questions with slight agitation. Ah, so this was his way of keeping me here.

"No. I am only here for one term. I must make the best use of my time. I do not want to miss out on this." I make the point to add, "I still have much to learn, much to uncover."

"I understand," he says, giving the floor his undivided attention.

"Alright then, let us get a move on. We have a day's travel to get across the territory and into the heart of the borough to find lodging," Thair preens. On his note, we stand to leave. Thair takes my bag from me to carry down the stairs. "I'll give you two a moment," he says, leaving us alone. The air in the room leaves with him, along with the resolve and boldness I carried with Thair as a middleman.

"Have you lowered yourself to outright thievery now?" he asks, pinching his cravat between two long fingers.

"I took it as restitution not only for your hideous behaviour but also for being gone when I came to your room to make amends and share something with you. I fell asleep at some point, waiting for your return. I still have a terrible ache in my neck from that beautiful yet disastrously uncomfortable settee. I figured this was fair. Though count your blessings that I did not take the fancy leathers with me. I could make myself something wicked with those."

His eyes glow with that, and he pulls his bottom lip in and bites it. "You are telling me, Miss Alder," he says, slowly stepping toward me, forcing me to step backwards. "That you went into my room without my permission, rifled through my things, stole from me, and slept on my furniture? Am I incorrect for recalling that was the very thing you accosted me for hawrs before?"

He's right, and I bloody hate it.

"Didn't I mention that I was coming to forgive you for that?" I say innocently.

"I cannot forgive you for that."

I scrunch my brows at him. "You cannot forgive me for the same error you made?"

He steps toward me again, towering over me. He takes my chin in those two fingers, bringing my gaze up to his. "I cannot forgive the fact that you spent a night in my room, lay upon my bedding, ran your fingers through my raiments, and I was not there. I *cannot* forgive myself for leaving you alone and wanting for me."

My mouth instantly dries, and I worry he can hear my heart ravaging my chest. His green eyes stare into my very soul, exposing me to the bone. I wonder if he can see the desire in my eyes—if he can sense that I want him. But I am leaving right now, and this is not the time, and there is still so much to say.

"I searched for you all wyth."

"You did?"

"Yes. I wanted to apologise. And now, I have to go," I whisper.

"I am the one who needs to offer an apology, Thorne. Not you. The way I responded to you on the shore. I–" He releases a huff. "Our dance needs new rules, it seems. I am afraid I got caught up in the adagio and missed my cue. I deeply regret my actions. I am not well-versed in the intricacies of...whatever this is."

My heartbeat quickens, driving the pace of this dance again. "I need to make it explicitly clear that I am no more educated in these subjects either, Dominus."

He tucks a loose strand of hair behind my ear, staring into the very depths of my soul. "I cannot express my disbelief in that adequately."

"No, you are mistaken. I–" I take his hand from my hair, wrapping it in my own. "I have never done this, Dominus. I have lain with men before, but I have never entered into a relationship with one. Ever."

His brows meet each other. "Why?"

"Because I cannot."

"Why not?"

I chew my lip in contemplation. Why am I suddenly compelled to bare my soul to Dominus Shrike? Now, I realise, is not the time.

"There have always been...circumstances in my life preventing it. I would tell you more, I will, but I need to hurry."

He offers a small smile. "Then perhaps there is something new we might both discover. Together."

Suddenly, I do not want to leave. Thinking of the distance between us sends pangs of sorrow through me. I abandon his grasp to walk around him to where my coat is draped across the arm of the chair. Hesitantly, I pull out the books. I spin and offer him mine. I cannot conjure the words to say to him. I cannot say that this time it is my choice. That I want to share these parts of me with him. The glazing of his eyes as he looks from the book to my face tells me that he understands. Somehow, he understands the offering.

"You do not have to do this."

"But I want to. I do. Additionally, I believe this is just as much my history as it is yours, Heir of Earth."

He steps back, bringing his hand to his chest. "No, Thorne. That cannot be me. I am not worthy of that. There is just as much about my past that you do not know. I am not deserving of anything. I—I am lost."

"I think you are. I have read this book hundreds of times. I know it more than I know myself. Trust me when I tell you, this feels like you."

He slowly takes it from me and runs his fingers over the worn leather cover. It is strange seeing it in someone else's hands but also lightening, like setting down something I have carried alone for far too long.

"We shall talk when I return. Read it all. I want to hear what you think, and I want more answers upon my return. I want them all, Dom." I reach to give him the other book, the journal that can only be his. "I found this in the library that night. I did not read it, and I will not. I thought you would want it back."

The realisation in his eyes nearly takes my breath away.

"Didn't you read it?"

"No."

"Good. Not that I wish for you not to, but I would like to give you the truth myself." He reaches out for me, bringing my face to his, resting our foreheads together. His scent, my favourite scent, covers me, and I ache to pull him closer, to drown myself in it. "I swear to you, I will give you everything you ask for. But in order to do that, you must return safely to me. Only travel during the day, and keep your wits about you. Eyes open, skean close. Am I understood?"

"Yes, Master," I offer sarcastically with a roll of my eyes.

"Thorne, I am serious."

"If you are so serious, why do you remain here?"

He releases a deep breath. "I will provide the truth if you promise to remain calm—oh, what is the point of asking you to do anything?" I release a chuckle, and he continues, "I discovered troubling signs of our local far liath. Generally, he remains harmless, and I allow him to live his life unbothered, but his antics have begun to affect daily life here. Scolers have been having trouble navigating the grounds."

A rather unfortunate snort escapes me as I put it together. Far liath. Grey man. The very reason for the constant, and recently growing, fog that surrounds the scol. They are malevolent beings known for mischief. Their main goal is to cover the land in fog so impenetrable that it causes humans to become lost or stumble and fall, potentially causing their deaths, where the far liath celebrates its triumph. I thump myself for not seeing it sooner.

"Is that humorous to you?" he queries, falling into a wide

smile of his own.

"Only in the sense that I have realised I failed to discover this myself. I should have pieced that one together far sooner. Will you dispose of him?"

"I hope not to. We have an understanding. I allow him to remain due to the fact that his fog often allows me...certain advantages from time to time." I shake my head, knowing now is not the time to question that statement. Dominus continues, "And do not press yourself too much for not realising. You no longer need to be the sole uncoverer in your life."

I release him and turn to leave without meeting those glowing green eyes that can tear me down to nothing. I force myself down the stairs and out into the yard. My heart aches as my feet take me further and further away from Dominus Shrike.

TWENTY TWO

The road to Eden is as magical as I imagined. We travel through forests and mountains, valleys and vineyards. Thair and I spend the day learning more about each other. He tells me of his time studying and how he has travelled through Eregahl in search of lost civilisations. I always thought I was an anomaly investigating rumoured people and lands, finding significant wealth in knowledge, but here in Eregahl, I am finally around others like me. We crave the unknown, going to desperate depths to unearth hidden truths.

I offer as much of my history as I can, explaining to him that I have always studied these lands. That it has been the only thing I have ever wanted. He, of course, asks about my family but does not press me when I tell him they are gone. He simply shrugs his shoulders and says, "Trust me when I tell you that

I understand the complexities and intricacies of familial bonds and how painful it can be to lose them."

We eat the food that Elowyn prepared for us, which is far too much for a single day's travel, but we are thankful for it regardless. Every few hawrs, we stop to stretch our legs and relieve ourselves. We arrive at sunset in Aigne, Eden's bustling centre.

"There is an old inn I have lodged at many times throughout my travels. 'Tis directly off the main street and offers a glorious view of the borough."

My legs are stiff when we finally arrive. I ease out of the carriage, inhaling the fragrant and hearty smells of Aigne. The heart of the city lies on a high point of land, offering an exquisite view. Narrow cobblestone streets wind their way through a maze of structures ranging from half-timbered houses to more austere stone and brick facades. Oil lamps cast a flickering glow over the streets as the night begins to fall, their light reflecting off the muddy puddles that gather in the uneven road surfaces. On the outskirts, the town gives way to a patchwork of fields and hedgerows. I can even make out herds of cattle far off in the distance.

The sign above the inn reads "The Raven's Nest" on a hefty piece of derelict wood. Thair removes our bags and speaks to the coachmen, mumbling about our return time. We will spend the full day here on the morrow but will venture back in the evening through the night, so Thair does not miss any of his duties. I suspect that order was given because Dominus did not want us alone for more time than necessary.

Before the carriage departs, I snag the basket of Elowyn's

provisions, refusing to allow the blueberry scones to go to waste. Thair grins as he witnesses me tuck my arm into the handle. "I had the same idea," he says.

"Supper in my room then?"

"Deal."

Thair checks us in, securing two rooms on the second floor across from each other, and I look forward to the view in the morning. My room is modest and somewhat cramped. I immediately recognise how accustomed I have become to the space and lavishness of Adonien, the sheer privilege of it all. The walls, covered in faded floral wallpaper, show signs of age. A narrow iron bed dressed in rough linen sheets and cotton blankets dominates the room. A small washstand with a ceramic basin and pitcher occupies one corner, while a battered wooden chest of drawers stands against the opposite wall. The floorboards, worn smooth by countless feet, creak with every step. A single window, its glass slightly warped, rests on the north-facing wall. The air carries a mixture of scents: wood smoke from the common room's fireplace below, the musty odour of old fabric, and a faint hint of the stables outside.

I place my bag and the basket on the bed. I bring Dom's cravat to my nose, trying to devour the fading scents of him. With a sigh, I wash up and decide to read as I wait for Thair.

He knocks a bit later, and we sit on the bed eating the remains of the fruit, creamed cheese, and cured meat, and we eat all but four scones. Thair was able to find a few decent pints of ale from the tavern across the street. We eat by candlelight, enjoying conversation and the sounds of the borough outside.

"So, now that you are away from his influence, tell me.

What is going on with you and Shrike?"

His question surprises me, and I quickly rework my face back to one of boredom. "Less than you might assume. We are, honestly, I am not even certain."

"Oh, come on. I would like to think of us as friends enough to be able to talk about our *rutting,* are we not?"

"You are quite the busybody, and I adore it, but we are not partaking in the delicacy of the flesh." Mostly. "I am truly unaware of what it is," I say, offering a small, honest laugh. "I hate the man, truly. But also, there is something that draws me to him. A moth to a flame, I suppose. I have no idea what I am doing, and it will likely end in war, but...he holds answers that I need."

"What kind of answers?" His face slides from playful to concerned, far too interested in this. I must be careful around him. Not only of what information I might give, but Thair is the closest I have allowed myself to get to another in yehrs. I think of Norine and Elowyn and Eamon, too. I am playing a perilous game here. One that will end in bloodshed if I continue to allow myself to get close to them.

I work my answer out quickly. "He knows immeasurably more than me about mythology. I wish to learn from him. That is truly all I want. I know that what has transpired between us might make this hard to believe, but I am not—" I pause, unaware of how to frame my thoughts. "I do not desire to wed. Or to share my life with anyone. Like I told you, I am unavailable for honest moments. I can lie with someone, but I offer no more than that." Lie. Lie. Lie. It has nothing to do with what I want and everything to do with my already-carved fate. But I cannot tell him that. I cannot tell him that every person I have ever loved is taken from me in violent, horrific ways.

"Why not? Is unconditional love not the single desire of all women?"

I throw a pinch of bread at him. "I would not think you so small-minded as to make such an ignorant statement as that, Torin. But, no. That is not what all women desire. Quite far from it."

"What do you want from life, then? From love? If that was what you sought, what would it look like for you?"

A rather good question, indeed. I take a deep gulp from the pint, considering. "Well, I want to continue my research. I want to find out what happened to the Seren. Where all the magic went. I want to discover something unknown. I want to spend the rest of my life writing and lost in research. Honestly, I could see myself doing that at Adonien. Maybe becoming a scolemaster or leading some other kind of research team."

He nods, clearly unsurprised. "And love. If it ever found you? What would your counterpart look like?"

"That is hard to answer because it is something I have never allowed myself to consider. Someone intelligent and bold. Unafraid of my veracity. I would not want them to be exactly like me so that we might have good, challenging discourse, but they would possess an equally hungry mind so that we might adventure together. Brave and unafraid. Helpful and selfless. Full of desire and life." I release a breath in consideration of the truths flowing from me. Thoughts I have never had to share.

Thair stares at me momentarily, and I allow the empty space to rest between us, letting him decide if his response will be filthy or honest. He simply nods his head and drains his tankard.

"What about you? What does your life–your love–look like?" I challenge.

He laughs. "I am afraid that I, like you, have not allowed myself to consider that in a very long time. I am afraid that if love did find me, I would not know it. I am not even sure if I would be capable of it."

"You would, Thair. Undoubtedly. And they will be very fortunate to have you."

"Maybe. But I am...working to undo things in my past. To make changes and become a better version of myself. I have done things I am not proud of. I have failed others. I certainly do not want that to be my legacy." He smiles a smile I have not seen yet. Small, terrified, and raw. A heavy stone of emotion lodges itself in my throat, full of empathy for him, but before I can answer, he adds, "Och, 'tis enough of that, my girl. I shall retire to my chambers lest you cut any more emotion from me."

I must agree with him. The conversation has turned too honest. "Goodnight, Thair. Thank you for joining me."

"Of course," he says, bowing deeply at the waist and closing my door behind him.

TWENTY THREE

Once Thair's door shuts, I wait for nearly an hawr before pulling on my dark, hooded cloak and walking quietly down the old, creaky stairs. Outside the door of the inn, I replay the conversation I had with Elowyn.

"On the south side of the borough, there is a lodge. You will know it when you see it because it is unlike any of the other structures in town. 'Tis black. Black, like it has been burned. Its roof is steep and sharp, like it aims to stab the sky above. It has strange white markings all over it as if they were painted with ash. That is where you will find her. Give her my name. You must bring her an offering. It does not have to be significant, but it must be handmade."

I pat the remaining scones in my pocket, hoping that they are enough. There are a significant number of indecent things

I would do for these scones. Hopefully, the seer has good taste. It takes me a moment to navigate where the inn is in relation to where the lodge might be. I take the main street south until the structures become scarce.

Like a beacon in the night, the lodge stands at the very end of a dirt path with orbs of amber light illuminating the windows like giant, haunting eyes. I rally myself before knocking, heaving in deep breaths. There is no way of knowing what will come of this or how this encounter might alter my path. I could find absolutely nothing here. This could all be time wasted.

But...I could learn *something*. Maybe she can offer me knowledge of my fate or point me in the way of one of Noreg's chosen who might be able to lift my curse. I silently send up a prayer to whatever god, Seren or no, who might hear my plea. Holding the scones in my left hand, I reach for the comforting weight of my skean with the other. Then, I take a final deep breath and knock one, two, three times. I wait so long that I am afraid no one will come. As I turn to leave, the door drags open behind me.

"What is it you seek, wain?" Her voice is low and rough and ancient. From a single question, it sounds as if she has lived lifetimes. I turn to see a short figure, her darkened silhouette cast by the inside lights, offering me no details.

"How do you know I am seeking something?"

A crow's laugh sounds from the shadow. "Everyone is seeking something. And you are here, are you not? Proof enough."

"I seek answers. About my past. About my future. I believe a curse has been placed upon me." As it leaves my mouth, the absurdity of it makes me want to run away in embarrassment.

"Aye, the usual. You may enter." Usual? How many people come to her with curses?

The interior is a sensory tapestry of the arcane. Bundles of dried herbs dangle from decaying rafters, their earthy scents mingling with the sharp tang of wood smoke from a crackling hearth. Shelves line the walls, cluttered with jars of glowing liquids and peculiar artefacts that I recognise as divination tools—rune stones and scrying mirrors. My blood begins to pump at the sight of them. Candlelight dances across weathered floorboards, casting long shadows that seem to move of their own accord. In dark corners, strange creatures chitter softly. The air is thick, tingling against my skin like an itchy sweater.

The figure moves me to a round table with four chairs, motioning me to sit. I do, and she turns to gather a tray of tea. Well, I am not entirely sure what could be in the pot. She gestures to me, asking if I would like any.

"No, thank you. I did bring something for you, though. A woman, Elowyn, sent me to you. She made these." I place the scones on the table and uncover them, allowing the fire of the hearth to illuminate them. As she sits before me, that same light shines on her face, and I jump, nearly tumbling from my seat.

It's her. The same bloody woman who visited my cottage an ocean away all those yehrs ago.

"So, you recognise me then. I never forget the faces of those I read. Regardless of time or ageing. I am surprised you lived this long."

Questions pebble my mind. "How? How were you there and now here? Where are you from?"

"I am from nowhere and everywhere. But that is not why you are here. I hope you have not travelled a long way because I will not give you what you seek."

"Please. I beg you. After you left, my entire family died. Each of them, the day before I had an episode, exactly three yehrs apart from the other. I need to know why. I need to know if I am cursed. If I can break it."

She laughs that hideous, sharp laugh again. "You are indeed cursed, wain, but not in the way you think."

"What does that mean?"

Her tone turns angry then. "It means there is absolutely nothin' you can do to change it. You are fated as the gods see fit, and they will do with you what they please. Now, leave this place and never return."

"I beg you. Please, try once more. Things have happened since then. Strange things. Maybe my fate has changed. Wouldn't you want to know?" My quick wit saves me again. This intrigues her, and she pauses for a moment. She picks up one of the scones and takes a bite, closing her eyes as she chews.

"You know Elowyn?"

"Yes. She is the one who sent me to your door."

"Damn her. Alright. Once more and never again. But it will take more than bones and stones this time."

"What do you require?"

"Your blood."

"How?"

"Nothin' egregious. A simple cut on the palm will do." She holds her hand out to me.

"I shall do it myself." I reach for the skean now resting at my side. As I remove it, her eyes widen, perhaps with realisation. Then she laughs, a sound I wish I could never hear again.

"Oh, this will be interesting."

I run the skean against the length of my left hand. Blood pools in the wake of its otherworldly sharpness. Without hesitation, the woman snatches my hand and licks the blood from my palm. I cringe as it drips down her chin.

Her eyes do the same as before. The whites turn cloudy. But then they shift again. This time to black. That's different from before. Familiar, suffocating energy pushes around me. It presses against me as if trying to find a way into my body. The floors creak. The creatures in the corner whine. The fire blazes in the hearth. Wind swirls around us, though all the windows are closed. That voice, my voice but not my voice, sounds in my head.

She is mine. You may look no further, seer. Release her.

I realise she is not speaking to me but to the crone, and I wonder if she hears her, too.

Release her!

The energy in the room snaps to nothing. All of it, all of the magic, is gone. Her eyes are normal again but are now filled with pure terror.

"What are you?" she whispers.

"What did you see?" I scream.

"You. You cannot do this. I will not allow it."

Her hands are swiftly around my neck, causing me to drop my blade to claw at them. She's strong, too strong for an old hag, and regardless of my fight, I cannot free myself. I beat at her face, but her grip only grows, obstructing my breath, and my lungs begin to fight for air.

"You cannot claim him if you are dead."

I try to speak, to yell at her to stop. The lights begin to flicker, or my vision does. Then, the door slams open, and the crone is momentarily distracted. I use the opportunity to raise my foot and kick her as hard as I can manage in the stomach. She flies from me, landing on the table and causing it to fall over with her.

"What the fuck are you doing?" Dominus yells at me, not the crone.

"What does it look like?" I ask, picking up my blade and taking a fighting stance.

"Getting yourself killed searching for things you shouldn't be searching for—again."

"Why are you here?" I scream at him.

"Saving your bloody life—again!"

"You will not claim him! You will not claim him! He is the heir!"

She comes for my throat again, but instead, she meets Dom's blade as it removes her head in one fell swoop. I am beginning to tire of his beheading people on my behalf. Her remains slump against the floor in a bloody mess.

I breathe heavily, exhausted by this. Exhausted by not having answers. Exhausted by death. What does it all mean? How will I claim Dominus? Why is it a bad thing? Does that mean that if I have him, if I love him, I will kill him, too? Oh, gods, no.

I drop to my knees and begin to sob. It was all for nothing. I will never be cured. I will never be loved. Dom catches me in his arms before I fully hit the floor. He picks me up and carries me outside the lodge and beyond. I sob and sob and sob as the fight leaves my body and defeat takes its place.

Dominus walks for some time. I can tell by the sounds of the woods that we are far from town. He sits me down in thick grass next to a large flowing river. He settles across from me, wiping my tears away. "Please tell me what you are thinking."

I sob harder because I know that, regardless of what I tell him, what I show him, or how I feel for him that this is doomed. We are destined to implode before we even begin, and it breaks me open.

He runs his hands over the sides of my face and brings our heads together. His scent overwhelms me. Slowly, it works through me, calming and unwinding me. My heart breaks more at how perfectly his nearness does that.

"I am cursed, Dominus. I have been for nearly half my life. Every person I have ever loved has died. And it is because of me."

TWENTY FOUR

"How is that because of you?"

"I—I cannot do this."

He pulls my face up, forcing me to look at him. "Thorne, please. We promised each other the truth."

We did. And if I am going to say goodbye, if I must let him go to save him, I can at least show him why. I inhale deeply and gather my thoughts. I turn away from him and face the flowing river. "I had a beautiful childhood. A loving, warm, hilarious family. There was so much love, laughter, and happiness in our home. My sister, Hyacinth, and I were tiny copies of our parents. Her of mother, and I of father. My father, Atlas, was light incarnate. He was as strong as he was soft. He always saw the silver linings, the lessons, in every good and bad thing. He worshipped my mother, Iris. Father loved that she had a floral namesake, and he chose Hyacinth's name before he even knew she was a girl. Though he always boasted about how he was certain of it."

I recognise the smile on my face as I recall my childhood memories. I was unaware it would be so cathartic to speak of them. To share them. I only thought the pain would shroud my memories forever, but there is joy yawning open in my chest thinking of them all now.

"My name, however, came about more organically. Father said that Mother's pregnancy with Hyacinth was effortless. I was a bit rougher on her. She said I liked to turn sideways and kick her in the ribs all day and night. 'You were a bloody thorn in my side, alright,' she said, smiling as she did. That became my little pet name, and when I was born, there was no other name that felt right.

"Father said that beautiful flowers needed the wicked thorns to protect them, and he indeed forged me that way. I followed his every footfall, cutting down trees, building birdhouses, spending hawrs duelling each other with wooden swords, and racing horses across endless fields. He was a leathersmith, and we would spend days in his workshop oiling, cutting, and moulding all sorts of things. He was well known for his sheaths. The attention to detail and pure talent he possessed were inspiring and an honour to witness. People would come far and wide to have Father craft all sorts of goods for them. Sheaths, saddles, bags, jewellery—he could make anything.

"One samhradh, I spent wyths making and drying sheets from used parchment for journals we created together. I kept complaining about always having to wait until we travelled to the market to purchase journals when I would spend my nights filling them with all my ideas and research. I remember now how nonchalant he was, stuffing his mouth full of eggs as he said, 'Do not fret, my girl. I shall make you some. All you had to do was say so.' And that is how he was. Everything could be solved, and nothing was a problem."

I lean into the memories, recalling their smells, their feelings, the way the sunlight sat on my skin, the way the cedar tree felt beneath my hands and bare feet. Wind howls around us, and Dominus leans ever closer to me.

"Hyacinth and my mother loved creating things, too. They spent their days baking, drying herbs for tonics and tinctures, collecting honey, and watching bees and birds from the open windows. They were pure love. Their souls were gentle and soft in the way mine was rough and curious. They cherished all living creatures and yearned to learn how the natural world works. We were a fortress, solitary in ways that I now understand were a true blessing. I will never be able to replicate that. I will never sit again with their company in the evenings, Mother making us balms in the kitchen, Father sketching designs by the fire, Hyacinth oiling my hair as I read to them all stories of magic lands across the sea." Tears roll down my face. The aching void in the centre of me ruptures open. But I can show him this. I need to.

"Then the episodes began after my sixteenth yehr. I can distinctly remember the way the first one felt. It was late at night; they're always in the bloody dead of night. I was reading alone in my room. My candle had nearly burnt out, but I was enthralled in a history tome.

"It came over me at once. The entire atmosphere around me changed. My breath flew out of my body. I began to sweat profusely, but my skin was prickled like gooseflesh. I vomited and sobbed. It felt like grieving a loss I was unaware of, such enveloping sadness. It felt like dying from a broken heart, a broken soul. It always feels like dying. Like part of my soul leaves my body. Like I am being called but cannot find where to run. Sometimes I wondered if I could run, if I could find what called to me, maybe I could fix it. Maybe I could stop it." I idly draw circles in the grass, watching the moon cast shimmering reflections off the water.

"They constantly searched for answers. They never stopped searching. They never made me feel like a burden, like I was less than. Mother spent all her time studying what herbs might help. Hyacinth was the one to always bring me back down, rubbing her gentle hands in endless strokes along my back. Father was always so certain that we'd figure it out. He never once let me see that it worried him." I clutch the grass beneath me as a tether to the here and now. I can see in my periphery that Dominus has yet to move his eyes from my face. I am thankful for the cover of darkness so that I might confess my sins without being too seen.

"After my eighteenth yehr, the episodes became severe. They affected everything. Touched every part of my life. In desperation, Mother brought a witch healer in to see me. She was a seer, but I did not know that at the time, fully unaware of the Seren or the gifts they bestowed. It would have been menoths after her visit before I found the book.

"She did a strange ceremony with bones and stones. I felt the magic that night, Dominus. I will never forget that feeling.

In fact, I chased it all the way here to that lodge and unknowingly to the very seer that came to my home." He tenses beside me, and the air shifts around us, warmer than it was before.

"She told me all those yehrs ago that I was a lost cause—that my fate was already carved. Since then, things have deteriorated. Mother became desperate. I retreated further into my research, hoping for answers in the magic land across the sea. She died the next yehr, the day before I had an episode. No one could tell us why. She fell over dead in the garden, healthy as she had ever been." I release a deep breath with the memory and wipe tears from my eyes.

"I suppose it was a blessing that Hyacinth went next because Father had always been my strength. He held me together. We held each other together. Hyacinth's death was much uglier than Mother's. She was run over by a herd of horses in the middle of the street in town. Someone had stolen some bread, causing a huge disruption. It spooked a group of horses the locals had tied up as they walked through the market. I still see her body lying in the dirt, muddy and purple and torn." Tears burn my face now.

"The hardest part of their deaths is that there is no reason for them; they were all just freak accidents and unexplainable disasters." I choke down sobs as I continue, "Hyacinth died three yehrs after Mother, and Father died three yehrs after her. On the exact date. All of them on the day before an episode. I thought the episode after Father's death would take me to join them. I thought it would completely end me, but unfortunately, it did not. None of their deaths makes sense to me, but Father's will forever be one I cannot reconcile. There will never be a way for me to understand or make peace with it."

Dominus finally breaks his silence, his voice raw and deep, "What...what happened to your father, Thorne?" There is a desperation in his eyes that I do not understand.

"I do not know. I woke one morning before him, which never happened. The cottage was still. The windows were closed, and I couldn't hear the birds. I could always hear the birds. I remember opening the windows and letting the morning air and light in. Still, I did not hear a single noise. I went to find Father. He was in his bed. It was covered in blood. I pulled back the sheets to find he had lacerations all over his body. Ones that he could not inflict on himself. They were countless. Endless. I didn't hear a single sound all night. I still do not know if someone came in. Still do not understand why I would not hear his screams. None of it makes any sense."

I finally bring myself to look at him. I expect to find pity, but instead, I see compassion, care, and even grief. "I know it's absurd. I have a logical, intelligent mind that tells me it is lunacy. But if I do not have this, if I don't hang on to this, then it is all for nothing. Their deaths were for nothing. Maybe it is fate or mere coincidence, but I need something, someone, to blame. And I am the only one left, Dominus. Me and my bloody madness." I drop my eyes to the grass, seeing his fingers flex into fists next to me.

"These episodes, how often do you have them?"

"Usually once a yehr. I had two of them during my twenty-second yehr. They mostly occurred toward the end of t-earrach. We have a festival in Albion to celebrate the coming of samhradh."

He inhales sharply. "Bealtaine," Dom whispers. "Bealtaine was right before you arrived. Did you have an episode?"

"Yes. The night before I left to come to Danumhar. It was different from the rest. There were visions—the one I had of you stabbing me and another one where I left moss-covered footprints on the floor."

He turns to look at the river now. His jaw flexes. "What did the seer tell you before I arrived?"

I weigh whether to tell him of the voice, of the other vision I had. I have already shared so much. I am not sure this is the time. "Same as before. My fate is carved. Nothing can be done. She saw something, but she refused to tell me what. She said that you were the heir and that I could not claim you. Then she tried to kill me." His eyes turn dark at the comment.

"Dominus, whatever lies between us must never be discovered. If I have you, if I claim you as everyone keeps calling it, if I love you...you will die like the rest of them. I am sure of it. And something has grown between us, for me at least, and I cannot have that. I will not have you if it means losing you."

He wipes tears from my eyes again. "What if that's not what it means, Thorne?"

"Dominus, you are the Heir of Earth. You are destined to rise against the bloody Seren and take your place on the throne— to rule this land for as long as you live. I am certain this will not end well. I am human. You are not."

"Precisely why this is worth fighting for. I am infinitely harder to kill." His glorious smile breaks through the darkness, a beacon in the night. "I have something I must confess. I would ask you to promise not to get angry with me, but I know that is unlikely. I need to preface this by saying that, though I did know what it meant, understand I could not tell you, not before you knew the truth about me. And though I still have every intention of giving you that, I cannot do so here. Not on this land." I nod at him, fearing that he might change his mind, craving whatever truth he offers. "The vision that you had the night of your episode and the night we kissed, it means something. It is not a vision of me killing you."

"What is it, Dominus?" My heart thunders in my ears.

"It is a ritual of my people. A bond. The tying of a knot. It is called a nodus. Something between chosen, lifelong partners."

The earth spins around me. A bloody mating ritual. My mind goes still with disbelief. "Why would a mating ritual require you to stab me in the heart? Is that not counterintuitive?"

He takes a deep breath, running his hands through his hair, making my heart ache to do the same. "My kind are immortal— or as immortal as you can understand. There are very specific things that can kill us. The nodus is a choice between two souls to be united forever. In doing so, we offer ourselves to one another—fully. The ritual requires that we consume blood from the heart of our chosen, and they consume our own. It bonds us together in ways I cannot explain. It intertwines our souls. We imbue one another, sharing gifts and intricacies, literally becoming one."

And we both had visions of us doing this. Becoming one. "Dominus, I cannot. I cannot allow you to tie yourself to me. I am tainted, corrupted, and cursed, and you are destined for great things. Things beyond my lifetime."

"Respectfully, that is not your choice to make. It is mine.

And if I choose to make it, if I want that, there is nothing you can do about it."

I am desperately close to falling. Seconds away from giving in to him, to claiming him, to allowing him to claim me. "I still need to know everything. I need to know who you are. Neither of us should make any decisions until then."

"That is a very sound and educated decision."

"Until then, I need you to stay away from me. Do not touch me or look at me with those haunting eyes of yours because I will give in, and I cannot. Not yet."

"That may be your most cruel request yet, but I will do it for you." He stands with preternatural grace and takes a few steps back.

I stifle a whimper, frustrated by my own damn choices. "I will need more of your raiments, though."

He smiles the biggest smile I have yet to see from him. "You know, that is a sign of a forming nodus—needing to be around each other's scent. It has been pure torture having you so close to me, even more so having you wrapped in mine."

I swallow, unable to respond to that. "Which, by the way, I learned from the headmaster that was *your* doing before I arrived. How was that so?"

"I had a...feeling?"

I push myself off the ground to stand with him, still allowing the distance between us. "Feelings, like visions? Visions from which you paint me?" His eyes flare to life. "I suppose that is confirmation enough. I was not certain."

He brings his finger to his lip as if to silence me. Then he taps his ear twice. "Not here. But I will say, it is rather impressive that you put that together."

I only nod, eager to learn what that means when we get home.

Home.

No, not my home. It can't be.

"Let us get you to bed. We have a big day on the morrow," he reminds me.

"Is it terrible that I want to resign from this trip? I am not confident that we will find new information and terrified that we might."

"I understand, but now that we have more specifics to search for, this might change things. I have much to tell you and much more I still yet know. Your book opened a new world for me. I have already scoured these lands for anything that might tell me more of my kind, but having this change of scope may alter that. It may supply us with something else tangible to hold onto. I will do the digging. I can sift through what might be new information here."

"Then let us find it. Together."

"Thank you. For sharing this with me. I had no idea the things you have survived. I am very sorry for your loss and for all the weight that you carry. And having to carry so much alone, well, I understand. 'Tis rather unfair, being forced to live such a lonely life. One that makes us angry, defiant, and too independent. Solitary even. You did not deserve to have those things happen to you. I woefully regret that your family was taken from you. For all the wretched things you have endured."

I do not have words for him. He has spoken directly to the pit of me, and I war to keep my insides together. I suck my lip in, holding back tears, and nod my head in thanks.

We walk back to The Raven's Nest in silence, only steps, yet miles between us. How have we come so far to still be here, standing on either side of a closed door?

TWENTY FIVE

As fate would have it, Thair and I took the last two rooms in the inn, and I roll my eyes at the horrible cliché of it all.

"Looks like you are staying with me," I say as we turn away from the front desk. The young lass, surely terrified by the talking statue wearing leathers and two swords strapped across his back, apologises for the third time.

"No. I will find somewhere else. Don't you worry about it," he brushes off. Except I am worried about it, and something ugly twists inside of me.

"I know I just told you to stay away, but I am not certain I can allow you to leave. We must make this work."

He hides his smile poorly, offers a low nod, and follows me up the stairs. At the top, I turn to him, holding my finger to my lips as we creep gently into my room. The quaint room looks laughably small with him in it. The magnitude of the castle somehow made him slightly proportionate. Seeing Dominus in this rickety, old inn is like seeing a child try to squeeze into a playhouse they've outgrown.

He looks around the room and no doubt realises the singular bed and lack of any other acceptable furniture to sleep on. The bed is indeed large enough for us both—if we wedge together and remain unmoving for the rest of the night. His feet will undoubtedly hang off the end, and the thought sends a grin to my lips.

"What humours you so?"

"You. In this room. You outside of that castle, really."

"The feeling is mutual."

"We will have to share the bed."

"I can sleep on the floor, Thorne. Trust me when I tell you it will not be the worst place I have lain my head."

Incomprehensible sadness sweeps over me. "Alright then."

"Or not. I will do whatever you need. Define your boundaries, and teach me where they lie."

"Can we try?"

"Certainly."

"Alright. I need to change. Turn around."

I expect him to craft a filthy jest or mention how he has already seen me naked, has already tasted me, but he spins quickly. For both our sakes, I assume.

I undress and rinse myself in the basin the best I can. I put on a fresh pair of underthings and a long, olive green silk gown. It's one of my more modest ones, and I am thankful I considered that in my packing. Though the cut goes nearly to the floor, the top plunges into a deep, revealing point at my sternum, and the straps are tiny bits of silk that tie together at my shoulders. I scrub my teeth with a bristled brush and mint paste and comb through my hair before walking to bed.

"You may turn around now."

Dominus turns to look at me, greedily consuming every detail he sees. He runs his hands over his face and turns back around. I smile as I pull the bedclothes back and climb into cold, scratchy linens. After I am in, he turns back around, not looking at me, and walks to the basin. I watch as he performs the same routine as I did, using my soaps and oils, a small gesture that means everything. Maybe he craves my scent, too.

He turns around, wiping his clean face with a towel. "I am going to do something, but I need you to remain calm. Do not react. Do not make a sound."

My blood rushes, and I clinch the woollen blanket in my fists, but I nod to him. His eyes begin to glow brightly. Then he closes them and whispers something I cannot hear. When I blink again, his leathers are gone, and his swords make a small clinking sound as they appear against the chest of drawers. Dominus now wears nothing but a simple pair of cotton sleeping breeches.

"I tend to run warm, especially when I sleep, but I can add a scyrte if I need to."

My mouth waters at the sight of him. His thick, broad chest runs into expertly crafted abdominals, and I follow the chiselled art all the way down to the corded muscles of his hips that disappear into cotton. I clear my throat and uncurl my toes, forcing myself to look away. "No, that is perfectly fine. Whatever makes you comfortable."

He turns back to the basin, and I notice a small satchel of toiletries has also appeared. He scrubs his teeth, too. When he finishes, he reaches into the bag and pulls out a small amber bottle. He tosses it over to me, and it lands in my lap. "I usually apply this to my face and hair at night, but perhaps you would like it."

I twist the dropper cap open, and the smell hits me immediately. I bring it to my nose, deeply consuming my favourite scent in the most concentrated form. I loosen a moan as it fills my lungs, my body, my soul. That dimpled smile forms on his lips, and I find myself slightly embarrassed. I squeeze the dropper anyway, filling the small vial up. I release the oil into my hands and rub it in. I run it through the ends of my long, thick waves, along my face and neck and arms. I close the bottle, place it on the small nightstand, and sink into the sheets, wholly satisfied and brimming with serenity. I open my eyes to see Dominus staring at me. One arm wraps around his middle, the other elbow rests upon it, and his chin rests on his knuckles.

"What?" I ask, suddenly hyperconscious of myself.

"You cannot imagine my experience of watching you find such euphoria from my scent. It is something I never thought I would see. Something I released hope for a long time ago."

A twisted concoction of pain and satisfaction fights its way through my chest. "I understand," I say. Because even though I do not know him fully yet, I have also lived a long time thinking I would never experience what I am right now. Regardless of how this ends, I am thankful for this. I can spend the rest of my lonely life knowing that I had this, if only for a brief moment.

Dominus walks around the bed and climbs in beside me. I immediately turn to my right, facing away from him. The bed groans under his weight, and I fear breathing might cause it to expire beneath us.

"I promise I will not be inappropriate. I have no desire to cross your boundaries or make you uncomfortable. I am a patient man, and if I ever get the chance to touch you the way I want, it will not be in a hovel." I beg my breath to slow and my heart to stop its incessant banging. "With that being said, would you allow me to hold you?"

Part of me wants to laugh at him for thinking I could say no. Instead, I offer a quiet, "Yes."

Dominus turns towards me then and wraps his long, muscled arm across my body. He pulls me close, and we instantly melt into one another. We stay quiet for long minutes, existing in this space we carved out. This space, where we can get intoxicated on the scent and comfort of one another without speaking about it. Without asking for more.

My mind whirls thinking of how strange it is to no longer consider him my opponent, to turn my back on him willingly. We have both laid our weapons at each other's feet, and though part of me wants to question if it will last, something else tells me he does not want to pick his up again.

Neither do I.

The rules have changed again. Perhaps dissolved entirely. And lying here, wrapped in the smell and warmth of him, in his presence, I have never felt such peace, such utter harmony within my soul. Not since the nights I spent surrounded by my family.

The comfort and fit of it nearly has me asleep when he whispers, "Thorne?"

"Yes."

"Can I offer one more truth tonight?"

I know it's dangerous, but I turn to him. His arm never leaves me, and when I face him, he begins to run long, gentle strokes up and down my back, exactly like Hyacinth used to, and I fight the void inside me to keep it from ripping open again. I meet those pale eyes, glowing slightly enough for me to see his face clearly and for him to see mine.

"I have a theory about your episodes." My exhausted mind perks up at that, and my eyes widen. "It is only a theory, and we can discuss it when we are back, but I wanted to tell you. I do not want to withhold unnecessary things from you." I simultaneously want to kiss and wallop him. I am thankful for his honesty, but now I fear I will not sleep for the wondering my mind will do. "We will talk when we are back, I swear it. Sleep, mo céasadh, sleep."

He tucks my head under his chin, allowing my face to rest against his warm, smooth skin. I inhale him deeply, allowing that blissful trance to cover me again.

"Why do you call me that? What does it mean?" I whisper, nearly asleep.

"My agony," he whispers back, kissing the top of my head, and then I am floating, sailing through worlds and time, feeling infinite. Feeling whole.

TWENTY SIX

We do indeed sleep the entire night without moving. I wake to callused, warm hands stroking my back. We intertwined our legs at some point. My right one is now hoisted over his waist, and one of his lies heavily over my left one, reminiscent of the twisted and tangled trees of the cave opening. I have woken embraced by lovers before, but never like this. Never with the intent of seeing them again. Never with this swell blooming in my core.

I open my eyes to find the blue light of a not-yet-risen sun casting a hazy fog around the room. We must have only slept for a few hawrs, but I am more rested than if I had slept for days. I meet Dom's eyes, and he brings his hand to the side of my face.

"What does this mean?" He knows what I am asking. This comfort between us. The melodical vibration. The way we cannot stay away from one another. How we push and pull, desperately fighting it for our own reasons, but still, unable to stay away.

"I have spent yehrs calling out to my family, begging for someone to hear me, to see me, to find me. Decades of praying, offering, and sacrificing so much of myself to be remembered. I think the Seren sent you instead. And I think it is up to us to determine why."

My mind devours the new information. He has a family—somewhere. He also thinks I was sent by the missing gods. I wonder if his disdain for me has meant that he presumes me to be an enemy—or once did. "Do you think I am here to destroy you?"

"No, Thorne. I think you are here to save me."

I want to spend forever here in this decrepit bed, staring into his eyes and breathing him in. Part of me craves the answers, but there is a part of me that fears the truth and what it might bring. An even larger part of me fears this intensity and its longevity.

A knock at the door pulls me from my exploration, and I remember Thair is here. I disentangle myself from Dominus and walk softly to the door and crack it open, only offering my face in the blooming light of the day.

"Good morning! I thought we'd get an early start since we only have daylight. I brought us up some bricfeasta. Might I join you again?"

The door is sharply pulled from my grasp, revealing a half-naked Dominus. I move my arms across my chest, attempting to cover myself.

"She is currently unavailable, I'm afraid," he answers,

crossing his arms. I roll my eyes and leave them to it as I scrub my teeth and face.

"What are you doing here?"

"Protecting my assets. Both of them. We will be out in a moment." Dominus takes one of the trays from his hands and closes the door with his foot. I let out a deep breath, and he places the food on the bed.

"I truly do not understand your hatred for him," I say with a mouthful of paste.

"There is something about him that triggers something in me. I cannot place it, but he reeks of dishonesty and secrets."

"And I don't?" I spit the paste out and rinse my mouth with water.

"No. You smell of lavender, sweet mint, parchment, and leather. You smell deliciously of danger and something else I cannot place. But not deceit. You keep your truths hidden, but you are sure of them. Thair is...veiled. Obstructed, like I cannot sense him fully." His admission of my smell brings a smile to my lips.

"I see. And...do you like my scent? Or whatever you sense from me?"

He moves around the small room to me, wrapping his long arms around my waist. He nuzzles his nose into the crook of my neck and inhales deeply. It reminds me of the moment we shared in his classroom. I watch in the looking glass above the basin as his pupils expand, hungrily eating up the space of his irises, and it causes my mouth to dry out.

"Your scent is unlike anything I have ever encountered. It's sweet." Another inhale. "Yet heady." Another inhale.

"And it drives me mad. It consumes my every thought. And it is infinitely more maddening when it is laced with my own." He sweeps my hair behind my back, exposing my neck to run his nose from my shoulder to my ear. "Had I known what a delicacy the antetaste of your scent was, well, let me simply say I have never, in all of my life, had to practice such self-control as I did on the shore of that sea."

His length hardens against my lower back, and I still in response, forcing myself not to lean into it. He senses the shift in me instantly, pulling away. He runs his hands through those damn midnight waves, and my palms itch.

"Thorne, you must forgive me. I need to cease being in your presence for a moment. I will respect your choices, but I am currently losing the will to fight."

"Do not apologise, Dominus. I only stilled for fear of what I might do myself. And we agreed, not here, not now. I want to abide by that."

His eyes rove over me then. My body, hot where we touched, begins to burn in this gaze. "Eat. Get dressed. I will meet you downstairs."

"Alright." My gut twists at the thought of him leaving. He closes his eyes, but my hands reach out to him. "Wait."

"Yes?" He answers, catching my hand in his.

"Can you...magic me a raiment of yours? Or whatever that was that you did." Concern drips into satisfaction with a deadly smile that I ache to consume. But I refuse. Not yet.

"I would love nothing more."

He closes his eyes and whispers something in another language. Its cadence is that of a dead, ancient tongue, but I cannot place it. With our hands still connected, the hum of magic runs through him and into me. I lean my head back as it courses through my body. I close my eyes, letting it wind around me, through me, like the caress of a lover.

"Thorne," Dominus whispers my name, bringing me back into the room.

I lift my head to look at him. A linen scyrte lies over his shoulder, and in his hands, he holds a pair of leather boots far too small to fit his feet.

"I think you need a far larger size."

"These are for you, daft one. Look at me." He takes my chin in his grip, staring into my eyes.

"What? What is it?" I ask as he studies my face for a long second.

"Nothing. I thought I saw something. Here." He hands me the boots. They are made from supple, full-grain, black leather. Sturdy, but will wear in over time, moulding to the foot as if they were designed for it. They are the most exquisite brogans I have ever seen.

"I cannot accept these."

"You cannot trudge around this territory today wearing those ill-fitted heaps of cattle you call boots that destroyed your feet last time. And I am currently not in a...position to carry you around all day."

"Fine." I snatch them from him and the scyrte from his shoulder. Then, slowly, I lean into him and place a soft, gentle kiss against his lips. "Thank you." My voice is low and warm.

"Bloody spirits," he echoes with equal gravel, and when I blink again, he's gone. I twist around the room, looking for him, knowing he's not here. His swords are gone with him. No trace left behind. I spin on my heels, searching for it. Relief floods me when I see he left the small amber bottle of oil.

I hastily dress and prepare for the day, layering Dom's linen scyrte under a sleeveless, traditional, deep amber linen dress, something fitting for Eden and the warm weather. Though I do let his too-large neckline hang off my shoulders. I look like what most people here would consider to be a proper lady, and maybe I even feel like one today. I oil the ends of my hair again and plait it back. The boots fit perfectly, light and agile, with the perfect amount of firmness. They even help to quiet my steps as I ease my way out of the room on creaking floors.

I meet Dominus and Thair in the foyer of the inn. Seeing Dominus make me more secure, regardless of how wrapped in his scent I am. He is perfect as ever, dressed impeccably in dark summer linen and cotton. We look like seemingly normal people, not at all haunted by our pasts and presents.

"Morning, gentlemen," I greet Dominus and Thair, and they both stand in response. "I suppose we can cover more ground today with the extra hands, and though I had a preexisting plan, both of you know this place better than I do. So, you two can decide what are the most valuable places to visit and who to speak to. I will be in the carriage."

I am significantly less excited about today. The weight of last night, nearly being killed—again—and my proclamations afterwards have me off-kilter. And the thought of spending the day watching those two eejits stick their proverbial tongues out at one another—maybe their actual ones, too—does not excite me as it normally would. I want to get back to Adonien. I want to learn everything Dominus needs to tell me.

I need to reassess myself and my life. I spent so long craving answers that as I begin to find them, I don't know what to do with them. My gut tells me to prepare. That I am barreling towards something, and I need to become ready.

Pick up your weapon. Accept your fate. The voice haunts me in my waking and my sleep. But what does it mean? And how can I begin when Dominus always swoops in to fight my battles for me?

I need to tell him about the voice and the other vision. If these are hallucinations I am having without episodes, perhaps my curse is coming to a pinnacle. Perhaps it is closer to claiming me than ever.

The two of them join me in the carriage, pulling my mind from my thoughts and my eyes from the beauty of the bustling borough. Though it briefly jumps back to the crone, wondering what will happen once her body is found, wondering if someone will come for me. I become irritated at myself for not asking about that last night, for being so consumed in a man that I did not immediately consider the repercussions of my actions. What is he doing to me?

The weight of them jostles me around in the carriage. Dominus sits beside me and Thair across from us. "Are you alright?" he whispers in my ear.

I only nod once, not breaking my gaze on the farmers loading mounds of barley into a wagon.

I spend most of the day in a haze, letting Dominus and Thair take the lead. They do most of the talking and questioning while I find my mind wandering, lost. I am ashamed of my behaviour and myself for not taking control and heading the expedition that was, after all, my idea for the journal I am creating, but I have gone numb. I can recognise my behaviour, but I am frozen; nothing to be done about it.

They pull me along to the library, then off to converse with acquaintances each of them knows, and I hear no new information from anyone. We visit Aigne's archives, where they load a trunk with books and scrolls for us to take back to the academy to study. I know when I get back, I will be thankful for the material to scour, but the longer the day stretches, the more internal I become. Fortunately, we are saving the archaeological unearthings for when we are all able to attend, along with Thair's assistant.

Dominus has remained at my side, ever the curious mind, undoubtedly studying my shift. I wonder what he can sense of it, what abilities he might possess that grant him untold knowledge of me. I wonder if he can tell me what ails me, for I cannot.

Then the thought hits me, a growing inkling in the pit of my stomach. It has only been menoths, and I have never had two episodes this close together, but the lethargy is the same, the grief that pulls me far within myself is familiar to me. What if this is because of my growing feelings for Dominus? What if this is a warning sign? I withdraw further into myself at the thought, spiralling down and around to that familiar, welcoming pain.

We visit the market at the end of the day, per my request

last night. I force myself out of the carriage. Maybe some fresh air and a stroll without having to discuss mythical legends and stories of the gods will pull me out of it. Almost immediately, we come upon the tent of a spicer. Her bright blue eyes and cropped sienna hair signal to me that this is Oona, the spicer that Elowyn told me about.

"You must be Thorne," she greets in her thick accent.

"You must be Oona," I smile back at her. Dominus and Thair both study us with confusion.

"I thought you wouldna make it. 'Tis nearly sunset after all."

"We've had a very busy day, but I am thankful we made it. I hear you have some items I might be looking for."

She looks at me cautiously for a long moment—long enough for me to consider if we are still speaking of spices. "Aye, perhaps, I might after all."

She takes us into her tent, countless smells fighting their way into my nose. I work hard to collect them all. Oona spends some time teaching us her processes. She explains that the planting of the herbs is critical to the success of reaching maturity. As equally important, the ground must be right: not too wet, not too dry. Once mature, they must be picked at exactly the right moment to preserve the essence and full body flavours. Then she goes on to spend wyths drying and curing them before they can be ground down into perfect consistencies. I realise the art of it—the harmony and balance it takes to produce something so precious to the people of Eregahl.

It seems small: providing powerful, delectable flavours to our food, a frivolous commodity certainly. But it provides much-needed reflection and perspective on my part. We all have a path, a destiny, something we were crafted for in the womb. Something that matters to someone, that alters the lives of others. Maybe many, maybe few. But if Oona can spend her days studying, growing, and crafting herbs to offer people the privilege of a delicious meal, then I want to be more like that. I want to have confidence in my path again and know that regardless of where I walk, I will blaze new trails for others to venture as well.

With renewed vigour cutting through the haze of impending doom, I thank Oona for the service she provides to us, and I purchase all the spices I have never heard of, which turns out to be many, since I come from Albion, and we have much simpler tastes. She packages up our purchases and hands the wrapped parcel to Dominus. She walks from around the table and, to my surprise, offers me a hug.

"Thank you for your hospitality. And for sharing your gift with me. It has meant more than you know," I say as we end the embrace.

She takes my hand in hers. "Och, 'tis is no worry at all. Also," she leans in and lowers her voice, "I included a small satchel of moon salt. 'Tis for conjuring. I sense you are very blocked. Use it to call to your maker," she whispers in my ear. Surprise causes me to chaotically mumble my thanks and pull away. "She was right, ya know. You are somethin' special."

Dominus pulls my hand away, and as he does, I see her eye him suspiciously, causing a wave of confusion to wash over me, sending me back into that space of uncertainty.

Back in the carriage, we begin the journey back to Adonien.

Shrike

I fall asleep immediately to the blooming sonation in my mind, louder than it has ever been, unable to fight against the swelling grief inside me.

TWENTY SEVEN

The jostling of the carriage pulled me from my slumber. We travelled through the night, and I dreamt of glowing eyes, sharp teeth, and a sea of blood. Both Thair and Dominus insist on getting me to my rooms, and quite frankly, I have half a mind to tell them both to sod off. I am beyond exhausted, and I need time. Time to process what the seer said, what Oona said, and what the sinking in my gut is telling me.

"Thank you both for your very unnecessary escorts. I have arrived intact, so congratulations to you both. Now, if you would be so kind as to make haste removing yourselves, I shall like to soak in boiling water and sleep for two days."

"If you'd like, I could come help you release some of that tension. I am told I possess an uncanny ability to coax delicious relief from a woman's body," Thair says.

Knowing he is only stoking Dom's anger, I respond by stepping through my door and closing it behind me. I slump against the other side for long enough to hear Dominus murmur, "Fuck you," and for Thair to only laugh at him before he leaves, and his footsteps soon echo down the corridor.

There is an immediate knock at my door. Wincing, I stand to open it. "Yes," I answer, completely not wanting to have this conversation.

Dom's eyes inspect every inch of me before he says, "Are you alright? I understand that was a considerable amount to divulge. Thank you again for sharing everything you did. I promise I am not going to be a prick about it if that is why you are pulling away. I have given you many reasons not to trust me, so my words likely mean little, but I bow out, Thorne. No more dancing or warring. I bow out."

His words thunder through me, but the victory tastes hollow, tainted by something else I cannot place. "Oh, Dominus. You have no idea what that means. But that is not what ails me. I– Something is going on with me, a new strangeness taking root. I still want to talk. I still want to know everything. Can we postpone? I need a few moments."

"What is it?" Concern laces those pale eyes.

"I feel like I do before an episode. Sadness, exhaustion, lethargy. I am numb, and underneath it all, completely terrified for what that means for you. They usually only happen once a yehr. I don't know how to handle this. I do not know what to do."

He reaches out for me, but I step back. "Let me be here for you. Let me protect you."

"It is you who needs protection from me, Dominus. Please go." The only sound is my tears hitting the floor as he studies me. I see him fighting with himself. "Listen for me. If you hear something worrisome, come to me, but let me try to protect you. Let me try to save you."

"I do not believe this to be an episode, Thorne."

"How would you even know?" Anger borders my numbness. How would he know how this feels? No one understands what I go through.

Shadows swell around him, and sadness creases his eyes. "Because I think all the times that happened to you were my doing. I think it was something I did. When you were telling me the story of your episodes, something struck me. Every yehr, I store up my magic to reach out to my family. Every yehr on the same day. Bealtaine, when the veil is thin. One yehr, I was so desperate, I tried twice. I think I am the one who has been... summoning you. I believe my call to my family, my plea, was unintentionally a call to you. I am so sorry. Thorne, I will never be able to forgive myself for the pain I have caused you."

Tears begin to pool in his eyes as relief, confusion, doubt, and fear all fight to consume me in a squall.

Sometimes I wondered if I could run, if I could find what called to me, maybe I could fix it. Maybe I could stop it. My own words haunt me. It was him. He was calling out to me. Summoning me with magic. Magic was tearing me apart at the seams, and I had no idea.

"But if I am here with you now, why does it still feel like I am dying? And that still does not solve the question of my family's deaths. That cannot be a mere coincidence, can it?"

He bites his lip and turns to look down the hall, at the floor, and then back up to me. "I think there are things far bigger than us pushing us towards one another. Maybe they always have."

Claim him, she whispers.

"A sign for me to claim you?" I bite with anger.

"Perhaps. I am not certain."

"Well, that should still be my choice—our choice."

"Who is saying this isn't my choice?"

I need to clear my head. I need to soak my aching body and consider all of this. And I still need to know what Dominus Shrike even is before I think about tethering my life to his. "I need to rest. I need to protect you, Dominus. I need you to live."

He releases a deep breath, and I can tell he does not want to leave. He wants to offer me his truths, and for once, I am the one refusing them. My head begins to spin.

"I understand. Call my name if you need me," he says, his voice nearly a whisper.

"I will."

Before I have time to undress, another knock sounds at my door, but thankfully, only a tray full of food sits outside. His thoughtfulness makes my gut turn with regret. It also rumbles with hunger, so I eat in silence as the tub fills. With a satisfied belly, I slip into the steaming bath, allowing the fragrant oils of lavender and eucalyptus to permeate my skin, hoping they might seep through layers of exhaustion and inexplicable grief.

The sun begins its incessant rising again, casting that familiar blue hue around the room. The water coats my skin like warm whispers, and my mind drifts to Dominus and how he held me. How tender he's been with me, how strange it is to be met with something other than disdain from him, and how I had shut him out when we had just come to a place of understanding.

He thinks he is the answer to my disease—the cure to my curse. He speculates that claiming him will rid me of it. But what if it does the opposite? And is it even my choice, or is something greater than me, this voice inside me, playing us like puppets?

Perhaps my insecurities are colouring my viewpoint a hideous shade of rose. Perhaps it's the fact that I have been lying to myself for menoths now. Maybe the grief is because of the loss I know I will suffer.

But...what *do* I want? I want to stop lying to myself. I want to acknowledge the fact that Dominus Shrike does not enrage me as he once did. Or perhaps he still does, but I like it. I like the fact that he does not coddle or fear me, and he does not find my intelligence intimidating. He pushes, challenges, and completely vexes me. He urges me to stretch beyond the boundaries I set for myself and to reach heights I have never dared dream of scaling. And in doing so, has he not revealed something of himself? After all, there is no one else here who pushes him back. That threatens his position and forces his thoughts and considerations. That knows as much of him as I do.

I crave our interactions. Each morning, I wake with a flutter of excitement, wondering what new intellectual battle we might wage. Our dance is intricate, passionate, sometimes bordering on furious—but always, always, precisely matched in force and fervour. And if I am being wholly honest with myself, I would never want a partner who didn't challenge me in these ways. I value true, raw honesty over false niceties. I intended to meet him step for step, and we have done that. As equals. If I were to ever allow myself to consider for a single moment the prospect of someone to love, they would include all of those qualities.

And gods, he is beautiful. Unnervingly, otherworldly so. No man should be able to look like that. Well, he's not a man at all, is he? Whatever he is, I do know that he is a perfect mix of hard and soft. Of intellect and discernment. A warrior's hands with a poet's mind. And the way he touches me...

I curse myself aloud for being so utterly immature and dismissive of my emotions, my very desires. I thought myself smarter than that, but perhaps I have been the sciolist all along.

Then again, that is how I have survived most of my life, pushing everyone away. If I love someone, they die. That is my macabre history. My twisted past. Perhaps my self-preservation has been hiding under the guise of feigned ignorance—all attempted murders aside. And whether this curse is real or not, if all this is some twisted fate of mine, I am terrified to tempt it.

The bath seems to turn cold at my thoughts, and a shiver has me absconding it. I tiptoe, still dripping, into my room to find a black tunic lying on my bed. I cannot help but smile at the kindness of it—that he's still considering my wants, my needs, even as I have sent him away. I drop the towel to the floor to pull it over my head. A blanket of him covers me as I do, that delicious, eternal feeling is soaking into the fibres of my being.

But something is different this time. It does not satisfy the growing hunger in me, nor does it calm the chaos brewing in my chest.

It spurs it, praises it.

The lethargy is gone. The grief evaporates into nothing.

All that is left is a desperate need. Something dead and cold crawling through dirt, craving the forbidden. I drop to my knees and push myself back across the floor until my back meets the wall. I close my eyes and cover my ears, attempting to breathe through the screaming sonation in my head.

Louder and louder, it pushes, stretching my skin, begging to burst through, begging to be fed. "Please, stop!" I plead. "Cease this. Now!"

Then silence. Pure silence. Silence so quiet it's deafening.

I open my eyes to find my wet footprints and trail of dripping water turning to moss before my eyes.

Then I black out.

TWENTY EIGHT

My eyes open to darkness. My chest heaves in breaths. I scramble to my bare feet, trying to make sense of what is happening to me. That thing in my chest growls with a different kind of hunger, with anger and rage.

My skean is in my hand, and I raise it in defence before realising I am outside. How did I get out here? How long ago did I lose consciousness? The sun had only risen during my bath. What is happening to me? I turn around and see the glowing lights of the castle. From this view, I make out that I am at its southern face, meaning the sea is behind me. I close my mouth, quieting my breath, and do indeed hear the crashing of waves to my back. My body shakes, though I cannot decipher if it is from fear or something else.

A horrible, low growl sounds behind me, and I spin on my

heels to see a flash of darkness dart through the trees. I hear the dragging of large limbs as it moves closer to me, close enough that I hear its breathing. Close enough that I can make out that it is significantly larger than me. That gnawing thing whispers to me.

Listen. Feel.

As before, I close my eyes, control my breath, and listen. As I do, I see a vision of it in my mind as it readies itself to attack me from behind. I twist into the attack, meeting it before it reaches me, sinking my blade into something, making a ghastly crunch ring through the trees. It gives a hollow scream as its clawed paw makes contact with my arm, sending sharp, deep pain searing into it. I strike, missing. I've lost it again.

Feel!

I close my eyes and attempt to hone in on its location. I hear my blood drip, drip, drip to the ground. I hear my heart beat like the wings of a hummingbird. I breathe deeply, trying to calm the fear taking control of me. Instead, a horrid, wet animal smell hits me, nearly causing me to gag. I force my eyes to remain closed, focusing.

A gear shifts, a door opens, and an instinct I did not have before floods me. I open my eyes, surprised to find that I can now see in the darkness. A pale golden glow illuminates everything. I see it now—the monster. It stands nearly twice my height. Its body is gaunt and skeletal, with pale, stretched skin, and little remaining fur clings tightly to its bones. Its enormous head resembles that of a hound but with sunken, glowing red eyes and razor-sharp teeth protruding from its elongated jaw. The claws on one of its hands are dripping with my blood. Its decaying scent hits me again.

I do not give it time to attack again. I charge it. Avoiding those deadly manuses, I dive through its legs, twisting to thrust my skean deep into its skeletal back. It shrieks again and whips me back and forth, trying to release me. It succeeds, but my blade comes with me. Landing roughly on my back, all breath abandons my lungs, and I gasp for the refuge of air as the creature stalks toward me. Thunder cracks behind it, causing it to pause briefly. Rain begins falling from the sky in a heavy, thick sheet. I crawl backwards, slipping on the wet ground, still breathless, still unable to fill my lungs to stand. It raises its gangly paw above its head, but before it swings to disembowel me, it stops as the blade of a sword plunges through its middle. The blade releases, and the thing stumbles back. It wasn't a killing blow, and it fights to regain some ground.

Dominus stares at me with furious, glowing eyes. He looks away from me to raise his sword.

"Stop!" I scream.

He whips his head to me with surprise. I finally fill my lungs with heaving breaths and stand. I walk to Dominus, pushing him out of the way.

"What are you doing?" he screams.

"Saving my bloody self for once!" I raise my skean and plunge it deep into the creature, right between its eyes. Fury, satisfaction, everything I have ever felt flows through me, and I release my blade to plunge it again.

And again.

And again.

I am screaming and sobbing, and large hands wrap

themselves around my middle. Rain, blood, and vengeance soak me to the bone. I don't know how to stop. I cannot release the rage.

"Thorne," he says, barely audible above the downpour. "It's alright. You can stop. Thorne. Mo céasadh, look at me." My arms pause midair, and I turn to him, blade still raised. His eyes widen at what he sees. The vicious, violent, uncontrollable woman before him. "Look at me. Feel me. I am here, Thorne. I am right here." I bring the blade to his throat, the anger beginning to evolve into that ravenous hunger again. His eyes glow brighter. "I know. I understand. Take what you need from me."

How can he know? How can he understand this when I do not? The thing inside me reacts to his words, twisting my insides to feel more animal than human. I stare at him for a long moment, waging a war within myself. I want to give in to it, but something else stops me. A long moment passes as I keep the blade pressed against his skin, yet he does not move. Long enough for the rain to wash me clean from the blood, though the gashes on my arm ache violently.

"Take what you need from me," he whispers again, and it sounds desperate. I dig the blade into his skin, causing thick, warm blood to drip down his neck. I do not stop myself from dropping the blade to wrap my hands through his hair and pull him against me to run my tongue along the open wound. His blood on my tongue is music to my body. It is blood and wine, sweet and tantalising, bursting with flavours I am sure no tongue has ever tasted.

His hands are instantly around me, and he leans into me,

offering me his throat. My licks turn to kisses, to bites, and a guttural growl sounds from him, reverberating against my body. "We must go, Thorne. Let me get you inside. Let me take care of you."

I cannot respond because I have forgotten words, forgotten how they form in my mouth and how to produce sound. I only climb and wrap my legs around his waist. He holds me so tightly against him that I think my bones may bruise, and I hope they do. I offer no reprieve from my exploration of his neck as he whispers in that language unknown to me. When he turns around to take us back to the castle, the creature is gone. Gone. Nothing left but a pool of blood swirling into the muddy ground, washing away toward the sea, and I become aware that the crone will never be found. This causes me to pause, to consider, to question.

As I lift my head, my senses become muddled. I blink, and my sight leaves me. No, just the ability to see in the dark. I start to come back down, and the blood lust falls away from me. The instinct, the rage, runs down my body and into the ground with the droplets of rain and mingles with the blood of the monster. I keep my arms wrapped around Dominus, ashamed of what I have done, of what I have become.

The voice in my head laughs. *You became everything you are meant to be.*

It's quieter than it has been—like it's no longer in my mind but far away from me.

Claim him. Barely a whisper. Then a long pause. And then, as if it floated on the wind and out to the sea, quietly, pleading... *please.*

I want to ask her who she is and where she's going, but I fear her answers. I fear what they might bring.

Dominus carries me through the tunnels and up and around the hidden stairs through our corridor. I stay quiet and shivering, my face pressed against the wet warmth of his neck. He takes us to his room, locking the door behind us. He places me on his bed and begins to assess my arm. "I need to heal this," he says with controlled calmness.

"No." My voice is raw.

"Thorne, these are deep." I begin to come back into my body again. His scent and nearness sober me like they always do. "

Leave it. I want the reminder. I want the proof of fighting back. I want the proof of victory." I am not certain why I say it, but it is true.

"Thorne, I–"

"Now. I want to know everything. Right now. No more waiting. No more reasons why. Give me your truths, Dominus." He sucks in a deep breath and runs his hands through his hair, staring at me for a long moment. "From the beginning," I say, goading him. He paces backwards, unbuckling the scabbard, letting it drop to the ground with a clang behind him.

"There is some truth in what you already know. We will start there. When the world was crafted, the four gods, Hellas, Noreg, Eden, and Caledon, created many things. But their very first creations were different from anything that came after. They forged warriors crafted from their blood and bone to watch over the lands and administer their will. They gifted them powers unlike their other creations—ones that allow them to live long lives, to fight with preternatural strength and speed, to heal, and to influence the earth and the creatures upon it. They were something other. Something in between the Seren and the rest of their creations. They called us Erads, but you will recognise from texts that we are often now called Mystics."

Blood rushes to my ears. Of all the creatures I hypothesised he could be, the gods' first and favourite creation did not cross my mind. Those, I was certain, I would never encounter.

"Only those born between the coupling of Erads inherit the gift. I, my father, Adonien, and my siblings, Fina, Camiel, and Icarus, are protectors of this realm. The Seren crafted our very own home, Eradia, in the clouds. We were forged by them all and crafted to protect the lands and the Seren and all they created."

He pushes his hair from his face. "Maybe I once thought I was a reverent soldier, but so much time in the darkness changes the way a person sees the light, and now I know that I was trained to be a glorified guard dog, crafted to answer their every need. There is an army of us, but only one family, four at a time, to represent each of the Seren, rule. Though one is always stronger than the rest. I was trained as my father's greatest warrior and showed promise of being that mighty leader. Then, he abandoned me here."

He begins to pace slowly, taking a turn in the conversation before I have time to question him. "Before my lifetime, there was a great war between the Seren. They created many types of creatures and lived in harmony with them for a long time. As you know, Hellas grew greedy. He wanted total domination. So, he used the similar magic used to create the Erads to create his own band of warriors that he could control."

"Deamhans," I whisper. Dom nods. I recall what Elowyn told me about the gods. What she said about Danu keeping Hellas on a leash. "Elowyn, Eamon's wife—I have become very close with them. Before we left for Eden, I asked her if she knew where I could find a seer. They are from Eden, and she is the one who sent me there. We had an interesting talk. She knows a considerable amount about the gods. She spoke of stories I have never heard, Dominus."

"Tell me everything." His brows pinch together.

"Elowyn said her father only ever told her this once and never spoke of it again. She told me that the Seren had another sibling in their homeland. Her name was Danu, and this very land was named in her honour." His eyes flicker, the same way mine did with some primal awareness. "She was the strongest of them, first in line for the throne, though Hellas was a sadistic second, and Danu worked to keep him in check. She died in a great war, sacrificing herself to let her siblings escape. They came here. After they arrived, she speculated that the lack of Danu's constant attention allowed him to gain power over the others. She said that each of the Seren represents something. Hellas as blood, Caledon as bone, Noreg as spirit, and Eden as fate. And Dominus, she called Danu the Heir of Earth."

The colour drains from his face. "How does she know this? I have never even been taught such things. I doubt even my father has. Your book was the only instance of this I have ever seen." He paces the room.

"I have no idea. She explicitly stated she does not know for certain whether the story was invented by her father or was a lost truth. But the seer called you the heir. The prophecy describes you perfectly. It must be true."

He scrunches his eyebrows, running through all the information. "It makes sense, though. Hellas used his deamhans to wage war, terrorise, and threaten his siblings, gaining more control of the land. They did not want to fight him. They begged him to let go of his greed, to rule together as they planned, as they escaped the horrors of their world to do. He eventually forced them out. Each of them created new lands for their creations to live in peace and safety from him. They keep them veiled from each other, though. The Erads remain a neutral species and are the only ones allowed to travel through each territory now that they have fled."

"How is it that you can fight against Hellas and his deamhans?"

"I told you that magic is all about intent. When the Seren created us, they intended for us to have the best interests of the collective in mind. Hellas has chosen to go against that. We still must protect the others. It is woven into us, threaded into our existence. We do not have a choice."

I nod, working to piece it all together. "How did you get here?"

"After Hellas drove everyone out, Eregahl, the homeland, became a wasteland. The humans that remain here were never intentional creations, Thorne. The humans that remain are what evolved from those that were left behind, one of the Seren's species that survived in the shadows for hundreds of yehrs. The Seren took the magic with them, cutting off access to the land and those left here. Eventually, their magic faded through each bloodline, though a few still possess some gifts. The seers and healers in Eregahl have not been gifted or imbued in this lifetime. They are what remains from their ancestors. I witnessed the evolution."

Shock courses through me. Humans were never even created. We evolved to survive. Magicless. "What about Albion? How is it that it is a separate island but not veiled from Eregahl? I was able to travel here."

"Albion was created when Hellas began his push against the others. It was essentially a place for them to meet without him knowing. He discovered it quickly enough. Many of those left behind were able to flee there as Hellas began his rampage."

I chew the inside of my lip, considering the information. "We have a different origin story, though. People there do not believe in the gods here. We are told as children that the goddess Cyfrif created our land out of pure love, and once we die, we join her in paradise."

"You are the only person I have met who has travelled here from there and vice versa. I have never heard the tale of this Cyfrif before. She does not exist to my knowledge. Perhaps she was a version of the story that the remaining species created to offer hope to their people throughout time."

"So, she isn't real?"

"I would assume not. Then again, I now have little confidence in any of my assumptions."

"Then what happens when we die here? Where do we go?"

"Honestly, I am not sure. No one died before the war. Everything just existed in perfect harmony. They never explained to us what happened to their creations when they ended. Perhaps the power goes back to each god. Perhaps they exist endlessly in the magic of the land. I wish I knew. I wish...I had been able to concern myself with such questions then."

"But the humans, the powerless, where do we go?"

He runs his hands through his hair, grief shrouding him. "I wish I had an answer for you, Thorne. I wish I could tell you that whatever happened to your family, they are at peace, but that is unknown to me."

"I understand," I say, trying to set that fact aside for later. I need to know the rest. "Why can't you leave this island?" I move to cross my arms and flinch, reminded of the woud. Dominus takes immediate notice.

"If you refuse to let me heal that, at least let me clean it to avoid it becoming infected. I am particularly fond of all of your limbs."

I offer a small smile. "Fine, but do it while you talk."

By the time I move myself to a more comfortable seated position on the bed, Dom is beside me with a bowl of water and a cloth. He begins to clean as he speaks. "I was mere decades away from taking over for my father. We had always been close, and it would not be arrogant of me to say I was his favourite. Everyone knew I was his champion, his prized possession. We were on a raid in Eregahl one day, fending off a savage scourge of failinis—what you fought off tonight." A moment of pride glistens across those pale green eyes when he says this, causing my heart to flutter. He rinses the bloody cloth and continues his meticulous mending.

"Hellas made use of Eregahl as his secret breeding ground for all his foul creations for too long before we caught wind of it.

He had been lying in wait, growing his army to hunt his siblings to their ends. Flushing them out was never enough for him. We had nearly dwindled the hoard down, dispersed enough to be able to retreat. I was burning the bodies when I looked back to see my father preparing to leave. I asked him why he was leaving when the job was not done. He told me that he intended for me to stay in Eregahl while he and my siblings returned to Eradia. As his heir and right hand, he wanted me to spend some time in solitude to find myself. A test, preparation to show my fortitude and ability.

"I was shocked, as were my siblings. Well, I don't think Icarus was at all. 'Tis hard to tell what slimy hand he had in it. Never wanting to disappoint my father, I agreed to stay and fight off Hellas' deamhans and wait for his return. But upon his departure, my magic...changed. It became dull and veiled. I became a fraction of the warrior I once was. I tried to shift, I tried to llif. Nothing worked. I am still unaware if it was my father's doing or if it was from being here for so long. Time passes differently here with the land being leeched of magic, and I have no way of knowing what has changed in Eradia or any of the other veiled lands, but I have been here for three hundred yehrs."

Three hundred yehrs. He's been stranded here for three centuries. The gods crafted him. He is endless and infinite and supposedly mine to claim.

He abandons me and my now-clean arm to my spiral as he walks to the bookshelf and procures two glasses and a dark amber liquid. He fills the glasses halfway and strolls over to gently place one in my hand as if this were a casual conversation over what we speculated the ancient runes might mean. Bloody spirits, I suppose he knows that, too.

He takes a deep breath, and I start to see the weight he's been carrying—how heavy this all must be. How lonely and tormenting. I take a long drink, letting the liquid fire burn courage down my throat. "What shifting could you do? And what does that mean—to llif?"

He waves a hand over his body. "This is not my true form."

TWENTY NINE

My eyes widen. "What does your true form look like?"

"Something not too far from this, but I was larger and significantly stronger, and I had glorious wings crafted from endless obsidian feathers. We are their most beautiful creatures. The perfect amalgam of beauty, power, wisdom, and terror. We are the only creation that possesses the essence of all the Seren. And with that perfection comes the ironic dichotomy of being able to shift into something with piercing teeth, scales, and talons. Something horrid enough to terrify creatures like the dearg due, afanc, and the failinis, Thorne."

He takes a sip of his drink and studies my reaction. My mouth turns bone dry. I try to picture him any larger than he is, with the wings and talons. I shudder at what my mind forms, knowing it is likely far more terrifying.

"As for the llifing, that is how I disappeared from the inn. 'Tis also called worldwalking, using magic to travel from one place to another, although it is a bit more alchemical than that. I can llif within the bounds of Eregahl, only within míles now, but I cannot leave these lands—on foot, by boat, or by magic." He takes a deep pull from his glass, his eyes glazing over from the memories. I remain quiet and sip from my glass, allowing him the space to unfold this in the way he needs.

"Conjuring is what happens when I *magic* you a raiment, as you call it. Summoning is what I used to call to my family. I cannot imagine what that felt like for you, Thorne." His eyes turn sad, and I cannot find it in me, even after all the pain, to hate him for it.

He walks to stare out the window into the darkness. The moon shines on his face, carving the shadows and chiselled bones into a masterpiece. "I was strong for the first century," he begins again. "I kept the deluded mentality that it was for my own good—that I would come out with so much knowledge and clarity of what Hellas had done, I would make the perfect leader. After those first hundred yehrs, I began to question. To doubt. I spent the second century raging, killing deamhans, searching for Hellas to no avail, and refusing contact with any other being." He lets his head fall, closing his eyes. "I became a monster, a different form of myself that I was unaware we could be. I have spent this last century dragging myself from that place."

He releases a deep breath, looking at me. "I started this scol as a way to save myself. My sanity. To never forget. Some poor attempt to preserve some of the story of my life that I was unsure that I would ever see again. I leave every decade or so and disappear on extended hunts, ridding the island of Hellas' ilk. I come back when there is no one here who would remember my face, claiming I'm a descendant of the last Shrike."

Another sip. "I built this from nothing. I pull all the strings behind the curtain while everyone thinks I am simply a wickedly smart, arrogant scolemaster that the academy needs more than they don't. I make myself indispensable enough that no one asks questions, and they leave me to myself."

He walks over in front of me and sits on the ground with his back against the wall and holds his glass in both hands, resting his elbows on bent knees. He leans his head back against the wall, offering me a moment to breathe. Millions of questions form in my mind. But even with all of them, I know that what he says is the truth.

My mind wants me to look at this logically—to tell this man he needs help and to run. But there's something else. Something at the core of me that hums to his words. Something that tells me what he says is true. Acknowledging that fact, I begin to ask the next burning question in line. "Why did he leave you here for so long?"

He huffs a deep, maniacal laugh at that. "That is the question that burns through my mind every minute that I am here." He drains his glass and places it down beside him before running his hands over his face, and I watch as darkness shadows his eyes. I become suddenly aware that I might be the only soul on this island, this world or realm or wherever we are, who knows his truth—who knows what he is.

Here it is. All I have asked for. The verity of Eregahl

unfolded at my feet. And I see the pain it causes him. My heart jumps towards him, but I hush it, needing more yet. "Do you want to go back? To Eradia? If they came now, would you go?"

He looks at me then through his dark lashes, bringing his head up from the wall. "If I am being wholly honest, and since this is the most honest I have ever been with anyone, I shall offer up some more." He leans up to his knees, nearly between my legs. I watch him as he takes my glass from my hand and drains it, too. He tosses it somewhere, moving to place his hands on either side of me, and leans in closer.

His muscles flex and roll beneath his warm skin. Heat radiates from him, and I smell the warm, sweet spirit on his lips. We are eye-to-eye now, and I remember that nothing but a wet tunic stands between my skin and his touch. The fire begins to burn slowly from my core, moving to my neck. I try to force it to extinguish. I need answers. I need him to spend the rest of the night telling me everything I want to know.

He brings a hand to my face and tucks loose hair behind my ear with the other. His fingers send shivers down my body as he drags them across my jaw, taking my chin between his thumb and index finger, pulling my gaze up. "I do not know what I would do if my father came back for me. What I do know is that I stopped asking, stopped caring, stopped begging for answers the moment you set foot on this godforsaken island. I have rarely thought of anything else. You have enchanted me, meeting me step for step in this ridiculous dance of ours. I lie here at night and think of your sharp tongue, of that delicious mind of yours, of the way you taste. I think about how, in three centuries of mindless, menial humans, this witty, brilliant, incredible woman shows up on my doorstep asking all the questions I have been utterly terrified to ask myself. So, I stopped. I ceased asking questions that you were not the answer to, Thorne."

Tears slide with infinite slowness down my face. He abandons the grip on my chin to reach around my waist, and both of his large, strong hands tightly grip me. Here we stand on the edge of an abyss, frozen with nothing but our breath and the rain outside sounding around us.

"I would like to try something if you would allow me. I have a theory. An absurd, unresearched, irrational hypothesis that I would like to test."

"I am not one to get in the way of good research, Master." Relief that banter remains my default floods me, even in the presence of this...glorious, immortal being.

"I think," he says, inching painfully closer to me, "that you might be more than either of us has assumed." Our lips are nearly touching now.

I dare to pull back, looking him dead in the eyes to say, "Underestimating me *is* your favourite thing to do."

He responds with a low growl. "Thorne, there is something at play here, something even I do not understand. I have been cut off for three centuries. My family, the Seren, no one answers me. I have no idea what has changed in the time I have been here, but you smell unlike anything I have ever encountered, and I have known everything the Seren has created."

Before the revelation has time to snake its way into my mind, I renounce it. "But you have never met anyone from my island. Maybe it's just that. Or maybe it is a curse someone placed on my ancestor."

He narrows his eyes at me. "Do you truly believe that? Is that what your blood says to you?"

It is becoming impossible for my mind to work with him this close to me, but I remember I have something to tell him. "When the dearg due attacked me, I went somewhere. I don't know if it was death. It felt like it. It felt like peace and comfort unlike anything I have ever known. But something spoke to me there. Spoke to me with my own voice. Since then, I think she has been...with me. She whispers things to me sometimes." I search his face for a reaction, hoping he might know something about this.

He pulls back to stand straight, shifting his gaze between my eyes and mouth. "What did it say?"

"When she held me, she told me I could not stay there. That my destiny has been carved. She told me all I had to do was pick up my weapon and fight. And Dominus, she keeps telling me to claim you."

His eyes widen. "And what does that make you feel?"

I stand to meet him, to look into those green eyes, the best I can from my height. "At first, I rejected it. I refused the idea because I do not want whatever is happening to force me into anything." He visibly shrinks at that, but I continue. "Because I hated you." I step toward him. "I hated the way you spoke to me. I hated the way you treated me. I hated the way you looked at me." He takes a step back. "I needed to know when that hate began to change, that when our war truly became a dance of something more beautiful, it was because we were choosing each other. I needed to know that outside of the deep, agonising need that I have for you, the cursed girl with the smart mouth who travelled across the sea to be here felt the same, too."

The light returns to his eyes then, blazing with hope. I continue, "You have summoned me for half my life if your theory is correct. I wanted to decide when to answer. I want to be the one who claims you. No other versions of us. No fate or destiny or worlds pushing us together."

I take a deep breath, trying to steady myself. "I choose you, Dominus, because you are my match. You are the one who sees me for all that I am, and you do not look away. You look with hunger and pride. I want to claim you because you are my equal. I want to claim you because somewhere in our dance, hate turned to love. I love you, prophesies and curses be damned."

Before the words fully leave my lips, his mouth is on mine. Gentle, exploratory, as if we were both waiting for something to happen. Another vision, a deamhan to break down the door, the bloody roof to be blown off. All seem like possibilities. I instinctively pull him to me, finally tangling my hands in his hair. He pulls me closer, our bodies uniting.

He lifts me tenderly, and I move my legs to wrap them around his honed waist. He walks us back toward the bed and gently sits me down again. His fingers are steady and certain as they take his tunic at my chest and effortlessly rip it apart as if it were nothing but thin parchment. I pull my arms free, leaving myself wholly bare to him. Raw, aching, yielding. I want to be his canvas. I want him to write poetry upon my flesh. I want him to form me into his very own masterpiece. I want his soul in the shape of his words. I want him to offer me the world with his lips and promise it with his tongue. Let his teeth guard my heart, and the thrum of his voice to sing me to sleep.

"Look at you," he says. I lean back on my hands and crawl back onto the bed. I ease onto my elbows and peer at him with eager eyes. He accepts my invitation, leaning over to begin a trail of kisses from my ankle up my leg. He kisses and rubs and kneads his way up my exposed body, leaving me breathless and needy. He pauses at my navel to look up at me through his dark lashes, the green of his eyes fully glowing now. My blood pulses in my ears.

Love, love, love, love.

"As you may have learned, Miss Alder, I am very thorough in my explorations. I leave no stone unturned. If you want out, tell me now. Because once I taste you again, I will not be able to hold myself back."

I know what he is asking of me and the fear that wavers behind his bravado. Behind his silver tongue lies pure terror because telling me his truth was an offer to his neck, and now he hands me his blade.

He's showing his hand.

All moves have been made.

All steps have been danced.

His grand finale.

And I know, somehow, deep in my core, that this will end me. That there is no coming back from what we are about to do. But I am already his—have already been his—and if my fate is surely sealed, I am going to die filled with love.

"You have offered me so much tonight," I say, running my hands through his hair. "There is still so much to discuss, so much to figure out, but thank you for sharing this with me. For entrusting me with these parts of you." His veneer cracks with every word I speak. "I also need you to know I am aware that I might not be much. I know I am just a frail human with a smart mouth, a stunning backside, and the ability to wield a blade." He offers a smile there, leaning to place gentle kisses on my gnarled, bloody arm. "But whatever I am, how little I might offer you, I am yours. Take what you want from me, Dominus. It has always been yours."

The time for gentleness is gone because Dominus is on me then. Hands and tongues and teeth everywhere. We are breathless, heaving threads of desire, aching to combine. We spend long moments running our hands over every part of each other, learning the dips and curves and softness of one another's bodies.

"Magic these bloody raiments off now," I demand. His laugh is heady and intoxicating, but he does so instantly. His warm, heavy body presses against me. Finally, there is nothing between us. I push him up to his knees to look at him fully. The gods truly did craft him, and he is every bit the carved specimen. The scars on his hands and arms are the only imperfections on his flawless skin. He is crafted, moulded, pulled directly from my dreams and given life. My heart breaks at the sheer beauty of him.

"Are you quite done with your intent observation? Do you find me to your liking?"

"No amount of time will make me tire of looking at you," I say, tears brimming in my eyes. "It makes my heart ache. My hands itch to touch your hair. My mouth waters to taste you. My body craves everything you are, Dominus, and that terrifies me. Thrills me."

He brings his arms around me and pulls me up to him, leaving us on our knees before each other. "That is because you were made for me, Thorne. You are mine; do you understand me? I am yours. Every part of me. I love you, my beautiful, gentle agony."

I melt into him then. Every broken piece of me slowly mends together, every wound stitching closed. Every fear of abandonment and every horror of being unloved floats away. "Then claim me, Dominus."

He lifts me, and I wrap my legs around him as he lowers further onto his knees. He is against me immediately, solid as whatever stone he must have been carved from. We release a shared moan through deep kisses. I run my hands through his midnight hair, tugging roughly at the roots, making him release a guttural moan.

"You are going to be the end of me, Thorne." I only respond by rubbing my pooling wetness against him. "Wait," he says, pulling me away from him slightly. I whimper at the pause. "I have never done this...with a human before."

"You mean to tell me you've been celibate for three centuries?"

"Mostly. 'Tis forbidden to couple with anyone outside our species to preserve the bloodline. Regardless, I had no such desires before you came along."

"I see. Are you sure you want to do this, then?" I ask, sadness beginning to pull me down.

"Of course I do. I want this more than I have ever wanted anything else. I am saying, we must take this slowly. I do not want to hurt you."

Oh. I see. A heated smile spreads across my face then. "For one night only, I concede to you. You lead, Dominus. I will do what I am told."

"You are granting all my dreams tonight, you know?"

"I aim to please." He kisses me then, slower, deeper than before, and I try to remain still. I try not to squirm in his arms. I try not to bury my hands in his hair. I try, but I need him. "Please," I beg between breaths.

He reaches around to grip my waist tightly in one arm and kneads my backside with the other. He moves down, squeezing and scratching as he goes. He places a quick, firm smack to my rear, and it sends heat straight to my core, eliciting a moan. Then he goes further, reaching to slide warm, large fingers down my core. I gasp at the contact, squeezing myself closer to him.

He growls, vibrating my entire body, and I think I might die from need. He runs long, firm strokes before circling my apex as he moves from my mouth to my neck. "Dominus," my plea is breathy and begging.

"Gods, I ache to hear my name on your tongue." As if to reward me, he plunges a finger into me, deep and controlled. I bite his shoulder to keep from screaming. "You maddening, infallible, woman." He adds another, and the muscles of my stomach begin to quiver. He moves down from my neck, taking each breast in his mouth, licking, sucking, and biting. His mouth and his fingers are nearly too much to take, and I wonder if I will be able to handle him inside me after all.

"I need you, Dominus."

He removes his fingers, replacing them immediately with his hardness. He slides it up and down the centre of me, sending me into a frenzy. "Do not move," he commands.

I try my best to be still. I bring his face to my chest and breathe in the scent of him, trying to calm myself. With brutal slowness, he guides himself inside of me, only slightly, and pauses. He squeezes my hips so hard I might bruise. I want to bruise. I want the outlines of his hands burned onto my skin. I whimper again, needing all of him, needing to be consumed by him. Another inch, another pause.

"Thorne," he moans.

"More," I demand.

He slides in further and pauses again. I squeeze myself around him, acclimating to his size. He loosens another moan, and the sound of it undoes me. I place my hands on the back of his neck, pulling his hair, and giving me his face. I look him in the eyes as I slide all the way down him until I'm fully seated, stretched, and finally filled.

His voice is rough and low. "You refuse to submit, don't you?" My only answer is to rise the long length of him and slide back down. I lose control then. My soul shatters inside me. My heart breaks completely. I am fully undone in his arms.

Dominus lifts me and places me gently against his soft linens, and I am entirely bathed in his scent. He tenderly moves in and out of me, testing my reaction, making sure I am not hurt. I move my hips in encouragement, meeting him thrust for thrust, release building in me already. As I do, he comes unravelled, animalistic, and I revel in it.

He fills me completely. His every stroke caresses that sensitive spot inside of me, pushing me closer to the edge. "You are more than I could have imagined, " I offer breathlessly.

"You are mine. Your body, your soul is mine."

"Yours," I agree.

"Say my name, Thorne." His command sends me to the edge of that pinnacle.

"Dominus." I pull his hair, tugging him down to me. I gently bite the lobe of his ear and whisper, "Dominus, I am yours"

With that, he slams into me without hesitation, sending me over the edge of my climax. Thrust after thrust, he sends me longer and harder. The pleasure is ceaseless, unending. I claw his back and dig my heels into him, holding on for dear life as I pulse around the thickness of him.

"That's right, keep going. I want every bit of your release."

His words send me spiralling into another wave, and it becomes too much. I want to beg him to stop. I want to beg him for more. The swell finally begins to recede, but with it, my need only grows. I bring his neck to my mouth and bite hard enough to make him wince, but the cry quickly turns into a moan of pleasure.

I have had great lovers before. I have spent many nights in exploration with tender touches and hungry hands. But this. This is different. To share your body with someone who has seen the darkest parts of you. Nothing will ever feel like this. I want this eternally. I want to consume him. I want to die beneath the weight of him. I want every place we touch to burn with the memory of this. I want to devour his heart.

Then I am reminded of the mating ritual. I tell myself that it is too soon. We only just confessed how we feel, and we need time. Something inside violently thrashes against my hesitance, then spurges forward, consuming me. I love him. There is no one else. There is nothing outside of this. We have laid ourselves open and offered our souls to each other. We have accepted each other for all our faults and darkness. He has summoned me, waited for me, prayed for me. Now, wyths, yehrs from now, it does not matter. I am his.

"Dominus," I say, placing my hand on his chest.

"Are you hurt?" He runs his hands over my body.

"Not at all."

"What is it? What do you need?"

I look into his eyes for a long moment. His beautiful, pale green eyes. Those onyx lashes, his full, beautiful mouth covering white, lupine teeth. There will never be anything other than him. He is my home. He is my destiny.

Yes, she whispers distantly, and the choice feels made.

"I want the vision. I want to bond with you."

He pulls up from me, removing himself, and backs onto his knees. My body nearly shatters with the lack of contact. "Thorne. I cannot ask this of you. I cannot ask you to bind yourself to me. I possess no certainty of what that even means or what it looks like for us."

"I know, I know. But that does not make me want it any less, and I have not allowed myself to want in a very long time. I am not sure I can stop it now." I rise and sit low on my knees, too. I place my hands on his thighs and lean into him. "I want you. Now, forever, for whatever time we have. I want to love and be loved. I want to own you and for you to own me. I want to share a soul with you. This is something I never thought I would have. I have prepared myself for the lack of love for a long time. I have it now. I cannot let that go. I cannot live without this anymore. Even if it kills me. I will go to my grave blissfully happy, loved, and wanted."

Tears fall from his stunning eyes, and I lean forward to kiss them away. "It is as if you know that I would rather die than deny your every desire." He brings his hands to my face, placing his forehead to mine. "Those are words I never thought I would hear. Especially not by someone so perfect for me. Someone I chose." He leans back to allow me to swim in his gaze. "I ache to show you how I can love you. I want you to wake each day knowing that you have me. Are you certain about this? Thorne, if we do this, there is no going back. There is no undoing of this. It will be us until the very end."

I consider his words, but then I question what my life would look like if I went back. Went back to what? Ghosts in a lonely home? I have found everything I have searched for here and more. He is the only man who might withstand whatever is brewing within me. "There is nothing for me without you." He pulls me in for a deep, long kiss. "Show me what to do," I breathe.

He stands to retrieve my skean from the settee. He carries it with a tight grip back around the bed. The light from the torches flickers across his skin, and I envy it for being able to dance upon him like that. To mould to every inch of him.

"We must be precise. I will not tempt your life, do you understand?" I nod to him. "I will go first, that way you are stronger with my blood inside of you. Then I will take what is mine."

Yes, yes, yes, my blood sings.

I blink, and he is back on his knees in front of me, handing the blade to me by the tip. "I never thought I would see this again. I honestly forgot about it. This was mine. From home. Fitting that you found it. You have been nothing but a constant reminder to me of who I once was. Who I hope to be again." He looks at me with centuries of memories in his eyes. Memories I crave to learn. "I am going to say something. You must repeat after me word for word."

"Yes."

He places his hand over mine and guides the blade to his rib cage, placing the tip upward between two of the bones. He takes a deep, shaking breath and stares with desperation into my eyes. "I give you my blood, my body, my soul. I bind myself to you for eternity. I grant you my power. I offer you my heart. I swear you my love. My sacrifice is yours."

Simple. Resplendent. Absolute.

Tears streak both of our faces, but our eyes do not dare to look away from each other. Dominus does not let go of my hand on the blade, and together, we push it through the bones, muscle, and tissue, and slowly, barely, into his heavily beating heart. He does not move nor give any indication of pain. No, he relishes it. We gently guide it back out, and he takes it from me. Softly placing one hand around my throat, he brings the blade to my mouth.

"Consume what is rightfully yours." The air around us hums. That static sonation thrums through me like the strike of a tuning fork. Time stills, waiting for me to move. Slowly, I open my mouth and, for the second time, lick his blood clean from my blade.

It tastes exquisite—euphoric. That wicked thing inside me thrills with satisfaction and grows with hunger. My head rolls back as magic rushes through every part of me. It reminds me of when he cast it in the inn, and I felt it. That was but a speck of dust compared to this.

Warmth floods my entire body, rushing my blood. I am powerful. I am infinite. Every emotion I have ever endured in an episode consumes me, but it's as if a missing piece has slid into place, and there is no pain. No agony. No grief. Only love.

Squeeze, swell, squeeze, swell.

I am empty; I am flooded.

I am nothing; I am infinite.

I am *his*.

"Look at me," he demands. When I lift my head and open my eyes, Dominus is lit with a warm, golden glow. I blink a few times, realising the lumination is from my eyes, shining like the sun across his perfect face.

"Finally." He beams at me with pride and love. I kiss him deeply, trying to convey the happiness he has given me. Then I pull from him and repeat his words effortlessly.

"I give you my blood, my body, my soul. I bind myself to you for eternity. I grant you my power. I offer you my heart. I swear you my love. My sacrifice is yours." As I do, I lie back on the bed, offering him every part of me.

He does not speak. There is no need. He leans down, the blade still in his hand, and wraps his arms around my legs. Then he tastes me. A groan escapes him, and his gentle licks quickly turn into desperate feasting.

"Dominus," I plead, begging for more, praising him for his

worship. He moves to run his tongue up my entire body, ending the trail with a demanding kiss. Pleasure washes over me as he sinks back into me again. The thrusts are languid and deep as he glides the blade across my peaked nipples. He guides it down to the same place between my ribs. Seated fully into me, he wraps his strong hand around the back of my neck.

I nod to him, and he places his forehead against mine as he slowly pushes the blade in, bringing my vision to life. Where I thought would be unyielding pain is only undeniable pleasure. The rightness of it sings in my bones. I feel the blade as it pierces my heart, as it tastes my soul, clinging to it. It lingers, even when he retracts the blade and licks it clean, never breaking contact with my eyes. I feel it as it enters him, as it merges with his own.

Then the thrumming comes to a pinnacle, a vibration so high, I fear my teeth might chatter, and where I existed, he now exists too. Where I was alone and broken, he now fills all the voids. We are bound, united in love, in power, and in soul. The vibration morphs into something else, something beautiful and haunting and wholly ours.

The thing inside me stirs to life, shining and shimmering in triumph. Words form in my mind. Words of a language unknown to me. They speak out to him, claim him, accept him.

"What does that mean?" he asks.

I do not know the words, yet their meaning is clear to me. "It means I claim you as my own. You cannot forsake me."

"I swear to you, I never will. I love you, mo céasadh."

"I love you, Dominus."

With that, his movement resumes. And we are floating. We are endless and infinite and together. I wrap myself around him, wishing we could merge our bodies as we have our souls, wishing I could climb beneath his skin.

He sucks my neck, my chest, and fully abandons his control. His coarse moans and punishing pace send me closer and closer, and when he climaxes, I do, too, his pleasure wringing me of my own. Dominus roars with satisfaction, clinging to me like salvation, and as he does, tremendous, glorious, midnight wings explode from his back.

PART TWO

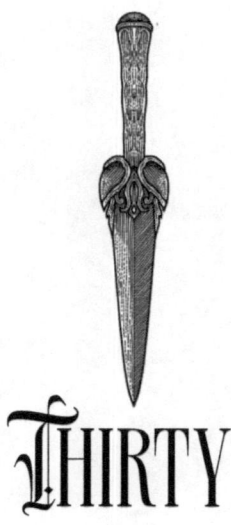

ᚦHIRTY

The walls shudder around us, but Dominus does not move. He only kisses me further, deeper, complete consumption.

"Dominus," I breathe. He doesn't say a word. Instead, he wraps his strong arms around me and sinks his face into my neck. We lay quietly, basking in the glow of what we've just done. The breadth of which I do not think is fully comprehensible to either of us.

"Shábháil tú mé," he says in that language I now understand. *You saved me.*

"No, my love, it is you who has saved me," I whisper into his hair. He finally brings his head up to look at me. When he does, a crown of black smoke haloes his head. My soul preens at the sight of him. Glory, honour, power. The beginning and the end.

"Is this new, or is this part of your true form?" I ask, reaching my fingers to glide through it. The dark vapour dances along my skin, up my arm, and forms a matching crown atop my head. Pure nirvana reflects in his glowing eyes.

"It is partially my original form, though it used to glow with golden light."

"And the wings. Have they always been this majestic?"

Closing his eyes and dragging in a deep inhale, he extends them out fully. Relief floods him as his massive wings cover us in darkness. "These are all me." He rolls his neck around and shifts the muscles of his back, adjusting to the weight of them.

Six angular wings dipped in obsidian feathers splay and twitch in the space above me. Dominus stretches them even further, revealing a single eye in the centre of each wing. Each of them copies of his own, pale green, intently aware, and blazing with divine light. They assess me, staring into my soul, discerning something of me, perhaps judging, weighing my worthiness.

I touch the uppermost wing on his left side, and he does not stop me. His eyes scour me, searching for my retreat. I can sense through this strange, new connection that he's waiting for me to flee. Waiting for this to become too much. My heart breaks that he does not know there is nothing that could turn me away from him.

The contact with the silky smooth feathers sends shivers through me. The impossible softness of them makes me want to wrap them around me. I want them to touch every part of my skin. "How fascinating."

"Can you imagine that these feathers can turn into the

sharpest of blades that I can fire and regenerate?"

My fingers hesitate, but I run them along the vast planes of them anyway. "That is terrifyingly impressive," I whisper.

He chokes a laugh at that. "You are taking all of this surprisingly well. Or you are pretending that you are, only to plan your escape the moment I am out of sight."

"It is rather presumptuous of you to assume I will allow you out of my sight. Ever. And you had better bite your tongue before I do. That kind of talk is forbidden."

His eyes, all eight of them, darken. "Forgive me. I only fear that this is all too good to be true. I have you. I have my wings. I have my power back. I have everything."

"Except you are still here."

"There is no other place in any other land or realm that I would rather be."

Pure love heats me from the inside out, and I launch myself on him again. When I do, it sends us hurtling off the bed. Two giant beats of Dom's wings stop us from colliding with the floor.

"What was that?" I nearly scream.

"Remember how I said the nodus allows us to imbue each other, to share certain intricacies? I believe you have already retrieved some of my qualities, though that is exceptionally fast. It usually takes menoths of us consuming one another for the effects to take."

Consuming. The word from his mouth is oil to my flame, and it sets me afire instantly. But before I can sink my teeth into him again, someone bangs violently on his door, our eyes widening with surprise.

"Get dressed," he demands, and I press my thighs together

in response to the command in his tone as I move to find something to wear.

"I have no raiments in—" I look down, and a long, velvet dressing gown, the same black of his wings, is wrapped around my body. "We just wasted a significant amount of time if you could have done that in the first place."

Bang, bang, bang.

Dominus closes his eyes and whispers in that ancient language that I now understand perfectly, and when he opens his eyes, our crowns of black smoke and his wings are gone. He remains dressed in nothing but a pair of clean, pressed pants.

"Stay there." Dominus strolls to open the door. To our shared surprise, Thair stands on the other side, fury ebbing around him in a hazy red aura. Before I have time to ask what that is, Thair pushes his way in and stops to stand between us. He sniffs deeply, causing my mouth to turn in anger. Dominus closes the door.

"What have you done?" Thair pleads. Dominus surveys him, and I can imagine all the wonderful and hideous things he is considering responding with. But then his brows scrunch together, and the energy in the room changes. Dominus retreats a step, and I can faintly discern confusion and doubt flood him. Then, slowly, Dom raises a hand in the air and traces an invisible symbol.

Glowing, bright light covers Thair, and when it shimmers away, someone else stands in his place: a male as tall as Dominus with pale blond curls and bright blue eyes. Thair's warm skin remains, but his features have changed, softening in places while hardening in others. Remnants of Thair only hazily linger.

He wears fighting leathers, similar to Dom's, but somehow, they are *more*. Slim, silver armour adorns his chest, shoulders, and knees. He whispers something, and feathered, ivory wings, a matching set to Dom's, emerge from his back.

Standing there, they nearly look like inversions of each other. Where Dominus is dark hair and pale skin, this man is his opposite.

"Icarus," Dominus whispers.

A crisp, rich voice responds, "Hello, Brother."

Icarus, one of Dom's long-lost siblings. Or, should I say, traitorous, abandoning, spineless pieces of—

"You have been here this whole time? What—when— Dominus takes a ragged breath. "You have two minutes to explain yourself before I disembowel you," he growls.

"Me? You need me to explain when you just formed a nodus with a fucking human?" Icarus turns to me then, "No offence, love. Trust me when I say I understand the temptation." Then he winks at me. He bloody winks at me. Oh, gods. I kissed him. I nearly...

My palms begin to itch. No, they begin to hum.

"Icarus!" Dominus storms him, wrapping his hand around his throat. "You should know better than to speak about someone else's notorum that way. I will boil your fucking bones and drink the broth, brother or not."

Notorum.

The word hums through me instantly with understanding. The one whom I recognise as familiar. The one I want to know and explore. Yes, he is my notorum. The soul I choose to navigate life with, whose depths I yearn to discover.

Icarus raises his hands in submission. "Apologies. I forgot how...passionate you are."

"I am certain you have, since you abandoned me hundreds of yehrs ago."

"Release me, and I will explain everything. There is much we need to talk about, Brother. There is much I need to tell you and even some things I must beg your forgiveness for."

That piques his interest, and Dominus slowly releases him. With it, his rage uncoils from my abdomen, allowing me to take a full breath. Then he is immediately at my side and wraps his arm around my waist. He whispers, *"Sedes,"* and a small table and three chairs appear in front of the blazing hearth. Dom pulls my seat out for me. The menial act nearly has me panting, and I work to regain control of myself.

"So, does Thair even exist, or was that just a skin you bore?" I ask, distracting and focusing my mind.

Icarus conjures his wings away, grinning at me. When he does, those armour plates dissolve as well, and he remains in leathers alone.

"Ah, Thorne, what's the matter? Grieving for poor Thair? You chose this one, need I remind you?" he says, waving his hand at Dom. "Though, do not doubt, I would have thoroughly satisfied that itch of yours."

I wonder if the arrogance and rakish mouth run in the family. Dominus loosens a warning growl at him. Icarus blows a kiss at him.

"Start talking," Dominus adds.

"Thair was just a skin. Sorry, love. I came here to spy on you," he says to Dominus.

Dom's answering laugh is cynical and terrifying. "Spy on me? Spy on me doing what exactly, *Brother?* Withering away, doing nothing besides slaughtering deamhans for centuries, lost to everyone and everything I have ever known? I hope it was a pleasing show for you. You have been here for nearly a yehr. Why haven't you made yourself known sooner?"

"I would not have made myself known now had you not just released some of the many binds on this island."

Dom's answering gape is response enough for Icarus to continue.

"Right, so I am going to attempt this in a single go, so secure yourselves. A few wyths before our raid here, I heard Father talking to someone in the throne room. He vehemently expressed his immense fear of little ol' you." He draws circles on the table with a long finger. "See, our dear father is not at all who we thought him to be. Surprise! Behind the facade of honour and grace, he cowers in fear and craves power. He knew your power was vast, and he knew it would surpass his own. So, in an attempt to maintain his hold over the Eradian army, he struck a deal to remain on the throne for a bit longer."

"A deal with whom?" Dom asks, the tension rising impossibly higher.

"Patience, little brother, I am getting there. Don't ruin my moment."

It become clear why Dominus called him slimy before. Icarus exudes evasive, lubricious behaviour. Even now, he mocks the fate of his brother's life.

"So, Father dearest devised a ruse: A raid in Eregahl to whittle the numbers of Hellas' growing deamhan army. We arrive, do our job, and he surprises us all with the charade that you are to be left here to earn your worthiness of the throne. I will be honest; I was tickled pink at first. Having my flawless, all-powerful baby brother out of the way for a while might allow some sunlight for the rest of us to grow. Fina and Camiel were not as ecstatic, you'll be glad to know. They pleaded with Father not to leave you here or to allow them to return to help you, but he was adamant. He served us well-prepared arguments that a leader must be ready to face any fate thrown at him, and he must gladly abide by the will of the Seren."

Icarus taps the table, and three glasses appear with the same decanter of spirits from the bookshelf. He magically pours us all a drink.

"Turns out, having you gone was woefully unsatisfying. Father took to work with the war band, aiming to build himself so high that, if you ever returned, you could not touch him. Mother secretly grieved for yehrs. In front of us, she mustered the strength she could to mimic his sentiments, but it fell on deaf ears." He sharpens his eyes, and his demeanour hardens.

"I began to do some research for myself then, curious to know what else Father might be lying about. I spent yehrs digging into the Seren's past. I travelled the lands, using my particular brand of cunning to learn what no one else could. Noreg and Caledon survived the war, but they are deep in hiding. So deep, they will not speak to me. The pain of it. The sorrow of your creators, your masters, denying you—ah, I suppose you know well enough what that feels like."

He tosses another drink back. "I *was* able to learn that Father was gifted with arcane spells that bound you here, stripping you of your magic. He had help, though. I followed that trail, and do you know where it led me, Dominus?"

"Where?" he deadpans.

The energy in the room pauses, watching, waiting, hanging on his every word. A pang of dread seeps from Dominus.

"Straight to Hellas' doorstep." He grins widely as he says it, as if this is all some hilarious, twisted farce.

"What do you mean?" Dominus nearly whispers.

"As it turns out, Brother, Adonien traded your life to Hellas to remain on the throne. You were to remain his entirely. A mhargadh. They would strip you of your power and bind you to this land, never to return, so that you may not lead the Seren's army against him. They both feared you so much that they cut off your wings and stuffed you in a jar. They knew the other gods would not sacrifice themselves to come to your aid, but if they did, that would suit their plan well enough. A prisoner, certainly, but perhaps bait as well." His smile is disgusting.

I cannot determine if it is Dom's anger or my own that vibrates through my body. Then I ignite, and I know that it is both. I expect him to explode, to flip this table, to strangle Icarus until he turns blue. But he does not move. He does not react. His hand shakes slightly as he brings the glass to his lips and drains it.

Icarus' smile fades slightly. "When I found out, I went to Father. I tried to oust him. Tried to get him to undo what he had done. He told me I was a witless boy dealing in things far beyond me. And you know what he did after that, Dominus?" His smile turns my stomach. "He offered me your bloody job." He wholeheartedly laughs then, edging toward maniacal. "He offered me everything I had ever wanted on a fucking golden platter, Dom. And it made me sick. It made my guts twist because I knew it was his offer of control. Stay, be quiet, and my dreams would come true."

I study Dominus as my blood pumps too loudly in my ears. He remains wordless as he stares at Icarus, who swirls the liquid in his glass. Then his smile fades, and he licks his teeth before continuing. He sets his eyes on Dominus. "What he failed to understand, my littlest brother, was that I watched you our entire lives. I watched you constantly outdo us all, progressing faster than any Erad before. I stomped my feet as you attended meetings and balls that the rest of us were not invited to. I studied and envied everything about you."

He pauses for a moment, allowing the truth to rest. Then he takes a deep inhalation. "But when he offered me your throne," he chokes, something else slippery lining his eyes, "well, I realised then that only one of us deserved it, had spent every minute earning the right to sit there. And I knew you would be the only one to stop him."

Dominus white-knuckles the glass, only a heartbeat away from shattering. On a new instinct, I push my love back in the direction from which I felt his emotions. The grip eases slightly.

"He plans something big, Dominus. He intends to join forces with Hellas to find and end the other Seren, allowing Hellas full control to reign forever. Father is deluded. He thinks Hellas will allow him to remain king indefinitely. I left before I had a chance to warn Fina and Camiel, but I know they would stand with you. I left willingly. I came here knowing that you would likely turn me away and not believe a word I said. I had to spend time with you, get to know who you have become here, and find a way to break the bonds this land holds on you. That was the plan, at least." He slides his focus to me briefly.

Dom's eyes glisten from across the table, and he releases a deep breath. "Icarus, you bloody fool. Have you learned nothing during your time here?" Icarus and I both recoil at that. "I have been stranded here for three hundred yehrs. I have prayed, summoned, and begged for someone, any of you, to find me. I would have kissed your fucking feet had you come to me."

I suddenly feel like I am imposing on something I should not see. Icarus fights to hold onto his mask. He coughs roughly and slaps the table. "But good thing I didn't, right? Because that left this minx enough time to swoop in and steal your heart and save the day. I do not know how, but your nodus broke many of the spells keeping you here and restricting magic." He gestures to me, and Dominus follows his gaze. We look at each other for the first time after Icarus unearthed all these truths. I take him in, all his glory. A king fit for a throne. The only one powerful enough to stand against his own traitorous father and a turned Seren. Two entities that gave him life, who were supposed to love and protect him.

It is truly selfish of me to sit here, hearing this, and wonder where I fit in all of it. I am powerless. I am nothing to him and his world. Shame washes over me.

Domimus places his hands on my face before I have time to finish my thought. "Don't you dare. Do not consider for one fucking second that this changes a thing between us. I will abandon every bit of this if it means losing you."

Icarus scoffs, and I strongly desire to smack his disgustingly beautiful face. I miss Thair.

"Absolutely not. I will not let you. This is what you were made for, Dominus. This is what you have spent centuries waiting for. I will not step in the way of your destiny."

"You brilliant, senseless fool. *You* are my destiny. None of this means a thing without you. I desire not to save a world you are not in."

Icarus be damned, I let the love shine through. I let it set my eyes aglow. I let him see what he means to me.

"Bloody spirits, what is that?" Icarus asks, his brows near his hairline as he stares at me.

"I assume she has taken on my traits. That is how this works, you know. Though I am quite surprised it is so soon."

"Dominus, you know that a nodus between an Erad and a human is forbidden, unsanctioned, unheard of."

Domnus whips his head to his brother. "Sense her, Icarus. Remove my scent and tell me what you smell."

I feel like a child sitting in an infirmary as two physickers poke and prod me.

Icarus roams my body briefly before responding, "The same thing I smelled as she stood on a boat still out at sea. Power, Brother. She smells like power, unlike anything I have ever felt."

"Precisely."

"This is dangerous. Whatever she is, your nodus released woven fabrics upon this world. We need to get to work testing what those are. We need a fucking plan. Because we cannot go back. You and me, Dominus, united at last. Well, and our girl, I suppose. 'Tis us against the world. Quite literally. Hellas will come for you. You are his. He will not allow you to slip from his grasp. He gave too much to keep you here."

My heart lurches at Icarus' words, but Dom continues, "Then you had better hope we snapped enough threads that I can shift. Do you have your full abilities here?"

Icarus drums his long fingers across the table as if he is weighing whether to tell the truth. "Yes and no. I have access to it, but I have veiled it. I did not want Father to track my magic here. So, I will keep it hidden until necessary. That is what I can afford. And you had better find a way to abate yours immediately. Gods know that will be difficult with the nodus. If Hellas thinks the change did not affect you, maybe he can stay hidden until his big move."

My mind warps and twists. Every hope, wish, dream, and desire I have had since my family's death was granted mere moments ago. And now, I sit here with everything in jeopardy. Maybe I am cursed after all. I thought my future would consist of long days of working on the journal and long nights wrapped around Dominus. I thought we would stay in this castle and fill our bellies with Elowyn's food and our hearts with the love we have for one another. We would spar beneath the giant willows in the forest. He would show me all the hidden treasures of Eregahl. We would write and continue to learn together.

Now, we stand in the middle of a war. The man I love is the rightful heir. The only one standing between every person on this island and the claws and teeth of Hellas' deamhans. I want to pity myself. I want to scream how this isn't fair, how I lose everyone I love, but then I remember... There are other people on this island that I love. Eamon. Elowyn. Norine. All these scolers. Then I am grateful that I have people to fight for, people to protect.

A family.

A new clarity dissolves into me, and I break the growing silence. "You two will train me. You will teach me everything you know in whatever time we have. We will do what we can to conceal the nodus. I will use whatever gifts I get from Dominus, and I will use them to fight until my last breath. I will fight," I say, swallowing the swallowing the permanent lump in my throat, "because I have something to fight for." Silence blankets the room as the words fall around us.

To my surprise, Icarus speaks first. "You blessed bastard. Only you would get dumped in a wasteland, stripped of your power, and left to your own devices to find yourself a fucking queen. I have endured enough of this. Enjoy tonight. Come dawn, we prepare."

Dominus gazes at me as Icarus abandons us with the weight of the world, slamming the door behind him. "How is it that the moment I think I have you figured out, you pull my bloody feet from beneath me and leave me in complete admiration and utter awe of you?"

His words crack me down the middle, but I try with all my might to pull the pieces back together, to be strong for him, for us both. "Because underestimating me *is* your favourite thing to do." I mimic my words from earlier in the night. The most incredible moments of my life, so distant now.

"'Tis my second favourite thing to do," he says, leaning forward to snatch me from my chair and place me in his lap. "And that is only because I relish seeing you go farther than what I even expect of you."

I wrap my legs around him and run my hands along the planes of his bare back. I want him. I need him like I need to breathe, but this is all so indulgent, so selfish when there is a world to save.

"Give me the night. Give me one night to ravage and consume you. One night to act on my deepest, wildest, most depraved fantasies with my notorum. I have waited many lifetimes for you. The end of the world can wait one bloody night. Come dawn, we will work to figure this out, I promise. Give me this. Give me you."

"You need not beg, Dominus, but oh, it is divine when you do."

We waste no time returning to our frenzied exploration of one another. With every starving touch, each tender kiss, and each desperate thrust, we lose ourselves more and more and more and become something of which the world has never seen.

ᎿHIRTY ᎾNE

We waste no time sleeping, and I watch the sun as it crests over the cliff. Its warmth spreads over my skin as I take Dominus languidly, relishing in the way he feels beneath me, inside of me, wrapped around me. I work to memorise every moment, not knowing what the future holds for us.

"You are the most stunning creature I have ever laid eyes on." His voice is raw, and it rakes across my skin.

"A grand compliment coming from the most beautiful creation to ever walk this earth." I let my eyes glow as I say it. I let his own perfect gift reflect on him. He rises to wrap his arms around me and stands, still seated within me. He walks us over to the windows and places me gently against the smooth, stone frame of the centre window.

"Let me see you shine in the light of the day. Let this world see how beautiful and perfect you are."

Considering his command, I place both arms behind me and drop my head back. My long, loose hair floats along the warm wind, and the sun heats my face. With my legs still wrapped around his waist, Dominus gently pulls out of me and sinks back in again, the angle offering him a deeper position, and I tighten around him with pleasure.

"Gods, look at you."

I bring my head up to meet his glowing green eyes. He glistens in the morning haze, too; a spotlight on a masterpiece. My core begins to shake looking at him. I let my gaze follow his to the divine point at which we meet, his broad hands along the generous curves of my hips, the way they dive in toward my rib cage now altered by a faint scar, all the way to my round, full breasts that bound with each of his strokes. I notice, though, that the muscles in my thighs have become more defined, that my arms are pillars beneath me, unwavering and not at all tired from holding myself up.

Dominus reaches to cup a hand to my face. I lean into it, breathing him in, and pebble kisses along his fingers before biting the heel of his palm. He rewards me by thrusting harder, immediately sending me over the edge. My entire body quickens and shakes beneath him, and I scream out his name, causing the shrikes flying above to disperse. My plea sends him to climax with me, and we spend a long moment suspended in ecstasy.

"Is this standard post-ritual behaviour? Because at this very moment, I could never tire of this. I could do without food and sleep just to have your body pressed against mine."

"Yes, mo céasadh. This is very usual. The nodus demands

it. It's to solidify our souls and help ease the blend of them. The closer we are, the better the nodus settles, and the more possibilities we have of sharing gifts. It is not uncommon for the nodus to manifest something new of its own, something created by shared magic."

"That is purely magnificent. What happens if we don't spend enough time...together? Does that jeopardise it in any way?"

"Not necessarily. We enacted the nodus, so it will always be there. There is no unmerging of souls, but the strength of it, and of what comes out of it, does correlate with the care that we provide for it in the initial yehrs. In the care we provide for each other."

I never thought I would be loved again. This—this goes far beyond my dreams. "I want to care for it. I want to nurture it as much as we can, with everything going on. You, this nodus, are important to me. I want to create the strongest foundation we can have."

"The way you throw earth-shattering words at me with such nonchalance is a gift in and of itself. I know this is my world, and this is all new to you. I would not fault you for a single moment if you needed time to adjust and take it all in. You have exceeded all my expectations, and the fact that you continue to lean into this, well, I cannot believe you are mine. We will nurture this nodus as much as you desire. You come before all else in my life. The moment you need me, I am yours."

"Smile, Dominus, so that I may see the remains of my heart in your teeth. Then, you may continue your worship of me."

"You had better stop talking, or we are never leaving this

room." He pulls me to him, skating his tongue across my bottom lip. The hungry thing inside of me spurs to life. Will it ever be satisfied?

"What happens if we deny the nodus?"

"We don't. Though beautiful and intense, the nodus can be intense and selfish. If there ever comes a time when it demands something from us, we must appease it. There will be moments for us both when we must have the other. We need to do everything we can to give in to that—to feed it. 'Tis quite similar to a newborn babe. We must take care of it and its irrational desires until it is established. It will not always be in control. Things will change in a few yehrs. That is why this is a choice. It is a tremendous responsibility. It takes time and effort and should never be entered into lightly."

"I do not think a few yehrs of this will be enough," I say, gripping his hair.

"Forever will not be enough, Thorne."

Without releasing me, he carries us into the bathing chamber where he washes us both. We soak in silence, running our hands over each other, memorising every dimple, dip, and bend, completely terrified to break this moment, unready to leave the sanctuary and bliss of this one night that we allowed ourselves to have.

Bathed, clean, and naked, Dominus leads us back into the bedroom where he whispers a spell, and my wardrobe appears next to his. "I took the liberty of filling the bottom drawers with my raiments if you wish to wear them."

"If you think I was a needy, scent-hungry monster before, you have no idea what you have unleashed upon the world. I will do my best today not to embarrass us both by burying my nose in the pit of your arm."

"You do as you please, mo céasadh. I am yours to do with as you see fit. That is one of the many beauties of you finally knowing the truth; you have nothing to hide from anyone anymore. You are mine, and I am yours, and I want the entire bloody world to know it. Except maybe Hellas. We may postpone that one for a while."

Ah, and there goes the moment, our one night. It is now time to figure out how to keep Hellas and Adonien from eviscerating the defenceless humans of Eregahl.

"I cannot help but feel this is my fault. Had I not asked to enact the nodus, this would not have happened. The people of this island would be safe. We would not be up against this. We could have taken our time," I admit.

"Though I appreciate your misplaced accountability, this does not fall on you. The snapping of the spells only—potentially—hastened the inevitable. The deal with Hellas and my father was made long ago. This was always going to happen. I only wish I had known sooner—had ever suspected..."

We stand together quietly, lost in thought and introspection. I stare at my raiments blankly, wondering what is appropriate to wear to such an event. Dominus must have the same idea, because my skin hums, and I look down to find myself wearing my very own fighting leathers.

"Though I am desperately curious about what wicked things you would have donned today, these seem most appropriate."

"It certainly does, and I love them. Thank you."

"I will always provide for you, Thorne. I will give you space to do things yourself and the resources to do so, or I will spend my days conjuring whatever you ask of me."

I am aware this might require some adjusting. As someone who has spent their entire life wildly independent, my gut reaction is to squirm. The old me would have told him to sod off and that I can take care of myself. But this, whatever undiscovered version of me is, appreciates the gesture. I am considered.

"Thank you," I say, but I know that my soul is his own, and I know he stands here now wholly understanding my past and knowing exactly that it means everything.

I oil the ends of my hair in Dom's scent and plait it back. My sense of smell has changed since the ritual. While the oil still scratches the itch, it lacks my favourite part: the smell of his skin. I do my best to stifle the need already rising in me and prepare for the distance.

As if the thought of dread summoned him, Icarus knocks on the door. Knocks, but then swings it open with his hand covering his eyes. "Am I interrupting?"

"No," Dominus growls.

"Damn it." He drops his hands and takes us in.

"Well, I came in here to devise a plan, but priority number one is masking this nodus, or we might as well hogtie ourselves to the front gates."

Dominus closes his eyes and whispers, *"Ceilt."* When he opens his eyes, the difference threatens to suffocate me. My insides feel wrapped in spider webbing. Where I felt sparkling and radiant in the new glow of my nodus, I now feel stuffed into a musty old trunk. And the nodus is outraged.

"Mm. That is a rather interesting sensation."

"I know, mo céasadh. But this is necessary. If it were not, I would not allow this. Trust me when I say, I could kill Hellas for this alone."

Icarus rolls his eyes. "Right. Your turn, darling," he says to me, waiting impatiently.

"What is it exactly that I am supposed to do?"

"Veil your scent, your nodus, and whatever else crawls inside of you that reeks of power."

I look at Dominus in confusion. "Are both of you aware that I am not an ancient magical being? Some guidance might be helpful to complete the task."

"One that I intended to help her with before you arrived. Sit down, and silence that insufferable mouth of yours, Brother. Your presence here will likely only make this harder."

Icarus gapes at us with feigned contempt, and I think that if I didn't hate him, I might find him humorous. Though the more I consider it, the more I see how that humour, a certain version of him, radiated in Thair. The parts I adored. He sits at the table and chairs from last night. Dominus moves to me, taking my hands in his.

"The use of magic is very complex and varies by its user. Though certain spells and usages are generic in a sense, the way they are cast depends on the individual. Our magic is extremely emotional. Intent and delivery are equally important."

"We don't even know if I can do this."

"And we will not until we try. Close your eyes and clear your mind."

I do as instructed, making a note to inform Dominus later

that he needs to bring his scolemaster's voice to the bedroom.

He growls.

"Sorry! Sorry." Not really.

"Clear your mind."

I close my eyes and inhale Dominus; the fastest way to peace I have found yet. I let his scent cover me and empty my thoughts.

"This is the unpleasant portion. I want you to think of me. Think of our nodus. Think about the connection between us." The nodus hums at the attention.

"Now, I want you to imagine a shield, a cover, a wall, whatever it looks like for you, covering everything that is us."

I do as he says, wrapping everything that is us in a thicket of moss and branches and deadly sharp thorns.

"Good. That's it."

Quiet down, you needy beast, I threaten myself.

"Now, tighten the branches, grow the thorns, make it utterly impenetrable. Cover every single crevice. Lock your scent in there with mine, cover it all. Imagine you are keeping it safe, protecting it, and no one can see or sense it. Yes, phenomenal job. Now, leave nothing but a cobweb, a trail of lichen, something small and unnoticeable. Make it a trail to me."

Sweat begins to form on my brow, and I push my mind to do everything he instructs. It's painful, not the magic, but covering us this way. Our mingled souls beg to be let out and to shine, but I promise the nodus that it will have its time and that we must keep it safe. It reluctantly stops pushing against the thicket, and I form a small shrike bird and place it at the entrance as my tether to him.

"It's done."

"Finally, I want you to think about what we are doing, why we are doing this. It is protection for each other, for our nodus, for our lives, and the lives of others. When you are ready, speak the word 'Ceilt' to seal it.

I consider his words, and I tell our nodus that I love it and that I will protect it at all costs. I think of Eamon and Elowyn. I think of the academy and the scolers. I think of everything I now have—everything I can lose—as I open my mouth and speak the word.

"Ceilt." Magic vibrates through my entire body, across our souls, and into Dominus. Grief floods me with the dulling of the greatest gift I have ever been given. I open my eyes, and the same sentiment shines in his eyes.

"I know, love. I know. When we are alone, I will teach you how we can open the space up between the two of us."

I lean in to kiss him, needing to feel the certainty that he is still mine.

"I will admit," Icarus starts, causing us to pull apart too quickly, "that was rather impressive. Dare I say you might be a natural?"

"It's the magic and the instruction of a phenomenal master. That is all. What's next?"

His smile is diabolical as he replies, "To the armoury."

Thirty Two

Hawrs later, my body convulses with exhaustion as I fight to keep the sword in my hand. They have tested my battle skills, and now they are pushing them to the brink. But I refuse to concede. I refuse to put down my weapon. Attack after attack, I block, I evade, I get knocked down, but every single time, I rise. I will until I cannot.

"Again," Icarus demands from the shadows. I think he is having a little too much fun with this.

It is not lost on me that I am training with bloody Erads, and regardless of my feelings for either of them, a deep yearning to make them proud pushes me further. These are the greatest warriors of this world. They were made to fight, and now they are training me.

I loosen a desperate grunt as Dominus swings again, and I

am thankful he has locked away his full strength because it takes every bit of power I have to block him. He twists on his heels, and in an instant, he is behind me. He wraps his strong hands around the insides of my elbows and pulls them tightly together behind my back as he bites me hard on the neck. The act does not elicit fear from me, but quite the opposite.

"You are doing very well," he whispers in my ear, and the encouragement renews my vigour.

I offer no response to or accept his distraction. Instead, I push off my feet as hard as I can, causing Dominus to land roughly on his back. I flip backwards and over his head to land on one foot and one knee, bringing the edge of the blade to his neck. I lean down slowly, drinking in the surprise in his eyes.

"You are going easy on me. Has your love for me stifled the desire to constantly have the upper hand and push me to my limits?" I grin at him deviously and plant a kiss on his forehead.

His growl reverberates through my bones. I blink, and he's behind me again, pushing me to the hard stone with his body. "On the contrary. It is my love for you that is allowing you the delusion that you hold any sort of ground here, mo céasadh. I figured it would be best to grow your confidence, but it seems my notorum is still fond of foul play. I am happy to oblige."

He pushes his knee into my back, forcing the air out of me. This is not going to work. Everything he does makes my insides itch to tear his raiments off. Sensing the flood of pleasure, Dominus rises, picking me up with him and setting me on my feet.

"Enough of that, you insatiable swine. 'Tis time to make you sweat a bit, dear brother."

Icarus rolls his neck around and steps up to the training space. I abandon the floor to lean against the wall and gulp the cool water of a full skin. Dom's smile makes my heart break. I realise that, regardless of the pressing dangers, this is a gift to witness. Dominus and his brother, sparring, talking, existing to one another again.

"Finally, a fair fight. The deamhans I have been slaughtering for all these yehrs have bored me."

Icarus offers a mocking laugh. "Have you abandoned your humbleness, you gloating cow? Something I never thought the pure and honourable Dominus could be capable of."

"That is your weakness, Brother. You have spent your life seeing things as they present themselves and not at all for what they truly are."

The air grows heavy, charged with their barely contained power. Dominus strikes first, snatching a golden spear from a nearby rack and hurling it with supernatural force directly at Icarus' head. He ducks, the weapon embedding itself in the stone wall behind him with a resounding crack. Retaliating, Icarus sweeps his hand across a shelf of shimmering vials. They explode in mid-air, releasing a cloud of swirling, prismatic mist. Dom's eyes narrow as he loses sight of his brother. In a flash of movement, Icarus bursts through the haze, wielding twin short swords of crystallised light. Dominus barely manages to grab a massive warhammer to parry the onslaught. Each clash of their weapons sends shock waves through the armoury, causing artefacts to rattle on their shelves and ancient armour to quake on its stands.

Dominus swings the hammer in a wide arc, forcing Icarus

back. The blow misses, instead striking a pillar. I wince as the impact shakes the entire chamber, loosening dust and small stones from the ceiling. Taking advantage of the momentary distraction, Icarus lunges forward, his blade slicing across Dom's arm. Thick, crimson ichor spills onto the stone floor, sizzling where it lands. The sight of it makes my body begin to vibrate where I stand.

Snarling, Dominus retaliates by unveiling his wings and unfurling them to their full span, knocking over racks of weapons and sending them clattering across the floor. The sudden move catches Icarus off-guard, and Dom's fist, wreathed in dark smoke, connects with his jaw. Icarus stumbles back, crashing into a display of ornate shields. As he regains his footing, his eyes blaze with cerulean celestial fire the way Dom's do. The way mine now do. He raises his hand, and the very weapons scattered on the floor begin to vibrate and rise.

Dom's own glowing eyes widen as he realises what's coming. With a gesture from Icarus, a storm of blades, spears, and arrows hurtles towards him. Dominus spins the warhammer in a dizzying pattern, deflecting what he can, but several find their mark, piercing his radiant form and sending fire to blaze in my blood, but the assault only fuels his ire.

"Please do not destroy the academy with childish play! There are scolers here," I struggle to remind them over the battle.

Ignoring me, Dominus channels his power. His wings beat with dark energy, creating a vortex that pulls the airborne weapons toward him. In a display of incredible skill, he holds the hammer with one hand and catches a gleaming sword with the other. Icarus' eyes widen in surprise as Dominus launches forward with blinding speed. The hammer sweeps low, knocking Icarus off his feet, while the sword arcs high, its tip coming to rest at Icarus' throat as he lies prone on the debris-strewn floor.

For a moment, tension crackles between them, the fate of their conflict hanging by a thread. Then, unexpectedly, Dom's stern expression cracks. A chuckle escapes his lips, growing into full-blown laughter as his weapons clang to the floor. Icarus hesitantly joins him, pushing him off. Dominus lands on his back, and they lie there together, their deep, rumbling laughter panging through my chest. I cannot help but smile at the two of them.

"At least you remember how to fight. You will need it," Icarus says breathlessly.

"I have not shifted in so long, I fear I will lose control when I do."

"Nonsense. I will not allow it. We will continue to train, and we will devise a plan. Something wicked and clever."

Dominus rises to sit, resting an elbow on his knee. Icarus joins him. "I have yet to ask, but what do you seek to gain from this? What are your true intentions here?"

In an instant, Icarus is on his feet, reaching out a hand to help Dominus rise. "Other than preventing the destruction of everything I love, you mean? Can that not be enough for me?"

Dominus clasps his offering hand, and Icarus hauls him up. "Was that ever enough for you before?"

Tossing his hand away, Icarus snorts. "Right, let us see. I suppose you cannot imagine your oldest, lacklustre, spineless, conniving brother deciding to be something different, can you?

That anyone other than Dominus the Great can be courageous and honourable." He runs his hand down his face, and when he does, he looks so much like his brother. Only where Dominus is darkness and shadows, Icarus is pearlescent light.

"You were not the only one who suffered in your absence. It was three hundred yehrs for you here alone and lost. It was thirty yehrs in Eradia for me under the scrutiny of our father." So, Dominus was right. The lack of magic in these lands does change the length of time.

"It was thirty yehrs of absence where you sat. And your fucking absence was a gaping black hole. And every day it grew. Imagine how perplexed I was, foolishly pining after you—if only to have a sparring partner back. Someone to push and prod, who offered that same spite in return."

My heart squeezes in my chest. That is exactly what Dominus and I had been at the start. We rivalled each other and relished in the game. Until it changed, and perhaps I am beginning to understand Icarus—beginning to understand the coldness that exists in the shadows of someone like Dominus.

"You have always been my adversary. You have always stood on the other side of me. I have envied you, cursed your name, and hated you because everyone else loved you." He paces the room, emotions boiling to the surface, and I press myself harder against the stone to not remind them I am here. "But I soon realised the victory was spoiled because you took all of that love with you. You fucking took my anger with you, too! I wished for you to disappear, and when you finally did, I bloody hated you for it. And I hated myself for not being thrilled by it. With Father showing his true hand, I was the only one to know the truth. I was the only person who could reach you, who could potentially stop this. And I stood at that brink with an opportunity. I could change, become something better, become something more like the little brother I despised. Or I could prove everyone right about me. I could take Father's deal and rule, regardless of the price I might pay. But by the end, Dominus, it was not about the price I would pay or even about what you would do. It came down to what would happen to our world, to all that the Seren created. Maybe it is simply the fabric of my being, or perhaps something else entirely, but I knew as I stood out into that abyss that I could not, would not allow them to destroy it."

Dominus begins to unravel through the tether. The legs of my small, fragile bird shake. I ache to comfort him, but I will not. This is not about me. This is a resurrection of a different kind of bond. This is an evolution. This is something that might shake the core of this earth.

"I am sorry," Dominus begins. "I am sorry that I ever treated you in a way that made you feel less than or below me. It is quite a difficult truth to hear that you felt that way when I was drowning in it, too." His features soften, and he continues. "I was killing myself trying to become what Father, what all of Eradia, wanted me to be. You cannot imagine the impossible weight of it all. I was created, born to be a warrior. To bend to the will and call of the Seren. Imagine how strange it felt, Icarus, when I came to maturity with a deepening disdain for being told who I was to be. We do not get to choose our destinies, Brother. We are mere fabrications of submission and loyalty, are we not? I warred with myself every day to quiet the voice of defiance that screamed inside me. I worked so hard, harder than anyone else, to be the best of us because within my core, I knew I was the worst. I was the error, the fluke, and I did not desire to rule or be ruled."

The room is silent as uncovered truths float around us like visible ghosts. I wonder if they never left, if the two of them would have ever had this conversation. I wonder what Dominus might have become to continue his facade. Chills pepper my body at the thought.

"I have never known you felt that way, Dominus."

He swallows thickly, glaring into Icarus' eyes and responds, "Then I did my job well, Brother."

Icarus crosses the room in three large strides and throws his massive arms around his brother. I beg my eyes to look away, to let them have this moment in peace, but I cannot. The reconciliation is too beautiful. The weightless finality of understanding, the likes of which I will never share with my sister, is a sight I will not lower my eyes to. I wipe my tears as Dominus slowly reaches his arms around his brother and holds him tightly. I unintentionally release a sniffle, causing them to break their embrace to look at me.

"Oh, don't be so bloody jealous, Thorne, you needy wench." We all laugh at that with the understanding that Icarus uses humour to cope with complex feelings.

"I am not envious at all, Icarus. My simple, fragile heart is only filled with pride." He rolls his eyes at me. "I will not stand here assuming that I understand a single thing about your pasts or your relationship. However, I do stand here as a woman who lost her only sibling to say: cherish this. Communicate and work out everything you have to work out. You both are worth it, and you both deserve the love."

Icarus clears his throat, and his eyes begin to shimmer with wetness. "Gods, I cannot believe I ever liked you. You are intolerable."

"Am I? That is not what I remember from the night you whimpered to touch me, offering whatever I wanted to take from you."

Dominus whips his head to stare daggers at his brother.

"Oh, come on. Look at her. We both know you cannot blame me for the affliction of my lust, Brother."

I add, "I also suspect that wearing someone else's face allowed you to be a version of yourself you have never been able to be. Perhaps a truer form. I was very fond of him, my dear friend. If you ever grow confident enough to let him come around, I would not mind."

Icarus beams at me, a quiet understanding passing through us.

"Subtracting the parts of him that felt like he could put his hands on my notorum. I would happily dispose of him," Dominus adds.

"Notes taken and tallied, dear brother. Now, where can we find a strong drink in this place?"

ᚦHIRTY ᚦHREE

We break for midmeal, eating in my rooms since they "lack the stench of our coitus," as Icarus so eloquently requested. I realise that this is the first time I have eaten since yestermorning, though hunger for food has been the last thing on my mind. As the smoked fish touches my tongue, the taste of it alarms me. Elowyn's cooking has never even been close to bland. This is lifeless, missing all those delicious herbs and spices.

"What is wrong with this?" I turn my nose up at it.

The two of them turn to look at each other and begin to laugh simultaneously. "Oh, mo céasadh, the Eradian pallet was a trait of mine I was sincerely hoping you would not inherit."

"Please tell me you jest. Please. Elowyn's food is the second greatest thing about this place. I have literally dreamt of her blueberry scones. Now, you tell me they will taste of dirt in my mouth?"

Icarus only laughs, but Dom's look is full of pity. I want to strike him for doing this to me. "We prefer things that are a bit more...fresh. And food only of the earth without much alteration. Our diets are different in Eradia. The food here is sustainable but not of the quality, type, or taste to that of our island. We can also go significantly longer without eating. Our bodies do not require much to survive."

"You bloody monster," I say, throwing my fork at him, which he, of course, catches effortlessly.

"You mean to insinuate, dear sister, that though your beloved has gifted you with magic and power beyond your imagination, you now thwart him for also evolving your sense of taste to that of a demigod because the bland and boring foods you once enjoyed no longer delight you? Do I discern that correctly?"

"Icarus, you are eerily close to discerning my boot into those perfect teeth of yours if you do not hold your tongue." To which he cackles.

"What *does* taste good here?"

"Apart from you, not much," Dominus says, forking his fish into his mouth and following it with a glass of wine. The wine, at least, is delicious. It's old in age and heavy with fermentation.

"Why does the wine taste good then? The fruits are altered, are they not?"

"Indeed, they are, but we have learned Erads like the taste of all spirits. Maybe it was a kind consideration from our makers. Maybe one of us negotiated that particular trait somewhere along the line."

Icarus steps in to answer my former question, "The rarer the meat, the better. The blood, the essence of life, satisfies us enough." I cannot help the shiver that crawls down my spine at that, or how I turn my mouth up at his comment.

"Here, try the vegetables. They were freshly harvested this morning; you can taste it." Dominus piles a heaping mound of potatoes, radishes, and carrots on my plate. I hesitantly bring a bite to my mouth and am surprised by the taste of them. They do not taste too significantly different than before, but now I sense the earth on them—the morning dew, the worms that crawled along them, the other plants that resided next to them, and the rain and sunlight that helped them grow.

"That's incredible," I mumble around my food.

"Wait until you've torn into a fresh buinín," Dominus says in a way that makes me want to tear into *him*.

"Easy, lass," Icarus warns. Dominus and I both shoot him a warning glare. "Before you two become completely carnal, let us discuss our next step. I will leave you to practice the disciplines of magic in the evenings together so that you can remain veiled. We can train from dawn to midday. That should leave you two zealots enough time to gnaw on each other at night. However, some nights we will need to familiarise ourselves further with the lands to understand all the ways in which he could attack. You can catch us up on all you've learned fighting deamhans these yehrs, Dominus. We may find something useful. I will work to see if I can somehow get a message to Fina and Camiel to join us."

"No, that will be too dangerous. Father will believe you disappeared without worry. The absence of the others will be too obvious. Additionally, we do not know if Hellas even plans to alert Father or if he means to come alone. Perhaps he watches for a while to determine if I have any power."

"We might not have an option, Dominus. We need allies. Any that we can muster will be needed."

"I understand that, but the moment Fina and Camiel disappear will be the moment Father looks to you."

"Fine. I will test the boundaries of what magic can be done now and see if Hellas has mended the wards. If I can slip away to one of the others, maybe I can bring back help."

I interject, my mind running alongside theirs, "Beyond that, what is our ultimate goal? Hellas has you here. He has a deamhan army ready to strike at any moment, only we are blind to when. Dominus is our hidden weapon. If we can keep the knowledge of your power and understanding of the deal he made with Adonien a secret until necessary, we may stand a chance of getting off the island. We will have to go somewhere to secure more allies. We are utterly alone here. The humans cannot, likely would not, fight. They do not stand a chance."

"If we leave, what stops him from razing the entire land to ash? We are the only things that stand between him and the humans," my beautiful notorum says.

"Then maybe Icarus is right. Oh, don't look at me that way—either of you. We need a way to communicate with the other Seren. With someone or something that is not Adonien or loyal to his cause who would come to our aid."

"I may have a plan for that. For now, we have our next orders. We focus on those and see what we learn," Dominus adds.

"Then I shall leave you animals to it," Icarus adds and quickly abandons us.

Finally, alone, Dominus and I take no time to reach one another. Words mean nothing when we share an ache, a hungry need. I imagine exactly what I want in my mind, and I peel his mouth from mine only long enough to whisper, *"Nocht."* I open my eyes to find us both bereft of everything but our flesh.

"I see you have been taking notes, mo céasadh," Dominus says before grazing his teeth across the lobe of my ear. It ignites me.

"I am a fast learner and a master's pet." I lick him from collarbone to chin.

"Mm, yes. I do vaguely remember there was something you wanted from me the next time I had you." He runs his fingers through my hair and pulls it roughly at the roots. I whimper in his mouth. "What was it, Thorne? You want my commands? You want to submit to me?" There is no point in responding when he feels my every desire. I only nod. "Good, then kneel."

I find myself doing as he commands, and as my knees hit the stones, his magnificent girth stands ready before me, and I take no time to wrap my hands around him and stroke, delighting in the smooth warmth of him. He responds with a moan.

"I feel how you ache to taste me, Thorne. I can feel the need trembling through your body, watering your mouth."

"Yes," I whisper because gods, yes, it is.

"Then taste me. Now," he commands in that tone that already has my core quivering.

I lap around his end before taking him fully into my mouth, using both of my hands at his base to stroke him. His legs shiver, and it drives me further. I take him in my mouth as deep as I can while running my hands along the mass of his mighty thighs. I look up at him through my lashes and take him at the base with one hand. I stare at him, lazily licking him from bottom to top.

He growls with pleasure, and in a heartbeat, I am standing with his chest pressed against my back. "You are a wicked beast, my notorum. Do you need to be reprimanded?"

I nod at him. "You better be thorough. You know I have a defiant spirit."

His laugh is smooth and soft as moonlight as he says, "And I revel in it."

He pushes me over, and I land on thick, cool bed linens. Dominus runs both hands through my hair. At the base of my neck, he begins to twist my unbound hair around his wrist. Then, without warning, he delivers a punishing slap to my rear. My body is already near shuddering with pleasure, but his work has only begun. He releases my hair to knead me with both hands.

"I have dreamt of these sinful, righteous, abundant curves of yours since the moment I witnessed them." Another smack, and my legs start to shake. "You are such a delicious agony. A torture I keep begging for, and when I saw this," a final blow, "in those leathers today, I did not think we would leave my rooms. Do you understand me, Thorne? You have me willing to abandon this world to kneel at your altar."

"Dominus," I whisper, needing more. Needing every inch of him.

"Don't like being tormented, do you, mo céasadh? Imagine how I felt looking upon you for wyths without touching you."

He spreads my legs to guide himself to my opening. He barely presses himself against me, and I lean into it.

He tsks at me, pulling away. "And imagine what I did, how I nearly bruised stroking myself after that night you took your gown off to try to get me to leave. You brutal, vicious thing."

I smile at the memory and replay it in my mind, only this time, the disgust I thought I saw resembles something more like pain. Pain laced with want. I try to twist on him, having had enough of his torture, but he places his hands flat on the bottom of my back, his thumbs touching and his fingers bruising my hips.

"Do you think you were the only sufferer, my notorum?" The air in the room changes, and I realise I have not called him that aloud yet. I take note of the reaction for when I truly want to madden him. "Look at you," I say, twisting to lie on my back, and he lets me this time. "The first time you walked into the room, I felt your presence wrap around me. I felt the hum in the air that I did not understand at the time. I watched as you bit into a grape and was bloody envious of the thing."

He leans forward, biting one of my breasts as if to repay the distant want. I thread my hands through his hair and arch into his onslaught. "I find myself slick with every single thought of you. I have dreamt of all the wonderful and terrifying things your sharp tongue can do to me." He flicks it across my nipple with a low groan. "And I have been blissfully happy to find out."

Without another second passing, he spreads my legs and plunges into me, relief spreading throughout both of our bodies, through our nodus. I cling to him, desperate for more, aching for every bit of his body to be pressed into mine.

"Think about the tether you made. I want you to change it. Create an opening for me, only for me. Wrap it in your thorns, secure it."

I nod, unable to form words as he slides in and out of me.

"Oscailt," he whispers for both of us. Our nodus unravels, liberated in the space between us while remaining covered and safe. The essence of him, full and unadulterated, rushes into me, and I begin to cry. I cry at the pleasure and relief of it. I cry because not having this today felt like existing in a void. Dominus kisses me softly, and our joining turns tender and passionate. He cups my head into his hands and presses his forehead against mine. I hold him tightly, so tightly I wouldn't be surprised to hear bones crack.

I wonder how a need like this can be natural between two beings. I am filled with pain and pleasure. With love and sadness. With fear and hope. Our souls begin to ache even harder, their desperate anguish in the pit of me.

"Thorne, I love you. I belong only to you." The words soothe me fractionally, but I need more.

"Dominus, I need you. I need all of you. I—" I do not know what I am asking. There is nothing else he can give me that he has not already.

"I know, my love, I know." He works me harder, deeper, squeezes me with his powerful hands, and presses more of his weight into me.

A thought, an inkling, a hint of something slithers into my awareness, but I cannot discern from where. I believe he senses it, too.

"Take what you need from me. I am yours. I will never

baulk at your desires. I will never turn away or deny you."

Without thinking, I bring my mouth to his shoulder, and I bite. As I do, the tips of my canines sharpen to a point, eagerly opening his vein. His blood flows freely in my mouth, and I moan at the taste of it. His essence pours into me, filling the chasm of need. It seeps into my bones, into my every fibre, and fills me completely. The same way it did when we bonded. I drink him deeply, the taste of him driving me higher and higher. I release his flesh to offer him my neck.

"Are you certain?" he asks.

"Trust me," I respond, and I do not know if this is a part of the natural nodus or something else, but I feel the desire grow within him, the want he has and how he craves me, too.

Dominus leans down to bite my neck, and as soon as my blood permeates his tongue, I shatter around him. He follows, pounding into me as he drinks from me. He leans up to meet my eyes before kissing me desperately. The taste of us mingling together soothes the needy nodus. Dominus was correct; it has a hunger to be rivalled, certainly.

We move to lie together on the bed, our limbs becoming twisted vines like that night in the inn, and I want to laugh at how much things have changed since then. Dominus runs long, soothing strokes up and down my back. We reside in silence, suspended again in that untamable euphoria, and though I can get a sense of what he feels through our souls, I need to know what he is thinking.

"I apologise if that was not something we are supposed to do. I—"

"Have nothing at all to apologise for. Nothing at all. I will never shy away from your desires. I will never shame you for asking for what you want. I will do everything in my power to satisfy you."

I take his words in, flipping them over, looking for any sign of deceit. None exists. "Is that common? For Erads or the nodus?"

"Blood sharing is somewhat taboo outside of the initial bond. I doubt it is something most couples take part in, but I believe it is different for us."

"Different in what way?"

"I was always taught that the bonding ritual was painful. The pain is signified by the sacrifice you make to give to the other. But ours was..."

"The furthest thing from painful."

"Precisely."

"And just now, it was the same for me."

"As for me. It was like that night all over again. A feeling I thought was only meant to be possessed once."

"The craving I have for you is unbearable, Dominus. I fear it may be the very thing that kills me."

"Do you forget we share a nodus? The desire is equally my own. But that, the blood, sated it more than I have felt since we bonded. I have been losing a battle not to whisk you away somewhere never to return."

"Well, perhaps we found a way to satisfy the nodus until we can take our time with it."

He runs his hands down his face. "Gods, I already dream of your flesh every waking and sleeping moment, now I have to spend my days begging like a hound to open you up and drink myself drunk."

"I do believe I have previously stated my approval of such grovelling."

I want to consume the laughter that escapes him as he leans over to nibble my shoulder before moving to my lips. He pulls back and runs warm fingers along my cheek, staring deeply into my eyes. "It is rather selfish of me, but I prefer that everyone you ever loved to be dead."

I look at Dominus with pure shock. "Did I hastily presume that the hate portion of our relationship was behind us?"

"Not at all. Let me be clear, Thorne. I do not imply that I wish you pain, grief, or loneliness. In fact, I promise any man or beast a violent end that might cause you such, but I have been alone for so long without my family, without anyone to love or love me. Forgive me if I find a certain mirror of that anguish in the entity that is my other half, that I find solace in our shared pain. Forgive me for wanting to be the sole object of your desires and affections. Forgive me for wanting, needing, you so much, for demanding to be the centre of your world. Forgive me for how that truth might make you feel. But please understand, Thorne, that I am not apologising for wanting it. I do not offer my concession for the greed of it. I can only offer my gratitude to whichever one of the gods who made you so perfect a match for my damned soul."

THIRTY FOUR

We spend the rest of the night consumed with one another. Between moments, Dominus gives me instructions to practice my magic. Small, basic spells like moving things around the room, summoning and banishing raiments and other small objects. He teaches me spells like *Bloc, Solas, Dorchacht, Rois, Spreagad, and Tine.* Together, we learn how to influence the nodus. We practice shielding ourselves and pushing our feelings into each other. We stand fully now in my room, snacking on freshly picked, still dirty apples.

"Icarus conjures light, while I conjure smoke. Fina conjures wind and Camiel bone. Every Erad channels their own element or variations of it. Whatever it is for you, let it call to you, speak to you. It already exists. It is not something you can choose; it is woven into your being."

"For you, but I was not born an Erad. Will it not be smoke like you?"

"Perhaps, but I will teach you as I was taught. That is all I know to do in this instance. And it likely will be. Let us find out."

I shake my head and close my eyes, the hum of magic flowing through me with a vibration I will never grow accustomed to. I guide it with my mind, giving it purpose, searching for the *thing* that is supposed to materialise. That same itch swells in my palms as it has before, but now, it grows. Magic vibrates my very bones as I call to it, bringing it to the surface.

"I wish I could say I was surprised, but I think I am learning that you will always do something no one else does."

I open my eyes to find my hands wreathed in sharp thorns, covered in deceptively beautiful, deep green leaves. I smile so widely that it hurts. I move my hands closer for inspection. The vines twist and curl around me from my fingertips to my elbows like living serpents.

"Is this not of you?" I ask.

"No, love. This is all you."

Scrunching my brows at him, I say. "But that day in the woods, when you healed me, the earth it—"

"That was not me. I cast a spell to heal you, but with my magic being constrained, I could not do it with my power. I thought it was the magic responding in the only way it could. I have never seen it before. I was not certain at first if it was killing or saving you."

I study the information, considering everything. I reach for the thorns around my wrists, and they crawl up my body and wrap around me as if to answer: *yes, yes, we protected you. We saved you.*

"You believe this was inside of me before we bonded?"

"Yes."

I do not know what you are or what any of this means, Dominus had said.

You are cursed, and you are blessed, the inner voice told me.

The same thing I smelled as she stood on a boat still out at sea. Power, Brother. Even Icarus noticed.

It seems everyone around me has some idea of what I am, though I still have no clue. My magic feels like magic. It does not feel like mine or Dom's. It just is, like it has always been.

You are mine, the voice whispers to me.

And what is that, I scream back at it, finally finding the courage to address it directly.

Silence. Endless silence.

"You haven't a clue, Icarus senses but cannot say, even the bloody voice in my head will not tell me what I am." I test the vines, moving them around my body, making sure they indeed listen to me. "You said that Albion was an island one of the Seren sent their species to. What if I am just an evolution of what was once there and somehow retained my power, and our binding just made it stronger?"

He slips a knowing smile and tilts his head slightly. "'Tis a very possible and likely guess. Absolutely what makes most sense." He nods his head.

I ignore his strange behaviour to digest the information. Magic. I have always had magic. The thought of it sends joy through my body. "Which of the Seren sent them there? Who would be responsible for my line?"

"Eden, actually. Once I had come to the same assumption, I thought that might be why you had such a reaction when we were there. Maybe you connected with the land somehow, and it stirred something in your magic."

It certainly felt that way. "Dominus, why didn't you tell me this before? Your theory."

"How do you tell someone you think they are a long-lost Seren descendant who might be exhibiting signs of growing magic?"

"How do you bed someone the way you do, then consume their blood, and think you cannot tell them such things?" I challenge.

"Well, my love, it is not as if I have had much time since the ritual, have I?" he questions. "Furthermore, watching you work through that understanding just now at such a speed, well, you like for me to beg. I like that."

His perfect mark lands dead centre, and I want to melt to the floor at his feet. Instead, I sneer at him because he is right, but I am still bothered that he did not tell me sooner. I am equally proud that I solved it myself.

He continues, "If you would rather we spend the small hawrs we have talking instead of what we have been doing, please tell me, and I will oblige."

"Shut your insidious mouth before I make good use of it."

"A threat I am eager to tempt."

I send thorns shooting for his chest, but before they reach him, they become wrapped in darkness, and his magic pushes against mine. It feels like him. Like him outside of me, and it is only now that I have been able to discern the distinction between our power. It's like the difference between our scents or our souls before they were one. Smoke and thorns. Two varying forms of nature. We stare at each other like two wolves sizing each other up.

Dominus glares at me with pure satisfaction and just enough rivalry to make me attempt another move. I try to twist my vines around his darkness, but he overpowers me again, stifling them out. I grow them larger and larger, but the smoke grows with them. Frustration floods me. Sharing a nodus with him is not enough to quell the competition between us.

Suddenly, an idea hits me. Our souls are intertwined. I am as much him as he is. I call to my magic, instructing it to shift, to become the very smoke that rivals it. To my surprise and Dom's confounded shock, it listens. My thorns slowly fade away, slipping into vapour themselves, becoming the smoke. It confuses Dom's magic, thinking it is its own. I wind my smoke around his body and with a close of my fist, I yank him to me, bound tightly.

"How did you do that?" he questions, pure amazement glistening in his eyes.

"I assumed since we are bound, since we share power, I could call to yours as well. Well, maybe not conjure your magic, but evolve mine enough to mimic yours."

"Can you release me so that I can tell you how incredibly brilliant you are?"

"Is that uncommon between notorums?"

"I am beginning to see that everything between us is rare."

I release him then, and he brings his hands to cup my face. "There has never been an Erad bond outside our species. We are a completely new creation. I have learned to stop having expectations and, of course, underestimating you. Perhaps you are our hidden weapon after all."

THIRTY FIVE

I question Dominus the next morning about the journal. "So, is all my work here moot now with the looming possible destruction of this continent?" I ask, rubbing my lips with balm and then begin to comb my hair. I stare at the flawless specimen in the looking glass as he steps out of the bath. Water runs down him in glistening ribbons. Now I envy the bloody bath water.

"I would like to say work on it in your free time, but that belongs to me now, and I am a greedy bastard." He smiles at me with that dimple, and my mouth waters to lick it. He wraps a towel around his carved waist, and I sulk like a child having their favourite toy taken away. "I have assigned all my duties to other masters as well. I want to make sure we have a scol for these scolers to remain at. I think focusing on that until our future becomes more certain is the best idea. Then you can have the entire bloody castle to do whatever you want with. 'Tis yours. Consider it a nodus gift."

Too many thoughts pebble my mind. "You are not gifting me an entire bloody academy, though I do think a remodel and a new name would be fitting since it is named after your traitorous father and all. More importantly, are nodus gifts a common practice, and if so, why have you withheld another thing from me? Also, what can I get you?"

His smooth laughter rumbles through me. "Gods, I love it when you're fraught with endless thoughts. The thing it does to your eyebrows makes my cock twitch."

"Do not distract me with thoughts of your endowment. Answer me." Heat floods my core anyway.

He laughs again. "I shall give you whatever I wish. And you can do to this bloody castle as you like, as long as this wing stays permanently closed off. And yes, nodus gifts are a tradition, though they are usually a bit more permanent than a castle."

"Permanent, how?"

Dominus steps behind me. He takes my comb from my hands and runs it through my hair. "The gift is usually a permanent marking on the other's body. Something that signifies the other. Humans wear wedding rings. Erads mark each other," he says, as he bites the comb before taking my freshly filled vial of his scented oil and running it through my hair, massaging my scalp. I know he is good with his hands, but this is a new kind of pleasure.

"Can we do that? Do you want to do that?"

He tosses the comb to the vanity and continues by dividing my hair into equal sections before he begins to plait it in a single, thick cord down my back. "Of course, I want to permanently mark you, showing the entire world you belong to me. I do my damnedest to bruise you every night." Both our smiles reflect in the looking glass.

"What prohibits us?"

He secures my hair and tosses it over my shoulder. He adds a bit more oil to his hands before massaging it into my neck and shoulders. I melt into his tender offering, realising how foreign it is to be touched in this way—not with hungry hands consumed with pleasure, but with care. Gentleness. I am used to being the person who gives, who sacrifices, but to receive is a new experience.

"Although our magic influences the mark, we do not necessarily get to decide what it is, where it goes, or even how large it is. I think it's best we wait until we confront Hellas. We are already fighting to keep our nodus veiled as it is. I do not need a giant mark on your forehead that tells him you are my greatest weakness."

"Can the mark not be veiled?"

"No. It cannot be hidden. 'Tis a gift, the outward showing of the inward nodus. It is inherently designed to be proudly displayed."

"I look forward to the day I get to bear your mark, Dominus." He pulls my neck back to kiss him. A knock sounds at my door, and I grunt, thinking it's Icarus. Only, when I stand and conjure my leathers, I sense it is not Icarus at all. I tally the days in my head and realise it's the bloody wythnos.

"It's Eamon," I say.

"I know."

"He retrieves me every wythnos to spend the day with him and Elowyn. He is a day early, but that must be why he's here."

"You shouldn't go. We have too much to do here as it is."

My heart sinks as I look into those pale eyes, but something else arises in my chest. A new feeling, or perhaps an old one I had forgotten. It takes me a moment to dissect it, but then it becomes clear.

Safety.

A space carved out for me to express my true wants, not ones masked by duty and expectations—or even ones to keep myself hidden, unknown. He can handle it, whatever I unveil to him. He has proved that.

I swallow the emotions and allow myself to speak before I change my mind. "I want time with them without the fear of my emotions. I have dreamt of this. They are a part of Eregahl that feels wholly mine. They are the version of me before you, and not that I ever want that to change, but I do want to enjoy the day with them. A single day when I am not concerned about the lump in my throat or the pounding in my chest. One day to truly appreciate them."

"Of course, Thorne. Forgive me. I was unaware of the true closeness you have shared. But I am going with you. There is no negotiating that."

I release the breath I held captive, waiting for the denial that did not find me. This must be what it feels like, being heard. Being seen.

The thought of seeing Dominus with them makes me feel things. Things like happy and hopeful. Things I am not accustomed to. My two worlds colliding.

I conjure more appropriate clothing for us both. Below my harness, I layer a crisp white button-down shirt tucked into high-waisted olive green trousers, and I remove the towel for Dominus. "There, my favourite outfit of yours," I tease, leaving him to open the door. By the time I walk through to the bedroom, Dominus is dressed in black pants and a light top with the sleeves pushed up to his elbows, and he's grinning at me.

"Heathen," he says through a delicious smile.

"Show off," I mock as I pass him on the now-made bed, and he stands to follow me.

I open the doors, and Eamon beams at me. "My girl, where have you been? We have missed you." He brings me in for a hug and notices Dominus standing behind me.

"Good morning, Eamon. How are you getting along?" he purs.

"Och, well, I see why you've been busy."

"Oh, Eamon, don't be so hard on the woman. She cannot help that she found more handsome company to spend her time with."

"You dream of the day when your bullocks drop enough to grow a beard like this," he says, gesturing to the impressive, oiled beauty.

"Eamon!" I laugh.

"He's not wrong, though, Thorne." With that, Dominus and Eamon join in with my laughter.

"I fear I have made a mistake," I say.

"Not at all. Bring the lad with us today; I could use the help anyway."

"It would be my honour," Dominus says, and we take off

down the stairs and out to the carriage.

In the heat of samhradh, the ride to the cottage is a needed refreshment. I sit in my usual seat beside Eamon, and Dominus takes up the entire bench behind us.

"Elowyn is dying to hear about your visit to Eden. We came to check on you one evening this wyth, but you were nowhere to be found."

Flashes of sweaty skin and midnight air from the greatest night of my life swirl in my mind. "Ah, I must have been walking the halls as I do at night." Dom's internal laugh tempts my composure.

"Well, I am glad you came today, if even you brought that ol' scoundrel with you," he whispers, leaning closer to me, though I know Dominus can hear him either way.

"Oh, he is only a bit rough around the edges. Trust me, you will be fawning over him by sunset, mark my words. It is quite an insufferable trait of his." I glance back at him to find him licking his teeth at me. I quickly turn back around.

We round the bend to the cottage, and Elowyn stands waiting as she did the first time I visited. That feels like that was a lifetime ago, not menoths. I hop out of the carriage before it fully stops, both Eamon and Dominus shouting at me, to take Elowyn in the longest embrace I have allowed myself to give to another person outside of Dominus since my family died.

"Oh, lass. Are you alright?" she asks, embracing me with just as much passion.

"I am far beyond alright, Elowyn, and I missed you." I pull back to look at her, our eyes both lining with tears as things far beyond words pass through us.

"I see you've been busy." She waves to Dominus as he releases the horse from the carriage for Eamon. "Come on then," she says, tugging me inside. "You must tell me everything before they catch up."

Elowyn all but throws me into a chair and plops down beside me. "Tell me how it came to pass that you brought the esteemed Dominus Shrike to my table today."

"Turns out we are far more similar than we cared to admit. So much so that we shone a mirror upon each other at my arrival. We brought out the bitter, broken, but equally beautiful parts of each other. We were both too prideful to admit that we had met our match. So, it got became uglier before it got better, but then, well, then things changed. We evolved. Became better versions of ourselves."

Her blue eyes shine at me, "Love does that to people. It tears them down and forces them to rebuild."

I only smile at her, fearful to admit it aloud. Eamon and Dominus appear through the door, Dominus shrinking to fit through, and they join us at the table heaped with mounds of food. I look around at each of them. Dom's presence changes the space. The days here usually resemble my childhood, brimming with food and warmth and the smells of blooming flowers and mint. Now, in this room, it feels like *my* home, like all the things that make me up. All the people I love in one space. In a cottage that has been a refuge. It smells of home and Dominus and...me. The blended scent covers everything like the blue haze of the first light of a new day. A day that I am thankful keeps dawning.

"Are you alright?" he asks, undoubtedly sensing my emotions.

"Yes," I smile, and for once in a very long time, I mean it.

I do not let Dom's presence alter my usual routine. We eat, and I help Elowyn tidy while Eamon drags Dominus outside to undoubtedly work him for all he has until we need to leave. The thought makes my heart swell.

"You two are... Well, I have not seen anything like it since Eamon and I met."

"I know it seems expedient, but I suppose working and living with someone for menoths causes you to get through a lot of things quickly."

"Och, Eamon and I knew the minute we laid eyes on each other that we would share a nodus. It happens like that sometimes."

I drop the wooden spoon I am drying, and it clatters on the floor. "What do you mean?"

"Well, I suppose you are bound then. It was hard to tell. You two have done a great job veiling yourselves, though it does not take one with magic to assess that you two are irrevocably in love."

My head spins, and I become nauseous. Dominus is at my side immediately, and Eamon appears seconds later.

"What's going on?" he questions, looking between us.

Elowyn looks Dominus right in the eye and says, "I fear we have some things we need to discuss, my child."

THIRTY SIX

"Start talking." Obsidian smoke wreaths Dom's arms, but Elowyn draws a symbol in the air, a rune, I now know, and it disappears after briefly shimmering with sapphire light. It makes me think of the bioluminescent mushrooms and how I was able to see the magic in them. The thing inside me, the thing other than the nodus, preens its head out.

"Sit down," she says, and as she does, she carries us on a wind to our chairs. Air must be her element. "I want to do this amicably, so if you promise to behave, I will release you."

"Elowyn," I breathe, dread twisting in my gut.

"Do not worry, my dear. I mean the two of you no harm. I have some things I need to say, and I need you to listen." I look to Dominus, and we both meet her gaze and nod. We relax into our seats immediately.

"I fear I have not been entirely honest with you, dear wain. And to be forthright, I never intended to reveal myself. But I worry the two of you have done something to change the fate of the world as we know it, and I must do the same."

Eamon pulls her chair out. "Are you certain?" he asks her.

"Yes, my bunúsachs agree." Bunúsachs. Spirits created by the Seren. Oh, gods. No. She cannot be.

Ellowyn is a bloody Seren. It all settles in me then, a certain clarity that rings true.

I form my assumption quickly, and my mouth speaks for me, "Eden," I whisper as if invoking her.

She whips her head to me. "You are clever indeed, aren't you, my girl?" And I suppose she truly is some sort of mother of mine.

"How?" Dominus growls.

"How are you here?" I ask in wonder at the same moment.

She takes a deep breath. "The story I told you did not come from my father. No, he was a horrible, wicked creature. It was the truth as I lived it, Thorne."

"Your f-father?"

"Yes. Will you allow me to finish the story for you?"

"Please do," I respond.

Naturally, she pours us all a cup of tea before beginning. "See, our father held fast to Danu because she was the firstborn. Hellas, the firstborn son, came next, and I suppose they were all he ever considered. We were not as powerful as Danu and Hellas were. I suppose maybe our essences were different, cut from different cloth. Danu was born with great power, and oh, did Father revel in that. He moulded Danu into a powerful, fierce warrior, destined to rule many worlds. Danu worked diligently to outperform and overachieve, fulfilling the duty crafted for her. She refused to sleep, to eat, to breathe without compliance. Only, her heart was not in it, but Hellas' was. He panted after Father, begging him to pay him attention, but it was Danu who was always the centre of his eye. This made Hellas grow desperate in his pursuit of power. He is so much like our father that I am surprised he left with us. But maybe Danu alone could carve out the good in him, and with her gone, who was left to stop him?"

She pauses to glance at Eamon, whose painful expression is a mirror to Elowyn's, and I wonder how long they have been together.

"In a new world, without Danu, it did not take long for Hellas to determine he had the freedom here to become whatever he wanted, and he chose darkness. We tried to stand up to him, but he crafted those deamhans the way we crafted you," she says, looking at Dominus with pride. "You know how unstoppable your kind is. Imagine that with dark magic running through them. Magic is so much about the intent, and Hellas' intent is purely evil. After we realised we would not succeed in defeating him, we ran. We dispersed and hid ourselves, promising only to contact each other if it were necessary. We took our beloved children with us, and we ran."

Her eyes glaze over at the memory with what I assume is regret. It bleeds into grief, a look I am well accustomed to. She takes a deep breath, looking at Eamon, and he nods, encouraging her. "It is not something I am proud of, but it was necessary for the survival of all those we created. And that was the reason we fled our own home. Each of us ached for a family in different ways, the family we would never get in Thoraí." I wonder if that is the first time the name of their homeland has ever been uttered here.

"I was hidden in Albion for a while until Hellas discovered it," she says.

My heart hammers in my chest. Elowyn continues, "Fearful of an attack, I left and came here. I veiled my people from him, though, convincing him we had abandoned the island. I remain here to keep watch and to signal for those in Albion to flee or come to my aid."

"Giving up the life you wanted, the one we hand-crafted, to become a beacon to them. To be the one who stands between their demise," Eamons says, refusing to remove his gaze from his beloved.

"How do you veil them?" My voice is quiet, fearful. I become too aware that I am standing on the precipice of my destiny.

"Their magic is hidden. Stifled to a mere ember. They have no idea who or what they are. They have had lives and children. They have been happy. I did not want them to cower in fear. I wanted them to live. On my command, they will awaken. They will remember who they are. New bloodlines will come alive with my magic, and they will rise. All of the Sídhe."

Thump. Thump. Thump. Thump.

I cannot bring myself to ask if I am one of those lost children. I cannot find the courage to step into the light. But she turns to me, cupping my face in her hands.

"Then you came along, my wain, and you sparkled, deep

within. A child of mine all the way from Albion. You reminded me of what I am protecting—what I have to fight for."

I cannot stop the tears as they stain her hands, but she wipes them away gently. "But like most of my children, you like to get into trouble and somehow found yourself bound to an Erad. Your nodus did something to this land. It reacted to my own magic."

"I think I can explain that," Dominus says, running his hand down his face. "My father is Adonien, King of Eradia."

"You jest."

"I thoroughly wish I did. He banished me here three hundred yehrs ago in the time of this world. I have been trapped here without my magic, confined to this island. How have you not scented or sensed me if you are Eden?"

"I locked my magic away a long time ago. The dregs I use now are only enough to allow me to get a message out if needed. It's untraceable. There would have been no way for me to know. You radiate power certainly, but until your union, it felt similar to the way bloodlines with remaining magic do. I felt the release of magic that night, and your nodus has changed your auras. That is what gave it away."

I find a small relief in that. Maybe Hellas cannot sense us either.

"You mean to say you have not gone looking for the thing eradicating all the deamhans that roam this island?"

"Honestly, no. We have our ways to keep them away from us. We rarely see them. Why are you here?"

"Right." He loosens a deep breath. "Adonien made a deal with Hellas to keep me trapped here. I was in line to take the throne, and he wanted to keep it for himself. He bargained me with Hellas. I stay here, Hellas does what he wants with me, and Adonien remains in power. We have also learned that they intend to use the Eradian army alongside the deamhans for another war. Except this time, he comes for you all, and he will not stop."

"They cannot do that. The Erads are bound to protect us and all of our children."

"I am not sure what sort of magic he has access to, but it is enough to keep one of the strongest Eradian warriors grounded for three centuries, so it is my assumption that he has learned a few new lessons in control."

She shakes her head, bringing her hand to her mouth in disbelief.

"I have no idea what Hellas has planned for me. He has not made contact with me the entire time I have been here. No one has. What I do know is that if I leave this island, if he finds out that my binds are broken and I leave, he will wage his war. My father will know that I am free as well."

"So, why not run? Why not save yourselves?"

I answer for him, "Because we do not want to. I don't want Hellas to end an entire people because we saved ourselves. There are people on this island worth fighting for." I look at each of them then. "People I love. People I will fight for."

"Eden," Eamon says lowly. "We have stood in the shadows for too long. We have let Hellas have his way with our world. No longer. We fight or we die, either way, we cannot allow him to continue this."

She nods to Eamon and turns back to us. "I can offer you

aid."

"We are going to need a whole army, Eden. An entire army of people who know how to fight," Dominus rebuts.

"What about an entire island?"

"'Tis a start. My brother found me. He is here with us. He aims to reach the others. Is there any way you can reach Noreg or Caledon, or is there a way Icarus can reach them?"

She pauses for a moment, dancing her fingers on her lips. Then she pops a finger in the air. "Yes," Elowyn, or, I suppose, Eden begins, "there is something we used to do as wee wains. We would send birds, native to our home, to each other if we wanted to speak or send messages. Get a shrike to one of them, and they might answer. Tell them, 'Tá sé in am.'" *It is time.* "They will know it's a message from me. My magic is in Albion. I will have to travel there to get it."

"Go. Get it and bring an army. We will need it," Dominus replies.

I add, "We will hold as many of your people in the castle as possible. We will dismiss classes, and we can create a safe place below the scol for them to stay if they choose."

Dominus continues where I stop, "Once we have enough magic wielders here, we can form wards of our own. We can block all territories from Hellas'. Leaving him blind might cause him to halt his retrieval of me long enough for us to form a plan of attack and to train those who need it."

"There is no guarantee Noreg and Caledon will join. They took the brunt of his force last time. They may not come out of hiding to sacrifice their people again."

"They will likely have no choice. Who knows what things

Hellas has created and hidden away all these yehrs? The things that roam the island are likely nothing compared to what he builds within his own walls. He could have the ability now to find them, too," Dom responds.

"Then we had better hope Icarus finds them and quickly. We will leave for Albion tonight."

They both stand to ready, and we follow suit. Elowyn—Eden—moves to wrap her arms around me. "When I release the veil, you might experience some things. There is no way for me to know who you are without my magic. I will call to you once I have it again. I love you, my daughter. I am very proud of you. Thank you for reminding me who I am and what I have to fight for." I come apart in her arms, menoths of emotions ripping free like the pop of a cork.

"I love you. I love you both." I reach out for Eamon, and he joins us, wrapping his arms tightly around us both.

"Go," she whispers. "We will see you soon. And I will bring our people with me. I will bring them home."

I nod and kiss her hands, and Dominus and I leave for the castle on foot.

ᛏHIRTY ᛋEVEN

"She has been hiding here this entire bloody time! Well, that is rather noble of her, is it not? For a bunch of gods, the Seren sure are cowards." Icarus is as surprised as we were to hear the truth of Eden. He met us at the gates just as the sun fell across the horizon, heavy with dread. There is a different buzzing in the air tonight. Like the trees are leaning in. Like the sea pushes further onto the shore. Like someone is waiting and watching.

"We do not have the time to discuss the morality of the all-powerful beings that created us, Brother—only the time to move. To hopefully change our fates."

"I will find them. Though I do not like the idea of leaving you here alone. Again. I have abandoned you once. I—"

"You will do what you can to save me and everyone in Eregahl. You will stand and fight with me this time. You will fight to save others because it is the right thing to do. You will bring us back soldiers. You, Icarus, will come back safely so that I can tell you how bloody proud I am of you, and how, because of you and the decision you made, others will live. *We* will live." Dominus pulls him into an embrace. The sound of their colliding bodies echoes like a thunderclap.

"I do not care what you must do; if there is any sign of trouble, call for me immediately. Do you understand? The borders are still warded. I will have to travel out to sea before I can either llif or fly out. Once I am out, I can work on breaking the wards. Maybe if I find Caledon or Noreg, they will help."

"Leave the wards to Eden upon her return. I think that will be something she can manage," I say.

"If communications open again, I will be in constant contact with you. I swear it," Dominus adds.

Icarus looks between us as doubt and regret shine in his bright, blue eyes. "I swear to the gods if you two stubborn arses die before I get back, I will raise you myself to kill you again. Do not fuck this up. And keep the training up. I want to witness the proof of it upon my return."

"We love you, too, Icarus," I say, placing my hand against his chest. He pulls me in, squeezing the breath from me.

"Show them what you are made of, Sister. Do not fear what you are. Be brave. Be ruthless. Be a bloody Erad," he whispers in my ear. A knot of pride lodges in my chest.

"Thank you. Thank you for everything you have done. I am honoured to know you, Icarus. Thank you for coming back for him."

He slaps me twice on the back and turns to leave quickly,

but not before I see a small tear glisten down his cheek. He walks a few paces and stops. When he turns back around, his face is dry and his eyes are deadly as he says, "Chun glóire. Chun ár n-onóir." *For glory. For our honour.* Dominus repeats it, nodding his head toward him. He watches him walk away from the castle, away from us, toward the sea. Towards the gods. Towards hope.

"He will succeed. He will come back to us."

Dominus remains silent as he watches and watches and watches. Long moments later, when he senses Icarus make it to the sea, Dom turns to me, desperation dripping from him. "We need to secure the scol. We need to dismiss the scolers and begin the work in the sublevels to make shelters, but...I need you. I need you right now, Thorne." He rushes me, lifting me, and I wrap my legs around his powerful hips instantly. "It is beyond selfish and unbelievably reckless. But I need the security, the strength you give me. I need to fill and consume you so that I can continue because I am fucking terrified that we might fail. And my own death is not of concern to me, but you—I cannot stand to jeopardise you."

His words ignite me, and I lean in to take his mouth in mine. "I am endlessly yours, Dominus. Take me."

A heartbeat later, we remain completely bare under the glow of the stars. Our joining is demanding and needy. We meet each other thrust for thrust, as we always do. The nodus hums at the greediness of it, delighting in the desperation.

The moon shines brightly in its entirety upon us, reflecting in the smooth, glorious planes of my lover. I watch as the muscles of his back roll and swell as he fills me so completely, so perfectly. Give and take. Ebb and flow. We are one. We are infinite. We are the beginning and the end. I realise this was the calling. This is what my soul was cleaving in half for. I was grieving the absence of his love as his soul called for mine. The thought of it nearly kills me. It has always been him. It has always been us.

With heavy moon-filled eyes, I come undone as Dominus sinks his teeth into my neck and laps at the pooling of my blood, my essence, as if he were a starved creature. The release of his satiated moan sends me over the edge again, and as I quake around him, he follows me, hauling me up and wrapping his arms tightly around me. Unsurprisingly, the ache within me only grows, never happy with what she gets. Dominus leans his neck to the side and pulls my head down to him. "Take from me. Now." His voice is coarse and deep.

I push him backwards onto the thick grass that he just ravaged my back on. His eyes gleam with faint, pale light as he watches me with anticipation. I climb off him to trail kisses down his body. I swirl my tongue against the skin at the base of his neck. I run my teeth along the thickness of his collarbone. Down and down I go, nibbling and sucking and scratching every bit of him. All the way down his corded obliques. I lift my eyes to his, and I let them glow for him as I lean down to bite into the powerful, lean muscle at his hip.

I watch his mouth open as I drink from him greedily. He shakes beneath me as his eyes glaze with pure delight. "You are agonisingly wicked."

In response, I pull my head up so he can watch with perfect clarity as I extend my tongue to lap at the remains of his already-healing wound. I close my eyes as I swallow, letting out a low, breathy moan at the taste of him.

"And you are agonisingly delicious," I say with that same drawl.

I blink, and we are in the same position we were in the grass but now in Dom's bed. "Once more," he begs. "I need you to taste me once more, then we get to work."

I wrap my hands around him and smile.

THIRTY EIGHT

I deduce Headmaster Connally was somewhat aware of Dominus and his authority. He only nods and eagerly goes on to act out his orders. I make a mental tally to inquire about that later.

Informing Norine and Orla that the academy is now being shut down to host an army of magic-wielding Sídhe that were just pulled from a few centuries of a very bizarre nap goes... differently. Norine, wide-eyed and gaunt, blinks rapidly.

"Thorne Alder, you have been gone less than a fortnight, and this is what you manage to get into? You...found them. The Seren. They are real?"

I realise the shaking this does to her foundation. Like me, she has spent years of her life searching for the proof of the gods. Here we both stand, without adequate time to scrutinise, study, or process. Only enough time to move.

"Yes, Odella. They are. And I cannot wait to thoroughly journey through this understanding together once we have time, but that is not now. Now, we must decide what part we play here. Will you help me?"

She shakes her head, clearing the emotions. "Of course, of course I will. Just tell me what you need."

This might be the first time I have ever seen Orla truly speechless, and I cannot say that the sight of it does not bring me joy.

"Dominus entrusts no one more than you two to inform the scolemasters as to what is going on while we work on what to tell the scolers."

"Let us go," Orla finally speaks before taking Odella by the hand and absconding to the upper levels. I hope I love long enough to figure her out.

I meet Dominus in the privacy of my chambers soon after.

"What are your thoughts here?" he asks, pacing the floor. "How do we protect them? Is that even a true possibility in this instance? There is still so much unknown to fear."

I chew my lip for a moment, considering what I would want to know if I were in their place. " 'The least initial deviation from the truth is multiplied later a thousandfold.' Our world—their world—is about to change in ways that can never go back. Magic is about to course through these lands again. All sorts of creatures are about to be housed here. I do not think trying to hide a single thing will benefit them. We tell them exactly what is happening. Let them decide what to do with their fates. They can go be with their families, or they can stay in the safety of the subfloors. The risk is equal either way."

"Then we shall tell them," Dominus responds, running a finger over my cheek. "You would make a glorious queen."

My heart stumbles. Queen. Until only recently, I never considered even being someone's friend, let alone someone's notorum. Especially one to a bloody Erad. But a queen. I am unaware of how to tell him that I find no interest in that.

Instead, I respond, "We will not know unless we succeed. Call an assembly. This is your scol. These are your scolers. It is time for you to withdraw from the shadows. Step into the light. Show them all who you are and claim your rightful place." He brings those fingers to my chin and pulls me in for a deep kiss.

"None of this would be possible without you. You see a version of me I abandoned long ago. You make me want to fight again. You make me want to be better. I love you."

"And I love you."

We stare into each other's eyes for a single moment, standing on a precipice, taking in the reality of what we have and what we stand to lose. This is the moment before everything changes.

We arrive at the assembly hall at twilight. Towering archways encircle the structure, their rhythmic repetition broken only by four grand entrances at the cardinal points. Tier upon tier of stone seating ascends skyward. Dominus prowls out of one of the entrances, and I walk tall behind him. His arrival quiets the chatter of scolers, demanding the attention of hundreds as he stands dead centre of the vast circular amphitheatre.

"Ampligh," he whispers, and when he speaks, his voice travels through the arena, amplified as if he were standing next to everyone in here.

"Scolers, thank you for joining us. I am sure you have heard some concerning things in the past few hawrs. I am here to offer you an explanation. The truth." He looks at me then, and I nod to him.

"My name is Dominus Shrike. I would like to think you all know my name since I have instructed here for many yehrs. I know many of you have your opinions of me, and I understand. I have worked very hard in the pursuit of remaining unknown. In doing so, I crafted a rather lonely life.

"There is no easy way to explain to you what is going on. I will preface this by saying that each of you is here because you are gifted. You are bright, intelligent, and discerning individuals. You are here because you love Eregahl and its vast history. You are here seeking answers, and I am here to offer them to you." He pauses, and the energy of the room sharpens, nearly whining in my ear. "The stories of our gods are true. The Seren came here from another world and created lands of wonder. With them, they brought magic. You know the lore, so I will not bore you with a history lesson now, but their creatures are indeed real. They are alive and among us."

Gasps sound from the crowd. Scolers reach for each other with wide mouths and gaunt eyes.

"You know the first and most powerful creations of the Seren, correct?"

A young man in the front row with deep brown skin and golden eyes like my own says, "Mystics."

"Yes. Though they were originally called Erads. They are warriors crafted to do the will of the Seren and protect their realms. I am one of many Erads." More gasps and worried chatter fill the room, bringing the energy to a pinnacle. "Do not fret," Dominus assures them. "I have no desire to harm you. In fact, I have gone to great lengths to secure your safety. That is why you are here now. As it turns out, Hellas turned against his siblings long ago. Since then, he has been devising an attack on Eregahl and the lands created by the other Seren to gain control of our world as we know it. I was sent here as a bargain by my father, King of Eradia, so that he would not be stopped by the Eradian army once his onslaught begins.

"I know this is a lot to accept, but I must explain further. I have been in contact with Eden. She aims to come here, to Danumhar, to Adonien, with an army of Sídhe to aid in the battle against Hellas. I am closing the academy to house them and to prepare for battle."

The room erupts then. Scolers cling to each other, their mouths all gaping in disbelief. Their screams fill the air, and they rise to their feet.

"We come to you now, offering you whatever we can. Go, be with your families, warn them of what is to come, or stay. Stay within the confines of the halls beneath the castle. We will provide you with raiments, food, and all that you need. We will shield and protect you. However, you will live alongside others who are unlike you. Those who possess the ability to wield magic. They will fight for you. They will fight for Eregahl, the land they were driven from centuries ago. Go or stay. The choice is yours, but it must be made today, and you must enact that plan come sunrise."

I step up to take Dom's hand in mine. I whisper the same spell, allowing me to project my voice to the arena. "We have no way of knowing when Hellas will make himself known. Things have changed recently, and his arrival is imminent. The people of Eregahl remain our single priority. Without magic, without an army, Eragahl will not survive Hellas. We are working desperately to secure enough aid to help. We want to provide you with the full truth so that you can make an informed decision on your own, but time is not on our side, and this battle will soon be at our very doorstep. Our lives—your lives—will never be the same again. We now stand before a momentous time in history. These days will be transcribed after this is all over. Whether we succeed or we falter, this will go down in books that your children's children will study. Today is the day that we choose what side we stand on."

The same young man speaks up again, this time with more vibrato, "And if we stay. If we choose to fight, what does that look like?"

"I do not ask you to fight. I only ask you to live. To let me do the fighting for you. You will be surrounded by Sídhe. I would only ask that you welcome them and treat them as you would one another. That you care for them and the sacrifice they will likely make on the part of all humans in Eregahl," Dominus answers.

"There is more you should know," I add, and Dominus looks at me inquisitively. "You are not fully human. No one the Seren created is. You are descendants of the species that the

Seren created after they arrived. We are all their children. Once Hellas began his attack, his siblings were not strong enough to defeat them. They took their people and went into hiding to protect them from Hellas. Countless classes of magical beings exist on hidden lands. Eden first went to Albion, my homeland. She hid there until Hellas discovered her, but she veiled her people before he could attack. She hid their magic, making them simple and harmless, so he would not attack. She is on her way to Albion now to break that spell and take up her place again. She will return with those beings. They will likely be just as disoriented as you are. We will teach them magic. We will train them. Classrooms will become battle rooms. The grounds will become sparring yards. This academy will become a practicum of magic, of war."

A girl higher up in the crowd with bright orange hair and a smattering of freckles asks, "What of us? Do we possess magic?"

I look to Dominus then, unsure of the answer.

He takes the lead. "We are unsure of that, though I suppose nothing is impossible. Once Eden returns, if we can reach the others, we can learn infinitely more from them. All we have ever had are stories, half-truths, and speculations. Soon, we will know the real history of Eregahl. Soon, we will become part of it."

We stay to answer any questions the scolers have. Only once they are fully informed do we leave to let the scolers make their decisions. I look forward to learning more of that truth and to sharing more of what we know with them—if we succeed and there is still an academy here. A thought occurs to me about a particular evolution if we do, and I make a note to discuss it with Dominus upon our victory.

THIRTY NINE

Adonien scolers are bold and brave. Two hundred students remain, nearly half, and the others make the equally brave choice to venture home to their families. Being from all parts of Eregahl, I am thankful we are spreading the word to the villages of what is happening.

Dominus has crafted official letters to send with the scolers. He also dispatches word to the prospective leaders of each territory. We fear that they will not believe us, but we cannot leave them blind to what may occur. I hope they take precautions, and I hope Hellas only comes for us. Most of the masters remain as well, almost twenty of them. All kitchen and castle workers stay; I assume on behalf of Eden and Eamon.

It takes a few days, but with the aid of those who remain and minuscule amounts of magic from Dominus and me, we create comfortable living quarters, well stocked with provisions, in the sublevels. The castle staff divide themselves so that some can provide for those below and some can remain to look after the arrivals. We move the contents of the armoury to the scolers' abandoned rooms for easier access for us and to offer more space below.

"We've done well with this," I say, wrapping my arms around his strong shoulders and burying my nose in his night-dark hair. Dominus sits at the desk in my study as we rove over maps, looking for areas of high ground and signs of places Hellas might arrive from.

"I hate it, though. As well as we've done, it still pains me that this is all I can do. We are trapped, and I cannot stand it. I temper my magic so that Hellas will not sense it, and that alone makes me want to pull my skin from my bones. The release you selflessly give me every time I ask is all that keeps me from blasting this castle to dust."

"If it eases your guilt any, know that it is not entirely selfless. I do believe that thing you do with your tongue is for *my* pleasure."

"That is debatable, but not the point. Something eludes me. There has to be more I can do."

Before I can respond, I am pulled to the ground by an unshakable wave of nausea. Dominus kneels over me, cupping my face and screaming my name.

I lose all my senses, lost in darkness for a moment before Eden's voice fills my head. "My children. For too long, you have been forgotten. For too long, I have cast you into darkness in hopes of protecting you. Now is the time to rise. Now is the time to fight. Remember, remember, wake, and remember."

I suck in a deep breath as my senses return.

"Thorne! What happened? Look at me. Are you alright?"

"Yes," I gasp out through heaving breaths. "Eden broke the seal. The Sídhe are awoken."

"How are you? How do you feel?" Dominus helps me to my feet as I work to assess any changes.

A wave of power flows through me as if I were standing in the tides of the sea outside. I sway forward with the force of it.

"Thorne," Dominus warns me.

"I'm alright," I open the tether between us, wrapping it tightly in my thorns so he can experience what I feel.

Like a lock has been turned on a giant iron door, pieces of my soul slide into place. Magic, arcane and endless, pours into me, quaking my entire body. My ancestors, all of them, their faces flash before my eyes, including my mother, my father, and my sisters.

We were all Sídhe. All of us.

We all possessed the power deep within us to wield magic—to change our fates. Eden, the Heir of Fate. She could have stopped this. This could all have been prevented had they fought back—had they chosen to stand for what they believed in.

Such sorrow rushes through me. So many emotions. All of them. All from those before me. The joy and power; the happiness and peace; the fear and terror.

"Thorne, hold onto me. Do not let go."

I dig my nails into his forearms, centuries of emotions surging through me. I fight to close the tether between us so Dominus doesn't have to witness this.

"No, don't do that. Do not shut me out, Thorne. Please."

I close it anyway, and then my body hits the floor, my mind already gone.

I am back with the light again. Its warmth cradles me, softly, lovingly. I embrace it like a child to its mother. This is home. This is everything.

Hello, my darling. Her voice has changed. It is no longer my own but something hauntingly beautiful and ancient, and it echoes itself.

Who are you? I finally ask.

You already know. You have always known. We have always been one.

Who are you? I repeat.

Let me remind you.

Memories flood my mind. Memories not my own. Images of a gory battle. Flashes of my siblings running.

"Go!" I scream at them. "I shall hold them off. Go!" I watch them run away from me. Blood, sweat, and magic pour from my skin. I do not take my eyes off them. I watch as they make it all the way to the tairseach. I watch as each of them looks back, grief flooding their eyes.

"Please come. Do not do this," Noreg, with her beautiful olive skin and pale green eyes, begs me. They cling to their desperation, holding the veil open with hope that I might slip through.

But Hellas is last, and as he turns, there is no sadness in his eyes. No downturn of his mouth. No, he smiles widely at me before turning and stepping through the tairseach.

I conjure every ounce of magic left in my body. I carve

runes into my skin with my thorns. I siphon the magic from the blood and earth surrounding me on the battlefield. I whisper my blessing, my curse to preserve my spirit, to hold it in time and space in case the day comes that my siblings turn from their promise of good and light. In the event that Hellas corrupts their minds or their land.

I tried to save him, I tried his entire life to turn him away, but he is too much like our father. I carve it into my heart to be bound until a soul honourable enough is born to hold my spirit. I will return. I will be the reckoning. I will end his devious reign.

Danu. I cry out, her grief filling me.

Yes, my heir. My chosen one. My soul, who has sacrificed, who has loved and lost, who has given, who has journeyed far. You are my heir. Oidhre an Domhain. I give you my power and everything I am. You may be a child of my sister, but you carry me within you. And now that you are fully awoken, together, we will lay waste to the wicked and the corrupt. Together, we will avenge my death and make my siblings remember my sacrifice.

I am Oidhre an Domhain? The book. It...it's always been me? Not Dominus?

Yes, my girl. Your destiny has always been within you. Though your fates are certainly intertwined. Hellas has grown stronger than I imagined. Dominus will be your aid. Together, you are something new, even to Thoraí. Something that changes the fabrics of the worlds. You are both children of my siblings, bound together, sharing and creating power. Now, you will have mine as well.

The warmth sinks deeper into me, filling me with a radiant, white light.

Promise me, soitheach. Promise me that together we will end him.

Yes. I swear it. And I mean it. I want to end Hellas. I want to live in a new world, or perhaps an old one, like Eregahl once was, full of magic and love and peace. Peace, like I feel with Danu.

What is this place?

It is called Mag Mell. When I cast my spell, it created a place to hold me. A new plane. One unknown to the living. I was here for a long time, alone, asleep, and waiting. It was when my siblings started to turn on one another that I awoke. I saw what Hellas had done. And I opened this place to all those he killed. The spirits of all Eden's, Noreg's, and Caledon's children rest with me here. It is peace and light. No evil can come in.

My family...

They are with me, child. I hold them, too.

I feel myself sobbing, not in the void but in my body. Something nuzzles at the corner of my mind, pressing in. Something I need to remember. It screams at me. A sonation. No, a bird's song.

Will you be with me?

Always. I am always with you.

That thing grows louder, pulling me back. Dominus. My notorum.

He will be safe. He cannot be used. You claimed him. He belongs to us.

I want to tell her that he belongs only to me. I want to ask her what she means by he cannot be used. But the warmth fades, and the light dims, and I am back in my body, and Dominus is screaming my name.

When I wake, the light comes with me, still soaking through me. Dominus holds my limp body with tear-soaked eyes.

"Thorne," he bellows.

I reach my arms around him. "Dominus." It feels impossible to express to him what happened, and part of me does not want to. We both believed he was the heir. What has that done for him? Holding onto that hope this entire time that he would fulfil the prophecy and end Hellas? What will it do when I tell him that it is me?

I take a breath and conjure the courage to begin. I tell him all of it except the final moment, withholding what Danu said about him not being used. I fear what that might mean and what doubt it might cause him.

He looks at me like his heart is breaking. I reach for him, searching the depths of our shared beings for what he feels, but he has hidden himself from me, receding in a storm of smoke. Just as my heart is about to break, thunder cracks from the darkness between us, and Dominus releases my hands to bow at my feet. Smoke wraps around my thorns through our nodus. His magic pours into me, whispering *goddess, goddess, goddess.*

I lift his face to mine, and I bend to my knees to meet him. "No. I am not. I am not a queen or a goddess or an heir of anything. I am yours and only yours. That is all I ever want to be. This power means nothing to me. You mean everything to me, Dominus." I am terrified of hurting him, terrified of what this means. Terrified of being the heir.

But then he smiles at me, raw and pure. "Yes, you are. You are a goddess, and you will be my queen, and you are the Oidhre an Domhain, and my heart could fucking break from the pride. You, Thorne. It's you. It has always been you."

"It is us," I echo. "Danu says it is us. Together, only together, are we strong enough to change fate. There is no me without you."

"And I am endlessly yours. My life, my will is yours."

The thing preens inside me, for once feeling wholly satisfied, but I am far from it. I do not want this submission. I do not want *this* loyalty. My mind envelops itself, swimming, racing, summing it all up in new, rapid speeds.

Danu is a Seren. What if his worship of me is instinctive? Does his blood sing for me because of the power that flows through mine? Because of the connection I have to Danu? Did he summon me...or her?

It is all too much. I cannot allow myself to break now. There is still so much to be done, so much for me to do. I refuse to question this now.

I become desperate, frantic, and wholly irrational. "Then show me, Dominus. Show me how you will worship at my altar. Show me how you will honour me and no one else."

He wastes no time in his eager need to devour me, but he doesn't use his magic this time. Instead, he takes my velvet gown and rips it to shreds, leaving me bare to him. I *Nocht* away his raiments, but I do it without having to speak the spell, only think it. That is a new advancement. Our hands roam each other's bodies like it's the first time.

This is different than before. I am different. Endless amounts of power barrel through me. Eden's, Danu's, Dom's, but it is all mine. A unique blend that is mine to possess. Mine to control. It becomes a part of me—sinks into my core in a way it had not quite done yet. Like I was missing an integral piece, needing to be awoken. I become one with it, accept it, and when I do, I understand it all. I begin to understand what Danu meant now when she said we created something new.

"Dominus," I breathe, the magic swelling and beginning to overcome me.

"Yes, my love."

"I need you." Without hesitation, he llifs us to the bed, and we rest knee to knee as we had done the night of our bonding, as we so often do, submitting to one another.

Not tonight. I push him backwards onto the bed and give him no warning before climbing onto his waist and lowering myself onto him. We release a shared groan at the sensation. I move, up and down, hard and fast, and he grips my hips, slamming into me. Thrust for thrust. Move for move. Dance for dance. I bring him up to meet me, and I pull my long, flowing hair away from my neck. Dominus takes it for me, twisting it around his fist behind my neck. I bring him to my chest, right above my heart.

"Take from me, Dominus," I demand, letting my eyes glow, and my magic hums through me so strongly, so powerfully, it becomes an audible noise. My own sonation. Whipping wind, rushing water. The earth, the moon, the sea. "Take it all, my notorum."

His eyes flash brightly, reflecting the power in my own. "Your wish is my command." And he bites. He bites so hard that my blood flows eagerly from my chest and pools between us, a red waterfall rushing into the moving current of our entwined bodies.

Danu's power flows with it, and I feel it enter him, sinking into the marrow of his bones. We come together in a new way, in a way that is somehow more than the bond we already share.

A new power. A new species. A reckoning is born.

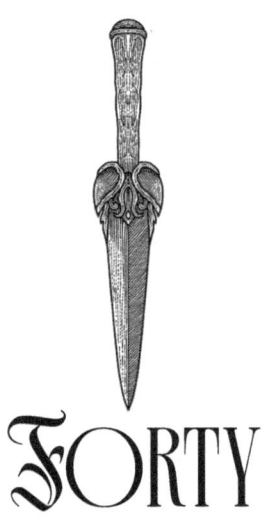

FORTY

We spend the next wyth training. I recall the sparring between Icarus and Dominus in the armoury and how enamoured I was by their skill and power. I laugh at it now, blasting Dominus on his arse for the—I have lost count of how many times. We are near equals now, though I think being the direct link to Danu gives me an upper hand.

"This is incredible. I thought I could fight as an Erad. This power is unmatched." He's right. It is. We still keep it and the nodus veiled, but it lingers in our bones, pushing through our skin. Using nothing but our hands and weapons for fear of drawing too much attention, we have bloodied each other for hawrs each day, testing the physical limits.

I have become relentless in my practice of magic, studying, working, and learning every element and nuance of it. I will continue to do so until it becomes as easy as breathing. Dominus has been blissfully happy to discover that my arsenal is advanced. I have earth magic. I can call to the ground, the trees, the mountains and bend them to my will. I can conjure the sea from its tide and rain down stars. I have divination magic. I can influence what others see, creating illusions that are not there, though it takes an immense amount of mental focus that is hard to maintain within the vicinity of my notorum. I am bound to a powerful Erad, possessing his battle mind and warrior strength.

I realise the stark differences in my life now and menoths ago. This is impossible, absurd, unimaginable.

And yet...

It is completely right. This was never what I dreamed of finding, yet I could never imagine my life any other way. Dominus is more wary, always speculating, concerned it might be too much. Indeed, there are brief moments right as I drift off to sleep and as I wake when I forget that magic floods my veins. But remembering is never laced with sadness. Only endless amazement.

"Are you exhausted with defeat yet?"

"No, but I am aching for you to spill my blood in different ways." He flashes that dimpled smile and those sparkling lupine teeth, and I am ready to take the fight elsewhere. Before we can move, my body freezes, and I can feel my eyes as they haze over.

"We have arrived. Ready for us. We will break the wards and meet you in Danumhar," Eden calls to me.

"Eden is back. They've made it," I say breathlessly.

We llif to the craggy cliffside, watching as ship after ship after ship sails towards Danumhar. Endless fleets pepper the water. The sight of it fills me with hope. We watch as they all come aground on the shore below. We watch as they pile out of the ships. Beautiful, ethereal, lethal creatures. The Sídhe.

Some of them look like the humans I grew up with but changed. More. Many of them bear wings of all different sizes and colours. Some are like the wings of a mayfly, shiny and translucent. Some are iridescent hues of blue, purple, and green. Some are round while others are more sharply defined. But they are all mesmerising in their beauty. There are wee little ones and ones as tall as Dominus. Others arise from the water with shimmering scales and long, dark hair. Their tails turn to scale-covered legs and feet as they emerge. *Merrow,* my mind whispers.

They all pause at an invisible border. Eden comes forth. Eden, in her full glory. She has changed forms, but my blood tells me it is her. Her flowing hair is no longer grey but vibrant, lush, and a rich umber in colour. Her blue eyes shine now in that way that mine, Dom's, and Icarus' do. She doesn't look much older than me now, and to my surprise, her face looks like my mother's did, and I understand why now. We were all her children. She's all sharp angles and full pink lips. She wears celestial robes of decadent gossamer, the same colour as her eyes. Her butterfly-like wings span broadly behind her, shimmering in the sunlight. Their brilliant blue hues glimmer like living sapphires. Tiny scales overlap like miniature tiles, creating a smooth texture traced by dark veins.

She holds a long, polished hand to the air. Closing her eyes, she begins to chant, *"Briseadh"* over and over. The others join in with her, and my heart dances to the beat of it. I close my eyes and join them. The magic swells and swims 'round the shore, the waters violently dancing along to the beat.

The pressure grows until a moment later, a pop sounds, and I open my eyes to see a shimmering line spanning the coast as high and wide as I can see, sliding down until it hits the ground and sputters out. My back itches at the release of it.

"Thorne." I look at Dominus to see him staring behind me. I turn my head to see that I have sprouted wings of my own. Not pale, luminous Sídhe wings. Not thick, feathered Eradian wings. No. Giant, velvet wings, dark and rich, dripping in earth tones. Danu sends me a vision of them to my mind. They were hers.

The forewings are drenched in the hues of autumn's last whisper. Like parchment dipped in sepia and brushed with the golden light of a fading sun. The warm brown bleeds into a deep green that spans throughout the lower wings. Green like the moss that crawled into me to heal me—green so dark it's nearly black. Each of the lower wings possesses a round spot in its centre. No, they are full, iridescent moons. The wings' edges are scalloped and rimmed with an inky black.

Inspired by the Polyphemus moth. They were my favourite. These wings were one thing I wholly loved about myself. The only things that were ever really mine.

They are beautiful, Danu. A true gift. I am honoured to share this part of your true self with you. Thank you.

'Tis a marvel to see them again.

I flutter them for Dominus, then I change them, allowing them to relax into a long train of silk down my back.

"A gift. From Danu," I say.

"She certainly knows how to give gifts. I must take notes."

"Do not think I have forgotten about the one you owe me. When this is over, I am getting my mark."

"I will give it to you once the wards are set if you wish. Mark or no, Hellas will sense you. And you will still be mine. Every glorious inch of you. I would rather display you proudly." He stalks over to take my throat and gently pulls me in for a kiss.

"You do know that I still want it, right? That I want every single moment of forever with you."

His eyes shine in a way different from the glowing. In a way that shows me what my confessions mean to him. "I know, mo céasadh. That is all I want as well. And I am sorry. I am sorry you fell in love with someone whose fate is as warped as mine. I never meant to bring you any of this."

"Do you not remember what Danu showed me? My fate has always been sealed. Long before I met you. Regardless of what our nodus will do for our power and the outcome of this battle, all I have wanted is to love and be loved. I made the decision the night we bonded that I wanted you for every moment I have with you. You, alone, Dominus, are more than enough. You are worth whatever we face together. I would rather spend the rest of my life fighting at your side than not have you at all." He embraces me, and we cling to each other, spending a long moment breathing each other in.

"To answer the question I can feel you are too scared to ask, yes. Yes, I was angry not to be the heir, but not for the reasons you think. I was angry that it was you." He pulls back, bringing one hand behind my neck and the other to tuck wind-whipped hair behind my ears. "You have already gone through so much, and this felt like more than you should have to bear. You should be spending your days working on your research and reading, and your nights tangled in sheets with me. You should be with Eamon and Elowyn, not Eden, on the wythnos, cooking and pulling weeds in the garden and laughing until your stomach hurts. You should be travelling through the vast, stunning territories of Eregahl, shining your light and meeting new people. You should be able to bask in the glory of our nodus, wanting for nothing. You should not be readying for battle, concerning yourself with gods and deamhans and protecting innocent lives. You deserve the most perfect life, Thorne, and I ache to give it to you. I did not want this for you."

I laugh, genuinely laugh, at him and pull back to look into his eyes. "As much as I appreciate that, and as wonderful as that life seems, it was not meant for me. Dominus, my path was carved long ago. I discovered this world twelve yehrs ago and never looked back. I have never stopped searching for answers. I have spent my entire life searching for this, for you, and I found more than I could have imagined." I cup his face in my palms. "I am the heir. I have always been the heir. From the moment I was born, this was my purpose. Using your very sentiment against you, I am sorry for the pain it caused you to be banished here. I am sorry that you spent three centuries here alone, lost, and scared. But I am also grateful for it. I am beyond thankful that fate brought us together. Look at the odds of us finding one another otherwise. We likely would not have, and I cannot imagine my life without you in it. Whatever our lives look like, whatever we must fight, whatever we must become to survive, I will gladly do it. Please, never doubt me or my love for you. I will love you in this life. I will love you in the beyond. I will always be endlessly yours."

He wraps his arms tightly around me before releasing a deep breath. "Thorne, my agony, you are a force of nature. One that will rival the gods themselves. One that will overcome darkness and evil because that is what you were crafted for."

The sounds of footsteps pull us from our moment as the Sídhe, my people, arrive home at last. I take them in, witnessing all their glory and vast numbers.

"Welcome to you all. We cannot begin to express the gratitude and happiness we feel to have you all here. I know that dark times bring us together, but my hope is that something much more beautiful will keep you here. This land is yours. Welcome home."

FORTY ONE

The Sídhe settle rather quickly. They scatter around the academy, choosing their rooms and beginning to familiarise themselves with the castle. I speak with as many of them as I can, learning their names and what parts of Albion they are from. I learn that the Sídhe were more commonly called luminaires. Our powers derived from Eden are those of concentrated light.

Like me, those who were unknown to the truth have full knowledge of their lives before. They've taken on the memories of their ancestors and the understanding of what they are and how to wield magic. Practising and honing it will be what we focus on, especially determining specialities. This is an experience new to all of us, and though I truly regret the events that brought us here, I find consolation in the fact that we are all in one place, learning this new way of life together.

Ever the researcher, I have begun to categorise their traits and powers in different journals. Buzzing with joy of newfound discoveries, I help them unpack and settle into their rooms. Bounding around a corner of the east wing with quilts in tow, I nearly run into someone. "Oh, apologies. I—Vivian!" I drop the quilts, fearing my eyes' deception.

"Thorne." She looks at me with her bright blue eyes. Eyes just like Eden, and it somehow all seems so obvious. We wrap our arms around each other, not needing words. Our embrace is long and tight.

"Look how far we have come from a tiny library, a world away. Look at what your eager, hungry mind did. You freed us, Thorne. We have magic again because of you."

"It was a joint effort," I say, smiling at her through blissful tears. "Have you found a room yet? If not, I would love to help you."

"I have. Walk with me there?"

"Absolutely."

"Good. Tell me everything."

I do.

We have wards up before nightfall. They likely will not stop Hellas, but they will protect us from his deamhans and alert us if anything gets through. This is the most security we've had against him, and we allow ourselves to relish the small victory. Though Danu has not fully revealed all her memories to me yet, her fear of Hellas rivals my own. There is darkness shrouding the memory of their father. She keeps it hidden from me in a stone vault, surrounded by thorns and shadows, but I can smell the terror that stands outside of it. I can feel the coldness of it. If Hellas is truly akin to that, then we need every bit of power we can get.

"Where did you go?" Dominus asks me, pulling me from my thoughts and the steaming warmth of my bath.

"Just considering things Danu has shared with me and things that she has not. Trying to assess Hellas' power, however futile that might be."

He wraps me in a soft, warm bath towel, kissing the water from my chest as he does. "Do you think we could table the doom and gloom for a moment of reprieve? I have a surprise. I promise we can resume our favourite wartime activities in a bit."

"A surprise?" This piques my interest. I allow myself to be giddy about it—how I should feel about a surprise from my beloved, not terrified of what might happen if we step away for a single moment.

"Mmhmm. Are you saying you accept?"

"I am unaware of what I am accepting, but if you are offering, then I accept." Gods, I want to live inside that dimple.

"Patience, my notorum. I will satisfy those needs shortly. *Éadaí,*" he whispers, and magic hums along my skin. I look down to find my body dressed in the most stunning gown I have ever seen. I run my hand along the softness of the gossamer, spun from ethereal whispers of white smoke. It flows like living water over my skin, its diaphanous layers catching in the candlelight.

The bodice plunges to a deep point, displaying the fullness of my breasts, while moth-like sleeves drape elegantly from my shoulders, their edges rippling with the gentle breeze floating through the room. The waist hugs my curves tightly, accentuating my shapely figure, but the skirts and subtle train billow outward softly, cascading to the ground in a pool of moonlight. I spin the skirts gently, and the gown comes alive, moving like mist over still waters.

Dominus is a wicked counterpart to my resplendence, dripping with darkness. His raiments, the same smoky material of my own, are the deepest of black. His top is without sleeves, displaying his honed, thick arms, and cuts into a similar deep point as my own, with the bottom portion mirroring the top, giving a view of the matching dark pants. A long train of smoke falls from his shoulders, trailing to the floor behind him. He looks like an angel of death, and I ache to see his wings free, to see the terrifying, glorious sight of him in his true form.

"How? Where?" Words abandon me, wholly enamoured by the exquisite, celestial raiment adorning my body as if it were crafted for me.

"I once thought of you as sunlight. A new day that dawned when I thought I was lost to the darkness. But then I realised you are not the sun, Thorne. You are the moon. You shone your light upon me, a beacon in the night. You sat with me in that darkness as if you belonged there, too. You did not expose me; you reflected me. And look at you now, dressed in moonlight, a perfect rival to my night." As he says it, he loosens the veil on our nodus, and smoke crawls from him, swirling and winding to form two perfect crowns above our heads.

Pride consumes me as Dominus reaches his arm out for me to take. "Shall we?"

Words abandon me. Rather than pittifully crafting a response, I carve the words on the walls of my mind and reach my arm to wrap around his. My blood sings at the contact.

Dominus llifs us, and we appear swiftly in the middle of the forest. I can tell by the way my magic clings to my skin in protection that it's the furthest we have travelled so far, and I wonder what the sensation feels like to move across islands, across worlds.

I shift my eyes to see in the darkness. When I do, it illuminates the dirt pathway that we stand on, which is barely wide enough to walk through, nearly overgrown with creeping vines and wild amethyst thyme. My eyes follow the path lit with those same illuminated mushrooms to a small stone cabin with a steep, moss-covered roof that gives life to a worn chimney. Warm, glowing amber light flickers from two small windows on either side of the arched wooden door.

"What is this place?" I look to Dominus, who is studying me.

"This was my home before I built the academy. This was where I stayed when I was more...human. After I decided the veiled cave was not a suitable home. This," he says, nodding to the cabin, "is perhaps one of the most vulnerable pieces of me. This is me with no one else, lost and forgotten, angry and grieving, without fear of who sees it. I want to show it to you."

This is the equivalent of letting him read my book. This is him bearing dark parts of himself not meant for others to see. An offering. Give and take.

"You built this?"

"Yes. It took me some time. Turns out the Erads are not masters of everything. I had to teach myself many skills. Woodworking, harvesting stones, and creating a mortar to set them. I have rethatched the roof a few times, made additions and updates. I return here when I leave the scol, or I stay in the wind, hunting."

"It looks so human. So beautifully simple."

"I suppose so."

I love that about it. I relish seeing what he's spent all this time doing. He did not surrender. He acquired new skills and worked to survive.

"Can we go inside?"

"Absolutely." His pale eyes begin to glow as he takes my hand and leads us to the door. His scent covers everything here, differently than in the castle. This version is stripped, raw. The earthy components of it are stronger, and there is a hint of fire to it, a heady smoke.

"*Oscailte,*" he whispers, and the door clicks as it unlocks. He steps in front of me to push the door open, then moves out of the way so that I may enter behind him. The space is warm and cosy, opening to a small kitchen on the left that houses scarce essentials: a wooden plate, bowl, and fork, a drinking vessel, and a cast-iron basin. A shelf above the basin holds glass decanters of various coloured spirits. The living quarters take up most of the space. Warm, wooden beams arch overhead. A grand, round window dominates the back wall. Its panes are divided into three arches with smaller circles like moons directly above the points. Through the glass, I can glimpse a lush forest beyond. Bookshelves line the walls on either side of the lit fireplace. The light of its flames dances across a plush, emerald sofa. Verdant plants cascade from every corner, some surely possessing magical properties. Tall, white candles flicker from low tables and drip from their candelabras on the wooden walls. A set of winding wooden stairs rests on the right wall, leading to the second level.

It is as if the earth crafted this place and pushed it out from the ground, a profound secret.

"The bedroom is upstairs," he says so quietly that I nearly miss it.

"It feels so much like you, but different somehow." He smiles at that. "Maybe we can come back here. If—when this is over." There is no confidence in my voice. Only hope. Because who knows what will even remain if Hellas gets his way?

"No, mo céasadh. This is not a place fit for you. Nor would I want you to live here. Seeing you here," he pauses, looking around, "heals something within me, but I would not want you here forever. I will build you something far grander if you wish."

I smile at him, willing fate to see this—to see him. To look at this soul who has lost so much and deserves to live. Truly live.

"Well, with that settled, I do believe there was a promise about satisfying certain desires of mine, Master."

He walks towards me with his hands in his pockets and that train of smoke trailing behind him. "Indeed, I plan on doing just that. After I mark you."

Heat floods through every inch of me. I search for deception in his eyes. "Are you certain? Is it safe?"

He steps into me, bringing my chin into his fingers. Night

dark hair falls around his forehead as he looks down at me. "I have never been more certain. I know not what our future looks like, Thorne. All I know is that we have right now. We have tonight, and I want to spend it showing you what you mean to me. I want to gift you with my mark so that you may wear it proudly, and I want you to leave your mark on me. I want remnants of you forever evident upon my flesh."

I think of the night we bonded, and I repeat my own words with a smile, "Show me what to do."

"Upstairs," he demands, his grin mirroring my own.

I slowly glide up the wooden steps as I run my hand along the smooth, worn handrail. The top of the stairs leads to a single bedroom through a round opening. A large bed lies in the middle of the back wall, which is covered in live vines and tree branches. The bed is crafted of harvested, raw tree trunks. Dark, plush bed linens adorn it. Endless amounts of candles line the walls, floor, and bedside table, illuminating the room in a gentle, warm glow.

"Are the extra pillows for me, or have you always been so high maintenance?"

"I slept on the floor of the forest with only a stump to rest my head on for a hundred yehrs. And you've seen the cot. I will let you draw that conclusion."

I snort at him. "Well, thank you for going through the trouble anyway."

The light of flickering candles caresses his white teeth as he smiles at me. "Nothing for you is ever a trouble of mine."

I reach for him, and he is in my arms instantly. "Will it hurt?" I ask.

"Would it matter if it does? I am sure you would find it pleasurable either way. The bonding ritual was supposed to hurt. Now look at us, tearing into each other's flesh every day for the delicacy of it. I relinquished all expectations of our nodus long ago, mo céasadh."

"Why do you still call me that?"

"Because I have grown fond of it. And you are still my agony, my endless torment. Only now, it is because you torture me with your body and your tongue and by wearing raiments," he says, squeezing the full curves of my hips.

"Do you realise you were the one who dressed me tonight?"

"Yes, and I regret nothing. You look ravishing. You look like a goddess. You look like mine."

"Mark me before I consume you whole," I demand.

His laugh rumbles through my chest where we touch. He brings his palms up toward me, and I mirror the gesture, running my fingers along the calluses of his hands and down his wrists.

"Where did you get these?" I ask, brushing my fingertips across the endless scars that smatter his forearms and wrists.

"Not long after I arrived, I went looking for deamhans. Something to take my anger out on, I suppose. I found a nest of abhartachs. They are like the dearg due in that they love blood, but they are, unfortunately, much harder to kill. They reanimate unless slain by fire or stabbed in the heart with silver. That is why I carry one sword of silver and one of steel. They are small, fast little buggers, though. I didn't know how many there were or how quickly they could bleed me out. They kept slicing me open, over and over, with their knives for teeth. They had me by my hands, and no matter how I fought, they held strong, continuing to tear me open. That was the closest I have come to death here. It took me days to recover, and since they kept tearing me open and the lack of my full power, the wounds scarred. The only scars I have, though I should be covered head to toe in them. They are a reminder of my weakness and arrogance."

"You are neither of those things."

"Not anymore. Not where it counts." He releases a long breath. "Are you ready?"

"Yes."

"Close your eyes, clear your mind, and take a deep breath. Good. Now, like before, when we cloaked the nodus, I want you to inspect it. Turn it over. Look at the parts of it that are me, that are you. Then consider both of us and how we fit together. Think of our relationship, all moments ugly and pure. Now, think of my body. Not that way, you hungry thing. Good. I feel it. Finally, without thinking, tell your magic to mark me. Instruct the nodus to take what it needs. When you are ready, speak, *'Brandálaim.'*"

I do as instructed, and the magic listens, bending to my will. I hear a small groan loosen from Dominus, and I open my eyes to see him staring at his arms. We watch in tandem as inky thorns begin to appear and crawl around his wrists and over his arms, adorning every one of those scars in my namesake. Though the scars remain, they are now hidden beneath sharp, twisted vines from his forearms to the tops of his hands.

I study him, calculating every movement of his eyes, every change in his face. "You would take something I hate about myself and turn it into something beautiful, covering it in your essence." He brings his marked hands to my face to kiss me deeply.

He pulls back to whisper the spell against my lips, and a sharp sensation blooms between my breasts at my sternum. I wonder if he planned it because when I look down, the mark now imprints my pale skin, fully visible with the cut of the gown. From my viewpoint, I can make out one vertical line with smaller horizontal lines running through it at various distances and angles. His pale green eyes shimmer in the low light.

"What is it?"

Dominus eyes the mark with furrowed brows. "'Tis a word. In a very old language. One of the first. It is called an Ogham." He reaches to run a thumb down the mark, causing me to shiver. "I haven't seen one of these in a very long time."

"What does it say?"

He drops his thumb and meets my eyes. "Baile. It means home." He huffs a small laugh. "Home. Because you are the only home I have truly known. The only one I will ever need."

He finally brings his eyes to mine, and we rest in a moment of silence. Of what we have done. Of what we learned from it. A single blip in time where it all rushes through. The doubt, the uncertainty, the overwhelming fear that this is too much happiness. This should not feel allowed somehow.

"I love you too," he finally whispers, and I know his heart is breaking, too. Breaking for the impending future, for the cruel reality we face. A reality where this could cease to exist.

I push the thoughts from us both on a wind of smoke, and slip on a comfortable mask. "Can you mark me another way now?" I ask.

His velvet laugh sends a shiver down my thighs. "It would be my honour."

It is still dark when we pull apart hawrs later. Blood litters the dark sheets, and my body is red and raw from the consumption. I wish I could scar. I wish his teeth and handprints would mark my skin forever.

"Maybe we can work on that," he says, panting as he runs his rough fingers over my mark.

"Promise?" I ask, collapsing on top of him. The beat of his heart matches mine.

"Yes, but not now. We must get back."

"Can we not resume here until dawn?" I ask, pushing back up.

"We can, but we will not be alone for long?"

"Why not?" I stiffen atop him.

"Icarus has returned," he smiles. We both jump off the bed, fully clothed, before our feet hit the floor. Icarus is back, and I pray that he brings help with him.

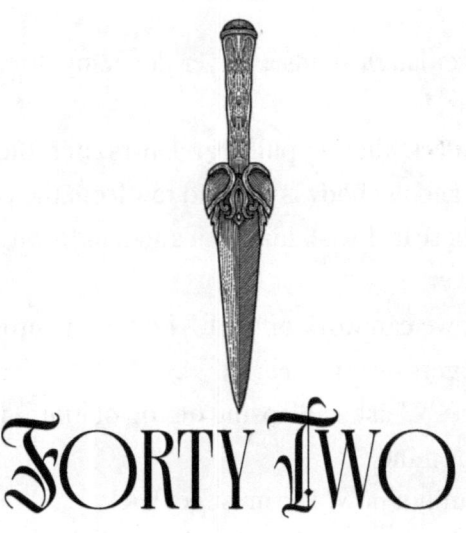

FORTY TWO

"Let me sort this out. Our tricky little notorum is actually a Sídhe—sorry, luminaire—bonded to an Eradian warrior and is also somehow possessed by a dead never-really-was Seren. Gods, brother, you know how to pick them," Icarus overviews.

Dominus tosses a dagger at Icarus' face, but he catches it with unparalleled ease. "So, does the goddess Danu offer enlightenment as to how she might help us win this war?" Icaurs adds.

They both look at me.

Well? I question her.

It will be made known when the time is right. He will not want to face me.

"She says trust the process."

"The process being what exactly?" He stabs the dagger

into an apple and brings it to his mouth to bite.

"Why don't you tell us what you learned, Brother, and we will go from there?" Dominus interjects.

He huffs a deep sigh. "I reached Caledon. Noreg is still lost to us, though I made some friends, and hopefully, word will reach her in time. Caledon was...not convinced. Though revealing the truth of Eden did send a little sparkle in his eye. Let us hope that sparkle turns into a flame, and he arrives in time to help. Forgive me. I...I did my best. Gave him the hero's speech and all." His facade flickers enough to reveal his self-disappointment.

"Icarus, you did wonderfully. The fact that you reached him at all is a testament to your skill. One I look forward to fostering if we make it out of this."

"And as much as I appreciate the sentiment, Dominus, the fact remains that this still will not be enough. We have no certainty of what we are up against. The Eradian army alone has an unfair advantage against a couple of half-wit luminaires. No offence, my darling, but that is what I see. And we are blind to every move Hellas makes."

"But we have them. They came to our aid when we needed them most. We can continue to spend every day training them. You can assemble your own rank to train now that you are back. Two and a half Eradian trainers are better than none. We have us. We have two gods on our side. Maybe three if we are lucky. Danu says he will not want to face her. That has to matter. It has to count for something," I say.

"It does, my love. It does. We just have to—"

Dominus and I stare at one another, frozen with sudden

fear. The wards have been triggered. The three of us move instantly, lliffing outside, weapons ready and magic humming.

The sky above the sea spins as the wind barrels violently toward us. Dominus and I lock our nodus deeper within us than we ever have, and I nearly lose all sense of him, causing a violent protest within me. In a flash, three people appear with the light of the growing day. By their looks alone, I immediately know who they are.

Adonien. Fina. Camiel.

"Well, at least I can finally say you have surprised me, Icarus. I did not expect to find you here." Adonien, the King of Erads, is terrifying. He's equal in size to Dominus, though he radiates a different kind of power, a darker one that commands reverence. A cascade of once golden, now silver hair frames his weathered visage and flows down into a full matching beard. His piercing irises are solid white and glowing. He's draped in dark robes with gilded seams. A winged helmet rests on his head, one that resembles his silver, eyeless wings.

Fina looks the most like Dominus with her long, dark hair. Where Dom's eyes are the palest of green, hers are a shining emerald, and where Dominus is pale, Fina's complexion is a stunning, radiant olive. Her armour is dark with silver sigils etched into it, and a single sword rests across her back. Her eyes roam over every inch of Dominus in assessment—in surprise.

Camiel does not move. He studies us all equally but does not show any emotion on his stoic face. His hair is a shade between Dom's pitch black and the pale blonde of Icarus', landing on a warm, soft brown that falls to his chest. His eyes are duller than the others, a deep steel, but they are highlighted by a smatter of freckles beneath.

My gut twists as I witness the inspections. I can taste the regret in the air. There is so much that remains unsaid and likely will with Adonien here. I remain frozen, fearing to even breathe.

"Father," Dominus spits. "Glad to see you finally found the time to pop by for a visit. I wish I could say it was welcomed."

"I suppose we can disregard pleasantries then since your good-for-nothing brother filled you in."

Icarus flashes his teeth at him.

"My loyal brother did, yes. Imagine how unfortunate it was to learn that my very father, the one who raised me in his image to become a ruler, sold me for everlasting reign."

Fina and Camiel glance at Adonien in confirmation, both battling to hide their shock.

"Regardless of what I did to prepare you, regardless of all my vast and failed efforts, you were still weak. I could smell the weakness on you as I do now. You were not made to rule."

Dominus bellows a guttural laugh. "You know what confounds me the most? Not for a moment did I possess the desire to rule. I ache not to sit upon your cursed fucking throne. If you ever paused to offer a choice, I would have gladly conceded my reign. It was all I ever hoped for. But you could not stop gorging on your greed and power to ever truly consider your children."

Adonien's eyes simmer with rage. "Beneficial for you to say now that you have been banished, but you likely would not have agreed to that then."

"I suppose we will never know. I will relish that fact. I hope it eats you alive, wondering if you could have avoided all of this.

Though deep down, I am sure you never cared enough about me to wonder."

"I forgot how full of passion and theatrics you are, my boy."

"I am glad your vision of me weathered while I learned what a spineless bastard you are."

"Ha! And to think, I come here out of love. Out of the selflessness of my own heart to warn you, to beg you to stand down."

"You came here because you fear me. You know you are playing a game that you might lose. After all, it was your fear of me that drove me here, was it not? A mhargadh with Hellas? I become his new plaything while you remain on the throne."

Adonien's eyes sharpen at Dominus. "You cannot defeat him. He has an entire army of deamhan warriors he created. Do you know what he calls them? The Slaugh. And, oh, are they hideously marvellous things. They are restless, hungry beasts. Do you know how he crafted them, Dominus?"

I despise the recognition of the same revelry in his face as I did in Icarus' during his diatribe. It drips with arrogance, knowing he has dominion of the moment.

He harvested the souls from your endless bounties all these yehrs. He changed them, moulded them, and evolved them into something that you cannot defeat. They are a wild hunt of winged foul creatures. Ones that fly. Ones that crawl. Ones that crave flesh."

Dominus stills beside me as a collective fear rakes down the three of us. How are we supposed to defeat an army of undead deamhans alongside the Eradian Army?

"I beseech you, my son, do not fight him. That will secure

your end. You will lose, and you will die. He cannot be stopped. He has a plan far bigger than us all. Stand with him. Stand with me. As it was always meant to be."

"Hellas' plan be damned. I will not stand down. I will not step aside as he lays waste to this entire world. I was born to prevent that. We all were." He glares at Fina and Camiel, and I see the doubt begin to form on their stone facades.

"You ignorant fool. It will not please me to see you gutted on the battlefield."

"It will please me, though, to wrap my hands around your insides, Father."

His laughter sends shivers down my spine. "At least you are brave. I suppose I did something right, then?"

"You did nothing right. You failed us all. Everything you crafted us to be, everything you stand for as a king is a fucking lie. I will dethrone you. I will rip the crown from your torn-away head if I must. You do not deserve to wear it. You do not deserve to lead our people."

"Stay bloodthirsty, my boy. You will need it." Adonien turns to leave, commanding Fina and Camiel to follow, but they both hesitate.

Dominus finally speaks to them. "I summoned you over and over. I endlessly looked for a way off this island. I never gave up. I have always tried to get back to you. You do not have to fight for him. You can choose to protect the children of our creators. You can choose your own path. I know you think you cannot, but you can."

"Fina, Camiel, come now," Adonien booms.

"I love you as I always have. Regardless of what you choose,

I understand. Forgive me for failing you. You deserve so much better."

Fina begins to crumble, and I see her fight to straighten her composure. Camiel listens intently, and I wonder what kind of person he is—if he is his father's son or not.

"Dominus—" Fina begins, but Adonien claps his hands loudly, and Fina and Camiel are gone.

"I do not take pleasure in any of this, but you are the price to pay for our future. A new world."

"No, Father, I am not. For in the darkness of this world, I, too, have changed. I have evolved and become something of your nightmares, and I look forward to showing you exactly what your chosen son is capable of."

Adonien stares at Dominus for a long moment, unable to hide a shiver before turning and disappearing into the clouds.

I gaze into the space that the three of them abandoned, wondering how it has come to this.

"Well, was that the reunion you dreamed of for three centuries, Brother?" Icarus sure knows how to read the bloody room.

Dominus turns to him and, to my surprise, laughs and claps Icarus on the shoulders. "More than I could have hoped for."

Icarus mirrors his laughter. "'Twas a great plan, reliving the story so that Fina and Camiel knew the truth rather than telling Father everything you wanted to. Clever."

"Let us hope it works, and when the time comes, they make the right decision."

I let out an exhausted breath, tired of all the hopes that we have hanging on others who determine our fate. They both look at me then.

"Thorne, our darling girl, did you enjoy meeting your dear father-in-bond?" Icarus asks with a raised eyebrow.

"I do not even think he noticed me," I realise. "Not that I am distraught about it. I am so sorry for both—for all four—of you. I cannot imagine what you have gone through." My thoughts slide to my own father. He was everything Adonien is not, and I could not miss him more at this moment. My whole family. I yearn to sit by the fire and tell them all that has happened to me. To tell them we are bloody luminaires and that I was never cursed. That my soulmate plagued me. It was all out of love. It was love, not darkness, that tore my heart to shreds.

They know, Danu whispers to me. *They see you, my girl.*

I ignore the onslaught of emotions in front of Dominus and Icarus. It is selfish to bask in the relief and joy of that realisation when they just had such a confrontation with their father. I banish my tears, locking away my emotions quickly from the yehrs of practice, and I tuck it away to pull out and study later.

Dominus walks over to wrap me in his arms and place a kiss atop my head. "Everything will be alright. I promise."

Icarus joins, wrapping his arms around us both. "And even if we die, at least we die together."

We share deprecated laughter.

Forty Three

Wyths pass without a word from Adonien or Hellas. We work tirelessly to train the Sídhe in combat and wielding magic. Though their instincts have returned, it is different knowing what to do and doing it. Being children of Eden, our specialities are divination, foresight, and light magic. Caolán, one of the appointed leaders of the Sídhe, possesses the power to see an opponent's moves in his mind before they transpire. He is one of the few who can hold their own against Dominus and Icarus. It has been outstanding to witness his magic manifest— watching them all and their many and varying skills. Breeda, another chosen leader, is fierce and driven. Like many of us, she can alter what people see, but Breeda has mastered her control and cannot be fooled by mind magic. She is unmoving steel, and I have found myself drawn to her, seeking her out as the perfect practice partner. I have learned how connected magic and personality are. Even with all this going on, Dominus and I have found a new, beautiful rhythm. Such rewards come from watching the faces of my family alight when their powers grow or make themselves known. I have developed quite a passion for it, and I think my Eradian warriors have found a familiar comfort in it as well.

Dominus, Icarus, and I spend our non-training hawrs searching for clues that Hellas might be close. We meet with Eden each day to strategise and learn from her experience with Hellas. Eden spends most of her time training the Sídhe to connect with their magic. She tells us stories of her time here before the war, working to help us strengthen the bonds we have with our true selves. Eamon is a large luminaire and a warrior in his own right. He dons a full head of long, golden hair, and his beard has become even more luxurious. He spends his days at the forge, crafting and imbuing weapons for battle, whispering secret, ancient magics into the white hot metals.

Though their forms have changed, I am grateful to learn that their hearts remain the same. I spend as much time with them as I can. Eden now cooks foods that we all prefer that outdo what I thought she was capable of as a human. We spend long hawrs into the night talking, drinking, laughing, and learning about each other again. The other nights I spend with Dominus, working vigilantly to memorise every curve, every sound, every taste of him.

Our nodus does grow, even stifled as we are forced to keep it. Though I long for the days to love him freely and wherever I want. I begin to resent the good days, knowing that we live them in fear and that they are finite. I tread the stone floors of whichever room we end up in, wondering if it is our last, as I do now.

"If you can pace the floor like that, I have not done my job thoroughly. Come here to me."

"You are thorough in all your attempts, my love. I just worry. I hate the waiting. I live in agony, begging for this to end and hoping it never arrives."

Dominus moves from the bed to meet me instead. "I know, Thorne. But regardless of what happens, we have now. Do not let the fear of morrow poison the joy of today."

"I try, I do. I love you. I love this life. If it were not for the impending, near-certain death, I would be so consumed with happiness. Just knowing that happiness is borrowed enrages me."

Darkness blots Dominus from my view, dragging its slimy mist over my skin. Coldness, unknown to me, snakes its way into my bones, causing my breath to ice in the air before me. This is not Dom's inky smoke.

"Dominus," I whisper. He pulls me into his arms tightly, and his wings explode from his back, wrapping around us both. Magic hums painfully inside me. It thrums below the surface with such power that my skin yearns to liquify and drip to the floor.

Hellas, Danu whispers to me. I tighten my grip on Dom. Hellas is here, in the middle of the night, in our room.

"This does not have to be the end of that happiness." His voice is deep and smooth like a finely aged whiskey, and it crackles my magic down my spine. I force it back, shielding everything that is Danu from him. Dominus moves me behind him, but I fearfully peek through his wings.

Hellas. Whatever I was expecting him to look like, it was not painfully beautiful. I see where the Erads were carved in the images of the Seren because, like Dominus, Hellas is expertly chiselled. Power seeps from him like rot from a festering wound, exuding equal parts danger and allure. His eyes burn red with intensity rivalled only by the inferno of his deep crimson wings, unlike any I have seen yet. Red, leather skin stretches across thick, gnarled bones, and they end in sharp talons. Flowing, wine-colored hair cascades over his shoulders, clad in intricately crafted black armour, the pieces interlocking like the scales of a dragon. The rich burgundy of his tunic peeks out from beneath the armour, littered with straps and buckles. He sits nonchalantly with his legs crossed at the table in front of the hearth.

"'Tis about time you showed yourself. I was bargained to you three centuries ago. I would think you would have introduced yourself by now." I am thankful Dom's sharp bravado remains because mine crumbles to ash as I cower behind him, quaking like a leaf.

"Ah, I find the wait to be tantalisingly delicious. Hate to hear you do not return the sentiment, my pet."

"No, I do not think I found the centuries with my hands buried in the entrails of your horrid beasts quite enjoyable. My apologies."

"Oh, but you were so good at it, were you not? Tell me, Dominus, did you not secretly delight in it? Did you not yearn for the sound of cracking bones and flowing blood?"

"Are you going to cajole me all night, or are you going to tell me why you are here?"

If I weren't so terrified, I would want to consume the laughter that croons out of Hellas' long, muscled neck. "Oh, Dominus, unlike these mere mortals, I grew fond of your violence while watching you all these centuries. Studying and waiting. You have impressed me, pet, exceedingly so. I have seen the many forms you have taken, and I have witnessed you defeat everything I have sent to you. You even shattered my wards." He tsks, waving a long, immaculate finger at him. "That has never been done before. Your essence is certainly powerful, made especially stronger by your notorum."

I am pulled from the shadows by a red mist that binds my arms to my body.

"Don't you fucking dare," Dominus growls at him.

"Oh, no. I would not harm a hair on her brilliant head. That would surely upend the plans I have for you both."

"What plans?" I ask, the fire inside me igniting again in the presence of an arrogant, self-righteous prick.

"Ah, she speaks! How entertaining would it be to give you everything from the start? That would hardly make all my work worth it. And I have been working diligently, my dears."

"Get to the fucking point, Hellas," Dom bites.

He laughs that enchanting laugh again. "My, you are delightful. Alas, I have come to make you an offer. A deal. Another mhargadh." His eyes alight with his own words alongside a terrifying smile. Dread coils through my frozen body. This is somehow worse than an all-out attack.

"I'm listening," Dominus responds.

"It pains me to say this, but nothing I create scratches my itch." He stands, towering over both of us. He tucks those blood-red wings in tightly as he paces the room the way I have done every night for wyths.

"Something is missing. Do not mistake, I tried tirelessly to replicate your kind. Unfortunately, nothing ever came out quite the same. You have bested all my creations. Well, all except one. I still have *something* up my sleeve, I suppose." He drums his fingers together in delusional glee. "Yet, my dear Dominus, you have grown on me, attaching to my mind like a barnacle. Slithered your way into my cold, dead heart, and now I want you. There is something within you that thrills me," he says, nearly rolling his eyes back. "Something my other children lack that I cannot recreate. It reminds me of something once told to me, spoken in the dead of night by a seer. A prophecy of my greatness:

'In shadows crowned with gilded light,
the Heir of Blood shall come to sight.
By dark of night and glory's flame,
the dark throne beckons them by name.
Through trials fierce and challenges great,
the heir must prove their royal weight.
As each test passes, veils will lift,
revealing truths, a cosmic gift.
Vicious eyes that pierce the night,
aglow with ancient, eldritch might.
All creatures of fair Hellas' land,
shall bow before the heir's command.
Blood of the ancients courses strong,

in the veins of one who rights the wrong.

For in the heir's bloody unyield,

Hellas' future shall be sealed.'

"You see, I need an heir, Dominus, a champion. Someone to lead my army and secure my victory. I like it as much as you do. I truly imagined my glory being solely my own. So it is written, and so it shall be. And you, my fallen warrior, are my chosen."

The earth spins beneath me, or I spin atop it; I am not sure. My blood clangs in my ears to the beat of a war drum, and my sight blurs. Their voices become muddled for a moment before they focus again with a sharp ringing in my head.

"Tell me you are not serious?"

"Deadly so, my pet."

"Must I verbalise my resignation, or will a 'fuck off' suffice?"

"He giggles. You truly are my child, dear boy. 'Tis quite refreshing. Listen, as any good father would do—well, maybe not since your father did trade your life for power, but I digress. I came to offer you a deal. Take your rightful place on my throne, walk beside me in the shadows, and I will let everyone on this island live, including your beloved."

"You cannot kill her; it will kill me, too." He shoots Hellas a murderous glance.

"You naïve thing. There are ways of untying that simple knot." The nodus bangs at my chest with his words, and my magic thrums through me, boiling over. Hellas winces and drops me to my feet.

"Oh, what was that, my little luminaire? That was delightful! What other tricks do you have?" I do not deign to answer him.

"The answer is no. I refuse to stand by and let you seize these lands. Why would you ever presume that I would help you?"

Hellas sighs extravagantly. "Heed my warning, pet. I came here to offer you salvation. I have witnessed what you have done. To my surprise, you found Eden. You managed to bring her mangy mutts here. You have surpassed all expectations I had for you. It is because of that and my grace alone that you still breathe. I will not be disrespected, nor will I ask again." His crimson eyes begin to glow with fire, and his face ripples and contorts into something made only from nightmares before fading back into the masterpiece of art that he is.

"My final answer is no."

"And so it is. As my progeny, you may now call to me if you change your mind." He takes a step toward us, and I hold my breath. "But do know this, Dominus. You *will* be my heir. Willingly or through the blood of your chosen people, I will claim you. The lives lost will be on your hands. Do think it over." He blows a kiss at me and then disappears into red smoke.

Forty Four

Dominus and I stare at each other for what feels like an eternity. I take the first step, walking towards him, but he retreats, and it floods me with anguish.

"Dominus," I whisper.

"Just. Stop. I need a moment."

"Don't push me away. Do not let Hellas and his false prophecy come between us."

"Do not touch me, Thorne. Do not even look at me. Because you will somehow convince me that this is all going to work out and that being the heir of a deamhan god is not the end of me—of us. And I cannot feel that right now."

"I don't want to make you feel anything but loved, Dom."

He runs his hands through his hair, pulling the ends into a wild frenzy of onyx waves around his head. His eyes widen with chaos brewing inside him.

"I do not deserve to be loved, Thorne! It turns out my fucking destiny is carved too, and I have dragged you down with me. I have done this to us, to all of Eregahl. He says I will lead the army that destroys this world either way." He laughs maniacally, "A rather fitting fucking fate since it was the very role I barely managed to slip out of. I am certain I have made my father proud now." His eyes become wild, and I fear he is on the very edge of breaking.

My heart aches for him, but I will respect his space and allow him to feel whatever he needs to right now. This is not my tactful, brilliant, diplomatic notorum. This is a terrified, cornered man with the fate of the world on his shoulders, so I alter tactics and rise to meet his needs for the moment. "Alright, assume this is the worst-case scenario. Let us play this out—all possibilities. What happens?" I step away and cross my arms, showing him I am willing to play the role of advisor.

He eyes me warily before standing taller. "If Hellas can claim me without my consent, then this is the end of everything as we know it. The only consolation might be that he spares your life, though he would undoubtedly use you for his gain."

"But he does not know about me yet—not about Danu. And that could be what turns the tide of this."

"Maybe. It could also push him further and faster."

Any thoughts here?

He is safe. He cannot be used.

Can you stop the riddles for a single bloody moment and help us fight your sadistic brother?

We claimed him, Thorne. My magic flows through him. He

can resist the claim to power, but he must choose. Hellas will not make it easy for him. You must be strong...for both of you.

My breath is an audible release. "Danu says that you can reject the claim. Her magic runs through you. You can resist it, but it will not be easy."

He drops onto the bed with relief and brings his elbows to rest on his knees. He rubs his eyes with the heels of his palms, and I watch as my thorns, my mark, undulate with the movement. His wings are still free, and they curve around him as if to comfort him. Their eyes whir back and forth between us, watching our every move. He looks like a stone carving sitting there, forever preserved in agony and torment. I burn to walk to him, but I stand still, hands clasped behind my back. I force myself to begin pacing to move my body away from him.

"Do you ever get tired of saving me?" he asks. His tone is sincere, and it breaks me, stopping me in my tracks.

"Never. I will never." My lip begins to quiver, so I suck it through my teeth.

"I am at war, Thorne." He drops his hands to look at me with reddened eyes. "I am fighting to find my place in all this. A place somewhere in the light. A position that helps us win this. It seems, at every turn, I find a way to make it harder. Bonding with you released the wards. It brought this fight to our home. Bringing the Sídhe here likely only pushed Hellas further."

"None of those were your choices alone, Dominus. I wanted the nodus. I begged you for it, and I do not regret that for a second, and it wrecks me that you do."

"I don't—"

"Bringing the Sídhe here was a great move for many

reasons. Sending Icarus to find Caledon might bring us success yet. Loving me with your entire bloody being has saved us both. It has created a nodus and power unlike any other that might very well be what we need to survive. So, forgive me, but I see what you call errors as miracles. I am not asking you to walk in the light, Dominus. I never have. I ask you to walk beside me, whether it leads us to victory or certain death."

I watch him visibly shatter before me, my words sinking dead centre of their mark. I walk to meet him, kneeling on the floor and wrapping my arms around his waist. He envelops me, wings holding us both, and the instant we are wrapped within, we break. We shatter into each other's arms, unstoppable destiny blazing toward us, gaining in velocity.

For a moment, forever, Dominus and I exist in a single, suspended exhale. A single moment laid bare. No titles, no ego, no flesh. A merged conciousness. A constellation of fate. My familiar, my chosen, my friend. This is dying and rebirth. This is a call and answer. A summoning. This is an echo. A memory. And yes, my love, I answer this time as I am awoken, and I can hear you.

Words sound, my words with my voice, as I slowly crawl back to myself. "Swear it to me. Swear your fealty to me and me alone. Promise not to forsake me again. Vow to never doubt yourself or what we can do together. You will not lay claim to the dark throne. You will rule beside me as blood of my blood. Together, we face whatever may come. Swear it."

His hand is steady as he reaches to pluck the blade from the sheath hanging around my neck. His eyes glow with power, with magic, and he takes the tip of it and runs it across the smooth skin of his broad chest, across his heart, and I watch as the blood slides down, dipping and diving along the contours of his honed body.

"I swear to you, my queen, my goddess, my notorum, I yield only to you. I am yours to command, and yours to use as you see fit. I will never forsake you. I will stand by you no matter the cost."

I slowly drag my eyes down him and lean to touch my tongue to the dripping blood at his waist and lick my way upwards to the now-closed wound. I kiss the pink skin there.

"Good," I say sternly.

Icarus blazes through the door, half asleep and half naked. "What was that?"

Dominus and I, still embracing, peek around Dom's wings and say, "Hellas," simultaneously.

He's wide awake then. "Tell me everything."

We do, and when dawn breaks through the sky shortly after, we find Eden and tell her as well.

"He has become too powerful. I fear this all was a mistake," she says.

Tell her. Tell her what I showed you. Tell her you are my child.

"Eden, I need to tell you something. It cannot leave this room. It is something we have kept hidden for when the time is right."

Her brows inch together in concern, but she nods her head.

"A dearg due attacked me when I first arrived here. I died for a moment, and when I did, I went somewhere."

Her eyes dart back and forth between my eyes and my

mouth, clinging to my every word.

"I was not made known to where I was, but it was peaceful—the most peace I have ever felt. Someone spoke to me. She told me I was her chosen. She has spoken to me at various times since, but she was veiled, locked away. When you awoke us, the return of my magic triggered something inside of me. Something that was always there, waiting. When it did, she took the opportunity to claim me...as her heir."

Her eyes widen, and she reaches over to place her hand atop Eamon's.

"When you left your home, Danu watched you all. She watched and whispered blessings upon you as you slipped through the tairseach. She held strong, fighting until her dying breath, expending every bit of her magic to see you through. Hellas was last to enter, and when he turned back to look at her, he smiled. He smiled a wicked, devious smile that she knew promised your downfall." Tears begin to stream from her beautiful blue eyes. "She cast a strong spell that created a plane for her soul to rest. She was there for a long time, waiting, lying dormant. Until Hellas betrayed you all. Her soul was awoken, and it called for her heir, for a soul that could hold her so that she might return to end him."

Her tears evolve into a full sob. "I had no idea. I—oh, Danu."

Go on.

"She felt Hellas was always her responsibility. She wanted to save him. She tried desperately to take the brunt of your father's attention from him. She saw the darkness in him at a young age—saw how desperately he worked to make your father proud. And she saw the monster it created when he always chose Danu instead. A price she willingly paid. She feels she failed you all, and she wishes she could have changed things—gone with you or found a way to end your father and save your world. This is her way of trying to right the wrongs."

"Doesn't she understand it was never hers to bear? She never had to do any of it. She never had to sacrifice herself to save us. We are grateful for the lives we have had because of her, but we did not ask it of her. I hope she understands that we would have loved her regardless. She was our sister."

Danu pushes her power through me, and golden light begins to slip from my hands. It moves over to Eden and strokes her cheek. She closes her eyes and leans into it, sobbing harder. "Oh, my dear sister. I have missed you. I have longed for you. We failed you. I am so sorry."

"No," I say, repeating Danu's words in my mind. "You lived. You created. You loved, Eden. That is all I ever wanted for you all. Hellas is mine to claim. I will finally save his soul from the shadows of Father's darkness. I swear it."

Forty Five

The days pass with an infernal dichotomy of grief and thankfulness. Each day, Dominus grows more distant from me, though he assures me there is nothing to it—only his mind spinning on the coming days. Something inside of me wonders if Hellas' claim has affected him. If darkness grows quietly within him now. There were signs of Danu's presence in my life long before she claimed me.

But his blood tastes the same, and he loves me with the usual desperate fervour. He spends long hawrs drenched in blood and sweat training the Sídhe. We have noticed how close the remaining scolers have become with them, and they often attend training, some of them even picking up weapons and following along with the movements Dominus and Icarus show them.

The young boy from the assembly hall, the one with copper skin and golden eyes, has taken to it well. I have learned that his name is Aengus. He often finds himself as Dom's shadow, a sight that I cannot help but adore. He has a fire in him, and I pray we both live long enough to watch it grow—to see what kind of man he becomes.

We sit now in the Great Hall, all of us eating together, united as a chosen people. I study each of them, marking them all to memory, appreciating every soul in this room. I watch as Aengus studies every move Dom makes. Norine laughs violently at some foul thing Icarus says. Orla speaks more freely than I have seen with the luminaires. I watch them all interact effortlessly as if this were the way it always was. The way it should have always been. Eden and Eamon look upon their people with such pride and joy. I look out upon my family, the spades of them, truly in awe that I found them. I think of the broken woman, standing at the threshold of her childhood home, aching for this very feeling.

My eyes find Dominus as they always do, and he studies me. That dimple creases in his cheek as he smiles with understanding. I want to bottle this moment. I want to squeeze the feeling of it into a vial that I can open and massage into my skin with each sunrise.

"You've done this, you know? You have given me all of this."

"*We* have done this, mo céasadh. Together, we forged a family. Our family."

Dominus drains the wine from his glass and wipes his mouth with a linen cloth before standing. He steps up onto the endless wooden table and walks to the middle of it. All eyes turn to him, and the room quiets.

"I have news for you all, but before I share it, I have a few things to say. Firstly, my thanks do not suffice for the contribution and sacrifice you all have made to be here. I know there is ancient magic at work, and I know each of you longed for this land. I offer my sincerest apologies that your return has been because of this. Although I believe we have all found a certain beauty in it, anyway. You have shown up for your creator. You have taken up arms against those who seek to destroy you. You will make history with your honour, with your glory. And I know that does not justify the lives that will be lost, but I hope it eases your soul into the afterlife. Into a place of peace."

He looks at me then. I wipe hot tears from my cheeks and nod at him.

"You have prepared well. You are strong in your magic and in your skill. I am proud to have such an army at my side. I am proud to lead you into battle."

Caolán stands three rows over from Dominus. "We are here because it was our choice. Our blood is not on your hands, Dominus. We came to fight for our maker, our home, and our freedom. We are honoured for you to lead us and are grateful for your preparations and for sharing your home with us, but do not misunderstand, it is vengeance that we crave. We have our own reasons to be here. We fight beside you, not behind you."

Babbles of "Here, here," and clapping litter the room.

"Thank you, Caolán. May the bravery and courage of your people stain the future forever." He casts his eyes on me again, running his hands through his hair.

"Hellas arrives on the morrow. He brings an army of Slaugh."

My mouth gapes, confused at how he would know this and had yet to share it with me.

He turns away, continuing, "He brings King Adonien and his trained warriors. We might have stood a chance against the Erads. I expect many of them might refrain from fighting once they know the truth. But the Slaugh...they are what Hellas created from the deamhans I have spent centuries killing. We do not know their numbers or their capabilities. Prepare yourselves tonight. Do whatever you need to do. Come sunrise, we fight for Eregahl."

Hellas comes for us on the morrow.

He comes for my notorum.

He comes for my family.

Burning rage scorches through our entwined souls. The room erupts in chatter and movement. Icarus rises stoically, awaiting orders from his brother.

"Ready the castle. Gather all the weapons. Our plan remains. We stand our ground here in the seclusion of the academy, resting high on the grounds. We keep the battle away from the mainland as much as possible. The strongest of those will protect the castle and those inside as long as we can. We will ward the antechambers in the morning, securing the scolers inside. Transform this hall into an infirmary for the injured. Bring all prepared tonics, salves, and potions in tonight. We only have nightfall to prepare."

Luminaires scramble at his command, immediately removing food and chairs. Others rush in with towels, blankets, tins of salves and healing ointment Eden crafted, and glowing bottles of shimmering liquids. I remain frozen watching them all. Frozen yet burning with rage.

Dominus gracefully hops off the table to speak with Icarus. He whispers something in his ear, but I cannot make it out through the clamouring of the crowd. Dominus speaks quietly with a few more sentries, and they all take off in a flash.

"You," he says, pointing a long finger at me. "Let us go." I rise to my feet, following him and Icarus out of the room.

"Dominus, how do you know when Hellas arrives?" I ask. Dread curdles in my gut with the understanding anyway. *As my progeny, you may now call to me if you change your mind.* Something exists between them now. Something I likely understand and wholeheartedly fear.

"He...reached out to me at supper. I thought it was best to tell everyone together and quickly."

I decide now is not the time to question further. Dominus leads us to the west wing and into his room.

"Though I am flattered and well prepared for this moment, I do not think now is the time to formally offer me a night with you and your notorum, Brother."

Dominus smacks Icarus across the back of his curly, blond head and pushes him into the room. I cannot help but laugh, fully relishing in his twisted sense of humour. It's my favourite thing about him. We all use words as weapons, and I consider myself a connoisseur in the craft, appreciating how differently it can be done.

"Keep dreaming, bellend."

"Oh, indeed I do," he winks at me.

We enter the room to find two wooden stands clothed in new, fine leather and armour. Battle suits. He had suits crafted for us.

"Where in Eregahl were you able to scrounge this up?" Icarus asks, moving to inspect his.

"I have been here for three hundred yehrs. I did make some friends." I snort at that. "Even used what magic I could to aid in the growth of certain plants, grains, and insects."

I think of my marking gown crafted from worm silk and woven moonlight and smile.

"They are no Eradian garb, but they will suffice. They are crafted from the finest materials in Eregahl, and I had Eamon imbue them for protection."

The armour and leather are sleek and black as night. So dark, it's hard to tell what pieces are what. Upon closer inspection, something glimmers on the chest piece. I step closer, running my fingers along it. It responds to my magic, and a shape reveals itself. Not a shape, a pair of wings. Danu's wings—my wings. A perfect likeness of them is etched in the centre of it. I run my fingers along them again, and they disappear.

"A symbol," he says, "of who we serve in this battle. A reminder of who is with us. The lost goddess here to save a land she never had the chance to venture to."

It's a beautiful gesture, and her warmth blooms in my chest. "She says it was unnecessary, but she appreciates your thoughtfulness. As do I."

He offers a bow of his head to me, and the action allows me to see him, all of him. His power, his honour, his selflessness, and love. I see every inch of him, and I love him entirely.

Icarus groans beside me. "Are you sure you do not want me to stay? We might die on the morrow after all. Would you want your bonded to leave this plane without knowing what pleasure two Erads might give her?"

His eyes darken, then widen a bit. Surely, he isn't considering this. Gods, he is. Before I shout at Icarus to get out, I pause, considering my next move. One last dance. A final move for the sake of it.

I prowl my way over to Icarus, not breaking eye contact with Dominus. His eyes dimly glow as he watches me. He clenches and unclenches his jaw as his hands pulse with white knuckles at his sides. I swallow my devious smile and run my hand up Icarus' arm and across his shoulders, coming to step on the other side of him.

Still looking at Dominus, I take Icarus' arm and wrap it around my waist. Dom's eyes blaze to life then, and I know this is pure torture. I am indeed his agony, but I still yearn to wind him tightly. I take Icarus' strong jaw in my hand, pulling him to me. His desire radiates from him and surrounds us in a cloud of vanilla and smoke. I gently touch my tongue to the base of his jaw and lick upward toward his ear. Power surges from Dominus. I turn my darkened eyes to him, pulling Icarus into me, and I speak lowly, lustfully into his ear, "Do you see that god before you?" He nods, breathlessly. "He is the only one who will ever touch me." I move my grip to his throat. "Only his tongue will taste me. Only he will fill me until I shatter so hard I cannot walk." Dominus begins to shake.

I lean closer, whispering, "Now, get the fuck out, Brother."

He turns to me, and our mouths nearly touch as he

responds, "You truly are a wicked thing. I know why he is consumed by you." He pecks me on the cheek and strolls out of the room completely unbothered.

"Find me when you're finished!" he lilts. Then he shuts the door.

I let the laughter roll out of me then, the delirious joy of causing my stomach to ache.

"I would have hated to kill my brother the night before a battle, but I was preparred to," he says, shaking his head at me. "You know no bounds, you cruel woman." He lifts me in the air and spins me around.

"Me? The only reason why I did that was because you considered it for a moment."

"Of course I did. If it was what you wanted, I would have assuaged my urge to pull his skin from his bones. I promised I would give you everything you wanted. If that is my brother, you can have him, too."

I pretend to consider it for a moment, and Dominus begins an assault of tickles where he holds me around my hips. "You're incorrigible."

I fight out the words between laughter, "And you...are... too selfless. It will...ah, stop...be your end."

"Then it would be a worthy end," he says, exchanging his fingers for his lips. Our lovemaking is quick but desperate. We cling to each other as if it would save our lives. The awareness that this might be the last time hangs around us in a near-visible haze, and we end in a bloody, tear-soaked mess.

"I love you, Thorne."

"I love you, Dominus. Endlessly."

He whispers the spell to clean and ready us, and we abandon his room and then *our* corridor. We abandon the place that has become our sanctuary, our home, adorned in armour and filled with hope to wage a war against Hellas himself.

FORTY SIX

The sun rises as it always does, casting that familiar blue haze across the top of the craggy cliffs that the academy rests upon. I look out onto the slow-moving waters, thinking of my arrival here.

I think about the lost, broken version of myself that came desperately seeking answers. I want to laugh at her. I want to toss my head back and howl at the unfolding of my destiny. The beginning days with Dominus rise to the surface. The way we hated each other. The way we immediately tore each other down to the bones. I think of the unfinished journal, and I make myself a promise that if we survive this, I will finish what I started here.

My mind wallows in the memories. The night of the cave. Laughing with Thair, now Icarus, up and down the halls late at night. My long discussions with Norine. The seer, Oona,

Elowyn and Eamon—before and now. Finding my skean, crafting my shoes. The thought that my family watches over me now. Our bonding ritual. Gifting each other our marks. I coil my memories around me like my own set of armour. A new armour, not crafted from self-preservation or deprecation, but with love. I let them coat my tongue and spread to my lungs. I lace them up to my neck like I once did with fear and abandonment. This is what I came here for. This was always my destiny.

Danu moves within me differently than she has before, and her power swells my rib cage. I run my hand down the pocket of my leathers.

On my signal. Not until then, she whispers.

I hope you know what you are doing.

Dominus and Icarus stand on either side of me, wings out and strapped head to toe with weapons. Eden and Eamon stand behind me, and an army of Sídhe litter the ground as well as the towers and inside the castle. We make our way to the west side of the scol, looking toward Hellas' territory. I take in my family, armed to the teeth with weapons and courage. I study Elowyn and Eamon, and before the fear consumes us entirely, I send them both the memory of my first time I came to their cottage. I show Eamon how safe and welcomed he made me feel, and I show Elowyn the moment I first saw her and how she immediately felt so familiar. They both beam with pride as the blue light of the dawn yawns into the golden hues of early morning.

And we all feel the moment the wards are shattered, like a sticky substance being pulled from my skin. We move into position and ready ourselves. I beg my heart to calm, heaving deep breaths in through my nose and out through my mouth.

But in the distance, a wall of darkness colours the horizon, a storm of shadows in the sky and on land, barreling towards us.

"Hold!" Dominus screams.

The black clouds hurl closer toward us. Dominus looks at me. "Release the nodus. Release me, mo céasadh. Release all magic other than what you need to hide Danu."

My magic swells in my chest at his words, and on my command, it shudders through me, through us both, and the ground upon which we stand. Power, unlike I have yet felt, courses through me, vibrating my bones. The magic of three dwells inside me, free at last.

I close my eyes as it covers me, and when I open them, I witness Dominus shift. His skin rips from him. His limbs twist and contort in all the wrong ways. His body expands to twice his size, and darkness ripples around him. His sets of wings merge into one, large, sharp set, and only one eye in each centre remains. Gone is his beautiful face. What remains is inky, swirling blackness beneath. I make out nothing but two glowing green orbs for eyes. A black, tattered hood adorns his head and flows into the robe covering his body, which is also shrouded in darkness, a writhing mass of smoke that devours light itself. His dark crown remains, floating higher and far more expansive above his head, a match to my own. His more skeletal arms extend from his sides, ending in razor-sharp claws that promise a cruel fate. Mist swirls at his feet, obscuring the boundary between earth and nightmare. He is ancient malevolence. Primordial fears. A harbinger of death. A reckoning.

For once, I fear him. My very being begs me to look away, but I refuse. I will not turn from his darkness. Never. I will look upon every vicious part of him. He turns his head to judge me, and though my knees quiver, I do not allow myself to fall. Does he know who I am in this form? Does he become something else entirely?

"I love you, Dominus. I love every version of you, my notorum. You are mine." My voice holds the confidence I wish my body would as I try to remind him of his fealty, his promise.

He slowly cocks his head to the side, studying. Some part of me hopes that whatever he sees, he finds me worthy. And I think he might because smoke loosens from him to come to my side. The inky vapour disperses into six swirling birds. Shrikes. Shrikes with glowing green eyes, and I know that Dominus might be another version of himself, but these are gifts—proof of his love and protection for me.

Icarus shifts next into something similar to Dominus, but where Dominus is darkness, Icarus is a pure, radiant white and holds a large bow made of light. I stand between the two sentinels in my comparatively small form. My magic hums, pleading to be released, so I extend my arms toward the sky and do just that. Lightning cracks, the sea swells, and roots, far beneath the ground, rise to wrap around my waist and lift me into the air to stand alongside my Erads. They look at me, and I speak the words they once did to each other, "Chun glóire. Chun ár n-onóir." Feral growls erupt from them both, reverberating with pride in my chest.

Hellas and Adonien arrive with a flash of light and a mist of red. The army comes into view behind them. Thousands upon thousands of them on the land and in the sky, Eradian warriors sail alongside the Slaugh beasts and march along deamhans on the ground. Adonien was not lying when he attested to their horror. They lack distinctive forms. Instead, they float in a flock above the hoard with leather wings, more souls than monsters. Wailing screams sound from them, and fangs and claws undulate in and out of their twisting darkness.

Eden steps around us, halting Hellas in his tracks. His eyes widen, and his smile turns terrifying. He steps up before his army, using magic to let his spine-chilling voice float to us. "Hello, my darling Eden. Oh, to finally lay eyes on you after all this time. What a shame it is that you brought your dear family to be slaughtered after all your desperate attempts to save them."

"You were once my family, too, Hellas. You grew beside me. What a shame you have turned into."

"Shame? Do you not think I have made Father proud? I think he would quite delight in my savagery."

Before Eden has the chance to respond, Dominus moves beside her.

"Look at your magnificence, my heir. You are a sight to behold." Adonien whips his head to Hellas, making it all too obvious that he did not know that Hellas claimed Dominus. I wonder if Hellas promised Adonien the claim in return for Dominus. I want to laugh at the deliciousness of it.

Dominus does not speak or move, though those wisps of smoke continually float around him.

"I beseech you only once more. Join me. Lead my army. Look at what all could be yours." He opens his arms wide, and Adonien's shift is only slight, but I still make it out. I watch far into the distance as Fina and Camiel step out in front of the rest of the line, still in their true form, wings out. Each of theirs is similar to Dom's and Icarus'. Fina's are a pale grey and Camiel's are burnt orange.

An enormous, pale spear appears in Dom's hand. He taps it on the ground three times. Then he extends the other arm, pointing a deadly, single skeletal finger at Hellas. He turns his wrist over and curls that finger inward, summoning Hellas to begin his onslaught.

He smiles at Dominus as if he were proud of him. Then he shoots into the darkening sky with those blood-red wings, and his army moves to attack. They come so fast, I must shift my eyes to see them.

They lay into us instantly. Erads litter the sky in confusion, half of them progressing toward us while the other half fall back, taking in the scene. That confirms that Adonien has not been honest with them. I wonder how he made them able to fight against their creator. Blasts of various colours soar through the skies from the luminaires. The clanging of weaponry from hand-to-hand combat sounds around us. We move into the onslaught.

My instincts sink into me again. I blast Erads and Slaugh alike with my magic. I use my thorns and branches to rip through the winged bodies, slinging them to the side. I move with such fluidity gained from my nodus. I parry and block, shredding everything in my path. I send visions to others, stopping them in their tracks to claw at their eyes. I strike others with bolts of lightning and pull Slaugh beneath the earth with thick roots. I drown others on land with water from the sea.

Regardless of my slaughter, of the slaughter of those around us, the numbers refuse to cease. After the first swell, Hellas' other beasts arrive on the blood-soaked battlefield.

Hordes of failinis, packs of dearg dues, and endless abhartachs claw at my skin. Three-headed beasts, creatures with gnarled, twisted horns and hoofed feet, giant serpentine monsters, they keep coming by the thousands. We quickly become vastly outnumbered.

I allow myself a small moment to look for Dominus, though I am aware of his safety through the nodus. The sight of him makes my mouth go dry. He vanquishes deamhans by the dozens, choking them with smoke, spearing five and six of them at a time, sending blasts of magic at others, and firing those terrifying, razor-sharp feathers from his wings. I am thankful Icarus stands close to him, fighting side by side. They forge a path through the centre of the dark army, straight to Fina and Camiel, who have both shifted as well.

When they reach them, they all pause, assessing one another. A flock of Slaugh swarms straight toward Dominus, but before they can get close enough, Fina blasts them to ash on the wind, only for them to form again. That must be all they needed because the four of them turn in unison to release death upon Hellas' hoard, causing most of the hesitant Erads to join them, to join us. I hear Adonien scream at them between the banging of his sword. He battles Caolán, and it brings a smile to my face that he will likely tire or die before too long.

A smoke shrike calls beside me, and I turn too slowly, receiving a battering of Eradian fists to my face. Her pummels are rapid and painful. It takes me long seconds to rally myself before conjuring thorns from the earth to wrap around her body. I watch her through bloody and blackened eyes as they squeeze the life from her. Tighter and tighter, until her head rolls off her neck and thuds to the ground. It does not bring me joy to kill the Erads. It pains me to do so, but there is no stopping them to talk nicely.

I spin on my heels, diving back into the assault. Time does not seem to pass at all as I wade through the growing bodies. More and more, and they are never-ending. Hawrs, days, forever. My arms begin to ache. My breaths become more laboured.

"Dominus," I breathe through ravaging breaths. I am so tired, so thirsty. He's upon me with my next breath, extending those decomposing hands to wipe the blood from my face. I lean into his cold touch. Why is he so cold?

I look around the grounds. There are so few of us left out here. Bodies littered with arrows drape along the spires and towers of the castle, though some of our own still cast blows from above. It is not enough. We will not last much longer. I look out into a sea of black at the beautiful, still-shimmering wings of my family. The reality of battle begins to crawl its way to me. I have lost them. I have lost them to this bloody curse again.

Behind Dominus, Eden raises her crystal staff and plunges it hard into the ground as she's done over and over. A pillar of blinding light bursts from the earth, clearing the immediate space around us and allowing a small reprieve.

"How many of those do you have left?" I ask.

"Not enough."

I hear Icarus' voice boom across the field as he runs to us in his true form. "Caledon," he screams between breaths. "Caledon has arrived with his forces. He brings shapeshifters, healers, and menders, but he's on the other side of Hellas' hoard. They are caught between us now. If we can hold them off long enough for them to get through, we might stand a fighting chance."

Hope blooms violently in my chest. I look to Dominus. His form slowly shrinks and melts away to leave my perfect, battered notorum in his battle armour. I wrap my arms around him as hot tears join the caking of grime and blood on my face.

"It's my turn," I tell him. "I can distract him long enough for Caledon's forces to reach us. We can do this. We will do this."

He pulls me in for one deep kiss and then rests his forehead against mine. "This is what you were made for, Thorne. Your whole life has led up to this moment. Everything taken from you, everything you suffered, every choice you made led you here to this very moment. Go show him who you are. Go show him what you are made of. I love you. I am endlessly yours."

"Endlessly yours," I whisper back to him and stalk off to the edge of the cleared space to call to Danu.

You're up.

I am ready, my chosen. It is our time.

I let the earth bring me high above the rest of the battle as it wages down below. "Hellas," I call with my magic, "I want to speak to you." He pauses his visceral destruction to laugh at me, but he saunters towards me anyway, flapping those now truly blood-drenched wings to meet me in the sky.

"Is the reality of war becoming too much for your heart to handle, my lumminaire?"

"On the contrary, Hellas. We are just getting started." His eyes squint at me then, his patience growing thin.

"Unless you are here to hand your notorum over to me, then I am afraid I need to get back to slaughtering the remains of your family," he says, spinning on the wind to return to the fight.

"And what do you know of family, Brother?" I ask, reaching into my pocket and pulling free a fistful of moon salt. I toss it on the ground beneath us and use my skean to slice my palm open, squeezing my fists and allowing the blood to drip and sizzle as it lands on the salt. I toss it on the ground beneath us and relish the confusion on Hellas' face. The salt allows Danu to take control of my body, summoning my maker as Oona said it would, and I become a passenger in my own skin.

"Oh, Hellas," Danu's true voice comes from my mouth. "You thought you would get away with this, did you not? You thought my sacrifice to get you from underneath Father's cruelty was a way for you to have control in a new world, to craft your version of his sinful palace. I freed you to give you a better life. I freed you so that you might see what you could become away from his darkness. You ignorant, simple fool."

"Danu." His voice is a near whisper, and all colour drains from his face. I see true fear glisten in his crimson eyes.

"I used powerful magic to preserve my soul for when you undoubtedly failed. Because that is what you do, isn't it, Hellas? You pawed after Father for him to only sing my praises. You were gifted a second chance, a new life to become anything you wanted, and you ended up just like him but nowhere near as evil. You cannot succeed at anything, can you?"

She's goading him, riling him up for something. It works because Hellas charges us with talon-tipped hands and his red mist. Danu expertly wields her magic, easily blocking him. She sends my thorns dipped in her golden magic at him, but he disappears into mist on the wind.

"That is right," she croons. "I forgot that when you realise how pathetic you are, you run away to lick your wounds. Stop being a child, Hellas, and face me. You never had the gall to do it before. Do it. Show me what an all-powerful god you have become."

He tries to attack us from behind, but she senses it and absorbs the spear of his magic, clinging to it and pulling him around to face us. His fear pours into us on contact. Danu claws him closer and closer. She spears golden thorns into his limbs and chest. When she digs them furiously around his throat, I become aware that she is siphoning the magic from him, draining him the way she did the land and dead things that day on the battlefield.

This must be the way to end him. Drain him of his magic and sever his head. She drinks it down quickly. Too quickly. My body begins to overheat. Sweat pours from my brow, but the harder she pulls, the weaker he grows in our grasp.

"You had every opportunity, Hellas. You could have done great things, but you refused to see the error of your ways. Now, you will die here alone with nothing to show for it, unloved and hated, just as he was. I hope you are proud of yourself."

"No!" Hellas screams, pawing unsuccessfully at my body wrapped in unyielding, ancient magic.

Danu pulls harder, and our vision begins to blur, and blood fills my mouth. It dawns on me then what is about to happen.

This will kill us, Danu—both of us and Dominus.

It will not kill me, girl. My soul will simply float back to Mag Mell.

Danu.

This was your destiny. This is what you were created for. To hold my soul long enough for me to end him.

It will kill Dominus, I say more to myself, the realisation of what is occurring settling violently.

Yes. A brave and honourable price to pay to save the lives of countless others. This world will go on, happy and full of peace, because of the sacrifice you will make here today. Do not stop me. Do not let the sacrifices of your family be in vain.

Sacrifices? What sacrifices? What does that mean?

I had to take them. You were not progressing quickly enough. You were not searching hard enough. Their deaths forced you down the path towards me to this very moment.

My mind spins. Their deaths—so unexplainable, so violent. She took them from me. She ruined my entire life to settle a feud with her brother. Rage, my rage, fills our ears.

Still, I consider her words. Even if this did kill us, it would rid the world of Hellas. It would allow the children of the other Seren to return and to live in peace and love. But how is it just for me to give up everything? Why am I the one who continues to sacrifice? No. I refuse. I refuse to lose another to this game of gods.

You have taken enough from me, Danu. You will not take him. He is mine. I call to the power. It hesitates, but slowly, it begins to bend to my will.

No! I have waited aeons for this. You cannot defeat him. Only I can.

Then I shall not defeat him today. But I will live. Dominus will live. My family will live.

Then I yank it from her with all my strength. Coming back into this much power knocks the breath from me. Hellas lies near lifeless in my bloodied hands, only a tendril of power flickering within him. Dominus is beside me, and I fight with all my might to continue the spell, to siphon the dregs of him the way Danu did, but she's gone quiet, and I do not know how she did it. My body begins to shake uncontrollably.

"His head," I chatter.

Dominus extends his fingers into the sharp, jagged bones of his other form, and he raises his arm to make the strike. He swings, making contact, but Hellas catches his arm before he plunges his claws the entire way through. I push my thorns and remaining magic further into his body, begging it to find something to rip free of him that will make him stop. Hellas digs his own taloned hand into Dom's arm. His eyes shoot open, and only a whisper of colour remains.

"I claim you, Dominus. You are my heir. Oidhre na Fola. I give you my power and everything I am. You are my champion. Together, we will claim our rightful place on the throne of Thoraí."

"No!" My voice is raw and broken. I will every bit of my power into him, trying to drain him, trying to find purchase on his cursed fucking soul.

He smiles at Dominus, and blood pours from his mouth. My eyes scour Dom for proof that it worked. His eyes roll back in his head, and his smoke turns from solid black to a deep scarlet.

"No!" I scream again. "Dominus, no. Please, I beg you.

Fight it. Do not accept it. Refuse his claim. You are mine! You are mine! I claimed you! You belong only to me. Do not break your bloody promise to me, Dominus. Look at me!"

He snaps his head to me, but it is not his pale green eyes that find me. Solid darkness pierces me instead. The depths of a pit. He angles his head to the side as if in recognition.

I reach for the nodus between us. I wrap it in our shared scent. I wrap it in love, in my own blood, in everything that is us. I push it to him, a desperate offering, a reminder of what we are to each other. His eyes flash quickly from black to green.

"Yes, Dominus. You are mine, and I am yours. My notorum, my soulmate, my rival, my agony. Please come back to me." Sobs tear through me, and I fall to my knees, my fingers and thorns still twisting through Hellas' insides. They finally release each other, and a tendril of hope rises in my core.

"Thorne," he whispers, his voice not wholly his own.

"Yes. Please, please do not leave me. Dominus, I need you. You promised. Stay with me." My vision begins to blur, and I reach deeper, searching for anything, but it's all gone. All my magic is gone, burned through by Danu. The bottom of what I thought was an infinite barrel. How naive. How ignorant. How careless.

I try to clear my eyes. I try to breathe through it, but the convulsions worsen, and I retract my limbs and release the earth holding Hellas. I fall to the ground. The last thing I see are glowing pale green eyes, and I slip into darkness with a heart full of hope that I might have saved him.

FORTY SEVEN

My mind wakes before my body does, and I open my eyes to find
the light of the moon glistening across my bedroom. I slowly
pull myself up. My body aches like it never has before. I look
down to find myself cleaned and dressed in Dom's raiments, his
scent enveloping me like a gentle lover.

For a single moment, I forget all that has transpired. I
forget the battle. I forget Danu and Hellas and all the dealings of
damned gods that I do not care to be involved in. I allow myself
to pretend I am waking in the night, as I often do, to reach out
for Dominus.

I do not need to look to know he is there. The nodus tells
me he is. I inhale deeply, truly terrified of what I might find when
I look at him. But then he's on the bed before me, pulling my
chin up to him as he always has. When I look, I find pale green

eyes, a dimple I could drown in, and full, beautiful lips that were made to roam my body. I bring my hand up to his. I run it down his arm and across his chest to wrap it behind his neck. I shatter into millions of pieces before him. Relief and pain and grief, all fighting to see who can destroy me the fastest.

"I thought I lost you," I sob, the thought of it sending me spiralling again. He wraps his arms around me and pulls me onto his lap. He shushes me, running long strokes up and down my back.

"You will never lose me. I swore to you. I am yours."

I allow myself to fully break. I let the grief and joy consume me. I think of all the Sídhe we lost. I think of Danu's betrayal and what that might mean for the rest of my life. I think of Hellas with his bloody grip on my notorum, and I let it all swallow me whole, unlacing my armour, displaying the remains of a shattered woman.

I scream and sob and cling to Dominus like an anchor in the eye of a storm. I let every emotion I have ever had wreak havoc on me. And Dominus lets me. He holds me and soothes me and whispers to me that he loves me. He wipes my tears and pulls me into his warm chest and holds the pieces of me together in his strong arms.

Sometime later, I finally exhaust myself. I rub swollen, salty eyes, my body still shaking, and my voice is hoarse. "What happened after I fell?"

"Are you sure you are ready for that now? You can rest. You need to."

"I need to know."

He releases a deep breath. "I will give you the truth, all of it. But can I give it to you with the sunrise? I want to hold you. I want to lie here and think of nothing and no one else. I just need you. Everyone is safe. We have a mess to deal with come dawn. Can we have the remaining hawrs with the quiet of the moon?"

I consider his words. The aching desire to know every single moment burns in my mind, but I urge it to smoke because he is right. We need this. This moment, just us, lost in one another, consuming each other the way we always have. I need his heart beating beneath my ear. I need his hands imprinted on my skin. I need him to show me that he is mine and that we survived.

I move myself to sit atop his waist, lifting his sweater over my head and tossing it on the floor. Dominus does not hesitate to reach out for me and pull me into his kiss. We allow ourselves to be lazy and indulgent for once. We let our nodus shine brightly, washing over us, and healing every pain and wound. It is more than I could ever imagine to be able to love him freely, to have him entirely unto myself. No more hiding. No more veiling. Just us in the rubble of our lives, full of love.

I want to die in it. I want it to consume me. But as Dominus sinks his teeth into my flesh, I cannot help but feel we are not alone.

ℱORTY ℰIGHT

DOMINUS

"I claim you, Dominus. You are my heir. Oidhre na Fola. I give you my power and everything I am. You are my champion. Together, we will claim our rightful place on the throne of Thoraí."

Thorne distantly screams my name. She coils herself around our shared souls. I taste her anguish and desperation, but it's not enough. Hellas' claim floods me, filling me with power I have never felt before. I want to become intoxicated by it. I want to drink deeply from the well and let it tear my soul in half. My soul. No, *our* soul. Her soul.

"Dominus, no. Please, I beg you. Fight it. Do not accept it. Refuse his claim. You are mine! You are mine! I claimed you! You belong only to me. Do not break your bloody promise to me, Dominus. Look at me!"

I have a choice. I can refuse this. I can reject this delicious and sweet magic. I can. I can.

I cannot.

"Thorne," I whisper, my voice not wholly my own.

"Yes. Please, please do not leave me. Dominus, I need you. You promised. Stay with me."

Yes, I will always choose her. I am hers.

There is much more to the story you do not understand yet, my pet. You will need me, or at least my power, to maintain this life of yours. Because he will come. Aed always comes. He will not let us live peacefully. He will not let us get away. It is only a matter of time.

I am so exasperated by this narrative. By this entire endless story. *That is not my concern, Hellas. You sought to destroy this world, my world, and you failed. Your reign is done.*

I sought to protect it, boy. I sought to build an army that could defeat him. You will need them. You will need me.

Gods, it never bloody ends. What if what he says is true? He could be playing the role perfectly, but something went wrong with Danu. Thorne ripped the power back from her for a reason. What if there is more at play here? I am slipping, sliding faster into the relief of Hellas' dark magic.

Danu claims me, too. Her blood is my blood. I have the right to choose.

A fact I regret that you learned.

Then if I do this, if I accept your claim, share your throne, I do it my way. I remain in control. You do not have the right to get into my head. I have free will. I will make my own choices. I share in your power alone.

Then I hope you can handle it without my control. It is done. You are my heir.

Thorne loses consciousness as Hellas' power flows into me. I want to vomit, I want to scream, I want everything.

Fully consumed with his power, I spear my longsword through Hellas' barely beating chest to hold him until I can get him in the dungeon. Caledon's people flood through the remaining Erads. On my command, the deamhans begin to retreat to whatever pit they crawled out from, leaving us standing in the hot, blinding light of the sun.

"Healer! I need a healer!" I scream. A young woman runs over to me, kneeling before Thorne. She places her hands over her body, and a bright, white light flows out of her.

"She will be fine. I have her." Relief floods me. Relief and all-consuming rage that Thorne was ever put in this position to begin with.

I spin on my heels, looking for my father. Hellas' magic continues to fill me, and I think my skin might melt off from the intensity. Adonien still fights, still screams at his remaining army to end us all. I let my wings beat, bounding me in the sky toward him.

He sees me coming, but it's not enough. I quickly get my hands around his throat. He claws at my armour, making no contact. "You have failed my people. You have sullied our name and our honour. You do not deserve to be king." With that, I send my magic, Hellas' magic, searing through my hands. His eyes widen in pure fear, and maybe even realisation at what I have become. "You are the reason for all of this. I hope you die knowing that I will be here to undo every horrible thing you did. I will be the king they deserve."

Bloody chokes sound from his mouth. "Son," he spurts through blood, but I do not care what he has to say. I let my magic burn straight through his neck, and his head and detached body fall from the sky and sound with a crack below me.

The rest of the battle stills. The remaining Erads take me in. They remain unmoving for a long moment, waiting. The magic snakes through the battlefield, assessing us all. It sinks within me a moment later, and I let my crown of smoke loose. One by one, they kneel, bowing their heads to their new king.

I watch Thorne as she sleeps peacefully, fully satisfied and covered in my blood and essence. The sight of it nearly overwhelms me, nearly brings me to my fucking knees. I could not bring myself to tell her what I had done. Not yet. I have failed her, betrayed her. I needed one more night of her thinking that I am good and honourable. I needed her soul to tell me once more all the things she loves about me.

Because when the sun rises, I fear I might lose her entirely.

EPILOGUE

In all the chaos of the battle, the awareness that Mabon had come and gone slid from me like an elusive lover. Those remaining at the academy have scheduled a festival tonight to celebrate the equinox, the victory, and to honour those who fell. I have spent my days aiding in repairs and my nights at the cabin with my eyes brimming with flashes of death and betrayal.

The days have cooled again, and the staggering mountains of Danumhar now glisten with warm hues of Fómhar, as if the colours were thrown from the palette of a grand painter, drenching the world in rich auburns and golds. The days grow short, allowing the celebration of darkness. Of harvest. I wish I had the guts to laugh at the horrible irony of it. Instead, I sit alone on a steep mountaintop, wrapped in a wool tartan and my own grief—a place I truly never thought I would see again.

I swear to you, my queen, my goddess, my notorum, I yield only to you. I am yours to command, and yours to use as you see fit. I will never forsake you. I will stand by you no matter the cost.

His words are ghosts, echoing in an endless cadence, beating along with my broken heart. Promises I believed. Lies that dripped like honey. Hollow vows. Doubt alone now consumes the spaces he occupied—the emptiness of me that he made a home in. I was prepared to lose his love, but only in death. I never considered the absence of all we had while my heart still beat. Never wanted to taste the horror of it. It makes me wish I had met my demise on the bloody battlefield. Gods, the thought of them all. The blood. The death. My stomach turns at it.

A faint scratching tingles the back of my mind at the thought, but I strangle it further, stifling it to nothing, as I have all communication with Danu since her betrayal. Our bond has altered in some way, lending me more control than I had, more clarity as well. Her magic still runs through my veins but not in the way it did before. Only in the way it does as I am her child. Is it possible to pull apart the things imbued by our makers? Are they infectious rot or something that can evolve?

Endless questions haunt me, but I cannot seem to muster the gall to ask her any of them. Questions like: Why me? Is there any purpose for my life other than to be a vessel for her? Are my choices even my own? Is my love for Dominus even real, or was it all part of her plan? I have never tasted love like this, and I quarrel with its normality. Not that any of this is a semblance of normal, but should it be all-consuming in such ways?

Danu's previous warning rings in my mind. Though your

fates are intertwined, certainly. Hellas has grown stronger than I imagined. Dominus will be your aid. Together, you are something new, even to Thoraí. Something that changes the fabrics of the worlds.

It certainly feels as if we were fated, but not for love. For a means to an end, maybe. And my family—I swallow, forcing the thoughts away. Danu took them from me, and she did it with my own hands. The tears are warm against my chilled fingers as I wipe them away, refusing to allow the weakness of them to stain me further. These thoughts have rattled my mind for the wyths I have spent in solitude in the hills away from Adonien. Now that Dominus commands the bloody deamhans, the lands are safe again, and I have stayed in them, allowing the land and the moon to nurse me.

I hate myself for abandoning my people when they need me most. I hate myself for not ushering Caledon and those who came to save us into the halls, seeing to their needs. How selfish this has caused me to be. Yet I cannot be there right now either. I cannot see his bloody beautiful face or allow his scent to comfort me. I know I will cave under the weight of it, and I have too much to sort through. Too much I need to understand before I make a move.

Dominus led me to think that I saved him. That our love, our nodus, was enough to keep him from submitting to Hellas' magic. Caledon had come. They were there. Had I only held on for a moment longer, he wouldn't have even had the chance to accept. Had I let Danu finish the job, then it would all be over, and we would not be facing even more evil from their homeland.

I would be with my family again.

The waves slap violently against the shore, and the grey skies begin to swirl. The clouds will release soon, giving way to the rain, and yet I cannot bring myself to move. I cannot give myself enough consideration to disengage from my thoughts to seek cover. I often wonder if I knew what was coming—if I knew what fate awaited me—would I still have boarded that ship to this island? Could I have lived happily in Albion, never knowing all that awaited me?

I would have come; I could not live without knowing. Perhaps it is naive to assume I had a choice. Danu would have done anything to get me here, whether I wanted it or not, and that makes me question everything. Has my love for knowledge ever been my own? How much of being an heir has influenced my life? Am I even my own person outside of this?

Only a void exists in response to my query, and that is why I require distance and solitude. To hopefully quiet my mind enough to hear the answers. Doubt has erected a wall between me and Dominus—between me and the world. One that I do not yet know if I have the capabilities to scale. I promised Dominus I would walk beside him in the darkness as I do in the light. And though the darkness, the harder work, scares me not, I must now, as I always have, first seek the truth. To consider if the love that swells within me like vitality, like the very essence of life, is truly my own or if I am simply a pawn, willfully sacrificing myself for the queen. Knowing my connection to Danu, I must consider whether his love for me is potentially driven by Hellas' influence. The thought of it makes me sick.

Who is Thorne Alder? Who could she have been outside of this fate? I was mistaken, assuming my questioning had come to a gentle reprieve. I thought that with Dominus by my side, it did not matter what we faced. How could I go another moment fearing my own life, my own existence, when I had found my purpose? When I had tasted, owned, the kind of love I was certain I could never hold. Now, I must sort through every moment of that life and question whether it was Danu. A thorough study of my internals is necessary. A discovery of what I am even made of anymore.

If anything remains.

I presumed I had found my way to some grand finality, having enough to be able to brave the unknown. Now, I sit alone with nothing but the certainty that the day keeps dawning, and I have to decide what I want to do with it.

ACKNOWLEDGEMENTS

My circle is small, so this should be brief; however, I feel I need a bit of a preface. I decided at the end of June 2025 to withdraw Shrike from submission to editors and publish it independently. I chose the release date of October 13, 2025, giving myself approximately three and a half months to complete the release and two months until the ARCs needed to be sent out. This was the largest step into the unknown that I have ever taken.

For the first time in my life, I can say that I did not complete this single-handedly. I have incredible, brilliant women who have held me up through every moment. My writing coven, Bianca Richardson and Danielle Drummond, kept me sane through this with their constant support and endless pep talks. Every writer feels like quitting at some point. That becomes infinitely more difficult to do with those who love you refusing to allow you to stop. I cannot express my gratitude, but we all know I sobbed while writing this.

Alexandra D'Amico, the agent of my dreams, you know all the things I want to say. Thank you will never be enough, but I shall make a feeble attempt. Thank you for seeing me. Thank you for loving my work and being my biggest fan. Thank you for your time, commitment, and passion. I am so honoured to know you. To my family and friends who have cheered me on along the way, thank you. Your support means everything.

To Silas and Ezra, thank you for being the best writing company

I could have. I hope that you look back at this time and don't see it as, "Mom was always working." I hope you watched me fight tooth and nail for every bit of my dreams, and I hope it encourages you to do the same. We can do hard things, and we always will.

And lastly, to Caleb. Without you, none of this would be possible. You are my constant. You are in every moment and memory. You alone have been my foundation, ceaselessly encouraging me, pushing me, and loving me through every version of myself. Thank you for being my notorum and for showing me what unconditional love, forgiveness, and grace are. Thank you for loving me so well that I had to write a book about it.

And as I write this, I have no way of knowing the outcome. My only hope is that it found you, dear reader, exactly when it was supposed to. Thank you for taking the time to spend in this world. I truly hope you enjoy every moment.

Endlessly yours,
C.

MEET THE AUTHOR

CHARLA AYERS is a multi-faceted creative who blends her passion for writing, editing, and visual storytelling. With a Master of Arts in Publishing and a Bachelor of Arts in Writing and Publications, she brings academic intrigue, a background in photography, and a passion for crafting stories about the intricacies of interpersonal relationships. As a college writing instructor and emerging editor, Charla channels her diverse skill set into nurturing other writers' voices while establishing her own.

She lives in Georgia with her husband and two sons, where she is likely listening to music and being inspired by nature and poetry. SHRIKE, a blend of dark academia and romantic fantasy, is her debut novel.

For more information, visit www.charlaayers.com